$ 19.95

GUIDING STARS

* * * * * * * * * *

A novel
By

JULIUS LING

Wire from Hungary

Dear Mr. Ling, in Budapest I have entered GUIDING STARS into a highly prestigious annual contest: THE MOST BEAUTIFUL BOOK OF THE YEAR! Its sole purpose of the evaluation was to select the best written stories for movie consideration. From over 3,000 entries the jury had chosen five (5) books worthy of consideration. I'm happy to report that your book is in the five!

In the final selection GUIDING STARS was classified into the third position! Accept my sincere congratulations!

Gyula Nyitrai, chief editor of Nation's Guard.

KNOWLEDGE IS POWER

GUIDING STARS

VICTORIA,..

2001, All Rights Reserved.

Name of characters in this book, except those of political figures, are fictitious or are used fictitiously. Any resemblance to actual persons, living or death, is purely coincidental. The places are real, although I have taken some liberties.

*

No part of this book may be used or reproduced in any manner whatsoever without written permission, except in the case of brief quotations embodied in critical articles and reviews. For information contact:
Julius Ling, 591 Delora Dr. Victoria, B. C. V9C 3S2. Phone: 250-474-5279; or E-mail: juliusling@aol.com.

*

National Library of Canada Cataloging-in-Publication Data.
Ling Gyula, 1925 - Guiding Stars. ISBN: 1-55212-680-3. 1 Title.

*

PS 8573. 1536G84 2001 C894' 5113 C2001 - 910460 - X

TRAFFORD PUBLISHING.

Suite 6E - 2333, Government St. Victoria, BC. Canada, V8T 4P4
Phone: 250-383-6864. Toll-free: 1-888-232-4444, Canada/US.
E-mail: trafford.com/robots/01-0079.

10 9 8 7 6 5 4 3 2 1

INTRODUCTION

In the early nineteen forties the Second World War was raging in full force on Soviet soil between Russia and Germany. When the Soviet army turned the Germans around, it was a matter of time before the fighting went on Hungarian soil. The Soviets reached Budapest at Christmas time in 1944-45. After the Soviet victory, the Soviets began to force its seeds of Communism on the Eastern European people. **GUIDING STARS** was built on this historical story that was blended together with fictional events brilliantly and indistinguishable. It sets against the Stalinist reign of terror in Hungary; an unbearable terror, that squeezed the Hungarians into revolution in 1956.

In the meantime a deep and powerful love story flourishes between Andrew Dombrady and Katie Erdelyi. But after the shocking Soviet revenge of counter-attack, which blows Budapest into flame—displaying a brutal lesson for wanting an impossible dream— *freedom,* tore the lovers apart.

Here the story leaves Budapest. Andrew (the freedom fighter hero) was forced to escape without having a chance to say goodbye to Katie. Fate takes Andrew to Canada, while Katie disappears in the confusion. Finding each other seemed utterly hopeless, and the question keeps linger on: *Will they ever see each other again....?*

Julius Ling spins the thread of the story between three continents with a skill of a magician, and the stunning conclusion will stay with you for a long time.

Naturally the erotic scene is not missing—nor should it be missing from a modern love story. It is an integral part of their innermost human feelings. It is written with good taste, and its powerful force, with which manner he is portraying true love — sad to say—it seems to be slowly fading out from our literature.

There is a moving passage in Hemingway's book: *For Whom The Bell Tolls,* when two lovers find each other. In *GUIDING STARS* there is no moving episode that would not match, or surpass Hemingway's novel, either in power or poetic beauty.

Gyula Nyitrai, chief editor of Nation's Guard.

Acknowledgments

While working on this book, I have met many good friends offering help and information. Amongst them were All Lebeau and Ray Sounders. My sincere gratitude goes to Cindy Goodman, who just for the sheer love of the story, has retyped the whole book into computer. To My dear friend, Harry Lund, the computer wizard, for his generosity to teach me the basic operation, and for his priceless contribution in making this book into the right format. Many thanks go to Cliff Wilde, the retired school principal, for his support, as well as Frank Keeling, the author of *Nobody's Son*. And last but not least, I am grateful to my dear friend, Peter Czink, professional journalist, for his proofreading of this book.

Furthermore, my thanks go to Leo F. Buscaglia for permission to quote an excerpt from his copyrighted book: *The Way of the Bull.*

I also wish to express my sincere appreciation to the generous and great country of Canada for giving us the equal opportunity to enjoy the good and free life.

* * *

Reader's view::

Mr. Ling, please, please, write another book! Guiding Stars was so enjoyable, it has written in a beautiful style. It is a giant story, I just could not put it down. If that book would receive proper marketing, it would be a world success! And if they would make a movie out of it— they should, you know—I would be the first one to go and see it. What a great love story!...
        Angela, from Victoria Bindery.
*

I'm very proud of you for writing such a valuable book. I, and my husband loved and enjoyed every page of it. I just could not put it down, and since then I have read it again because I'm still discovering so much beauty in it. Those wonderful people in the story became our friends—we love them. Our only hope is that a follow-up will coming...
        Mrs. Ilona Krauhs, Trenton, N.Y.
*

*Mr. Ling, Congratulations for your excellent book. In **GUIDING STARS** the story rolls smoothly. The pages are "run-ning away" and I could not stop reading until I finished it. It is too bad that there is no continuation. I'm happy to have **GUIDING STARS** in my 2,500 valuable book collection.*
        Zsuzsa Erdos, N.J.
*

...My wife literally fell in love with your book. It is so real. There is a magnetic pull in the pages, as one stunning chapter rolls into the next. It is a rare book that is truly begging to be read. Thanks for the few hours of thrill.
        Mickey Cornish, Ottawa, Ont.
*

Mr. Ling, thank you for the gift of your talent. I don't remember enjoying a book this much. It is bursting with life. But it is more than just a beautiful love story—it is a story of decency; of being human in the deepest sense of the word. I agree with the jury in Budapest: If there ever was a movie material, by God, this novel is!
        Steve Borosh, New York.

... Your book was marvelous, I enjoyed it thoroughly. I'm 94 years old, please keep writing, I want to read your next book.
        Mrs. McMeeken, Victoria, BC.
          *

Mr. Ling,
 Being an avid reader, it is not easy to find a good book. I was just starving for a good story when I received Guiding Stars. The style was refreshing, easy to read, it was brilliant! It was good food for the spirit, and for the soul... Everybody should read it....
        Peter Short, Vancouver, B. C.
       *

Dear Mr. Ling,
 I am retired, and I was reluctant to buy Guiding Stars, but was I ever wrong! It is a darn good book! Right at the beginning I have realized that Guiding Stars is in a class with Olympic giants amongst fiction. I was hypnotized by the force of "read on," as the story had a grip on my curiosity: what is coming next? I truly had a hard time to put it down. It was exciting and beautiful; one must read it to believe it. Thank you.
      Andrew Montgomery, Vancouver, B.C.

This letter is from Tom Lantos, Honorable American Senator .

Dear Mr. Ling:
Thank you for sending me your delightful book, "Guiding Stars." My wife and I very much enjoyed reading it. It is unusual to see an English-language novel that takes place in Hungary, and I applaud you for making the wonders of our shared homeland accessible to people who don't speak Hungarian.
I wish you the best of luck with all your endeavors.
Cordially,
Tom Lantos, Member of Congress, Washington, D.C.
(The Author is honored by all views received from the readers.)

CONTENTS:

PROLOGUE
BUDAPEST..11

PART ONE
1 - Coming of age..17
2 - New world..21
3 - Face of Communism................................26
4 - Crossroad..39
5 - Lake Balaton..44
6 - The Erdelyi family....................................60
7 - Youth and love...69
8 - New Year's Eve Party..............................83
9 - Dream of the Nation................................89
10 - The revolution..96
11 - Bitter awakening..................................113

PART TWO
12 - God bless you, my son........................121
13 - It's a cruel world..................................136
14 - All alone...145
15 - Under Australian Sky..........................155
16 - The Wanderer......................................166
17 - Niagara Falls..177
18 - New hope...184
19 - If there is will......................................196
20 - In school again....................................202
21 - Struggle of the soul.............................212
22 - Love affair...222
23 - Alex's store..230
24 - Miracles still happen...........................241
25 - Shocking news....................................249
26 - Guiding Stars......................................265
27 - Beautiful to be alive............................275
28 - Ultimate pleasure................................286
29 - It's a Small World...............................295

THE CONCLUSION

30 - It's incredible!...................................313
31- Happy years in Canada.......................322
32 - Fate of the Grandparents....................337
33 - Sweet home: Canada..........................346
34 - Reminiscing..353
35 - The Canadian Rockies........................362
36 - From Heaven to Hell...........................376
37 - Deep hidden secret.............................387
38 - Dear God, let it be true.......................399
     EPILOGUE....................................404

This work is created by labor of love,
dedicated to my wife who stood by me with
love and encouragement..

BUDAPEST
PARLIAMENT BUILDINGS & FISHERMAN BASTION

MOTTO

"There is nothing more essential to life than hope; without it a man may be breathing, but he is dead.
Hall Lindsey

PROLOGUE

BUDAPEST

ON A DULL, CLOUDY April afternoon in 1955, the university students were having their ten-minute recess. In the huge yard, among the drifting, jostling crowd Andrew Dombrady was practicing some of the new boxing techniques with George Pusztai, one of his friends. As they discussed the finer moves they had learned from their trainer, Andrew noticed that Frank Csokros, one of his schoolmates was picking on someone again. Frank was an ignorant, loud-mouthed bully, an empty boaster that made him unpopular—a lonely character. He enjoyed tormenting other students, particularly the ones he knew were timid. This time he had chosen John Dobos. Although his meanness irritated Andrew, he was reluctant to get involved, for he was sure that it would end up in a fight.

John, being a spindly and a shy boy, tried desperately to get out of Frank's way. His timidity, however, just made Frank more aggressive.

"Well, what's wrong with you, clothespin? Are you scared of a little fight? Try it, you might like it," he said, laughing derisively.

"Just leave me alone, will you?" John said, backing away from him. "I...don't like fighting, all right?"

By nature, Andrew was sensitive to unfairness, so Frank's insolent act made his temper flare. "When that bastard recognizes the chance, his limited brain and manner takes a hike. Nothing despise me more than when this arrogant jerk opens his mouth and spews his venom," he murmured, casting a disgusted look at Frank. "He makes me sick. I wish he'd try his tricks on me."

"Oh, don't let that idiot creep bather you," George said, making a contemptuous gesture. "Let him have his fun. Although I agree, he is a lousy brat, but one day he will meet his match, I'm sure."

"Yeah," Andrew muttered, though he wasn't paying much attention to him. However, when he saw that Frank was actually pushing and tossing John roughly to provoke a fight, Andrew could not stand it any longer. "That's enough!" he mumbled, and with a sudden move he jumped over and placed his hand on Frank's shoulders.

"Look, Frank," he said in a no-nonsense tone, "why don't you just leave John alone and pick on someone of your own size?"

Surprised, Frank turned his head and glanced at Andrew with an annoyed look, then his face changed into a sarcastic smile. "Well, look who is playing the guardian angel! But why don't you mind your own business? I suggest you to butt off and get lost before I'll smash your nose. Then you can run home and cry to your F...Mother ..."

The blood running to his head, Andrew gasped, and with a quick move ripped his shoulder to face him and landed a powerful blow on to his nose before Frank could finish his scurrilous sentence.

Frank staggered backward and crashed to the ground. He shook his head wildly and jumped up to fight back. At this point, however, George jumped between them. "All right, Frank, cool down," he warned him, "and don't act like a smart ass. Or else Andrew will tear you to pieces if you are giving him the chance. So for your own sake, you better to take your lumps and beat it."

After tilting his head in an attempt to stop the bleeding, Frank, disregarding the warning, pushed George aside fiercely, and attacked Andrew. But he was ready, and skillfully ducked and hit Frank again on the left ear. Dazed, he fell down for the second time. Feeling dizzy, slowly he picked himself up and cast a hateful glance at Andrew and sneaked off.

"And that was just a warning," Andrew yelled after him. "Next time better if you choose your words more carefully about my mother."

A roar of laughter broke out in the crowd that had been gathered to watch the fight. It proved that they rooted for Andrew who had a friendly personality with a good sense of humor. And also he was popular for his participating in many kind of sports, while the class generally despised Frank. Leaving the scene with George, he heard someone saying with a satisfied tone, "At last that bully found his match and got what he deserved."

*

A few hours later, hading home after school, Andrew was sitting on the tram. As it passed over the Franz Joseph Bridge, he looked out the window in a day-dreaming mood, admiring the picturesque sight of the Danube that separated Buda from Pest. His beloved city of Budapest already has been recovered from the barbaric destruction of the Second World War, but the memories from his childhood—the loneliness, the fear and hunger he had experienced—still vividly lingered on. Those beautiful bridges, some of them were more charming than the new ones, were blown up and dangled in the river, the two ends yawning painfully towards the sky. Destruction and ruins were everywhere. During the war years he lived with his mother, for his father was a soldier fighting the war on Russian soil. More images from that era flashed through his mind. He saw himself as a little boy walking the streets of Budapest in ragged clothes, looking at food in the grocery stores with longing, for he knew he could no have them.

He remembered living in terrible hardship, because his mother could provide only the bare necessities—just enough to stay alive. How some memories stay with you to the end of time! Recalling some of those days when the force of life tempted him so strongly to steal... With certain shame, now he could understand with a flicker of smile on his face. He was glad that something always held him back. Perhaps it was because my mother was able to instill in me some strict moral values, he thought.

Then the war was finally over in 1945. Hitler's Germany was defeated by the Russians and Americans, but who could have believed that it will be replaced by the most sinister era Hungary and Eastern Europe had ever known: Soviet Communism.

PART ONE

WAR — AND LOVE, IN THE ERA OF MADNESS

1942 — 1956

1

COMING OF AGE

IN 1942, ANDREW WAS barely six years old when his father was drafted into the army. After three months of training, Mike Dombrady received a three-day pass, for he was declared ready to go to the battlefield. Hungary was fighting on the side of Hitler's Germany, against the Soviet Communism. By now the Second World War had been going on for three years, and the Germans were advancing deep into the Soviet Union.

Mike was six feet tall, a broad-shouldered ruggedly handsome man of thirty-one. His thick, black eyebrows matched the smooth hair that he combed back, carefully parting it on the left side. Standing in his uniform at the platform of the Eastern Railway Station amongst the swarming, noisy crowd, he glanced around the dirty, soot-smelling building with a grim face, observing the mood around him. By their dejected faces it was easy to see that most of the people were waiting for the train for the same reason. It is the sign of the times, he thought. Margie, his wife on his right side, clung to his arm quietly crying. Occasionally he stroked her hand gently in a consoling manner: "Don't worry about me, sweetheart, I can take care of myself. You take care of yourself and Andrew. I'll be back, you will see." But it brought little result.

Andrew stood dejectedly beside his mother, waiting for the train to depart. Lately he had heard a lot about the war and knew that the train would take his father to Russia, but he was confused about what's that meant. Sad as he was, he did not cry like his mother, although he felt he should, because loving his father as much as he did, he knew that he would be away for a long while. It bothered him, but he just had to accept it.

Then, when the conductor's sharp whistle finally gave the signal for boarding, the noise amplified into an almost panic-like shouting. With throbbing heart, Mike kissed his wife good-bye, and turned to Andrew. Bending down, he cleared his throat, trying to put on a brave front. "Well, Andrew, as I told you, it is my time to go and fight for our country. I can't tell you how long I'll have to be away but one day I'll be back. That's a promise. So, be a good boy and take care of yourself and your mother." Then the train made a noisy jerk, he kissed him and jumped aboard just in time, for it slowly started to move, leaving a screaming and waving crowd behind.

Bewildered, Andrew had no idea how he would go about taking care of his mother, but he felt proud just the same, for his father trusting him.

* * *

Without his father's reassurance, the days that followed were very confusing. The relentless sounds of the shrieking siren-warnings for the bombing, which came more and more often that was followed rushing to the air-raid shelter. The almost daily routine of huddling each others, clutched by the icy hand of fear was terrifying. It seemed like hours went by listening to the thunderous shower of bombs falling mercilessly down on the city.

Under this horrendous pressure Andrew tried bravely to console his mother when she was crying. Not always succeeded, but when she finally smiled, it filled him with pride that he was able to fulfill his promise.

Then during this horror, Margie received the first letter from Mike, which contained only the essentials, like his safe arrival to the battlefield, and how he missed and loved them. Then his letters stopped coming, and she had no idea of what happened. The only information she could glean was from the newspapers—but the stories were unreliable and confusing. The headlines dealt mainly with the hardship of the cruel Russian winter, and the inhumane conditions the solders had to endure...Casualties, shortage of ammunition and food—nothing but trouble and suffering. There were mostly contradictory accounts about "victories", "withdrawals" and "systematic military maneuvers," and Margie could find no reason for hope or consolation. The war was dragging on far too long.

Then, after the long-long stretch of months, out of the blue Mike suddenly appeared at the door. He came home on a furlough due to him for fighting on the battlefield for over six months.

"Mike!" Margie screamed, rushing to him with open arms. "Oh, Mike, thank God you're alive."

"Oh, yes, sweetheart, no bullet can touch me," he said, trying to put it lightly.

"Please, don't talk like that!" she said with horror, just when Andrew stepped in. Surprised, he ran to him shouting. "Gee, Dad, you are home!" his eyes sparkling proudly. "Wow, you look thinner but great!" he said as they hugged each other.

"Thanks, son, you look great yourself."

Margie smiled. "Yes, Daddy is thin because he misses not only us but my magic kitchen," she said, observing how much weight he had lost. "But I'll take care of that."

Mike laughed. "Honey, I don't think you will have time to do that in three days."

"Oh!" Margie cried out in disappointment.

As if Andrew read his mind, he knew what to do. He ran out to tell their friends and relatives the good news of Mike's arrival. They came immediately. After the warm and cheerful embraces, Mike had to answer to the flood of questions. He talked about the senseless killing and destruction, the overpowering might of the Soviet Army, and how thousands of soldiers had to walk tens of kilometers in deep mud, sometimes pushing broken-down army trucks, while they had hardly anything to eat for days. He had seen thousands of dead soldiers and civilians along the way, and witnessed the total deprivation that human beings had to suffer....

But those bittersweet three days were running out fast, and it was time to return to the battlefield. In spite of Mike's protest, Margie indulged herself in baking his favorite cakes, enough to last him for days.

Then again they stood at the Eastern Railway Station, exchanging tearful farewells. Before Mike kissed Andrew, he said, "Well, my son, your mother said that you were a very good boy; I'm proud of you. Just keep up the good work."

*

Then suddenly, in the chain of events, Miklos Horthy had announced in the radio that Hungary withdraw the army, for he believe that the further bloodshed is senseless. For a day or two the country was overjoyed. The withdrawing army ecstatically started to sing patriotic songs, shouting: LONG LIVE HORTHY, DOWN SALASY!

But the March 19, 1944 was a historical day in Hungary. Although Hungary was officially Germany's ally, the German SS army unexpectedly seized the power, threw the ruling Horthy out of the office, and overthrew the Hungarian government. They immediately put the power into the hands of Ferenc Szalasy, the leader of the *Arrow Cross*, which was the Hungarian Nazi Party, who announced that *"we will fight Bolshevism to the end!"* Soon more anti-Jew laws followed, and the hatred and cruelty toward the Jews had increased. They were forced to wear the yellow stars on their garments. It was a tragic sight witnessing helplessly the cruel ways by the *Arrow Cross* has treated them, worse than animals, And it was just a matter of time before those innocent people ended up in cattle cars, being deported to those infamous concentration camps in Austria..

From now on more ominous tension gripped the nation. The daily routine of watching the danger-sign sirens and rushing to the air-raid shelters became the temporary lifestyle, as the nerve-racking intensity of the bombing increased, bringing more and more fear, panic and dead. The rumbling, earthshaking explosions of the chain-bombing promised Armageddon, leaving its dreadful devastation behind. One day a bomb dropped too close to Andrew's building, making an indescribable ear-splitting sound. He watched with horror as people dropped to the floor, his mother among them. He quickly lay down beside her, shaking so badly that this time his mother had to calm him.

The newspaper headlines were screaming: *Brutal Western bombing attack over Budapest!* By now, as the Soviet war-machine irresistibly advanced toward Hungary, the letter from Mike stopped coming completely. Along with the advancement the desperate news-reports were spreading of the horrifying destruction by the Soviet army, raping and robbing mercilessly along the way. They arrived at Budapest in the winter of 1945, and the bitter siege for the capital began. The desperate street-to-street, sometimes even house-to-house fighting went on with heavy artillery and rattling machine guns that forced the people to move in the shelters permanently.

2

THE NEW WORLD

AFTER THE GERMANS SURRENDERED the almost leveled city, the occupation by the Soviet army followed. After two weeks of starving, people finally came out of their hated air-raid shelters. Fortunately some trains were still in service, so the invasion of the villages for food had begun. But what chaos received them! Day after day people waited for hours, and when the train arrived, the huge crowd overran the platforms. In the pandemonium the struggle for a tiny place started by pushing, screaming, cursing—almost killing one another at the train entrance. Eventually the train was overfilled, people squeezed in like herrings is a sardine box. Even the rooftops were jammed, yet hundreds were still left behind.

Those graceful bridges over the river that linked Pest with Buda, were torn apart and yawned hopelessly towards the sky, because they were blown up by the Germans in order to gain time. While the Red Army's priority was to build some temporary bridges, the war was going on, and the renewed papers were screaming their hatred against Hitler: *"Only an insane lunatic would fight against the whole world....!"*

Beside lack of food, the most urgent problem was the desperate fuel shortage. By now Andrew was 10 years old. In his youthful restlessness it was a relief to be able to move around again, and he spent days collecting firewood from the rubble. Then, with the bundle on his back, he would carry them home. However, his favorite place was the supermarket where he enjoyed roaming around between those inviting food-stands, admiring the beautiful meats. At the same time he was trying to find casual work, for which he would receive food, because he was always hungry.

One day his mother went to the market, and asked Andrew to go with her. Andrew tagged along for a while, but her slow pace did not suit him, so they parted and Andrew mingled with the crowd. By now he knew the place well. As he roamed about casually, listening to the black-marketers shouting, offering their inviting sweet-smelling treasures, suddenly on one of the stands he saw the most beautiful piece of bacon in the world. He stared at it for a while with his rumbling stomach and parched throat, longing, like a starving beggar. He had some money, and on the spur of the moment, he wanted to surprise his mother. He knew what the *black-market* meant, but he didn't know that lard and bacon were priced their weight like gold—figuratively speaking. So, when he asked the man how much he wanted for a quarter of a pound, the astronomical price sent the blood up to his head.

"That is too much!" he cried. "I can't pay *that much* for such a small piece of bacon!"

The man sniffed and bent down condescendingly. "Well, kid, if you don't have the money, you should not want to eat bacon."

Andrew's pride was deeply hurt, and his remark brought out all the outrage a ten-year-old can feel. He clenched his fist and threw a punch at the surprised man's mocking face.

"You dirty cheater!" he shouted, and ran away.

Those were indeed hard times. To survive, people ate anything edible, wasting nothing. When Margie was able to find a job at a Laundromat, it was a great relief. She was able to arrange a sitter for Andrew with her neighbor, and after that life was a little easier. Life without Mike was still miserable.

When the war has finally ended in May 1945, a huge happy celebrating crowd was marching on the Great Boulevard. But the economic situation became more and more catastrophic. It caused the Pengo (the Hungarian currency) to collapse, and the black-market sky-rocketed. Imagine that one week's pay of 100 Pengo jumped to 1,000 Pengo the following week. Soon the workers received one million, ten million and then billions. Eventually people got tired of saying "million" or "billion", instead they called it "mill-pengo"and "bill-pengo." Keeping up with these astronomical numbers was impossible, and the workers started to demand food for payment. A few litres of cooking oil, a couple of kilos of potatoes, flour and sugar were the most welcomed items for a week's pay.

*

It was in these tens and troubled days when Margie's sister, Barbara, unexpectedly visited her. She lived in a small village with her husband faraway in the North-East. They had a beautiful teenaged daughter, Sylvia. Margie could not believe the drastic aging she went through since she saw her.

The purpose of her visit was that at this time this was the only way to let Margie know what had happened to her husband and Sylvia.

"Because we have heard about the Russians robbing and raping women was rampant, we dug a hiding place for Sylvia. But in an unexpected moment they saw her and tried to rape her. She started to scream and my husband grabbed the axe to defend her. The other Russian shot him on the spot. Then they both raped her," she said, sobbing in pain.

"Oh, my God!" exclaimed Margie, crying with her.

"My...poor...baby, she was engaged to a fine young man, but in her heartbreak she broke up the engagement and joined the convent to be a nun."

*

Margie had not heard from Mike for almost three years, so ending the war did not bring much happiness for her. Until that is, when one day Mike suddenly appeared at her doorstep. He stood there in ragged dirty clothes, unshaven, all skin and bones, looking like a beggar. Margie frowned, but when she recognized him, tears of happiness filled both their eyes. They fell into each other's arms. "Mike, oh, Mike...,"she cried. "I can't believe it. Welcome home."

"Margie! Dear God, how good to see you. Thank God, at last I'm home again!" he said with trembling voice, while his eyes were glued to her happy face.

After sitting down, Mike recovered his composure. "You look as lovely as ever. Where is Andrew? Is he all right? Gosh, he must be a big boy by now..."

"Oh, yes, he is; and he is fine," Margie said, hardly able to take her eyes off of him. "He sure has grown a lot. Right now, he is collecting some wood for the stove. He'll be back soon. Oh, but I talk too much," she said sheepishly. "And you must be hungry..."

*

Now, with the war behind them, they also had a chance to build a new future. To have peace again was a sweet welcome. During the following days Mike told stories about his life during the last three years. He sure had his share of suffering, running away from the Russians' heavy attacks, ending up in an American prison camp in Germany.

"Well, despite the hardship, thank God you look healthy," Margie beamed.

Yet there were noticeable changes in Mike's behavior, which she could not ignore. His nerves were shot, and he was easily irritated and more impatient, which was alien to his nature. Even Andrew noticed it, and one day he mentioned it to his mother.

"Yes, Andrew, I know. But it could be worse, you know. So we have to do all we can to get him back to his old self."

As time passed, the worthless Pengo was replaced by a new currency: called *Forint*, which, due to severe legislative measures against inflation, miraculously kept its stability. The economy was on its way to recovery, so they were optimistic.

The first priority was to forget the past, and the destitution the war had brought upon them. The people's outlook on the Soviet army being around was annoying, but it was considered an unpleasant necessity. People believed that this nuisance was only temporary. The patriotic optimists believed that the war had ruined the country, but we'll build a free and healthy society, where searching for the truth will not mean concentration camps and mass murdering... The left-wing communists said that the Soviet heroes freed the country, and comrade Rakosi will lead us into a flourishing socialist society, free from western capitalism...

One day Andrew witnessed an argument on the street. "If this is the paradise the comrade want to fight for, better if you put a rope on your neck and hung yourself. Maybe you will save the nation by it."

But the people of Hungary did not expect, or believe that the Western World would agree with the generous peace-treaty, which allowed the Soviet to swallow up the Soviet-Bloc countries. So Hungary became a Soviet satellite.

Up until the 1947 election (which was the last one in Hungary), people had enjoyed a reasonable political freedom. But here was a crushed, beaten-to-the ground, robbed and exhausted nation that was an open prey for the Soviet world-power to play games with for their pleasure. So regardless of the open anticommunist mood, a dictatorship was born and the Stalinist election tactics put an end to *freedom* in the country.

First, the Communist Party (which actually had the real power), struck many of the "undesirable" voters names off the list. Second, in order to ensure the victory, they created those "GREEN CARDS" which was distributed to all members of the Communist Party. These cards were an official ticket with which they could vote *anywhere* in the country, and at as many places as they chose. So, caravans of trucks and buses were loaded with party members, and traveled from city to city—*voting*. Naturally a well-prepared explanation was given that these people just *"happened to be working there at the time."* People knew the truth, but there was nothing anyone could do about it. Then it happened: the Communist Party—or actually the GREEN CARDS claimed victory!

Stunned by the horrendous boldness, this victory crushed their freedom forever. The nation's law and order turned upside down, and things began to happen fast: Hungary has entered into a *lawless state* that was called: **The Stalin Era.** Through his fanatic followers, a secret police method was imported from Moscow to establish the terror. That being done, murdering of innocent people became a way of life.

*

Under this dictatorship the world went crazy. The members of the Communist Party were empowered to embark on the most vicious manhunt to eliminate the *enemy*. It provided them a free hand for getting their revenge. There were enough conscience-ridden lunatics willing to do anything to climb to power. If they reported someone to be an "anticommunist," God forbid, it was only a matter of time until his/her disappearance occurred in the middle of the night. A party member's words were sufficient, proof and evidence was not needed. So this insidious terror wrapped thousands of innocent people into its iron web.

As Stalinism engulfed the nation, fourteen-year-old Andrew watched in confused horror what was going on. He began to learn fast that it was suicidal to express one's opinion against the system or leaders. The only choice that remained for people was to withdraw into their homes and witness in utter despair as the country was sinking deeper and deeper into destruction.

3

THE FACE OF COMMUNISM
(In the Reign of Terror.)

THE DOMBRADY FAMILY LIVED in an old apartment in the VIII-th district, on Baross Street. Although the place was old and primitive, with the desperate housing shortage, they felt blessed to be able to live there. They loved it for the good location, although they didn't have the luxury of a bathroom or a refrigerator. But at least they had indoor plumbing. The apartment consisted of two bedrooms and a kitchen with a wood-burning stove, which was used for cooking as well as heating. They had an extra small room that one could call the living room, though it was used as a dining room. The walls were faded and dirty and the air was stale and smoky, partly from the wood-burning stove. But it was almost useless to open the window, for the smell was everywhere; the whole city was breathing polluted air.

In spite of all that, Mike looked around the apartment with peaceful satisfaction. Fortunately he got back his old job at the National Transport Company as an auto mechanic. His eagerness to work again soon paid off. After a few months one of his co-workers urged him to apply for a transport driver position. Mike did not believe he would get the position, because he was not a party member. By now it was known that one of the Communist Party's priorities was to give the better positions to party members.

On top of that, he had some adverse points to consider. The system already had established a secret file, from which the Personnel Office knew that Mike had returned home from an American prison camp in Germany. (By now America was the

Soviets' most hated enemy.) Anyone who had any connections with the United States *in any form* was considered suspicious, even dangerous. Therefore if someone had relatives living in America, it was best to keep it a deep secret, or else he/she could have been considered an American spy.

Also Mike's file revealed that the Dombrady family attended church occasionally. Although it had not yet been openly declared as a crime, but practicing in religion was mark a "sin." His file also revealed that Mike's father had been a policeman in the early 1930's. (If any member of a family had served an anticommunist system, was considered an anticommunist,) and their past had affected the present family members. So Mike learned that he "inherited" these sins, which unforgivably became *his sins.*

But in spite of all these, to his surprise, he was granted the transfer to the transport department, because the company badly needed experienced drivers. However, his *background* still caused limitations, for he was not trusted to make international trips like bonafide party members. Even so, it was a better job, and he was glad for the opportunity to make a more decent living.

* * *

At the same time Andrew was attending university in Buda. At the beginning he liked the atmosphere and enjoyed going there, but in dictatorship he learned soon that here too has been built up a network by which the authorities kept the students behavior under scrutiny. They already knew Andrew's background, and watched that he did not display much enthusiasm for communist activities.

So it was only natural that one day George Bistray, the school principal, called him into his office. When Andrew entered, the first thing that had assaulted his eyes was a huge picture of Stalin and Rakosy (Stalin's right-hand man in Hungary) on the wall behind comrade Bistray, with an inscription underneath.

**WITH COLLECTIVE EFFORT WE WILL
ACHIEVE THE WORLD POWER!**

Andrew glanced at it with supreme contempt. Bistray sat behind the desk like a judge with a grim face, and motioned Andrew to take a seat. He was leafing through the report, then he began lecturing him.

"Comrade Dombrady", he began, "I have reports on my file that you don't show enough enthusiasm during your participation in the youth organization. I must remind you that you should display more gratitude toward the glorious Party for the opportunity that has given you. You don't seem to realize how fortunate you are living in a free and prosperous country where you have a great future. You should take advantage of the benefits you could enjoy, by changing your passive attitude. We have to work for our future with all our strength, in a collective spirit. Your future is in your hands, but you must show also unconditional appreciation to our glorious Soviet liberators. They sacrificed their lives for our freedom, and in exchange, the only sacrifice the Party is asking of you is that you show us more enthusiasm. We all must work hard to achieve our goal. But so far you're not doing your share, and you haven't proved that you're worthy of living in this glorious society."

While those loathsome lies rolled out from his prostituted mouth, Andrew could feel perspiration trickling down his spine. It took a superhuman effort to keep himself from shouting, *"What is the goal?"* Instead, sustaining his gaze, he said, "Comrade Bistray, I came here to learn, and I don't think I have to prove anything. I'm not a criminal."

Frowning, Bistray moved closer to Andrew and looked at him menacingly. His condescending voice had a deadly undertone.

"Listen, Andrew, you better think twice before you say things like this. You can consider yourself lucky, for this time I will overlook what you just said. But for the future I strongly advise you to choose your words more carefully. I could interpret your remarks as an insult to the Party, but for now I'll let you get away with it."

Andrew expressed his appreciation for Bistray's generosity and said that he will try harder. When he staggered out with a sigh of relief, he mumbled to himself with disgust: *Good God, some glorious freedom!* He took a deep breath as if to clear his lungs from the spiritually polluted air he had left behind.

Then it involuntarily crossed his mind that this brainwashed principal had probably been trained in political seminars to wipe off the joy and happy laughter from people's face, for this happy countenance must constitute a menace to a soulless Party. It was clear that the communists are making all the effort to form a robot society to ensure a total worship for the Party! It was increasingly obvious that the Stalinists did not acknowledge the concept of conscience and human emotion. They were constantly filling the brains of the youth with trenchant slogans, instead of enriching their souls with love, trust and respect. Andrew could see clearly that they were creating figments for people to hate—making enemies between friends. They were forcing them to take sides for or against the system. Achieving that, it was easier to eliminate the ones who were **not** *with them*. Adhering to the ideology was the only way to survive.

There were some over-ambitious communist teachers, like Bistray, urging students to report anybody, even their parents, if they hated the system. The students were told that to do so was not only their duty, but also an honor. When the Party obtained complete power, another of their task was to build up an absolutely reliable Secret Police, it was called the **AVO**. They became a pampered bunch of hoodlums and heartless fanatics, whose top priority was to build up a network of informers in the factories, offices and schools. They were always been able to find people willing to work for them, in return for generous privileges—or just out of fear. It was organized in such insidious ways that no-one—not even the spies—could relax for fear of having a spy spying *on them*.

* * *

Peter Kardos was a perfect example of how the communists achieved their goals. Whenever a student was called to the principal's office unexpectedly, a pang of suspicion always agitated his/her nervous system. Peter Kardos was no exception. He was a good student who was also active in the youth organization. But, unfortunately to him, his enthusiasm was not driven by political ambition, only for having fun, and for his love of being active. However, because his parents were *working-class* people, with that excellent background the officials thought that his enthusiasm must be due to his interest in becoming a communist.

In the principal's office he was greeted by two plain clothes AVO men, and George Bistray who sat at the end of the table with a fixed, simpering smile on his face.

Peter looked at the two men. One looked more like a village peasant than a policeman; but the second one looked quite the opposite. He had a polished but unpredictable look on his face, which in one second could reflect kindness, and the most terrifying look in the next. Naturally he was the one who carried most of the conversation. He started with a friendly little chat about Peter's activities in school, then he asked him about how he was getting along with his schoolmates. Unsuspecting, Peter bragged proudly that he had no enemies as far as he knows.

"Oh, then it would be no problem for you to be working for us."

Peter's face turned white. "What do you mean?"

"Oh I think you know what I mean."

With a shocked hesitation, Peter said, "You want me to be a *spy* or something?" spitting out the word "spy" as if it were a poison. *"Never!"*

"Come on, Peter, it wouldn't be that bad. Of course it's up to you, but you should consider the reward, the great future you could have. Naturally we're suggesting that you think it over before giving your final answer. Since the kids trust you, it would be relatively an easy job for you."

Peter's face was red. "You're right. They trust me, and I want to keep it that way." At this moment he glanced at the huge picture of Stalin and Rakosi on the wall, and suddenly he had the feeling as if they were able to see into his mind.

The two men exchanged a surprised glance. "Don't be too hasty, Peter," the polished one said, putting on a supercilious smile. "Look, we are your friends and hope you'll co-operate. On the other hand, we have *ways* of making people to co-operate, but we hope it won't have to come to that. The choice is yours. But if you provoke us, you could get yourself into a great deal of trouble."

From the next day on Peter silently carried his terrifying burden. The sudden change made him feel like he was an outcast, a living dead. He would say "Hi" to his friends and then went on his way. He became moody, hardly could eat, yet he would not talk about what was bothering him. If someone tried to confront him, he became irritated. "Just leave me alone, I'm okay."

But Andrew knew that he was not okay. Yet, even that he was one of his friends, when he tried to approach him, he was evasive and rude. Andrew, however, was persistent and Peter gradually told him the whole sordid story, begging him to keep it a secret. Andrew was shocked beyond words.

The third night two plain-clothed AVO men appeared at the Kardos's home. When he identified himself, Pal Kardos was arrested in spite of his protest. He guessed that it had to do something with Peter. In the AVO headquarters they came up with the spurious allegation that his son had reported him for listening to **Voice of America** radio program. (In those days it was a serious crime listening to any foreign news.)

He didn't believe them, but fortunately other then lecturing they, did not torture him. When they finally let him go, they warned him in no uncertain terms never to tell anybody, not even his family, where he had been taken. For if he did, his son would disappear in the middle of the night.

Meanwhile comrade Bistray asked him about whether he had changed his mind. Peter's answer was a definite *no*!

Soon after his father returned home, the two AVO men paid another visit to Bistray's office. When Peter was called in, he noticed that Bistray was not in the room. He cast a quick apprehensive glance at the two men, and a foreboding shiver rushed through him as he sat down. The polished one greeted him, a smug smile lurking in the corner of his mouth, as if saying, *"I told you so."* Then he asked Peter about his decision.

A dark scowl clouded Peter's face as he bowed his head, recognizing that they were actually enjoying playing with his emotions. He felt suffocated by the intimidating atmosphere that surrounded him. Struggling with a terrible inner shaking, he turned his head with a nervous jerk as if in protest, but said nothing. The two men mistook Peter's silence for hesitation and tried to encourage him to make up his mind. His act and tone of voice was full of humiliation, condescending, and superior. "Well, Peter," the polished man said, "we can understand, but if I were you I wouldn't hesitate. You should see my point by now." He kept talking as he walked around him, then he stopped, his menacing frame towering over him. "My point is that next time your mother might disappear," he said with a malicious smirk, his voice as cold as ice. "Now, you would not want *that* to happen, would you son?"

His words were dripping with joy of playing the power game without any trace of human concern, and Peter was boiling inside. But threatening his mother was the last straw. His face darkened and he jumped into a raging explosion. Like a cornered animal he jumped up, shouting: *"Leave my mother alone, you dirty..."* Then he broke into shuddering sob. The other AVO man jumped to strike him, but the polished face held him back. "Okay, Peter, we can understand and will let you get away with it this time."

They have planted the suffocating poison into his brain so effectively that it was driving him insane. Facing with the impossible demand of causing suffering to innocent people was such a shock, he could not have recovered from. Peter went through unimaginable anguish, crying through many a sleepless nights until his mind was numb. He knew what the stigma of "spy" meant, which would follow him to the grave. He was so overwhelmed by desperation that it made him reach the end of the rope: Peter Kardos sacrificed his life—he hanged himself.

Even knowing what Peter was going through, Andrew still could not believe what he had done. "God, what a disgusting world!" he said to George as they were heading home from school. "This system scares the daylights out of me. But what can one do?"

"Yeah, I'm speechless, too. Members of the AVO are not normal people. No sane people could ever belong to such a soulless profession. As you know, my Dad was deeply involved in politics, and he paid for it. He sure knew how the AVO operates."

"Yes, I know he was well informed."

As they walked along the promenade on the Buda side, George looked around to make sure that nobody was following them.

"He loved to talk about politics," George said, "and one day I overheard him telling to one of his friends that the AVO carefully selects their members for the purpose of holding the terror with iron hands. In the seminars the instructor's goal is to destroy their conscience in order to follow the Party rule. They fill their minds with hatred and distrust against anything that is decent. They must prove to the Party, that they would execute *any orders* without question. What's more, by the time they're completing the course, as a result of their training, the inspectors extinguish from their souls all the moral fiber, if they had any. Having done the brainwashing, they're incapable of feeling any guilt or remorse. And as long as they prove of following the Party's ideology, they're above the law—they're empowered to play God."

"That is just what we're experiencing," Andrew said, his curiosity aroused.

"Yes. Actually, they're given the license to kill...So what had happened to Peter doesn't surprise me."

Andrew shook his head, boiling. "It is horrible!" he said. "We're seeing it, and have to pretend that it's all right."

Arriving home, the tragedy was still raging in him over what had happened to Peter. Sitting at the table, Andrew poured out the tragedy to his father. "How could they put perfectly innocent people through something like this without the slightest chance of defending themselves?" he fumed.

"You know, son," Mike said, folding the newspaper he was just reading, "It's a complex matter. I have come to believe that there are people, Party fanatics, rather gangsters, dictators and opportunists who are born heartless, and hopelessly rotten-to--the-core individuals. Falling into Communism, we're experiencing firsthand how a system operates under political fanatics like Hitler and Stalin. Since they're criminals themselves, they grant the criminals more rights and protection than their innocent victims. Having lost all freedom, unfortunately the victims have no choice but to take the law into their own hands."

"Yeah...Well, I don't care what those "know-it-all" swaggerer big-mouths say, but sometimes I wish I could take the law into my own hands," Andrew said, clenching his fists to demonstrate the act. "We are sure learning it the hard way that in a total *police state* there are people in high positions who should be in jail. Instead, they're enjoying making people miserable. These misfits would do anything for power just to satisfy their viciously sick egos."

* * *

Mike had a close friend who had joined the Communist Party solely to protect his job. But he knew well that his friend was far from being a communist. During one of his visit he told Mike that one of the Party's main priorities was to destroy patriotic sentiments, because they were against the communist ideology. Then he pulled out a book from his hidden pocket that he had managed to put his hands on secretly. He explained that this woman had lived through the Russian revolution in the early twenties. She wrote a book in Vienna, called: *The diary of Rachmanova.* He had underlined some sections he wanted Mike to read. The powerful revelation described the limited ways in which the communists' mind are working.

"...It was a peculiar way the communists solved the people's life in Russia. Their solution was so incredibly primitive like themselves. Because basically all of them—even the most "brilliant" individuals have nothing more than dark, narrow brains. But their primitiveness is exactly in which their power lies. For the masses seldom accept

the real truth but rather what they pumped into their limited brains. In the communists' minds there are no such concept as human being or soul, only proletariat and capitalist....

*The most distinctive characteristics are their lack of understanding humanity, therefore they have no mercy for human feelings. As far as they are concerned, actually there are **only slogans**, and people are nothing more than robots that execute those slogans. In Communism, - this dry and empty ideology, - the power is built on those slogans. Without those their ideology is dead. It is their **predestination** what they call: "We're taking care of you, so shut up and be happy!" They want to build a paradise, but they haven't the faintest idea who could be happy in that paradise..."*

* * *

During these troubled years it was the constant terror that produced a nonstop fear. The name of *Communist Party* became a symbol of menace that hung over people's head, like the sword of Damocles, ready to strike at any moment. The systematic brainwashing reached every corner of the nation. By destroying all human rights and common decency, they purposely injected suspicion and distrust in everybody, and this way they achieved another important goal. *In this atmosphere* people would not dare to rebel, so they wouldn't have any problem controlling them.

As part of the daily life, workers were forced to participate in *"volunteer"* activities after their regular work. One of these activities was the political seminars where they would *"learn"* (instead of *feel!*) how free and happy they were. Those people who grew up in a free society, could not believe the notion that all those compulsory activities were brushed with the bright color of *pretense* as happy *"willingness"*—meaning that this is what they really wanted to do. It was an art of the greatest deceit in distracting reality.

First of May was declared a Workers Holiday. On this day huge marching event was organized for the purpose of glorifying the Party and the heroic Soviet Liberators. The Party secretary was responsible for **everyone's** participation. On the way to Hero's Square people had to carry Stalin's and Rakosi's pictures, while chanting Party slogans, glorifying the leaders and the great Soviet liberators. Stalin was god, above all gods.

Ah, indeed, Communism was such an unbelievably simple system! After this non-existing freedom, there was nothing but fear of

thinking, of speaking the truth, of wanting to be free, of hoping; *fear of everything and everybody—fear of being human!*
That is Communism my friend!

In this depressing atmosphere Andrew managed to withdrew into his studies and, as a safety valve, he turned to his favorite sports. He joined the boxing club and swam regularly, but most importantly he belonged to a soccer club. In the European countries soccer was considered a national sport. During these years Hungarian soccer was one of the best. At the Helsinki Olympics Hungary had beaten Brazil 4 -2 in overtime. In another great soccer event, Hungary had beaten England 6-3 in London's Wembley Stadium. And in Budapest, Hungary won 7-1.

In the eyes of the Hungarians, the Puskas-Kocsis "golden-foot" soccer stars were the real heroes of the country.

* * *

Before the Second World War the Communist and Social Democratic Parties existed only illegally. George's father, Miklos Pusztai had been a member of the Social Democratic Party since 1939. While after 1945 the Communist Party was swamped with complete hate, the S.D.P. was popular. But since both were considered working-class parties, in an unpleasant but obvious reason the communists flattered the S.D.P. by calling them *"Sister Party".*

During the 1947 election campaign, the communists' strategy was to advocate the coalition, which the S.D.P vehemently opposed. Pusztai made some heated public speeches, using strong words, referring to them as the menace of Stalinism. "The idea of Communism was fabricated in Moscow by a group of demented monsters", he said. "They have killed millions of peasants in the process of breaking them into an inhuman system; then after the Second World War they carried their extreme "dream" idea, their mental disease into our country by force. We know that it is an inhuman system because it is based upon a carefully planned terror, in which uttering the wrong word evokes the deepest suffering a human can endure. Its aim is to eliminate the humanity in us, to mutilate the human spirit, making robots out of us. Is that what we want? *Never!"* he shouted, hitting the table with his fist.

He received tremendous applause and a standing ovation. Naturally his speeches were in the AVO's secret file. After the Communist Party came to power, they immediately forced the

"*Sister Party*" into coalition. It boosted the party's membership; however, many S.D.P. members refused to become communists in this convoluted way, among them Miklos Pusztai. But it made no difference. He was branded a *right-wing* democrat, the communists' confirmed enemy. And during the manhunt for anti-communists, one night in 1948, two plain-clothes AVO men came for him.

Although he knew the answer, he risked the question anyway, "What is the charge you're arresting me on?"

Their answer was a blow to his abdomen. "How dare you ask questions, you filthy traitor of the proletariat?"

After this they dragged him into a waiting van.

They took him to Andrassy Street, into one of the most infamous AVO torture chambers in Budapest. Behind those thick doors there was another country, a hell on earth, run by the KGB from Moscow.

After throwing him into a concrete cell, to the very bottom of the pit of human degradation, he had no time to collect himself. Without a shred of humanity, two AVO men were pounced on him like hungry dogs on a bone. Night after night they tortured him, demanding the confession of being an American spy, a traitor of socialism and the enemy of the working class. These charges were on paper already; all they wanted from him was his signature.

When he refused, the AVO's fist smashed his face throwing him against the wall. Then they would kick him everywhere. For a few days they continued beating him with Billy clubs. His blackouts were a welcome relief but they brought him back with buckets of icy water. Occasionally he let out a muffled grown to suppress the pain, and he gritted his teeth to stop from screaming.

It was one of Pusztai's misfortunes that he was born with a face that seemed smiling. Even when his face was contorted with pain, it still appeared to be smiling. This happy countenance irritated one of his torturers, for he interpreted it as "defiance." To solve it, he simply punched out six of his teeth with his Billy club, making sure he would never smile again.

After a week of beating, Pusztai was taken to a secret death-camp, called *Recsk*. Six hundred prisoners lived in this camp, all for political "crimes," under the most dehumanizing conditions. They slept in tiny sheds on stinking manure with no window, heating or water; only a narrow door that was locked with an iron bar.

Fifty-eight watchtowers surrounded the camp, the guards with machine guns and vicious dogs for obvious reasons. One of the prisoners' worst deprivations was lack of water. Not only were they unable to clean themselves, but they were dying of dehydration. Contagious diseases were crippling them. But despite all this, the prisoners worked hard every day with sledgehammers, crushing large rocks into rubble, which would eventually end up as part of a road. With systematic methods the skeleton-like prisoners were sentenced and killed by slow death. Sickness was no excuse for being absent, only death. If one had to be hospitalized, the AVO doctors were instructed to cure the prisoners, so that they could endure more sufferings.

In this state of lawlessness the only laws were existed which the AVO had chosen to enforce. If a prisoner dared to stop for rest, the guards would beat him down. The gruesome work and the constant beatings had not only turned them into dreadful-looking skeletons, they knew that the AVO did not give a damn whether they lived or died. They knew also that they had no hope of ever getting out of there alive. In sheer desperation the prisoners ate anything they could find: leaves, grass, even insects. But they had to do it in secret, for if the guards caught them, the special Punishment Brigade would beat them up for cheating. What was there about life that they still valued? What gave them the strength to carry on when peaceful death would free them from this torturous hell? It must be one of the mysterious force of life.

There had been written many books about the subject of: *"The choice is yours to live your life the way you want to; it's up to you!"* Oh yes? Perhaps in a free country. But how about all those desperately oppressed miserable innocent millions of people in the world living in Eastern Europe and elsewhere, where there is no chance to have those choices! Their hopeless lives are pre-determined to the very last move as to how to live and die—unless they are willing to sink into the *oppressor's* level !

Then, to the great relief of all decent human beings in the world, the infamous Stalin died in March, 1953. The Stalin-worshiper Matyas Rakosi was replaced by Imre Nagy, who dissolved this dehumanized death-camp in the fall of 1953.

* * *

During Pusztai's imprisonment George's mother searched for

her husband. In her desperate inquiries at the AVO headquarters they gave her a cruel reply: "When the time comes, we'll let you know," the AVO man said. "So until then save yourself the trouble and don't bother us."

Miklos Pusztai had survived it all, but when he came home, he was unrecognizable. At forty-eight, he was an old man, his face lifeless and gaunt. His once strong body was emaciated; toothless with infected gums; he was a grotesque shadow of his former self. The years of torture and starvation had created the moral gangrene that destroyed him. Sitting alone, slouching in a chair, silently staring into the void with pain-haunted eyes, coughing violently and jerking in convulsions; the horror of suffering had robbed him all desire for living.

Watching what the *Arrow Cross*-turned sadist AVO criminals had done to his father, words cannot describe the murderous rage George felt against those sub-human murderers. What kind of God would create such monsters? It was beyond him to even consider calling them *human beings.* They had lost every right to belong to the human race, he thought.

Miklos Pusztai died in the spring of 1954.

* * *

After Stalin's death, Mike had received a surprised call from the Personnel Office. Now they politely told him that suddenly the communists had recognized his "trustworthiness" and from now on he was permitted to travel throughout Europe!

At first, he was happy, but he soon found out that it was an exhausting occupation. Being away for weeks from his family did not suit him well, but he continued until he succumbed to the job-related stress. He became tired easily, which he tried to hide. But it was getting worse and he could not fool Margie for long.

Finally, after her constant urging, he went to see the doctor. The verdict was harsh: his heart condition did not permit him to continue his job as a long-distance driver. So, after almost two years he was forced to accept a transfer to a lighter office job. This is how he became an office clerk—a position he accepted reluctantly.

4

CROSSROAD

ON THAT PARTICULAR APRIL day in 1955, when Andrew arrived home from school, he had almost forgotten about his fight with Frank. Closing the door behind him, he dropped his coat carelessly on the arm of a chair. His mother was busy in the kitchen, and he greeted her cheerfully.

"Hi, Mom, I'm home!"

"Oh hi, Andrew. I'm glad you're home. Before you do anything else, I want you to run to the store and bring some bread and milk. You know the kind we always buy. Your father must have his sandwich and coffee ready for tomorrow. Otherwise you know how fussy he can be if something isn't just the way he likes it."

"Sure, Mother, I know what you mean," he smiled, as the enticing aroma of the spicy chicken paprika hit his nostrils. "Hmmm, something smells good," he said, kissing her. Then he flung his coat over his shoulders and ran down the steps.

As soon as Mike started working again, Margie quit her job at the Laundromat to become a full time housewife. That is where she had been the happiest: taking care of her family. She was 40 years old, still young and pretty.

Just as Andrew came back and put the things away, Mike arrived. Closing the door gloomily, he said in a tired voice, "Hi everybody," then hung up his light overcoat.

"Hi, Dad. You seem to be in a bad mood," Andrew remarked. "I hope they didn't hassle you too much in the office."

"Well, whatever it is, it can't be so bad that my delicious chicken paprika and a glass of fine Hungarian wine would not fix," Margie interjected, trying to cheer him up.

Mike sat down heavily like a tired traveler at the end of the road.

Somehow even the nice welcome did not seem to cheer him up. He gave a tired sigh, then waved his hand distractedly. "It's a madhouse over there, I tell you. Everyone wants to play the big shot and give orders, and no one wants to do the work. There are more shepherds than sheep."

"What else is new?" Margie shrugged, laughing. "It sure not worth losing sleep over."

"I know, I know. It's just that I can't stand carelessness, which is the trend everywhere. I don't know where the pride in one's work has gone. There are no work ethics, no soul, no joy, no nothing. They're just doing their time and try to get everything they can for nothing. But that's enough of this," he gestured resignedly.

"I've heard that even stealing has become part of the game," Andrew said. "But that is the system, Dad, like pay, like work."

Mike smiled feebly. "You're probably right. So how was *your* day? Is everything all right in school? I guess you have to study hard these days with exams coming and all that."

"Hmm...Well, yes. The studying is all right, but unfortunately I ran into a little trouble at the schoolyard. It started when one of my classmates was picking on someone. I just can't stand it when one is bullying another just because he knows that the other guy is timid. So I told him to leave the boy alone. Then he made an insulting remark, so I punched him in the nose."

"Oh, Jesus, Andrew!" Margie exclaimed, clapping her hands desperately. "Did you have to get into another fight again?"

"O, come on, Mom!" It's not a big deal. I didn't mean to fight, but these things happen. Besides I only hit him when he insulted you. And no one can talk like that about my mother," he said, trying to justify himself.

This time, however, Mike decided to take the matter into his hands. "Andrew, listen to me. Your sentiment is fine; fighting for fairness is admirable. But my point is that sometimes your hands move faster than your brain -"

"Now wait a minute, Dad..."

"No, you listen to me!" Mike said firmly. "It worries me that you don't consider the price you could pay. One of these days you'll get into big trouble if you continue fighting against people's stupidity. I know some people should learn the lesson for their boorishness, but you also must learn to control your temper. It is one thing to stand up for what is right, but quite another to use common sense. You must remember that violence incites revenge. Anyway, did you get in trouble with the authorities?"

"No, although Frank reported it. He said I started the fight, which was partly true. However, three witnesses were willing to stand by me and they told Mr. Boros, the new principal, that Frank caused the fight. So he dismissed us by saying that in the future he won't tolerate fighting in the schoolyard."

"Nonetheless, your father is right," Margie maintained. "You just cannot take the law into your own hands like you did the other day on the tram. If only you have minded your own business, that fight would never have happened."

Andrew raked his black hair with his hand impatiently.

"But Mother," he protested, "you're really unreasonable. As I told you, I could not help being angry when I saw that a young man was sitting while a very old man stood right in front of him. He had the nerve to pretend he did not see him. This lack of consideration irritates me to no end! That punk would have ignored even a woman with a baby in her arms."

Mike chuckled but said nothing.

"So I asked him politely if he would be kind and give up his seat to that gentleman. What was wrong with that? And what did he do? He gave me an angry look and said, 'I've paid for my ticket just like everybody else, so get lost.' Then he hit my stomach with his elbow. Should I have thanked him that? Of course I punched him in the head maybe a little too hard, for he slid off the seat unconsciously. So they had to call the police. I was scared but I was lucky. People stood up for me and the policeman decided that my conduct was based on humanitarian concern." Andrew chuckled. "Well, he had to give me a 100 forint fine (approximately $3.00) for disturbing the traffic."

While Andrew recounted the event, he noticed a faint smile on his father's face. It was apparent that Andrew was a man of action. Although he didn't think he should encourage his child to settle things with his fist, but as far as he was concerned, deep down Mike trusted him and was proud of him. He knew that Andrew was stubborn, but also thoughtful, if the circumstances presented itself. He had a knack in judging people. Nevertheless, he warned him: "Well, just remember you cannot catch a bee with vinegar." Then he paused for a moment. "Anyway, let's change the subject and talk about something more important. You're nineteen years old, and I want to know what your plans are after the summer holidays. I've been hoping you'd stay in school, but are you still toying with the idea of quitting school for learning a trade?"

"That's right, Dad. You know my dream had always been to become an electric technician," Andrew said, his eyes gleaming. This was his favorite subject, and was proud that he had a clear vision of what he wanted to be. He was confident, and his determination created an air of excitement.

"In the fall I will find a company where I can learn the trade. You know, electricity is in my blood, and with my ambition I shouldn't have any trouble finding the place. The way technology is developing, the twentieth century will be an electronic era, especially for radio and television, and I see a great future in it," he said.

Andrew's enthusiasm touched Mike. "The way you put it, I admit the idea sounds good. It is very essential to believe in what you want to do. There are too many people who stagnate because they're miserable with their jobs. Just imagine how much happier life would be if we could do what we really liked." Then he put his hand on Andrew's shoulder.

"However, there is something that I had intended to talk with you, and this is as good a time as any. Since your whole life is ahead of you, it might be a good idea to pass on whatever experience in life *I went through*. When you will enter the world, you may meet people who will look down on you for your religion, your lack of education, nationality or whatever. You might will meet people who will hate you without knowing you, just because you're *different*. I have stumbled into some so-called "educated" but the most uncivilized, disrespectful, and narrow-minded individuals who just enjoyed hating. Generally their sense of humor is equal to a piece of dead wood. On this train of thought, I'll never forget what one of my teachers said: '*Courtesy is an attitude. And avoid those who have read but one book only in their lives*'. Remember also that being educated is not always synonymous with being intelligent."

Andrew was awestruck. He looked at his father as if he were a man he did not know. He felt honored that his father shared his inner thoughts with him. Talking to him as an equal brought about the deepest respect in him.

"Gee, thanks, Dad, for sharing your thoughts with me. It was beautiful, I appreciate it. Boy, wouldn't it make a great difference if parents would take the time to talk with their kids about important things like this! The world would be a much better place to live."

That may be true, son, but the trouble is that young people don't always listen to the advice of their elders."

* * *

In the middle of July Mike Dombrady came home with the good news that the following month they could spend their vacation at Lake Balaton! This was remarkable news, indeed, because finding decent accommodation at such a popular holiday spot in the middle of summer was almost impossible. Not that they had ever tried, for they could not have afforded it.

"As luck would have it," Mike explained while eating, "one of my co-workers had to cancel his holidays because of an emergency. He had leased a nice cabin at Balatonfoldvar for three weeks starting the last week of July. I don't know why, but he came to me saying, 'Mike, I thought you might be interested. I have this cabin reserved and you can have it if you want, but you must make up your mind in a hurry.' Naturally I jumped at the opportunity to get away from it all. 'My mind is made up' I said without hesitation. 'I'll take it.'"

"Yahoo! "Andrew shouted. "Now that is something, Dad. And the guy picked you! You must be a popular man there."

The prospect of going to a dream place they only heard about was really special, and they were delighted. Especially Andrew, to whom Lake Balaton was only a mere blue spot on the map. They knew that Lake Balaton was a resort for the rich and famous, so his imagination ran wild just thinking about the great adventure the trip might provide.

5

LAKE BALATON

THIS REMOTE WORLD, glittering with glamour had a haunting beauty about it. Lake Balaton, (Miami Beach of Hungary,) had been once an upper-class holiday resort. In this fairy-tale-like atmosphere a mysterious excitement permeated the air—it certainly had its magical effect on the visitors. It provided them a dream-like lifestyle that was, for many, far beyond their everyday life.

It was a hot day. The sun shone brightly from an incredibly blue sky, and its rays reflected on the softly rippling water. This was the Dombrady's second day at the beach. They stood at the shore for a while, leisurely looking around, as children were playing in the water, screaming and jumping, throwing beach balls to each other. Young lovers and people of all ages were enjoying themselves.

Adventure-seekers gauged the depth of the water, testing their aquatic endurance and swimming skills, while others were satisfied just enjoying the lukewarm water, letting it wash away the memories of the dreary existence that was their lives.

Then Andrew decided to go into the water and coaxed his parents to follow. He went into deep water, exuberantly showing off his swimming skills while his parents splashed about. When he stopped to catch his breath, squinting into the bright horizon, he saw some sailboats close to Tihany, floating lazily on the gentle undulating water.

His parents soon grew tired of the water, as Margie found it a little cold, so they decided to seek refuge on the grassy, shady shore. But Andrew stayed a little longer, swimming further out into the lake and offering himself to the sun.

When he had enough of swimming, he joined his parents, teasing them for being "chicken." Then as he turned, he saw a man

behind him reading the party paper: **Szabad nep** (Free People), of which front page read:
THE SOVIET UNION PROTECTS OUR FREEDOM BY FIGHTING AGAINST IMPERIALISM!

Disgusted, Andrew turned away. The poisonous lies follow us everywhere, he thought, and went wandering around a while aimlessly, watching the sunbathers. He saw some of the women wearing ridiculously tight bathing suits with a sheer determination to get a tan from the beating sun at all costs. (He already had a tan by playing soccer in the school field.)

As he walked slowly among the sunbathers, he noticed a girl on a blanket, her eyes closed, the arms and legs spread out to receive the sun. She had rich black wavy hair that had an iridescent bluish glint. She was a trifle skinny with a flat abdomen that rose and fell with her breathing. In her bathing suit she looked almost like a little girl. At first glance the only thing that impressed him was her chestnut-color skin, which made him think of gypsies. He could not say why, but her disposition intrigued him. Occasions like this brought out the mischievous impulse in him. So, with a sly smile on his face, he decided to "accidentally" bump into her foot.

The girl's eyes fluttered open with surprise and blinked from the blinding sun. "Oh," she said, staring at Andrew questioningly.

This was the moment when a magic power took Andrew's breath away as he stared at an innocent, radiant face of a youth with a cute turn-up nose, sparkling, dreamy black eyes, her pretty breasts above her flawless tiny waist that reminded him to a delicate flower bud. All in all, her purity seemed like the falling snowflakes before the dust of the road soils them. Hypnotized by her beauty, it was as if— beyond physical observation—he was seeing her with his soul. He never could imagine that a sensation like this is possible. The notion was akin to the feeling that he had found his soul-mate he was searching for.

Looking curiously at the handsome boy standing before her, she was pleasantly surprised. The attraction was immediate, and suddenly the desire for each other was swirling between them like invisible magnet. Sitting up, a daring thought flashed through her mind: *I think I could love him.* "Hi," she said, breaking up the silence.

"Hi! Please excuse my carelessness...."

"Oh, it's quite all right," she said, looking at him with her laughing eyes. Andrew blushed, but withstood her provocative scrutiny. He sensed that she liked what she saw. "Considering the crowd, it probably wasn't your fault. Anyway, it's just about time for me to get out of this heat before my skin fries."

"It's a good idea," Andrew agreed. "Seeing your lovely color, I don't think you need any more of this scorching heat." Then for a few seconds he was tongue-tied, struggling for words. Making an awkward move, he said, "Well, it was my pleasure to meet you. By the way, my name is Andrew Dombrady."

"Katharine Erdelyi," she said, extending her hand in a manner of inviting him to help her up. "But usually people call me Katie," she added, a lovely smile illuminating her face. Like a bright sunshine that brings out the sparkling beauty of a diamond, it transformed her face into an even more glowing loveliness. *It's incredible what a smile can do*, Andrew thought.

"Katie?...What a lovely name! It goes well with your beauty," he said, wanting to please her.

"Gee, thanks. Although I can't take the credit, for we don't have much say in choosing our names, do we?"

"It's true, but I meant what I said." Then, trying to prolong to stay with her, an idea struck him. "Katie, would you like to have a drink with me? I wish to make up for my clumsiness."

"Well, if you ask me out of *duty*, then the answer is no."

Andrew was taken aback. "Oh, I didn't mean it that way. Then let me rephrase it. I'd love to have a drink with you."

Katie's face brightened. "That's more like it! Only I hope that I won't bore you to death."

"No, no. How could you say that? I'd be very honored to have your company."

After they walked a few steps, Katie suddenly stopped.

"Wait a minute, please." Then she jumped back and picked up her blanket, and took it to one of the benches under a shady tree where a middle-aged couple was sitting. She exchanged a few words and turned back. *Probably her parents*, Andrew thought.

"I don't think I will need it for a while," she said as she came back to him.

"I assume they are your parents?"

Katie nodded, "Yes."

"They look so young."

Katie cast a pleased glance at him. "I'm sure they would appreciate hearing that."

A long line stood at the snack bar, so they stood in line. They were resorted to small talk, feeling some discomfort in their ability to talk. Their struggle to chose the right words was a sure sign that the attraction between them was strong. When received their drinks, they sipped them slowly, pretending to be engrossed in watching people around them.

"It's a lovely day, isn't it?" Andrew said, determined to break the silence.

"Oh yes, it's very nice."

"You know, I've been spending two days here already and wondering around, so I have no idea of how was it possible to miss you."

"Well, we have a large crowd; besides I don't go around much."

Andrew nodded. "Anyway, I'm glad for having bumped into your foot. Otherwise I'd still wandering around aimlessly. I have no friends with me, except my parents. So it seems my lucky star was with me today and changed my loneliness."

Katie smiled. "I'm glad you feel that way; it is the same story with me. Although I enjoy being here, I agree having a friend sure beats boredom."

"Very true. And thanks for considering me a friend."

Katie cast a friendly smiled. "Seems that it is easy to please you. So you like it here?"

"This is the first time for me, but I love it. It's a great place."

"Same for me. Lake Balaton seems like a sea, which fascinates me." They started to walk back, and gradually their conversation became more relaxed. Turning to personal questions, suddenly Andrew realized what was missing. It was the lack of humor! So he soon switched to a lighthearted tone of conversation, and the formality melted away. They soon felt as if they had known each other for a long time. Katie confided in him that her dream was to be a teacher.

"I always loved being with children," she said. "I think I would have the love and patience it requires."

Andrew nodded. "I'm sure you'd meet the challenge, and the reward would come naturally."

"Besides the three R's, I would try to teach them the love of music, for it refines the soul, and it is an excellent communicator of love."

"Oh yes, I heard that music is the food for the soul and the spirit," Andrew said.

"That's right. And what about you?"

With a musing face, Andrew said, "Yes, I have my plans too." Then he told her briefly about his involvement in sports, and that he quit school to pursue a trade, to be an electric technician.

"That sounds interesting, I wish you good luck."

When they reached the place Katie's parents were sitting, Katie introduced Andrew by explaining how he had almost broken her foot just to get to know her. Her cheerful disposition warmed his heart, for it was an indication that she felt something for him.

A slender, youthful looking man in his late thirties extended his hand, "Joseph Erdelyi," he said, " It's nice to meet you."

"Andrew Dombrady. It is nice to meet you too. But Katie exaggerates a little," he said.

"Naturally," Erdelyi said. "We know they make a mountain out of a molehill."

"Oh come on, Dad. Look who is exaggerating."

Andrew turned to Katie's mother. "Hello, Mrs. Erdelyi, pleased to meet you!"

"Pleased to meet you too," Annie said, stretching her hand. "By the way I saw you walking by us yesterday," she said. Her voice was friendly but her serious look was a contradiction.

"Oh really? I don't remember seeing you. I must have been kind of a sleepwalker."

As Katie listened to them, she rubbed her forehead. "Ah, it's so hot. Mom, Dad, wouldn't you like to go for a little swim?"

"No, not now my little girl. You just go ahead," Erdelyi said with an understanding hint of letting *them* go.

Andrew grabbed the opportunity. "Then I would like to offer a challenge for a friendly competition."

"Sure, be my guest."

But before they went, Andrew said, "Wait a second, Katie. Mrs. Erdelyi, would it be all right with you if I call on Katie tonight? We could take a walk and enjoy the beautiful sunset."

"Oh that's a splendid idea!" Katie exclaimed eagerly, her eyes shining with anticipation. She turned to her parents with a beseeching look on her face. "Mom, can I go?"

Annie and Joe looked at each other with a knowing smile. "Sure, have a good time," they said. They did not want to reveal the bad news why they agree to let her go.

"Thank you!" they shouted happily and turned quickly, racing into the water like two carefree children.

* * *

In the evening, sitting at the supper table, Andrew could not resist bragging about the beautiful girl he had just met at the beach. "Not only that, but I have managed to make a date with her in the evening," he added enthusiastically..

"Her parents are nice people too," he beamed. "I'm sorry I did not have a chance to introduce her to you, but I certainly will do so tomorrow. I know you'll like her. She is just the kind of girl you'd wish to have for a daughter."

"Wow! The way you describe her, she must be some movie star, or a jewel of a girl, " Mike said.

"Oh, boy, is she ever!"

"Well, you couldn't have picked a more romantic spot to find a nice girl, you lucky devil. You definitely didn't waste time in getting a date with her. This must be a record, congratulations!"

"Okay, okay, you two, slow down a little, will you," Margie interjected. She just could not get over how enthusiastic Andrew was. He had gone out with girls before, but he never raved about any of them. "So you have a date. So far, everything sounds sooo wonderful. But tell me this, how old is this so-called *dream girl?*"

"I don't know. She could not be more than sixteen. But that doesn't matter because she is so beautiful, and smart too. She reminds me of a delicate blooming daisy. I've never met anybody like her. One day I'm going to marry her, that's for sure!"

"Marry her!" Margie exclaimed. "Well, that's a hasty decision if I ever heard one. Are you *that* desperate? You better take a cold shower to cool down. Besides, I don't care how beautiful she is, to me she is still just a child. If I had a daughter *that* young, I wouldn't allow her to go out alone with a strange boy, that's for sure. *At night* yet!"

"Oh come on, Mom! Why not? For heaven's sake! This is not the

Dark Ages. You mean you wouldn't trust me with your daughter?"

"That's different. *I know you*. But her parents don't."

"Somehow I feel as though I have been insulted. Anyway, what do you think that could happen to her?"

This time suddenly Mike hit his knee and burst into laughter. "Well, Margie, as long as your son put up a question like that, you have nothing to worry about. She is safe!"

"Oh come on, Dad, I know what you mean," Andrew said, blushing with embarrassment. "I wasn't born yesterday."

"Okay, son, I was just kidding," Mike said amicably. It was true, the two of them never discussed sex before.

After supper Andrew went to change, painstakingly choosing his best suit. Then he said, "See you later," and he was on his way.

"Have a good time, son," Mike called after him.

* * *

This was the first time that Andrew had gone out of his way to make a good impression. He was good-looking with thick, black hair, and a pleasing smiling face. He used to blush when someone referred to his good looks, but he was proud to hear when people said that he was clever. His view point was that a person's worth should be based upon his inner values, rather than by physical appearances.

However, this time he appreciated combining the best of both, hoping to captivate Katie's heart. He smiled as he remembered the way she had stared at him this afternoon. She certainly seemed to be impressed.

When he arrived and knocked on the door, Katie let him in with a welcome smile. "Hi, Andrew. Come in."

"Hi, Katie. Good evening Mr. and Mrs. Erdelyi."

"Hello, Andrew. Welcome to our modest family circle," Erdelyi said, as they shook hands. "Sit down please," pointing to a chair.

"Thank you."

Katie disappeared into the next room to get ready, while Andrew exchanged a few words with the parents, analyzing the lovely evening. Looking around, he praised the pretty place they have rented. Then Katie reappeared, ready to go. Before they stepped outside, Mrs. Erdelyi reminded her to be home in time.

"Don't worry, Mom," she assured her, and they slipped out the door into the warm summer night.

They strolled down the street solemnly, feeling the special occasion in their steps. Seeing her dressed up for the first time, Andrew's mind was buzzing with new admiration. She wore a tastefully embroidered flowery summer dress that accentuated her tiny waist and the delightfully provocative curve of her dainty breasts. The way she looked, the thought crossed his mind that she must have had the same desire to impress him. Well, she certainly had done it: she was a work of art!

The magic power of her closeness awakened his desire to embrace and kiss her. Erotic fantasies had intruded his thoughts; feelings which he wished to express, bud did not have the courage.

"You're beautiful," he said instead, and surprised how naturally it sounded.

"Thank you. You look good, too," she said shyly. "Ah, isn't this a lovely evening ?"

"Yes, it's perfect," Andrew said, while musing over the mystery of life. Life is crazy, he thought. What kind of wizardry empowers a girl that can steal a man's heart in such a sweeping way? Yesterday he didn't even know her, yet today she is stirring up his wildest emotions; feelings that he did not know existed. *Is this what they call love at first sight?* But glancing at Katie's calm face, he could not tell if she felt the same way. *Does she have any feelings for me?* He wondered.

Walking down the street by holding hands, seemingly enjoying the peaceful surroundings, while they were immersed in their thoughts. Then on the spur of the moment they turned into a side street, which led them to the waterfront. Standing by the bank of the breathtaking expanse of the water, they noticed a bench nearby, hugging the shore. They went and sat down, facing Tihany, and in the distance they saw the dimly outlined hills of the Badascony region.

The romantic calmness spoke for itself. As they looked beyond the mountains, the descending sun filtered through the hazy air, fading into the arms of twilight. Admiring as the golden rays were drilling into the smooth surface of the water, Katie said dreamily, "Oh, Andrew, look, isn't it lovely? The sight of the sunset makes me feel like there is a magic scent in the air that soothes the soul. Don't you feel it?"

*Andrew...*She certainly said it before, but his name had never sounded this beautiful to him. It was like heavenly music to his ears.

"Yes, I feel it, and much more," Andrew smiled. "I feel the magical vibration around us which is hard to explain. It is like we could almost touch the tranquility that surrounds us. In my imagination I hear soft music that rippling from the distant shore like a whisper. One only wishes to be able to stop time, so that this moment would last forever."

"Oh, yes, that is just how I feel," Katie said. "Look at the sun! How red and large it is as it descending behind the hills. This view alone made it worthwhile to come here."

Sure, the sunset was beautiful, but Andrew derived more joy from looking at Katie's lovely profile. To him she was the sunshine, and nothing else could have rivaled her beauty. So beyond all the surrounding beauty, at this moment he wanted to forget all the beauty of nature, and concentrate on the most important subject: exploring *their* feelings for each other. He was nervous, but he had to change the subject. "Yes, Katie, everything is beautiful, except...I want...to talk about something else..."

Katie glanced at him quickly, as the sudden change in his voice was a warning sign .

"Oh?..." she said with a surprised look.

Andrew gulped. "Khmmm. What I would like to talk about is you and I, for I find you more beautiful than all the setting suns in the world, including the clustering stars in the sky. What I mean is that I'm so happy to be with you."

Katie blushed with relief, for she expected something worse. With a pleasant excitement she said happily, "I enjoy being with you too, and I'm glad you asked me out."

"Thank you. I'm pleased to hear that." he said, bending closer and gently kissed her cheek.

The unexpected surprise made her an involuntary protest, for her strict upbringing told her that kissing on the first date was a little out of line.

Seeing her confusion, Andrew turned his head with embarrassment. "I'm sorry, but I just couldn't help it." Then awkwardly he tried to explain. "I guess what I meant to tell you was that I'm falling in love with you..."

Katie let out a short, confused laugh. "Oh, come on, Andrew, you must be kidding. People don't fall in love so quickly. Don't you think we're too young to fall in love? Besides, we hardly know each other..." Now it was Katie who felt strange, for she recognized the sharp contradiction with her own feelings.

"I agree that we're young, and hardly know each other, although I feel that I know you enough to live with you in the rest of my life. It may sound impossible to you, but I assure you I could never have imagined being able to fall in love this suddenly. But age has nothing to do with love ... "

Listening to him in disbelief, Katie interrupted. "Oh yes, I've read about these things like: 'love knows no barriers, be it religion, color or age, and this is happening to people since time immemorial."

"That's exactly right!" he said. Then, as if he came to his senses, he shook his head. "However, seeing it more rationally, I'm sorry. I shouldn't reveal how I feel, as I can see that you're not interested. So I apologize. Let's just forget the whole episode." But as soon as he said it, he felt angry. He did not like the way he was handling the situation. But Katie's answer surprised him.

"Oh but I don't want to forget it. I mean, how can you forget a beautiful moment like this? I did not really mind your..." She stopped and turned away to hide her blushing. Actually she almost made a confession of her own. After all, she loved Andrew's confession. To make amends, she added: "but if that's what you want...."

"I've already told you what I want. I want a mutual love relationship. I want to explore whether we really have a future together. Because if we haven't, why waste time? Because I have the distinct feeling that you want *a friendship only* relationship with no strings attached...."

"Dear God, of course that's what I want."

"I don't think it is possible. Along with being friends, men and women are meant to be lovers. That's the law of nature—even the books say so. I don't want to play the part of being your brother, for heaven's sake!"

Katie liked it and laughed. "Why not? I never had a brother, it could be fun. But I don't want to talk about this any more. It's ridiculous. We're having such a lovely evening, why spoil it with silly arguments?"

"First of all, I don't consider it a *silly* argument. But if you think it is, it means that you don't love me. Therefore this evening is worthless and not lovely at all. It would be lovely only if I could tell you how beautiful, how desirable you are, how much I would like to kiss you forever; that when you are smiling I feel like I'm in heaven. Otherwise, to be honest, if we don't love each other, this evening is dull, dull, dull, and I want no part of..."

"Andrew stop it!" Katie cried. "Some logic *you* have. If I didn't like you, I wouldn't be here. Yet I don't want to talk about the rest of it. It's embarrassing," she said, her voice trembling.

Andrew's heart melted. "Well, at least we got this far, although I wished to hear the word, *love*, instead of that lousy *I like you*. But before I stop, I would like to clear up one thing. You said before that you 'didn't mind it.' What did you mean by that?"

"I don't know."

I don't believe you, but I'll let it go. It means only that we won't talk about love."

"Good!" Katie said.

"So, since my choice of subject is closed, you tell me, Miss Princess Erdelyi, what would you like me to talk about. I'd hate to talk about politics with you on such a lovely, romantic night. Wouldn't that spoil it all?"

Katie laughed. "Very funny," she said, feeling almost guilty, as if she were spoiling the evening..

"Well, if you don't have any suggestions maybe we should go home," Andrew said, feigning deep disappointment. Then he added, "Anyway, thanks for the memory."

"Oh come on, Andrew, that's not fair."

"So we're still friends?"

"Of course we are."

Then you won. But according to old traditions, when a bargain is made, it's supposed to be sealed."

"But how, we have no wine or anything."

Andrew's mood changed, and with a mischievous smile, he made a bold move. "Like this," he said and kissed her hard on the lips. Although she tried to resist, her body had a mind of its own. Her lips opened to his kisses with equal ardor, like the thirsty flower welcomes the morning dew. Andrew's kisses became more demanding, and he could feel her body respond. He had never imagined that she was capable of such burning desire and passion. Lost in the vortex of love, her breath quickened and her heart throbbed madly. "Ah, Katie, my love," he moaned.

The beauty of the moment swept them into unbearable desire, and although they wished the moment would last forever, Katie reluctantly pulled away. They sat for a long moment, both of them trembling from the pure delight, staring into each other's eyes.

Then silently they rose, and hand in hand they walked up the narrow path. Darkness had already fallen and the silvery moon was rising slowly, vying for dominance over the brilliantly twinkling stars. As they wandered along in perfect harmony, Andrew's head was buzzing with happy thoughts. In that state of love they did not need to put it in words, for they understood the words of the soul just as if their lips were saying them.

Encouraged by their new closeness, Andrew spoke of his feelings that were born out of their passionate moment, saying how grateful he was to fate for the chance of meeting her.

Katie's feelings also came to life, which was inspired not only by her love, but the surroundings, and suddenly she started to talk about the love of nature. "I adore the soothing effect of a quiet landscape, the glowing sunset as it slowly disappears behind the mountains, carrying with it a bitter-sweet good-bye, leaving behind the mountain with the promise of a brighter tomorrow."

As Andrew listened with startled amazement, Katie looked up at the starlit sky, collecting her thoughts. "With my soul's eye I see a vast panorama of mountains, lakes and valleys that are filled with wildflowers, ornamenting the world. You know, these are God's beautiful gardens, which were created for giving life to all living creatures. Our lives are too short to see all the beauties the world can offer, so we must be grateful for what we can enjoy."

Sharing her amazing spiritual adventure, Andrew luxuriated in the beauty of her dream world. It was a special delight to see how her physical and inner beauty went hand-in-hand with her. Although she shone in the light of innocence and purity, she seemed to possess the wisdom of the aged. *No wonder she wants to be a teacher,* he thought.

Katie that was beautiful! "I never ever heard a lovelier description of nature," he said. "Now I can see that you are as lovely inside as outside."

"Thank you. But you know, I find it strange that I never said things like this to anyone. Probably because I haven't met anyone who deserved it."

"Thanks a million. I feel honored."

As they kept wondering around, suddenly a popular song popped into Andrew's mind about a blue-eyed girl whose name happened to be Katie. And he began to sing.

"My Katie is a dazzling beauty
her eyes are as blue and cutie
as the sky on a lovely summer day..."

Katie burst into laughter. "But my eyes are not blue."

"I know, but nobody can have everything. Besides, I like yours more. To be honest, your eyes are the most charming I have ever seen. My dream girl always has been brunette, like you. Black wavy hair, round dark eyes just like yours. I think that is what I fell in love with at first."

Katie smiled. "You're too much."

"But that's true. I love that fire in your dreamy dark eyes, your ripe, heartbreakingly inviting lips. When you're smiling, your eyes telling me tales about heaven on earth. Lost is the man who has the chance to look into them. I feel fortunate that for this moment I can share their rapture."

Katie turned her head, for Andrew's words were somewhat beyond flattering—they were embarrassing.

"Good heavens, Andrew, I think you should have your eyes examined."

"I already have, they are perfect."

"It's amazing the way you come up with these compliments."

"Seeing you it's easy. Besides, honesty comes from the heart. In our hearts there is a sensitive device called feelings that register the thoughts. Your beauty provides the words, and my brain is reading them."

Katie changed the thought process. "Well, we can't see into the future," she said. "Who knows, that 'fortunate' man may be living on the moon, for all we know."

Andrew looked surprised. "Well, I thought...Anyway, I don't give up easily. If I'm to conquer your heart, I'd go to the moon gladly."

"Would it worth the sacrifice?"

"If it were for you, it would be a joyride."

Suddenly Katie wanted to know more. "So, if you would 'conquer' my heart, would we have a chance to live happily ever after?"

"Very funny. All right then, do you want to know what is in my heart?"

"Y-e-e-s."

"Good! But I warn you, you asked for it."

"Oh, my! Am I to hear my death sentence?"

"No, no; you'll love it," Andrew chuckled. Then assuming a pose of a romantic lead on the stage, he took her hands in his. "As I'm holding your hand," he began, "my heart is saying that you're the girl of my dreams. I feel more about you than I've ever felt about anyone in my life. If there ever was true love at first sight, then this is it. I feel as though I've known you in all my life. I love you, and if you would love me too, I would be the happiest man on earth. So now you know. Well, now it's your turn to pour out *your* heart's content."

Katie was stunned. Listening to his words, a wave of pleasant warmth washed over her, for Andrew's words were the answer to her dreams. Yes, she loved him just as much, and tremors of happiness fluttered around her heart. But everything was happening too fast; and she wasn't ready yet for such a confession. Her eyes downcast, she stammered, "I don't know what to say. Now I can see that we should never play games with our emotions." And with happy tears she admitted, "Oh, Andrew I love you too."

Andrew felt drunk. Not from alcohol, but from something far more potent: from being in love and being loved. His eyes shone from the wonder of it. He felt he had indeed conquered the universe. Then he stood before her, put his arms around her gently, sending a tingling sensation through her body, and kissed her. "Now, my sweet love, tell me, was it really so hard to say it?"

"Yes, it was, but I do love you, Andrew," she said shyly. She felt so alive and somehow freed, and wanting to dance from the pure delight of it. They kissed each other again, passionately, exploring, feeling one another. "This could be a lovely habit for the beginning," Andrew moaned, looking into her shining eyes.

The hour grew late and they turned and started to go home. As they walked down the path, abruptly Katie became unusually quiet to the point of crying. Andrew glanced at her, surprised.

"Katie, what's wrong? Did I say something?"

"Oh no, nothing like that," she said, and took a deep breath. "Andrew, hate to tell you this, but we're going home tomorrow."

Andrew's face turned white and felt a sudden lurch in his heart. "Good God, no!" He exclaimed. "Why didn't you tell me this before?"

"Because I didn't have the heart to spoil our lovely evening. I'm sorry."

"Hm...That's awful," Andrew said, staring at the ground, rubbing his chin with his fingers. "Well, saying that I'm sorry is an understatement. But we can look at it from the bright side, hoping that nothing is lost. At least we've met. I know you live in Matyasfold, give me your address and I'll visit you as soon as I get home. That is if you want me to."

"What a question! Of course I want you to." She reached into her purse for a piece of paper and wrote down her name and address in Matyasfold. It was a suburb, about thirty kilometers from Budapest. It was reachable only by subsidiary train from the Eastern Railway Station, Katie explained.

Andrew nodded. "I know." Then he told her that he lived in Baross Street, which was almost in the heart of Budapest. They were half way home when Katie said, "You know, I feel as though leaving Lake Balaton will exile me from an enchanted world."

"I couldn't have said it any better myself." Then suddenly an idea crossed Andrew's mind. "Katie, let's go back to our love seat and make this night as memorable as we can."

It was late, but they turned and walked back on "Memory Lane," as they called it. Their feet fell into even steps, just like their hearts were beating in harmony. Aside from the scattered street-lamps, the peaceful town was dark. They observed the sleeping houses silently, reflecting how a simple thing like walking together could make life so beautiful.

At the shore they sat together, enjoying the tranquility, with their heads touching. They felt as if they were on their own island of paradise, isolated from the rest of the world, wrapped up in their innocent love. As they watched the scintillating stars, a falling star streaked across the sky. Hazy, scattered clouds floating slowly to infinity, behind which the moon appeared as if playing hide-and-seek.

Just above the water the evening fog hung like a virgin bride's veil. The breath of the countryside blended with the warm flavors of the night. Perhaps the depth of the forest would breathe such a peaceful calmness. The gently muffled hum of the rippling water lingered in the stillness, sustained by the light breezes. The two lovers sat there in the vortex of their perfect world, trying to prolong the magic circle of intimacy. They felt as if they had just been born.

"Katie, this is the most beautiful day in my life," Andrew said. "I'm beginning to understand what life is all about."

"Yes, I feel the same. Happiness is the ultimate goal in life, and I couldn't be happier. I'm almost afraid that I'm dreaming this."

"Oh, but I can prove it is real," Andrew said, kissing her.

Finally they stood, arms around each other's waists, headed for home.

When they arrived at Katie's cottage, they stopped at the gate. As she turned, the moonlight illuminated her profile and he was moved by her beauty.

"The more I look at you, the more I want to kiss you," Andrew whispered.

A mild breeze crept into the air. They kissed passionately, while the orchestra of chirping crickets played around them.

"You see, sweetheart, even nature is singing for us," Andrew whispered, pointing to the grass. "Helping to celebrate our newly found love."

"Yes," Katie signed. "Isn't it beautiful?"

Finally they parted and Katie said, "It's too late, sweetheart, I must go, or else I will get into trouble."

"Yeah, I know. Thank you for the lovely evening."

"And I thank you. Meeting you made it my happiest holiday."

"You took the words out of my mouth."

"I wish I could take you with me," Katie sighed.

"You'll always be in my heart. I wish you a safe trip."

"Thank you. I'll wait for you."

"Good. Come hell or high water, I'll be there my love. Until then sweet dreams and keep smiling.

6

THE ERDELYI FAMILY

AS SOON AS THE TRAIN pulled into the station, the Erdelyi family settled into one of the berths. Erdelyi placed the luggage up on the shelf then settled back into his seat. Soon, the train jerked forward and gained momentum as it headed toward Budapest.

Katie, holding a book in her hand, sat across from her father at the window.

"Ah, this is nice,"Erdelyi said, stretching his arms behind his head. "I think I could get used to this lifestyle," he added.

"It will be a little strange to go back to the everyday life," Annie said.

"Yes, the last two weeks was like a dream. But Dad, you could not stand being lazy all the time."

"That's true. Well, it was nice while it lasted," he said. But a few more words later the subject was exhausted and they let their minds wander. Katie did not feel like reading. Instead, following her father, she looked out the window and watched the landscape as the colorful stripes of crops flickered as the train sped by.

This contentment reminded Erdelyi that not too long ago their lives had been hell. The memory was fresh and the nightmares still came back to haunt him. The most infuriating aspect of it was how unjustly the communists had treated him. Oh, he knew why he had received such a harsh treatment, but how could they be so dirty? His "crime" was that he was a police officer during the war years, serving an anticommunist regime. He was considered an enemy of the working class, and was labeled as a traitor of the proletariat.

* * *

Erdelyi always wanted to be a police officer, and his dream came true in 1938, when his application to the police force was accepted. He was twenty-three years old and already married. After completing a special traffic regulation course, he was assigned to be a traffic controller in Budapest. He loved his work and was proud of it. It not only provided him with a decent living but also exempted him from the draft.

By the time the war ended in 1945, they had a six-year-old daughter and a nice home in Matyasfold.

After the communist came to power, total confusion set in. In the social-political change, there was considerable upheaval within the police force. Changes in the hierarchy brought chaos where once had been order. There was reorganization, new regulations, and reshuffling, and often incomprehensible instructions to follow. To compound the confusion, over the experts, politically appointed commanders were assigned to positions they knew nothing about, for they had been trained to be officers in political seminars. Many of them were overly ambitious, jealous and plain ignorant. Erdelyi tried to adapt to the changing trends but he soon realized the futility of trying without political compromise.

Up until the last election in 1947, voicing one's opinion had not seemed to be dangerous. So before the last election Erdelyi made a fatal mistake by not keeping it a secret of his political feelings, never believing in a communist victory? He was a Smallholder Party supporter. Unfortunately, he paid for his frankness. After the election any opinion he voiced in the station, it was there in the Secret File. They began to watch him closely. He was criticized for everything he said or did. The communist commanders deliberately twisted his words and his actions, so that it was almost impossible for him to do anything right.

One day his commander came to him, seemingly upset.

"Comrade Erdelyi," he said, "I have been informed that you broke the regulation during your duty."

"Oh?...and how did I do that?" Erdelyi asked, surprised.

"When you're on duty, Comrade Erdelyi, your first and foremost responsibility supposed to be controlling the safety of the traffic, instead of allowing yourself the luxury to be distracted by having conversation with the public."

"Oh that! He was a tourist, asking for some directions. I couldn't refuse. The traffic was light and it was perfectly safe to give him the information."

"Don't lecture me on what is safe. Your sole duty is to direct traffic, period. So I warn you, as long as you're wearing that uniform, you're not your own boss. Is that clear?"

"Yes comrade Kaposy," he said, his fists clenched. Erdelyi realized that the truth was irrelevant; the dictating factor was whether or not it served ***their*** greedy purposes. So, as a rule, he could not have been right.

Gradually the conflict escalated to the point that Erdelyi has decided it was time to wise up and resign before he ended up in deep trouble. Probably this is what they wanted anyway, he thought. Nonetheless, it still hurt that his career as a police officer was over. Although by that time, the once honorable institution had degenerated into a hate-mongering, power-hungry terror.

* * *

After his resignation, Erdelyi went looking for work, only to discover that his past had been thrust to the forefront. By this time all the positions were in the hands of the government, so wherever his name came up, like a shadow, his past followed him. Finally, he had to make do with dirty manual labor jobs for the lowest wages. He had become a second-class citizen.

During this era of lawlessness, the communists often came up with shocking news to make people more miserable. The newest wave of terror that swept through the nation was in 1951, when the Communist Party initiated a nationwide deportation against politically undesirable people.

The disaster began when the communist's policy forced the hard working peasants into Sovietized collective farming, called ***kolhoz***. As a result, the country was soon hit by an alarming shortage of farm workers. The good old Stalinist method came up with the solution of deporting those politically undesirable people, forcing them to work on the farms.

By this clumsy bureaucratic move (absolute legal robbery), thousands of families were uprooted from their homes—highly qualified office workers, ex-military personals and politically suspicious people. They had to leave everything behind, which then became government property. It conveniently solved (partly) the desperate housing shortage for some high-ranking party officials.

When Erdelyi's name appeared on the deportation list, he

had been working at an optical factory as a delivery man. The deportation paper gave him two weeks notice to relocate him and his family to a farm in Csongrad County, about 200 kilometers from Budapest. It meant that they would lose all their possessions to the communist authorities.

Erdelyi immediately started to move some of their valuables to Erdelyi's brother, Bela, for safekeeping. But they did it very secretly at night, for fear of someone might find it out and report them.

In the communist system there was a Party Secretary's Office set up at every workplace, right beside the Personnel Office. These party officials were highly trained political watchdogs, holding the most powerful positions within the premises.

It was Erdelyi's luck that his supervisors were satisfied with his reliability. He knew he was watched, but pleased him to see that *this* party secretary liked him for his diligence. When Erdelyi presented him the deportation paper, the secretary intervened on his behalf. Using his influence, he told the authorities that Erdelyi's contribution to the factory was more valuable than working on a farm.

This is how he got away with the deportation, although Erdelyi knew nothing about this interference. All he knew was that "miraculously" his name had been taken off the deportation list. Secretary or not, this time the Erdelyi family was saved by a decent man from the trouble of losing their home.

Then in 1952 Erdelyi was able to track down a better job at the General Renovation Company. It was here that he had the opportunity to learn a new trade as a house painter. By the time he had received his diploma, Stalin was dead. The terror slowly began to ease, which meant that the communists destroyed that damning Secret File. Now Erdelyi was free to work in his trade without restrictions.

* * *

That was the ugly past. The change was gradual, but it was comforting, for now he was able to provide a more decent life for his family. It came just in time because he needed more money for Katie's education.

Katie..Well, she occupied a soft spot in his heart. Her attitude during those hard times had been understanding. Being an only child, she could have been spoiled, but in spite of her parents' protective circle of love, Katie did not take advantage of it. They tried their best to provide her what she needed, even if it meant denying things for themselves. They had every reason to be proud of her. She was beautiful, intelligent—everything they could have dreamed of. Naturally she was the breath of their lives.

As their lives improved, they began planning the holiday trip to Lake Balaton. It was a huge step but an exciting one, and it turned out to be a happy occasion for all of them.

Now, as the train advanced toward Budapest, Erdelyi glanced at Katie with concern. He noticed a conspicuous change in her mood. He knew she had come home late last night and he wanted to discipline her. But he decided to let it go. Now he watched her from the corner of his eyes as she was staring out the window with a faraway look in her eyes. She seemed to be lost in her thoughts.

Indeed Katie was going through some emotional turmoil. In the aftermath the shock seemed even more sudden. She was not prepared for Andrew to capture her heart in this powerful way. Up until now no-one was able to arouse such deep love in her. Even now, looking out at the landscape, it was Andrew she saw. Overnight she had gone through a complete change, as if she were a different person. Leaving Andrew behind felt like a part of her heart stayed with him.

Sure she had some crushes over boys in school. There was Peter Kertes, for example, with whom she fell in love. He was handsome with blond, wavy hair. At the beginning he was sweet and considerate, and she was trusting. In retrospect it was easy to see that he was a self-centered, conceited braggart, and a liar. She did not have to wait long before she realized that he was the kind of person who wanted a girl only for one reason. He became more and more demanding, so she cut him off quickly. After that she wanted nothing to do with him.

When her mother warned her to be careful with boys, she replied with a flippant, "Oh, Mom, you don't have to worry about me. I'm not about to lose my head over any boy—yet. I want to have fun first. Besides, wouldn't that be a drag?"

Annie stifled a knowing smile.

It was easy to say—then. But now that Andrew has entered into her life, life did not seem to be a drag at all. In fact, it promised lots of fun. There was *something* about Andrew that set him apart from all the boys she knew. Aside from his good looks, there was a magnetic quality to him. He projected an air of trust and self-confidence. But what she valued even more was his healthy sense of humor. And she liked his kissing too. She remembered the powerful sparks of electricity between them—the chemistry was definitely right!

Nevertheless, she was confused. She never believed in love at first sight, but yesterday had changed all that. Also, it brought with it some unseen responsibility, scare and worry—feelings that her secure world might be shattered. But by all means it was a challenge, a change that she could not just ignore. Still, the truth of the matter was that she was too young to take their love seriously, she argued with herself. It was one thing to have a boyfriend, but the way they felt about each other, would *friendship* be enough for Andrew? They had met too soon, for she did not want to get married at sixteen, for God's sake! Common sense dictated that even if they were meant for each other, she was not supposed to fall in love yet, period! They were too young, too young...So what? She rebelled. She simply had to change her mind and say, *so what*! Because she could not bear the thought of losing him, not ever! She was definitely deeply in love. Oh God, how confusing life can be...!

"You seem to be in an odd mood, my little girl." Erdelyi said, interrupting her thoughts. "Did something go wrong between the two of you last night?"

Katie looked at her father, startled as if she had just realized that she was not alone.

"Oh no," she said attempting to smile. "I'm just a little tired, that's all."

"I can imagine that. Well, you'll be able to catch up on your sleep when we get home."

A minute later Katie left the coach for the washroom and Erdelyi took the opportunity to whisper to his wife, "Annie, our daughter is in love."

"Yes, it seems that way, doesn't it. My hope is that it is only puppy love. After all, she is only sixteen. At her age, I was still playing with my dolls, not with boys."

"Ah, yes?" Erdelyi teased. "Then, I strongly suggest that your memory is fading, my dear, or else I have to wonder who was the girl I was kissing so passionately all those summer evenings. Yet, it's true, the world is changing, isn't it. Compared to the thirties, it's amazing how fast this generation is maturing. Kids today would laugh at your puritan attitude, that's for sure."

"Well, let them laugh. I think it's too soon for Katie to get involved, going to school and everything..."

Erdelyi chuckled. "Too late for that."

"There is a proper time for everything, including love."

"Oh sure! But you cannot change human nature. Besides, the timetable is changing. Everything around them is in a rush, which makes kids grow up faster. They learn too soon that life is short and they don't want to miss out on anything. Anyway, as far as Andrew is concerned, you must admit he is a fine looking boy. I like him."

"I like him, too, as far as that goes. But the point is Katie is not ready for a serious commitment as yet."

"They're just kids, Annie. Why does it have to be a commitment?"

Annie sniffled. "Because she is serious about him, I can tell. However, Andrew reminds me a little bit of you when you were in his age."

"Well, thanks honey, I needed that. But there is another thing I must say for him, he has mighty good taste in girls." Erdelyi chuckled. "That reminds me, do you remember what our neighbor, Mrs. Szekeres used to say when Katie was about three years old?"

"I sure do: 'Well folks,' she used to say, 'one thing is sure. This little girl is going to break the hearts of some men'."

* * *

After Katie left, Andrew no longer enjoyed his vacation. All the enthusiasm he had come with, suddenly vanished. Without Katie, Lake Balaton did not have the same magic appeal. She was in his mind constantly—he missed her so. He wished he could have gone home with her; he would have done it happily. Instead, his spirit broken, he was lingering around restlessly, feeling lost. He could not understand himself. How could such a short time turn his life upside down in such a mysterious way? His cheerful temperament sank into moodiness and he became introspective. *What a wonderful evening it was!* With his soul's eye, he saw her walking beside him, heard her innocent voice, which promised happiness.

But like Katie, Andrew was also confused. Being in love goes hand-in-hand with a lot of responsibility, he thought, as he was lying on the grass. And he did not even have a job yet, for heaven's sake! It just did not make sense. Living in an oppressive regime, what kind of future could he offer her? Surely Katie deserved more than just a tentative relationship. Being as smart as she is, she probably had figured this out herself already and came to the same conclusion.

However, his conscience jumped to the forefront and called him a coward. He was not a quitter, and could never tolerate lying. Deep in his heart he knew that there was no way he could stay away from her.

Naturally, it did not take long for his parents to notice the change.

"Well, son," Mike said, "something must have gone sour last night, otherwise you wouldn't be this miserable. Would you like to tell me about it?"

"Well, yes...you're right. We had a lovely night, but Katie's vacation has ended yesterday. She, I mean they returned home this morning," Andrew said dejectedly.

"Oh my, that's too bad! I'm truly sorry to hear that, for I was really looking forward to meeting her."

"Well, it isn't the end of the world," Margie said. "Knowing Andrew, I'm sure the friendship has not ended with it and it won't be long before we see her."

Andrew managed a wry smile and kissed her. "You're a mind reader, Mom. How did you guess?"

Just before it was time to go home, Andrew went to see their love seat once more. He had attributed so much significance to it that he just could not go home without saying farewell to it.

He sat there for a long time, imagining Katie sitting beside him. As he listened to the softly rippling water, many thoughts crossed his mind. What a nostalgic place this will be! His attitude went through a great deal of maturing. Never before in his life had he appreciated life in such a profound way. No matter what might befall him, nothing could take away the sweet memories of Lake Balaton. Their love had been born here, and this bench would always be a symbol of their special happiness.

Before he left, he squinted into the slowly descending sun behind the mountains. "I adore the glowing sunset," Katie had said. This time it seemed as if the sun collided with the mountain, painting the sky with beautiful scarlet. "God, how Katie would love to see that," he said to himself.

He looked back once more, then with a deep sigh, he reluctantly walked away.

7

YOUTH AND LOVE

ARRIVING HOME, ANDREW immediately sprang into action. He went to the gym to talk to someone. Although he had many friends there, he was looking for Paul Korondy, his boxing coach. He knew that Paul had good connections with people in important positions.

Paul was a giant of a man with piercing blue eyes under shaggy brows and a battered nose that gave him a menacing look. But contrary to his looks, he was a gentle, friendly man.

"Hi Andrew, good to see you," Paul said, greeting him with a handshake. "You look great. Did you have a good holiday?"

"The best," Andrew said. Then, after some small talk, he went right to the subject he came for.

"So, you want to learn the electric trade? Sure, Andrew, I think I can help you. Let me see..." He took a notebook from his breast pocket and jotted down a name and address.

"This guy is a good friend of mine. He is the manager of a small electrical firm. Go there tomorrow and tell him that I sent you. Meantime, I'll phone him, so he'll be expecting you."

Andrew thanked him and at home he repeated the happy news.

"Well, the good old golden rule is still valid," Mike said. "It's not what you know but whom you know that counts."

"That's how it is!" Andrew said.

The next morning he went for an interview. The firm was located on Visegrady Street, about a 20-minutes ride by tram. He arrived early so he had to wait. When Mr. Lugosy, a short, stocky man called him into his office, he seemed very friendly, which Andrew felt as a good sign.

After the introduction he pointed to a chair, "Please sit down."

He asked Andrew politely about his interest in sports, and then a few questions about his idea of the electric trade. Andrew's eagerness noticeably made a good impression.

Two days later, he went to work. Since this was his first job he was shy, but the workers were friendly and helpful. Although he had studied the trade in the library, he soon found out how much there was to learn. His enthusiasm, however appealed to the workers, and in no time he felt at home and made friends.

As soon as he had settled into a routine, he was in a good frame of mind, ready to call on Katie. There was no such thing as a private telephone in Hungary, so all he could do was hope that she would be home.

It was Saturday when he jumped on the tram for the Eastern Station. From there, after a long wait, he transferred to the sub. train, called HEV, and an hour later he was on his way.

Matyasfold was a quiet garden suburb at the outskirts of Budapest. It was a village-like place, a sharp contrast to the din of the big city life. Agoston Street was easy to find. Katie's house was a lovely cream-colored brick house on a corner lot, enclosed by a white picket fence.

The gate was locked but there was a little red push-bell above the handle. As soon as he pushed it a dog started to bark.

"Hush, Bokrosh!" Heard Andrew, and his heart leapt with joy, recognizing Katie's voice. He saw her coming, while quieting the dog.

"Oh, Andrew, it's you!" she exclaimed, her face lit up with delight. "What a nice surprise!"

"Hi, Katie," he said. "Your nice welcome alone made the trip worthwhile, not to give the credit to Bokrosh. I hope he won't tear me to pieces."

"Oh no, no," she laughed, "don't worry, he is a friendly dog. Besides, he's on leash."

She took his arm in an intimate fashion and they walked to the backyard. Erdelyi was standing on a stool, pruning the branches of a fruit tree. Edging the neatly kept flowerbed around the fence, crouched Mrs. Erdelyi weeding; and obviously enjoying the fresh air and sunshine. The pleasant scene made Andrew realize how much he was missing by living in a mass-designed apartment.

"Look, Dad and Mom! Guess who came to visit us?"

"Good afternoon, Mr. and Mrs. Erdelyi. How are you?"

"Hi, Andrew. Nice to see you again," Erdelyi said, putting down the pruner in order to shake hands. "I'm glad you found us at last."

"Well, it took a while, but here I am. You have a lovely home." Andrew said, admiringly. "The fresh air and the nice greenery is a pleasant contrast to the concrete jungle I came from."

Erdelyi smiled, pleased. "Thanks, Andrew, I know what you mean. Yes, we sure love it here and wouldn't move into the city for the world. But Katie, why don't you bring another chair to make Andrew feel..."

"Thanks just the same, Mr. Erdelyi," Andrew interrupted. "But I have other plans. If it's all right with you, I'd like to take Katie to a movie or a play."

Katie's face brightened. She looked at her parents with a radiant smile. "Oh, Andrew, I'd love that," she said, clasping her hands in an endearing, childlike gesture of delight.

"Well, now, I'm not so sure about that," Erdelyi said, glancing at his wife for support. Katie's late homecoming at Lake Balaton still lingered in his mind.

"Can I go, can't I, Mom?" Katie turned to her pleadingly. Although usually it was the other way around: Katie considered his father to be the "softy."

"Wouldn't that be a little too late to come home?"

"Yes, it would be, Mrs. Erdelyi, but I promise I'll bring Katie home safe and sound the minute it ends," Andrew said, unmistakable candor in his eyes.

Smiling, Mrs. Erdelyi feigned a brief hesitation. "All right," she said. "It's Saturday and besides, school hasn't yet began. "

Katie did not wait for her to finish. She dashed into the house to change while Erdelyi took Andrew around to show him the house. Andrew was impressed by the clever placement of shelves and storage spaces in the basement, which Erdelyi made them himself.

"Very neat," Andrew commented. "I don't think you have time to get bored here."

"Oh, no! And that's the way I want it."

Soon Katie was ready and off they went. She wore an

embroidered white and black dress with a silky black belt. After half an hour of waiting, they were on the sub. train. Her spirit came to life like a bird when set free. She was blessed with easy laugh; witty and delicately feminine. When she turned her head, sometimes she would toss back her curly black hair with an exuberant energetic gesture. Her flame-colored lips could rekindle the flame from the smoldering embers. There was a lightness and vitality about her; the very air seemed altered in its composition.

"You look as lovely as ever," he couldn't resist saying, "I'm delighted to see you again."

"Thank you. I'm glad to see you too. But what took you so long? I was beginning to worry you had forgotten me."

"Don't you even think that. But I'm pleased that you missed me." The next moment Andrew suddenly hit his forehead. "My God, I could not figure out what I was missing. Do you realize that I haven't kissed you yet?"

Katie laughed. "I wouldn't have been surprised if you had started kissing me right in front of my parents."

"Well, as a matter of fact, maybe I should have. But they're not here, may I kiss you now?"

Katie stared at him, shocked. "In front of all these people? You must be kidding."

"Why not?" he teased her. "Love is contagious; they might find it encouraging and follow us. After all, the song says that everybody needs to be kissed."

"How would you know? You said you have never been in love before."

"You don't *have to be* in love to know things. Anyway, I can't see anything wrong with kissing you. I hope you're not allergic to kisses."

"Oh, come on! What a silly thing to say. But I tell you what. I'll kiss you nice and proper when we say good-bye tonight. That should settle it. Until then the subject is closed, period."

Andrew glanced at her, feigning a sulky look. "My heart is bleeding. So, you want me to sweat for a little pleasure. Well, I won't play the *'give me a little kiss game'*. I know you will come around and offer it yourself."

Katie stared at him, surprise. "You are not a bit conceited, are you?"

Andrew chuckled. "Not at all; only confident. Anyway, let's change the subject. I want you to know that I've missed you terribly."

"I missed you too. I hope I didn't spoil your holiday by leaving you so suddenly—unintentionally I might say."

"Well, you may take it as a compliment, but I was awfully miserable without you. Life is funny, isn't it? One day, you're happy just being there, and then you meet somebody you never knew existed and bang! Your life is completely turned around. I must confess, now I couldn't imagine life without you."

Katie blushed. "Oh, Andrew, you are so sweet."

"The trouble is the way things are, I can't even offer you anything concerning the future."

"Oh, Andrew what's the rush!" Katie said annoyed, "we have time to think about all that later. Let's not spoil our day over something you can't change."

Pleased, Andrew smiled, "You're right."

"As I see it, life is full of mysterious coincidences," Katie said. "Call it fate or destiny, which is beyond our control, and the sudden change can rearrange our priorities in life."

"I forgot I have a beautiful philosopher. Do you want to know how I feel right now?"

"Yes."

"I feel that when I'm with you, I'm floating over the clouds where the sky is always blue. With you, I feel like I'm in a dreamland."

"Andrew, what a beautiful thought. Thanks for sharing it with me. I'm happy that I make you feel that way. My only hope is that I'll always be able to keep you over the clouds."

"As long as you're with me, I'll always be there."

"And I'll be with you as long as you want me to."

How Andrew loved her innocent honesty. He wanted to sweep her off the seat into his arms. Instead, he bent over and whispered, "Katie, can I say something?"

"Y-e-e-s..."

"I love you very much."

Katie laughed happily, then she whispered back, "Is that all?"

"You know sweetheart, just before we came home, I went back to see our love-seat. I imagined you were there with me and I was kissing you."

Katie's eyes glistened with moisture. "Oh? How sweet of you to do that. Yes, our love seat...it means so much to us. Too bad it is so far away and we cannot go there more often."

"Well, there is a solution to that, we simply have to find a bench closer that's all. Let's say somewhere by the shore of the Danube."

Yes, we could, but it would never replace that one."

"That's true. I'll always remember it as the cradle of our love," Andrew said, glancing out the window. "Oh, my goodness, I almost forgot to tell you my good luck. I'm working at an electric company."

"Andrew, that's wonderful news. Congratulations!"

"Thanks, love. So, if I'm lucky, I'll be an electric technician."

"I'm proud of you. Now you have something to work for. It will be a challenge, I'm sure. I wish you all the luck."

"Thanks again. But I must say, my father is a great inspiration," Andrew explained. "He used to say that to achieve something in life that would give you a feeling of pride, like you're a productive member of society. We are all born into this world *for a reason,* and you have to have a purpose to strive for. I believe in that."

Katie smiled. "I believe in that too. Your enthusiasm has a magnetic quality. Anyone who has so much ambition is destined to be successful."

Finally, they reached their destination and walked briskly to the Boraros Square, which was a large traffic circle in front of the Eastern Railway Station. Then they took a streetcar to the Metropolitan Operetta Theater. Fortunately, there were still some tickets available, and they were able to see one of the most popular shows of the time: *The Chardas Princess.* It was a hilarious comedy show, which they enjoyed very much, especially Hanna Honti's charming voice. They laughed along with the audience at the witty performance by Robert Ratonyi.

It was midnight when Andrew escorted Katie home. At the gate, Andrew told her that on the next weekend, he would introduce her to his parents.

"I'm looking forward to the occasion," Katie said happily. "Thank you for the lovely evening. It was a superb show."

"It was my pleasure. I too enjoyed every minute of it." Then they kissed good night the "proper way" as Katie had promised.

"So until next weekend, I wish you sweet dreams."

Traveling to see her was exhausting and time consuming, but

that was the price he had to pay for dating Katie.

* * *

The following Sunday Andrew arrived early, and to his surprise Katie was alone. After some passionate kissing, Katie was getting ready to visit Andrew's parents.

"I can hardly wait to show my parents my beautiful gypsy princess."

"Now come on, Andrew, I'm not a gypsy princess," Katie said—not really objecting to the title, rather it was out of modesty. "Anyway, what should I wear for the occasion?"

"W-e-e-ll, let me see," Andrew said with an impish grin, "courtesy by yours truly, I suggest that you could wear a flimsy paper dress, or some palm-leaves stick on here and there...You'd look perfect in them, I'm sure."

"Andrew!" Katie exclaimed, hitting him playfully. "What a big help you are!"

Andrew laughed. "You're so sweet when I manage to ruffle your feathers. Anyway, my love, all I want you to do is present your sparkling self, be naked or dazzling in diamonds. I know my parents will love you either way."

"Aha! With your suggestions they would throw me out together with you so fast we wouldn't know what hit us."

The way she looked at the end, Andrew beamed with pride. Approaching Baross Street, Katie was apprehensive. This was the first time she would meet his parents and it was important to make a good impression.

"Here we are," Andrew said, turning into a large gate of a three-story building. There was no elevator, so he led her up on the dimly lit staircase to the first floor. Andrew opened the door and ushered Katie in.

No matter how gloriously Andrew had described Katie to his parents, it still surprised them to see such a lovely girl. Katie's modest manner was the first impression. She had a magnetic quality about her that made people love her at first sight.

"Well, Mom and Dad, here is the nicest girl in the world a guy could ever hope to find, Katie Erdelyi."

"Hello, Katie, welcome to our home," Margie said, embracing her. "It's a pleasure to meet you."

"I feel the same."

After Mike's greeting, he couldn't help saying, "Seeing you in person, now I can understand why Andrew speaks a lot about you. Which means we know you as long as he has."

"Don't spoil her, Dad, for heaven help me later," Andrew said, winking at his father.

"Well, I could say the same thing about Andrew, he talks about you with great love. I'm only sorry we couldn't have met at Lake Balaton."

"We were sorry too, but as they say, better late than never. Nonetheless, this is just as pleasant," Mike said.

They went into the small family room, which was facing the street.

"This is a lovely place," Katie commented. She went to the window and watched the street below that was bursting with activities. Trams were rushing in both directions, glittering in the sunshine, rattling and jingling noisily, which were increased by the speeding trucks and cars.

"It's very interesting to see a busy street from above. But isn't it too noisy at night?"

"Yes, it is, but we have got used to it by now; it has become part of our lives."

"Oh yes, like the rope for a hangman," Andrew said.

While Margie was in the kitchen making coffee, Andrew took out the family album. Leafing through the pages, they laughed at some of Andrew's baby pictures, making crooked faces. Then Margie called, "All right, children, the coffee is ready. Come and sit at the table."

"Hmm, this is delicious," Katie said, enjoying the steaming aroma, and the apricot cake. As they sat there, the conversation became more relaxed. Margie asked about her plans, mainly how much effort it takes to become a teacher. And Mike wanted to know what her father did for a living. Katie was pleased with their showing of interest.

Knowing how serious Andrew was about Katie, Mike observed her charming nature. It pleased him that Andrew could find such a lovely girl.

Then it was time to go. Before she said good-bye, the Dombradys expressed their appreciation for coming. "You are welcome to our home any time," Mike said.

Katie was happy. Back on the street she said, "Andrew, your parents are really nice people; it took only a minute to like them. Not that I had any doubt."

"Thanks, love. You see, they didn't even bite your nose off."

"Andrew! I never said they would!"

"I didn't say you said. But all kidding aside, we got along great. They're a little strict but I love them very much. And I know they love me. They set a good example and I have enough sense to appreciate it. If you were my wife and we had children, I'd like to maintain the same relationship with them."

"Me, too. But Andrew isn't it a bit too soon to discuss family matters," she said, turning her head.

A cloud drifted across Andrew's face. He knew by now that contrary to her eagerness, actually Katie was shy when the subject touched sex. Considering that he might have problems in breaking through her inhibitions, he decided to approach the subject from a different prospective. He took her hand and said softly, "Sweetheart, I may have jumped ahead a little, but can you think of a more wonderful subject than talking about our dreams and future? We're young and our whole lives are ahead of us."

Katie nodded with agreement but said nothing. Seeing her discomfort, Andrew took another approach. He assumed a hoarse voice of an old man and started to talk with a slur. "All right, mama, then we can talk about something else. You know, dear, I was finally able to fix your broken rocking chair, so now you can use it the moment we get home."

Katie looked at him dubiously, as if he had lost his mind. Disregarding her silence, Andrew continued in a simpering composure.

"Oh yes, thank God, the rheumatic pain in my knees hasn't bothered me lately. It's strange because it always reacts to that blasted rainy weather. Also, I hope your hot-water bag helped you last night and your kidney didn't act up. It's so hard to sleep when you have to get up so often, I know. Thank God, we're free of the kids and have our privacy. There is another thing. I must tell you we have to learn to be more careful with that old-age pension check so the darn thing would last a bit longer..."

Suddenly Katie burst into laughter. "Andrew, stop it! That's enough. Dear God, you're terrible!"

"I know, my mother used to say: 'I hope one day you'll have a son like you'."

"Very funny," she laughed again. "Anyway, if I have to choose, I'd rather talk about babies."

Andrew's face lit up. "That's more like it! So now, since we're young again, I tell you that one day I want to marry you. And if you want to marry me, I hope you will want to have children."

"Yes, I think so."

"Well, you have to be more definite than that. My next question is, which one would you prefer, a boy or a girl?"

"It wouldn't matter to me, but if I could choose, I would like to have two girls and one boy."

"Two girls? Well, for heaven's sake! What else would a woman wants? I'd prefer two boys and one girl."

"But Andrew, this is silly. You can't predetermine such things. I would never argue about things I have no control over. Suppose we could not have children at all? That could happen, too, you know."

"I know, I know, but please, don't play the devil's advocate. What kind of marriage would that be?"

Katie let out an annoyed laugh. "Why, for heaven's sake? It still could be a happy one. I know a couple that just cannot have children. They were advised to adopt but the husband would not hear of it. If it came to that, would you want someone else's child?"

"Now you're putting me on the spot." Andrew said. "That's a difficult question. I'm not sure. To be honest, I don't think I have that so-called *'unconditional love'* in me. Like I heard about a man who was a cold-blooded, vicious murderer who killed just for the pleasure of it, worst than an animal. And his mother said, 'I still love him no matter what.' That is what they call unconditional love."

Katie glanced at him, musing. "Yes, I think you have to be put to the test to really know how you would feel."

"In any case, I have sympathy for that man. Adopting a child isn't the same as having your own flesh and blood. You have no idea what kind of disease the baby might be carrying. You could get yourself into a lot of trouble."

"Oh, you could get into the same trouble with your own child," Katie said. "So you should do a little homework on that. However, before it would come to that, I'd want to know all the history of the parents."

"Yeah, you could be right."

* * *

A week later they decided to visit the Royal Castle, one of the most beautiful sections of Budapest. As they wandered through the century-old historical buildings, they felt as if they were in another world. Passing by the beautiful statue of King Mathias, they stopped at the lookout of Fishermen's Bastion. They admired the view of the city, especially the spectacular architecture of the Parliament Buildings, located at the Pest side of the Danube.

Then they turned toward the King Mathias Church, another of the most ornate buildings of the Royal Castle. After admiring it for a while, they decided to walk to Margaret Island, a distance of two kilometers.

It was a marvelous autumn day. The sun shone from a clear sky and its warm rays bathed the relaxing visitors. On the promenade young lovers strolled leisurely, holding hands, amongst them Katie and Andrew. Others with their arms around each other, carried with them small hints of hidden pleasures. Their smiling faces reflected the feeling that this was one of those days that were made for romance.

As Andrew looked around, suddenly he caught sight of an exceptionally beautiful curly-haired child, about four years old. She was dressed in a bright little summer dress, which was in charming contrast to her black hair. She was jumping around a flower bed excitedly like a giant butterfly, shouting, "Mommy, Mommy! Look at this!" and stroked them.

Andrew had never seen such a beautiful child. He could not help expressing his admiration. "Katie, look at her! Have you ever seen a child this beautiful? Oh, perhaps when you were her age. But you couldn't remember. If we have a little girl some day, I hope she'll look like you."

"Thanks for the compliment. Yes, I saw her, and she *is* beautiful. But look at her parents. What a contrast! They're such plain-looking people. You couldn't imagine them producing such a beautiful child, which just proves that children don't always inherit their parents' looks. "Why, our poor daughter might look like you," she said with a sly smile.

Andrew laughed. "I hope not," he said good-naturedly. Suddenly he let out a short chuckle. "That reminds me of an anecdote about an American movie star, a sex-symbol who met with a genius scientist at a party. As they danced, she said, 'Just imagine, with your brains and my body what an exceptional child we could produce!' After a pause the scientist replied, *'Oh yes, but what if the child gets my body and your brain?'"*

Katie laughed heartily. "That was cute." Then she glanced at him again with that teasing smile. "But I could not help noticing how spell-bound you were by the beauty of that little girl. I was almost jealous."

"Jealous? Now that's another interesting subject. Are you a jealous person?"

"No, at least I don't think so. I mean...."

"Well, that's good, because I'm not a jealous person myself. To be honest, I believe that jealousy is a sickness, which comes from lack of self-confidence. If you have a reason to be jealous, that kills the love right there. My judgment may be harsh, but I think jealous people are dangerous. Besides, what can it solve?"

"Now wait a minute, Andrew. Things are not as black and white as you make them sound. Suppose jealousy is really justified?"

"That's more to my point: imagined or real, *it kills love.*"

Katie shrugged and snuggled close to him. "I think you're over simplifying it. I'm not sure, so I'm not going to argue about it. Nevertheless, you don't have to worry about me. For just as you said, if I fall out of love with you, you'll be the first to know."

* * *

Autumn was the time when young people were looking for dance studios for Sunday dance. At times Andrew visited some places with George and he liked it. Knowing a good place, he told Katie about it and asked if she would like to visit one to see if she likes it. Surprisingly, Katie's parents agreed, and they went to a place called, *"Yellow Canary".*

Katie liked it very much. It was an inviting place with its romantic dim lighting. It had a large L-shaped dance floor, and a band played on an elevated stand in the corner.

Most young girls came chaperoned with their mothers, but many came alone. The lonely boys asked the single girls—usually sitting at the side—for a dance. It was a meeting place. But if there were no available girls, they went to an already dancing couple and with a bow they asked the girl for a dance.

It was an old social custom for socializing; a way of forming some friendships. Generally the boys did not know the dancing couple, so Katie has been asked from Andrew many times. Being free, Andrew followed the same routine.

The first time they came, Katie told Andrew, "I went to parties before, but my mother had always chaperoned me. This is the first time she has not come with me."

"Oh, really? I'm delighted that it happened with me. It proves again how lucky I am," he said, kissing her forehead. "But it is so unfair. If my mother ever wanted to chaperone *me*, I'd have taken it as an insult, a violation of my rights," Andrew said. "Oh they made it clear when they expected me home, but other than that, I was free as a bird. It just proves how much easier it is to be a boy."

"You can say that again. Although my mother would say that girls need more protection, implying that there are no bad girls, only bad boys."

"Now just a minute! I hope you don't believe that. Does she mean I'm one of those *bad* boys?"

"No. She would also say that there are exceptions to every rule."

"Well, if you need protection, I'm here. From now on, I'm your bodyguard. I shall protect you even from mosquito bites."

"Thanks, my bodyguard. But I know that I'm safe with you."

* * *

After going there a few times, something happened that ended it. The dancing started as nicely as always, then at one point a young man came up to them and asked Katie for a dance. Andrew had seen him before but didn't know him. Giving Katie to him, Andrew went to dance with someone else. At the same time—he was not sure why, but he did not like the boy's manner, so he kept an eye on Katie. His instinct was right, for he soon noticed that the boy was a little fresh, trying to kiss her. Katie tried to fight him off, but did not want to make a scene. The boy, sensing that, became even bolder.

When Katie had the chance, she gestured to Andrew for help. Seeing everything, Andrew murmured: "I'll kill the guy!" He jumped over quickly, shouting, "Hey, you punk, what do you think you're doing?" And with wild fury he pushed him to the floor and a fight broke out. Girls jumped out of the way screaming. Suddenly one of them shouted, "Watch out, he has a knife!" Andrew saw it just in time, and kicked it out of his hand, then he kicked him again in the stomach—it was all reflex, without thinking.

Meanwhile the owner called the police and all three of them ended up at the police station. Andrew had some bruises, but the other boy was in bad shape. After the paperwork was done, the boy was kept there till the morning to sober up, but Katie and Andrew were released.

On the way home Katie was still crying, blaming herself. I'm so sorry, Andrew, "I'll never ever go there again," she said.

"Relax, sweetheart, you didn't do anything wrong," Andrew consoled her. "It was merely bad luck that the punk picked you."

By the time they arrived home, Katie was calmer. Feeling grateful, she kissed him with all the love she felt. "Thanks for protecting me," she said at the gate. "Good night my sweet, beautiful bodyguard."

8

NEW YEAR'S EVE PARTY

BECAUSE OF THE BRUISES, Andrew couldn't keep the fight a secret. But to his amazement, this time Margie agreed that Andrew had done the right thing. Time was rolling on, and they hardly noticed that the weeks had turned into months and autumn was gone. In December, snow-filled winter clouds hung over the city, and freshly fallen snow covered the gray buildings and the dirty streets with its sparkling whiteness.

As Christmas approached, Andrew wondered what kind of present he should buy for Katie. But the solution usually presented itself and he decided on a golden necklace with a pendant, in the shape of a heart. When the time came to give it to her, he said solemnly, "Dear Katie, with this modest gift I wish to say that my heart is yours forever."

Katie gasped with pleasure. "Oh, Andrew, it's beautiful, thank you," and she kissed him, with her parents as happy audience. "And now it's my turn," she announced, running into her room. Returning a moment later, her hands behind her, she insisted that Andrew close his eyes. Then she placed a heart-shaped box, tied up with red ribbon, into his hands. When Andrew opened the box, Katie's beautiful face smiled at him. His face turning red, he was convinced the picture was a masterpiece—he couldn't stop admiring it. On the back of it Katie had written:

To Andrew with all my love, Katie.

"Katie, this is the most beautiful gift you could have ever given me. Thank you. I'll treasure it as long as I live."

With a beaming face, Katie sighed happily. "I'm glad you like it.

I could not think of anything better to surprise you with. But come to think of it, what a coincidence! It reminds me of a proverb: *'My heart is given for yours with pleasure'."*

"Indeed, my deepest sentiment," Andrew agreed.

* * *

The next day Andrew learned that his father's company was organizing a New Year's Eve party. It was an old tradition that for this occasion factories would provide entertainment for their employees According to customs, the workers organized a play, rehearsing it for months. Then when the show was over, they rearranged the seats to make room for dancing, and the festive mood would last until dawn.

Unfortunately, Andrew learned about it too late to be able to prepare Katie, and he was afraid that her parents might object to her going. Nevertheless, he dressed for the occasion, to make all the convincing impression that he expected Katie to go there. Then he rushed to her, hoping that Katie could convince them. He was excited because this would be a real special occasion.

Burt his fear was justified; Mrs. Erdelyi strongly opposed to it, saying that it would be too late for Katie to come home.

"Remember, the reason we had agreed on to take Katie to the Dance Studio was because you were able to bring her home by midnight. But three o'clock is too late."

"But Mrs. Erdelyi, it goes without saying that you're invited too," Andrew said, displaying his most persuasive charm.

"Good try, Andrew, but we can't go because we're expecting some friends over tonight. But thanks, just the same."

Andrew looked at Katie with frustration, his face silently apologizing: *Sorry my love, I tried.*

Up until now Katie listened quietly, but now she put up a fight. "Oh, come on, Mom, be reasonable. After all, it is New Year's Eve, and I'm not a baby anymore!"

Seeing her displaying persistence, she began to relent. Yet it was Andrew's final attempt that disarmed them.

"Oh, Mrs. Erdelyi, please show us you have heart. You don't really have to worry about Katie. First, my parents will be there; second, I take full responsibility for her. If she happens to drink too much and can't walk straight, I assure you I'll carry her home slung across my shoulders." He winked at Katie with an impish smile.

Katie gasped, rolling her eyes in protest. "Andrew, you know very well I wouldn't do a thing like that." But even when seeing the joke, she added: "I'll get you for this!"

It is amazing how a little humor can relieve tension. The Erdelyis looked at each other and burst into a roaring laughter.

"All right, all right, you crazy kids, go ahead and have fun," Erdelyi said. "Just make sure you get home safely."

* * *

Unfortunately it was too late to see the show. The huge ballroom had already been rearranged for dancing. Above the crowd of noisy people the room glittered with colorful lights. The ceiling was decorated with silky paper ribbons, skillfully entwined into an intricate shape of a spider's web. And, to complete the occasion, there was a huge Christmas tree in the corner.

Andrew looked around and picked out his parents immediately. They were sitting at one of those long tables, talking with friends. When Mike saw the young lovers, his face lit up. After greeting each other, Mike introduced them to his immediate friends and said, "I'm glad you could make it, but it's too bad you missed a good show."

Andrew glanced at Katie. "You can imagine how hard it was," he said.

But they hardly had a chance to sit down; the band started playing the *Tales of the Vienna Woods.* The elevating music of the Strauss waltz carried the expression of beauty that made them eager to go to the dance floor.

It was heavenly to be in each other's arms again. The sound of music, their embrace and the fairy-tale atmosphere all enriched their love for each other. Katie's eyes glistened with rapture. She floated with the music, enjoying every moment.

"This is one of the happiest days of my life," she said blissfully. Andrew smiled and squeezed her closer to him.

When the music stopped, they went back and sat beside the Dombradys.

"Ah, it was wonderful!" Katie said to Margie. "Mrs. Dombrady, how can you sit through a nice number like this?"

Margie smiled. "Well, Katie, as the years go by it gets easier. But I enjoyed seeing how much you liked it. You two dance beautifully together."

"Thank you." The table was filled with beer and wine, and an assortment of food. During some friendly exchanges, Andrew picked up a bottle of Tokaj wine and absentmindedly tried to fill the glasses without taking out the cork. People began to laugh, commenting that Andrew discovered a safe way to keep them sober.

After a second of embarrassment, Andrew recovered and laughed with them. "That's right," he said, "the darn thing is expensive, so we might as well use it sparingly."

Befuddled by alcohol, a man across the table boasted with a hiccup-faltering slur, "Yes, but it sure makes me feel high and mighty." Then, with a friendly gesture, he offered Andrew a cigarette.

"No thanks, I don't smoke."

"Oh, another future millionaire," he said.

Katie glanced at Andrew proudly. "That just reminds me how pleased I am that you don't smoke. It's not only a filthy habit, but a health hazard."

Andrew chuckled. "That's true. I was about sixteen when one of my friends wanted me to try. I was almost choked and that was the end of it."

The band began to play again, and Katie's face lit up with delight. This time they played: *Should Auld Acquaintance Be Forgot...* This was her favorite song, and dancing to it with Andrew made it even more special. The beauty of the melody was like rippling moonlight on water; it had its magic.

While Katie hummed the tune, the slow rhythm drew their bodies together as if they were one. When it ended, Katie let out a happy sigh. "Ah, that was beautiful!"

"It was, my love," Andrew said. But instead of sitting down, he suggested a walk in the fresh air to "ventilate his head," as he put it.

As they stepped out into the empty street, their breath cut frostily into the cold air. Katie linked her arm into Andrew's and walked gracefully at his side. Glancing at her happy face, Andrew adjusted to her steps. They were silent for a while, then Andrew started to talk.

"You know, Katie, the political climate is changing in our favor. So if we really wanted to, within two years we could get married, presuming that we still love each other."

"It's funny," Katie said, "but I never thought about marriage that soon. Then suddenly adopting a sulky tone, she jerked her head, "What do you mean: *'if we still love each other'*?

"Does that mean you still love me?"

"Oh, come on, Andrew, be serious."

A faraway look came over his face. "You're right, of course. Just remember sweetheart, whatever fate the future holds in store for us, we'll always belong to each other. Physically many things can happen to us, but our hearts are chained, nothing can tear our love apart. These are big words, but I just cannot imagine life without you."

"Oooh, Andrew, that's exactly how I feel. I could never stop loving you. But please, don't paint the devil on the wall. Remember, *after the rain the sun is always shines...*"

Andrew stopped and looked piercingly into her glowing eyes. "I will remember," he said, and kissed her.."Oh, Katie," he moaned huskily, "You've no idea how much I love you."

"No more than I do," she said, locking her arms around his neck. As they drowned into a sea of sweetness, their feverish breathing intermingled with soft moans, heightening their desire to a painful yearning for relief.

"Katie, I want you so much, it hurts."

"I want you too, sweetheart, but we must be strong. It's not easy, but we must wait. You know that, don't you?"

Andrew sighed, "Yeah, my mind knows, but my blood is screaming in protest. Two years! Can we wait that long?" he asked, but he expected no answer. He glanced up at the sky. The silver circle of the moon crept from behind the clouds, opening the way for a galaxy of twinkling stars. Then he put his arm around her waist and said, "Let's go back sweetheart, it's getting a little cold. And I'm responsible for your well-being, remember?"

"Oh yes, of course. You're my bodyguard," Katie said, snuggling to him.

Walking through the laughing crowd, their nostrils were assaulted by the unpleasant odor of smoke and perspiration.

They came back just in time, for the band started to play the *Beer Barrel Polka.* The throbbing rhythm filled the air and the cheerful audience's feet followed the crushing beat of the polka. Again Katie was swept onto the dance floor by Andrew's guiding arms.

Shortly after the polka, the room became darker and the speaker started the traditional countdown. The excitement grew to a peak as the speaker shouted, "Happy New Year, everybody!"

It was 1956! People started hugging and kissing each other with ecstatic fervor, laughing and crying, wishing for a happier new year.

The announcement caught Katie and Andrew in the middle of the hall. This was their very first New Year's Eve together, and they kissed each other with special emotion."My sweet love," Andrew said huskily, "if I could, I would give you the whole world on a silver platter. But since I cannot do that, the next best I can do is to wish you the happiest New Year."

"I, too, wish you happiness and prosperity and the best of health from the bottom of my heart."

Then, while they wished all the best to Andrew's parents, the band began playing the Hungarian national anthem. The room fell into silence, and people began to sing: *God Bless the Hungarians.*

Who could have known then what a decisive year was awaiting this tiny nation? Who could have foreseen the tragedies, the heartaches, and the grief that was waiting for them?

9

DREAM OF A NATION

BECAUSE OF HER ARDUOUS studies during the winter months, a limit has been set to Andrew's visits. But when he was there, they had fun working together on Katie's homework. It did not matter how they spent the time, as long as they could be together. Sometimes she would take out some of her games, like Monopoly, and they spent long hours playing. But by far the most enjoyable times were when Katie put some records on the turntable. They would either sit and listen with swelling hearts to those beautiful sentimental Hungarian folk songs, or dance to the tunes of the lively Latin American music. Sometimes the irresistible rhythm would inspire even the Erdelyis to join them.

At other times they would sit around the table—just talking. That is how Andrew learned more about the Erdelyi's past, and about their hardships in the early fifties. It was the intimate hours they spent together that made them a close-knit family. Indeed, for Katie and Andrew those winter months were the happiest and the most memorable as the years passed by.

In the year of 1956, an irresistible growing pressure was in the air for more positive actions, and drastic changes began to take place in the country. It was a pretentious way of life with an unreal quality to it, as if floating on a temporary cloud; waiting and wondering what would come out of this daring dream. The mood seemed to indicate that it was just a matter of time before something would erupt. Without Stalin the system slid onto shaky ground. The communists had lost their iron grips on terror, and people felt the leaders' hesitation. Yet it was a slow trust condemning the past.

After all, people had a fear-injected mind, and the nation was far from being free, although no longer feared from one another. Gradu-ally people began to air their feelings more freely, which period became known as *the thawing time*. It was stunning news to be able to criticize Stalin, more so because the encouragement came from Khrushchev, who openly condemned the crimes of his corrupt regime. This was unthinkable to utter in the past. That much *freedom* was like rays of blinding sunshine after years of living in a dark tunnel.

Analyzing the state of the nation, Andrew realized that a group of fast-maturing intellectuals took the country's fate into their hands, and with a great risk that was still lurking around, making every effort to save from being further destroyed. Leading intellectuals like George Faludy, Tibor Deary, Zoltan Benko and many university students formed the *Petofi-Circle* (named after the greatest Hunga-rian poet). Andrew was delighted to see that the whole country was behind them and have given all the support to their efforts. The motive rooted by the fervent desire for more political and econo-mical freedom, nurtured by patriotic pride.

Andrew and George were strong supporter of their endeavors, and they were attended their meetings. Listening with deep interest to what they had to say; it was an eye-opener and an education. The speakers talked passionately about the painful wounds from the past, painting vivid pictures of the suffering that completely innocent people had gone through over the years. Hundreds were murdered by fabricated crimes; when in fact their only crimes were that they have disagreed with their oppressors. Even if people knew about some of the cold-blooded murders, the *Petofi-Circle* reveled many more horrors perpetrated by the Stalinists.

On the tram, going home, George said, "Just imagine, all of these that surfacing mean that finally the communists must be realizing that they can't blindfold us anymore. Oh, they must have known all along that we didn't believe those outrageous lies about what a glorious freedom we are supposedly enjoying. Or, if they did not know, they are more stupid than we gave them credit for."

Andrew laughed, "That's right! The idea they built that if they give us a communist upbringing would be enough to *make us communist*, must come from sick minds. Now the poor bastards are very disappointed. What a darn shame!"

George took over the mocking. "And after such a *happy life,* how dare we enjoy the failure of their brainwashing. God, they did everything to mutilate our national pride, and make it a crime of being a patriot. Outrageous! And now they're probably wondering what the hell they done wrong? Amazing!"

"Right you are!"

*

When Andrew arrived home, he talked enthusiastically about the meeting. He quoted the speakers' demands for political and economical reconstruction, to free the political prisoners and restore the freedom of the press. "What a refreshing subject! You feel reborn just by listening to them."

"These points are long overdue," Mike agreed. But he didn't believe that this new movement would be able to change or achieve them under the present circumstances. "A few words to the wise, son," he said. "First, I am sorry to say, but you are swimming in a pool of fog. You seem to forget that the Soviets are still in this country, and we're still living under the rule of Soviet Communism. The Hungarian leaders are mere pawns on Khrushchev's chessboard. Every move that is made here is initiated in Moscow. That means the wind could turn at any day and the Soviets could put all those speakers in jail."

Andrew refused to believe that. "But Dad," he argued, "you forget that Stalin is dead and Moscow can't turn the clock back. Do you really believe that Moscow can wipe out a whole country and put its people behind bars?"

"To answer to the first question, who will stop them from turning the clock back? Second, it would be enough to lock up the leaders. Just remember, Khrushchev is still a dictator and you had better believe that he will do everything to retain his power."

"I think you're too cynical. Can't you see what is going on in the country? And what about the fact that it is Khrushchev himself who condemns the crimes of Stalin?"

"No, not cynical, merely realistic, my son. As for your next question, he knows that the world hated Stalin with a blistering passion, so his maneuvering fits in with his political tactics. One day you'll learn that politics is the dirtiest business there is," Mike said, patting Andrew's shoulder.

As the days passed by, Andrew became convinced that his

father was right. After two years, in the swirling political storm, Prime Minister Imre Nagy suddenly has been dismissed by Khrushchev. The reason given was that he had become a *"right-wing lenient"*.

*

One Sunday afternoon Katie and Andrew were strolling on the Great Boulevard, enjoying the lovely spring sunshine. Suddenly, Andrew spotted George in the crowd, immersed in his thoughts. George knew about Katie but they never met. So, this was a good chance to introduce them.

"Here comes George," Andrew whispered to Katie. "Stay quiet, for I want to surprise him."

A moment later he grabbed George's arm. "Oh hi, old boy. What a coincidence! I was just on my way to visit you, but of course, I should have known better. You're never home on weekends."

"You're right for a change," Andrew joked, then he introduced them. "George, this is Katie, my girlfriend. Katie, this is George Pusztai, my good old buddy."

"It's my pleasure to meet you, George," Katie said, extending her hand.

George stared at her with great admiration. "I'm pleased to meet you." Turning to Andrew, he remarked: "Now I know why you're never home." Glancing at Katie, he added, "And I don't blame you, you lucky devil."

Andrew beamed proudly.

Katie smiled. "But George, there are lots of pretty girls around who would be more than happy to have your company, I'm sure."

"Well, you could be right," he said. "Seeing you is quite an inspiration. We could make a good foursome."

Andrew turned the subject into ambiguous joking.

"Splendid idea George! I was beginning to worry that the opposite sex is not interests you," he said, winking at Katie.

"Oh, come on, Andrew! I am not that kind of a person. Besides, thank God, perversity is not my coup of tea, anyway."

"Now that's a relief!" Andrew smiled. "Of course I am just teasing, you know; I know you better than that."

"I hope so. By the way, if we are already at it, I have read some extremely sadistic whipping cruelty that had connected to their sexual pleasure. If that is not abnormal, I don't know what is. You may can't help having a cancer, but you are still a sick man."

Katie did not understand much of it, so she said nothing.

George continued walking with them, making small talk. Moments later some beautiful dresses caught Katie's eyes in a large shop window and she stopped for a second. "Oh, I want to see this," she said. Seizing the opportunity, George whispered to Andrew with a crafty smile, "Listen, buddy, I know my chances are limited, but as beautiful as Katie is, I'll try to seduce her whether you like it or not."

Andrew laughed. "All right, you're on. I want you to try. I would like to see how Katie reacts. But I wouldn't guarantee which of your legs I would break first."

"Gee, thanks for the choice."

They were like brothers, knew each other inside and out. And in their friendship it was natural for them to joke without hurting each other's feelings.

*

The mood in the nation alternated. Under the pressure for constant demands, more changes were made. The system was beginning to resemble to a fast turning kaleidoscope. In the late summer months the intellectuals in the *Petofi-Circle* presented their strongest demands for more changes. One of the sour points was that there were still too many *hard-line* Stalinists in top positions, which made it harder to free the country from the Soviet oppression. The other was to get Imre Nagy back into power.

During the next meeting, Andrew looked around the crowd and thought that there were times when many of these people would have swallowed the verbal garbage and sung the song of communist promises. But as the years passed by, some of them lived through Recsk and other torture chambers, for the lies and party slogans insulted their intelligence. They learned that those slogans were nothing but lies that meant more work only for less money. Meantime Andrew also read the **Diary of Rachmanova**, and his mind had connected to many of her great statements.

As for this moderate freedom of expression, it served to ripen their realization that they can't take the dictatorship any longer! It seemed the time had come to make their dream come true, so it was here and now that the decision was made. Having came this far, they cannot let the success wasted! The climate was right, and people believed that a new dawn was rising.

*

The movement peaked when the new leaders gave an honorary state funeral to Laszlo Rajk, an old-time communist who had been Minister for Domestic Affairs at the beginning of the Rakosi era. In the late 1940's, Stalin had a hateful conflict with Marshal Tito of Yugoslavia. Although Tito was a communist, he had his own idea of Communism and resisted Stalin's interfering. They became enemies. And since Rakosi worshiped Stalin, it followed that Hungary too became Tito's enemy. But Laszlo Rajk sided with Tito. He had been executed in 1949, under fabricated charges of treason.

But now, in this thawing period, when Stalin became a despicable criminal, the communists made every effort to whitewash the dirty past. By revealing the truth, now Laszlo Rajk became a hero.

The funeral was held on October 6, 1956. It was a gray, dismal, misty autumn day. The leaves had already gone and the trees stood naked, the branches pointing to the sky like dried-out spiky sticks. On this drizzly day, Andrew and George marched along with the thousands of bewildered people thronged to the cemetery.

Once there, the huge crowd heard the most outrageous charges against the inhuman Rakosi era. Layers upon layers of pure lies and cover-ups were revealed. "...These criminals who disguised themselves as leaders of the country, built a pattern of insidious, sickening criminal abuse of power. Thousands of innocent compatriots fell into their corrupt, power-hungry web—no one was immune to their cruelty."

The revelation was shocking. This was a spiritual riot, one that added more sparks to the smoldering fire of the revolution.

*

ON OCTOBER 21ST news began circulating that the university students were organizing a mass demonstration on October 23$^{rd.}$ Their daring demands were worked out in fifteen major points, among which were the withdrawal of Soviet troops from Hungary; free elections, freedom of speech and literature; removal of the loathed statue of Stalin that had been erected on the site of a demolished church, and the restoration of Imre Nagy as Prime Minister.

At the *Petofi-Circle*, heated arguments broke out between the more conservative intellectuals and some hotheaded students over some of the "too strong" demands, arguing they were unrealistic, which would not bring the desired freedom but rather bloodshed and more oppression.

But the wounds were still fresh and the students were not about to compromise. They wanted to get rid of those who had inflicted them, once and for all.

Andrew and George sided with the students. At the end of the meeting the organizers gave them a package of declarations to display on public advertising poles. The two friends took it eagerly and went to do the job.

It was a Saturday. It seemed as if all the people of Budapest were on the street: the city was in the grip of electric mood. When Andrew finished distributing the declarations, he stepped aside and watched as people read them. Some elders inched their way closer to be able to read the words, while others shook their heads in disbelief. Not too long ago they would have been given a lifetime of torture and execution for reading these words. Now, they were reading such words as **"Russians go home"** and "*we want freedom*". This was incredible! How could this happen? He turned his head, *"This will lead to bloodbath, for the Soviets won't stand for this."* They read the manifesto over and over again smiling and whispering: "I just can't believe this! But still, thank God, we lived to see the day it happened!

As Andrew observed this highly emotional mood, the gleaming rays of sun filtered through the tangled branches, soothingly caressing his face. Blinking with pride, he thought how the communists could imprison the body, but the spirit could never be bound within prison walls.

He felt he was among true compatriots.

10

THE REVOLUTION

OCTOBER 23rd FELL ON a Tuesday. The demonstration started in Buda. First they went to honor the statue of Bem, the legendary Polish general who had fought in the Hungarian war in 1848. Marching over to Pest, the avalanche of demonstrators rank swelled into hundreds of thousands, flooding the main boulevards. Above their heads, a forest of waving posters and national flags sparkled in the autumn sunshine; others marched arm-in-arm, singing and chanting patriotic slogans. Their infectious enthusiasm captured Andrew. It was all there: the sparks of pride in their eyes, the challenge and contempt toward the oppressive system. The magnetic spark triggered an approving reaction, and people cheered and waved flags from the apartment balconies. The timing seemed right. Traffic came to a complete halt as the crowd headed toward the Parliament Buildings. But instead of resenting, the drivers cheered and some even joined the marchers. One could feel the electricity in the air.

Arriving at the Parliament, the crowd filled up Kossuth Square and all the side streets. In the vibrant atmosphere, they demanded to see Imre Nagy. It was a long wait, but finally he appeared on the balcony. When the thunderous cheering died, he greeted his supporters with a brief message, warning them to be cautious with their demands, thanking them for their support.

Then the enthusiastic sea of humanity sang the national anthem and began to disperse into groups. One group went to see the toppling of the statue of the infamous Stalin, another group swarmed into the *Szabad Nep* (Free People) building where the daily newspaper of the Communist Party was printed. There they threw out all the communist propaganda literature from the library into the middle of the Great Boulevard, poured gasoline on and burned them.

Andrew and George joined the group that went to the *Radio Budapest,* located in the Brody Sandor Street. Dusk had fallen by the time they arrived. A noisy crowd of students had already gathered at the heavy wooden door, confronting the two AVO men guarding the building. They demanded the right to broadcast the fifteen-point manifesto to the people of Hungary.

The AVO men laughed, saying that their demand was impossible to carry out. But seeing the grim determination on the students faces, one of them proposed condescendingly that if they leave the manifesto with them, they might broadcast it at a later hour.

The students refused to fall for such an obviously dishonest promise, and made an attempt to force their way into the building. But the AVO men pushed them back. Their roughness made the crowd furious, and provoked some more scuffling.

Eighty AVO men stationed in the building, watching the heated actions. Observing the conflict, they started hurling teargas bombs into the crowd from the top of the building. The acrid smoke stung their nostrils and forced them to seek fresh air at the nearby park. However, determined to accomplish what they came for, it forced them to return.

Realizing that the teargas had not frightened them, the AVO flashed a powerful beacon light onto them. A new rage of protest arose from the crowd and they hurled stones at the lights. The AVO would not tolerate this, and began firing real bullets into the crowd.

By those bullets a spontaneous revolution was born; history was in the making, as people started to drop to the ground, dead or wounded. Stunned, and in the roaring, paralyzing anger they tried to roll out of sight. While the machine guns rattled from the roof, in the pandemonium they buckled, sprawled, trampled over each other. The Brody Sandor Street became an instant battlefield.

"They're killing us!" the crowd shouted in shocked disbelief. The blood froze in Andrew's veins.

That is how the carnage started, what ignited the bitter fight with the hated secret police. The shooting continued, and more people dropped dead. They were the first martyrs for attempting to free Hungary from Soviet Communism.

"Oh, the cursed bastards!" George hissed between gritted teeth. "Come on, Andrew, run under the gate!" he shouted, grabbing his arm. Meanwhile the raving, boiling crowd was vowing revenge, exhorting others to fight back.

The news spread through the city like bush-fire and, as if by magic, a line of trucks appeared. With a resounding cheer, the crowd recognized the workers from Csepel, a large factory town at the outskirts of Budapest. The workers came from the gun factory, bringing arms and ammunition with them.

The sight hit Andrew with fascination. Here was the so-called pampered Csepel factory workers, the inhabitants of the industrial world, the "elite" of the proletariat, pillars of Communism. The hard working people that was breathing the soot-polluted air, but whose brains were filled with slogans by which the factories, the country, everything were theirs; they were working for themselves, and for the glorious future... But now these "pillars" of the nation are here, turning their backs against those lying slogans, which were in fact choking and jailing them.

The weapons were quickly distributed to people eager to fight. They became the first freedom fighters. Andrew got hold of a machine gun, George a rifle and many others received pistols and hand grenades.

"We will destroy the AVO," a voice shouted.

They still did not have enough guns, but what they had improved their chances of taking over the radio building. Fast thinking students ran over to the nearby army headquarters, the Kilian barracks, for support. It was known that the army felt the same hatred for the AVO as they felt for the infamous Nazi Gestapo. Naturally the students were not disappointed; the soldiers were glad to fight against the secret police.

Studying the gun for a short time, Andrew joined the fighters and helped organize their strategy.

At the same time the Csepel workers assembled a heavier gun on the truck and wiped out those blaring beacon lights. Meanwhile an ambulance arrived with a Red Cross flag on it. The grateful crowd cheered with relief for there were many wounded lying on the ground that needed help. But as people gave way for the vehicle to pass, the pale-faced driver silently kept driving past the wounded bodies. Watching with growing horror his apparent disregarding of their cries for help, they got suspicious.

"Hey, man, where the hell are you going?" shouted one fighter. "The injured are here. Can't you see?"

Reluctantly the ashen-faced driver rolled down the window and said, "My orders are to pick up the wounded from inside" and with that he made an attempt to drive through the crowd.

With raging fury, one fighter tore the door open and dragged the driver out of the vehicle. This was when they realized the truth—they had taken him for a real ambulance man. But this one carried not medicine but guns, hand-grenades and ammunition for the AVO. A wave of shock swept through the crowd. *"My god, he is an AVO man.* **Look!***..."*

A moment later the crowd, in their outrage, went wild. Hundreds of hands tried to reach him, and in spite of his horrified pleas, they tore him to pieces. They captured the vehicle and its contents. And the rattle of gunfire from both sides continued.

Hours went by, and it was getting late. Besides being hungry, Andrew worried about his parents, for they knew nothing about his whereabouts. He hated the thought of leaving his compatriots, but he felt he must. George also worried about his mother, who had a serious heart condition. So they decided to go home.

They could not have taken more than a dozen steps when a fighter hit the heavy door of the station with a hand grenade and they heard a huge explosion.

"Let's smoke out those bastard AVOs!" they shouted.

"It seems we'll miss out on some good action," George said.

"Probably, but we'll have our fair share of it tomorrow. I think your dad would be proud of you, could he see you fighting against his murderers."

George nodded. "Yeah, he'd be here with me, I'm sure."

The darkness engulfed them, and the rattle of gunfire slowly faded away like a dying echo.

*

Andrew's parents were aware of the revolution that had broken out in the city. The apartment building was buzzing with excitement as all kinds of wild stories were flying about, regarding what was going on at *Radio Budapest,*—and how the city had been turned upside down in such a short time. They also heard Home

Secretary Erno Gero's speech on the radio, saying, "...*Some unruly fascist mob,* traitors of the Hungarian people, flooded the streets of Budapest..."

But they were not prepared for what they saw when Andrew came home. Machine gun slung over his shoulder, and with a determined face he said, "Hi" and sat down. Margie gasped, "Oh, God! Andrew, are you crazy?" Then a stunned silence fell in the room.

He looked at his parents calmly, almost defiantly. "No," he said, "I'm just doing my patriotic duty."

The tension that hung in the air could have been cut with a knife. "You lost your mind," Margie cried.

Mike too was shocked beyond words. Never before had he seen Andrew in such an adult frame of mind. His transformation within mere hours was unbelievable. Listening to his son, he made a nervous jerk.

"Look, Andrew, I know how stubborn you can be. I also know that you're fighting for a just cause. But I must convince you that what you're fighting for is unattainable and suicidal. I respect the motive that drives you, but--"

"There are no buts about it, Dad."

"But can't you see that other than costing too many lives, nothing good can come out of it," Mike continued, disregarding Andrew's interruption. "Why don't you consider the consequences?"

"Dad," Andrew said, his voice faltering, "You know how much I love you. I appreciate your concern and I'm sorry if I disappoint you. My compatriots fighting for the freedom of this country, I can't turn my back on them. I may be stubborn but I'm not a coward."

"Oh, God!" Mike said with a painful frustration. "What's that got to do with it? You don't have to be a coward to use your common sense."

Andrew shook his head defensively. "Dad, I can't even begin to describe you the viciousness of that slaughtering. How those innocent people were dropped to the ground dead or wounded. If you had seen those traitors unmerciful killings, you'd agree that they've killed all common sense tonight. We didn't want to fight; what's more, our demands were reasonable. Yet they didn't give us any choice," he said heatedly. "This is our fight now, and we'll finish what they started. It's about time we show the world that we don't want to live under Soviet oppression—or any kind of dictatorship. It came to the point where finally we had enough: if we can't be free, we're ready to die."

(Words, great, lofty, patriotic words! Isn't it a blessing that we don't know how many lonely nights and suffering those words might bring and come to haunt us.)

Margie lost all her strength to argue. She could only sit there sobbing bitterly. It was as if she were burying her son already.

Mike's hands were shaking with frustration. He would have admired his son's determination if the situation hadn't been so hopeless. After a long silence, he tried a new approach.

"Well, son, you're talking about being reasonable. Do you think Katie would approve your decision?"

Andrew looked up. "I knew you'd bring her into this. Maybe not, but as a matter of fact, I'm fighting for her freedom as well."

"Fair enough. But I still say that fighting against the Soviet tanks is like banging your head against a brick wall." He paused, and in that split second he suddenly saw things in a different light. "All right then, if I can't stop you, then I must say this: even if I don't believe that you're doing the right thing, I respect you for following your heart. So, painful as it is, I won't stand in your way, though God knows I feel I should. But now I look at it in another way. Should I stand in your way, one day you might resent it and I might regret it. You're an adult and you have to go through the experience, just like all of us, in order to learn whether you were right or wrong. There is no way of escaping our fate." As the emotion overwhelmed him, he managed to say. "All I ask is to be careful... and God bless you."

*

The early morning sun shone brightly over Budapest, oblivious to the desperate struggle that had just taken place for freedom against Communism. After hugging his parents, Andrew went to the Corvin-Block. That building was one of the head-quarters, which the freedom fighters had chosen, because of its proximity to the Kilian barracks.

George was already there. He introduced Andrew to the commander, Gerald Portas. He was about thirty-five years old with a sharp, alert look in his eyes. After exchanging a few words, Andrew realized he couldn't find a more honest, no-nonsense man.

George also told Andrew that in the middle of the night there was an attempt by the AVO to take over the Kilian barracks. But the Hungarian army, which stood by the revolution, put up a fierce fight and the attackers were beaten back.

News was now circulating that Russian tanks will attack the Kilian barracks. Young, eager fighters, some of them only ten or twelve years old, came with their guns from all over the city, offering help in any way they could. There was a death defying, an almost suicidal determination on their faces to destroy the Russian tanks. What gave these young kids the awesome courage when, figuratively speaking, they were fighting almost barehanded against one of the world's powers, amazed the world. Part of the reason must have been their *nothing-to-lose* desperation. In the vortex of their hatred for dictatorship, their feelings were dominated by strong patriotic pride to achieve a just deed. Grabbing the chance to fight for freedom, history will classify it as the ultimate and unsurpassable courage. But wait! Fighting for freedom? Most of them did not even know what freedom was. *What they really knew was what they did NOT want: Soviet Communism.* Also they had an immense desire to show *them* that they were not mindless sheep —by God, how they wanted to show them!

A boy, serving as a lookout, suddenly ran in shouting, "They are coming!"

Seven tanks advanced on the cobblestone boulevard with total menacing assurance. Then the fighting had begun. With thundering noise, as if the sky was crashing down, the heavy guns punched holes into the huge four-foot thick walls, splintering them into dust-clouds, inflicting huge amount of damage. The surrounding buildings reverberated from the shots, killing many soldiers and civilians. They kept pounding at it as though they intended to demolish them into rubble. It seemed that the Russians had the upper hand in this inferno.

Desperation inspires special measures, and the fighters from Corvin-Block sprang into action. Talk about bravery! They suddenly appeared on rooftops, crawling to the streets armed with *Molotov cocktails* and hand-grenades. They circled the tanks and hurled gasoline bombs and hand-grenades at them. They fought barehanded against the tanks with all human determination. There was no limit to their ingenious ideas. Andrew ran up to the tanks and stuck pieces of metal into the track, causing them to jam. Once the tanks were immobilized, they threw gasoline bombs on them and blew them up. This way they managed to destroy four tanks. Finally, the remaining three tanks withdrew, as if saying: *That's enough for today.*

The streets of Budapest become a battlefield. The buildings were shaking from the explosions and two million people lived through this life-and-death horror. But in spite of all the ruins, the Hungarians had that stubborn, undaunted will to fight to the very end. This determination put Hungary on the map, at least for the time being...

Danger and desperation brings people together and creates a unique bond between them. During one quiet period, Andrew told George that it is a thousand-year Hungarian tradition (and tragedy that we have to keep fighting the evil forces to maintain our existence as a nation.

This revolution was spontaneous. Its sole discipline was self-discipline and deep dedication. There was no question about it: at this historical moment Hungary became a "laboratory" of heroism and sacrifice!

The next day John Karoly, an eighteen-year-old freedom fighter, told Andrew that he wanted to go to Republic Square because a big battle was going on there. This is where the AVO headquarters were, and he wanted to take part in the action. John invited Andrew to go with him and he agreed, but George decided to stay.

They had to walk a distance of three kilometers, which gave Andrew time to think about Katie. He wondered what she was doing and how worried she must be over fact of not being able to make any contact with him. The whole city was a war zone, and any kind of communication was impossible.

The Republic Square was a heavily wooded area, which presented good possibilities for organizing the attacks. When they arrived, fierce fighting was already taking place. Wishing each other good luck, the two friends parted and looked for positions to join the fighting. There was a theater building across from the headquarters that provided some good and safe view of the AVO building. Andrew found a good spot and started shooting at the windows from where the AVO men were shooting back. Wounded and dead bodies lay on the ground and an organized unit was trying to carry them away on their stretchers.

As a result of the heavy pressure from the street, the AVOs

finally were forced to take refuge in the cellar where they have kept some prisoners. One of the fighters noticed a water tap and a great idea hit him. After some discussions they collected enough rubber hoses to thrust them through the cellar window. Water began flooding the building and the AVOs were forced to abandon the place. They began to appear in front of the building, pushing the prisoners in front of them as shields.

Seeing that cowardly act infuriated the fighters immensely. When the AVO men were captured, many of them were beaten to death, or hung on trees by their heels. Andrew saw people spitting on them with all their pent-up hatred.

"Finally they got what was long overdue," John said. "Rakosi, Gero, and all these Stalin-worshipers, they're not Hungarians but nation-traitors—enemies of the worst kind." Then he turned and said: "Listen, Andrew, I just heard that tomorrow there will be a huge demonstration at the Parliament Buildings. Do you want to come?"

"I think I'll go back to the Corvin-Block," Andrew said. "But I want you to give me the true account when you come back. Good luck."

*

Meanwhile, George Pusztai was engaged in a bitter street fight. The group he was with was trying to round up some AVO men who were shooting from a building. As George tried to run from one cover to another, a bullet hit him in the back, killing him instantly.

When Andrew heard the terrible news, the tragedy hit him so deeply that he slumped into a chair and sobbed. "Oh, dear God!" he cried. His conscience bothered him, thinking that had he been with him he might have saved his friend.

It was impossible to keep the tragedy from his parents. When he told them, their worry increased to an almost unbearable pain. Now they lived for the brief moment when Andrew came home to sleep. The rest of the day they spent by the radio, hanging on to every piece of information. The radio broadcast, now coming from a relocated station, was still in the hands of the communists. After three days of fighting, exhausted, they wondered when this destructive madness would end.

The following day, thousands of people gathered at the Parliament Buildings, repeating their demands to reinstate Imre Nagy as Prime Minister, and remove the fanatic Stalinist, Erno Gero from his office.

As John gave a detailed account of what took place, "in answering to the demonstrators' demands, the AVO, hidden on top of the Supreme Court Building, opened fire on the defenseless crowd. Hundreds of people fell to the ground —like dominoes on a huge board. I could not believe that is possible to see such a cold-blooded savagery. Luckily, I was safe behind an advertising pillar. The rattle of machine guns kept pouring their deadly bullets even when the ambulances arrived. In fact, they shot down the attendants the moment they stepped out."

"Russian tanks were stationed around the Parliament Buildings. Observing the massacre, one of the rank captains directed his gun at the roof of the Supreme Court Building and shot those crazy AVOs out. He must have been disgusted by the senseless massacre. This was the first incident in which Russian soldiers turned their guns against the Hungarian Secret Police."

"The very same day Imre Nagy was reinstated as Prime Minister and Erno Gero was replaced by Janos Kadar. People on the street mourned, 'If only this had happened one day earlier, how much bloodshed could have been averted!'" (*)

Imre Nagy made a moving speech on the radio. He promised a meeting with the Soviet officials to discuss their imminent withdrawal from Hungary. Then, the dream of all dreams, victory was celebrated! The red-white-green national flags flew loftily in the autumn breeze on thousands of buildings, with a huge hole in the middle, for the hated Soviet emblem of the sickle and hammer had been cut out.

On the walls and shop windows, slogans were painted: *Russians go home!* The statue of Stalin was hauled to Akacfa Street, a distance of three kilometers, where people smashed the huge figure with hammers, releasing their pent-up fury and frustration. Then on the fourth day of the revolution, victory was officially declared!

Soon Imre Nagy confirmed that the negotiation with the Russians had been successful, and they had agreed to withdraw

(*30 years later the new Hungarian government erected a statue in the middle of Kossuth Square to honor the memory of hundreds of innocent victims who were killed by the bullets of the insane AVO murderers.)

their troops. Andrew was with a large group of fighters in front of the Corvin building listening with rapt attention as Nagy ended his speech with a triumphant:

"*Long Live the Free and Independent Hungary!*"

A loud cry of happy cheers vibrated in the air. The strains of the Hungarian national anthem followed.

People stood and listened solemnly, their heads held high singing together with bursting pride and emotion. It was a moment of supreme realization that Hungary was the first nation behind the Iron Curtain that dared to defy Communism successfully.

At the Corvin House, where people used to stand in line waiting for a show, now teenage boys and girls, Hungary's newest heroes were smiling proudly, machine-guns slung over their shoulders. They were joking, laughing—life was suddenly all joy and happiness.

Deliriously happy himself, Andrew went for a walk. It was a balmy autumn day. The breeze stirred the fragrant yellowing leaves as if endeavoring to rid the city of the stench of corruption brought upon her by Soviet Communism. Everywhere jubilant people thronged the streets, celebrating their true liberation. Andrew watched as complete strangers opened their arms and clasped each other, congratulating, kissing, crying and laughing with sheer disbelief—renewed hope on their faces. Being on the street after hiding in their homes for days, this sudden new world was truly unforgettable—a glorious day!

Andrew lifted his face to the arching blue sky and let out a deep sigh. Dear God, how wonderful it was to be alive! *If only George could be here with me to celebrate this victory*, he thought with sadness. Then on the spur of the moment, he decided to erect a monument in his honor:

An honest man was born in this corner of our tiny world. He was a decent human being who never had the chance to taste the grace of freedom and what it can offer. He had to die too young, so that others could enjoy the victory. I'm so sad, my friend, that you cannot be with me to share this wonderful victory. I wish my dear friend that your soul will rest in peace and happiness.

Next, he wished that Katie was at his side to reassure her that he was all right. It was hard to believe that only a week ago, they had been walking on these streets, laughing and dreaming.

What a change one week can make! Well, those extreme times, the fear of terror are over, he thought, and they soon could make up for the lost time.

Physically and emotionally exhausted, Andrew started to walk home to share this historical moment with his parents. On his way, he observed the burned-out tanks, shops and demolished buildings. He saw scattered Russian and Hungarian dead bodies on the pavements. There was an overturned streetcar in Kalvin Square, and electric wires dangled over the streets.

The city was grounded to a halt. The sight was almost as bad as after the Second World War. It seemed like a cruel joke as curious youngsters were sitting on top of the burned-out Russian tanks in Ulloi Street, toying with the dead monsters that probably had killed hundreds of people. Yet a new Budapest was beginning to emerge from the rubble. This was a true victory—our freedom, Andrew thought proudly. Not only the people of Budapest, but the whole country was celebrating. Everybody felt that they had arrived at the threshold of heaven.

In spite of the crumbling law and order, many broken display windows were unguarded, but the merchandises were untouched. Cardboard boxes were placed at the main intersections with a hastily scribbled line: *Please Help the Parents and Families of our Fallen Heroes*. The boxes, also unguarded, were filled with bank notes, as people had been contributed generously. But no one would even think of stealing them. In this cruel world we are living, what could illustrate the poignant human spirit more beautifully? Andrew thought. This historic moment brought out the pinnacle of honesty, the peak of morality and the patriotic pride from the Hungarians.

When Andrew arrived home, his parents welcomed him with enormous relief. As they embraced him, all eyes were filled with tears of joy. Andrew was triumphant. **"We've done it!"** he shouted. "I wish I would be a poet, but all I can say is that it was madness, but we have achieved something that seemed impossible."

"Indeed, my son. All I can say is that with your awesome courage, you made a miracle come true," Mike said, trembling with emotion. "You have proven me wrong, and I congratulate you."

"Thanks, Dad. Though I must confess, I was afraid you might be right. Well, Mom," he turned to her with swelling pride, "What do you think, was it worth it?"

"I don't know," she said. "I think the price was too high."

As they were sitting at the table, Mike's old suspicion hit him again. Scratching his head, he struggled with his thoughts. "I'm still not sure," he said, as if to himself. "I hate to be a party pooper but I think the unrelenting defense baffled the Russians. I wouldn't be surprised if this so-called withdrawal is just a Russian ploy to gain time. I hope I'm wrong but I think as soon as they collect themselves, they'll be back for a counterattack. In other words, their promise means nothing. We must not forget that they're notorious liars and promise-breakers. Not to mention that they're one of the world's strongest powers whose prestige has suffered an unforgivable affront. There is no precedent in history to suggest that the Soviets would permit such an insult without retaliation. So, I'm afraid we have not seen the last of them."

Andrew's confidence wavered because he respected his father's clear-sightedness. "But what about the West, the free world?" he said with an impatient gesture. "If what you say is true, do you think America will tolerate it without interfering? I'm sure the UN would also condemn the aggression."

Mike laughed. "They'd condemn it, all right. Look, Andrew, for eight years the Russians trampled us in the mud. But when we rose to fight against them, what did the huge American propaganda machine do for help? Nothing! Their encouragement choked into silence and let us commit suicide. It is my experience that the world's most powerful nation don't give a damn what happens to small countries, unless there are business interests, especially oil is involved. Then they act fast!"

"I can't believe this," Andrew said. "I hope you're wrong."

"I hope too. Of course, from a purely logical point of view, you're right. If America would have a farsighted president, he would realize that standing up to the Russians would be the correct things to do. They should show the Soviets that the Free World would not tolerate forcing Communism on other countries. But with all due respect, I'm afraid the Americans don't consider us important. So, other than expressing their deep regrets, they will find all kind of excuses, to do nothing."

"Well, even if it's true, we'll still fight to the bitter end."

"God forbid. I hope that won't be necessary."

*

During the victorious days, peasants from the villages flooded Budapest with truckloads of food to ease the shortage. It was their intention to show how grateful they were by contributing to their effort to free the country.

Meanwhile Andrew took a new post for serving the nation. Dressed in a faded khaki coat and the popular blue beret, tilted to the right side, with army boots and machine gun slung from his shoulder, he walked up and down, guarding the entrances of strategic buildings, such as City Hall. He was a proud man and felt the respect from people walking by.

He was also thinking about Katie, how he could see her? Considering the complete halt in public transportation, she could have been living hundreds of kilometers away. But he must know if she was all right.

Then quite by chance, he overheard one of the freedom fighters saying he had to drive through Matyasfold. Andrew could hardly contain his excitement, and asked if he could go with him. It was as simple as that!

On the way, sitting beside the driver, the city seemed strange. Before he got off at Matyasfold, Andrew fixed the meeting time and place with the driver. Looking around, it was a relief to see that the arms of the revolution had not reached the suburb. As he rang the bell, Katie came to the gate. Seeing Andrew, she gasped. "Oooh, Andrew!" she cried out and rushed into his arms. The rest of the words were choked back by happy sobs. Andrew stroked her hair.

"Hush, my love, you see, I'm all right..."

"Thank God, you're alive!" she said, pressing her head to his chest. Then, together they went in.

The Erdelyis couldn't have been more surprised either. They welcomed him as if he were their lost son. "Andrew! How good it is to see you. How are you?"

"I'm fine, thanks. It's good to see you. Well, what a change four days can make! Would you believe it, **We Are *Free!*** " he said enthusiastically.

"That is what we're hearing but it is hard to believe," Erdelyi said. "It seems we're dreaming!"

"Believe it, it's true! You should have seen the happy people in the street of the city."

"Yes, but we heard such terrible things," Katie said. We were safe here, but you'll never know how much we have worried about you." Then, as if this was the first time she was seeing him, she stood back surprised, looking at him suspiciously. "But Andrew, you've changed so much. You never dressed like this before. Don't tell me you took part in the fighting?"

"Well, yes. I did a little..."

A look of pure disbelief spread across her face. "Andrew! Oh, my God!" she cried out, repressing a shudder.

"Really?" Erdelyi exclaimed, just as surprised. "But I should have guessed." Excited, they all sat around him with great curiosity. "Then you must have some story to tell. What happened out there?"

Taking a deep breath, Andrew started to talk about heroism and fear, the senseless killings and the terrible destruction. He spoke about seeing the terror on innocent people's faces as they cut down by the bullets of the rattling machine gun fire, pleading to God for help...About a fifteen-year-old boy who had been struck by a bullet while running across the street. The boy stopped suddenly, staggered a few feet and then collapsed to the pavement.

"Before the revolution, the image of death was a huge and horrifying monster," he said. "But the rattle of machine guns killed the notion of immortality. You learn fast that human life is so cheap."

Erdelyi was outraged by the vicious slaughter that took place at the *Radio Budapest*.

Later still, he spoke about the desperate fighting at the AVO headquarters at Republic Square, where they literally flooded the AVO out of the building. Then, with glowing eyes, he spoke about his inexplicable happiness on Victory Day. People were delirious on the street. The only time his voice faltered was when he spoke about George, who was among the fallen heroes.

"Oh, no!" Katie gasped. "Poor George, he was such a loveable person." She wept for George and for his mother who now had lost both her husband and son. Then she stood up abruptly, and nervously walked up and down till suddenly facing Andrew. "But you, Andrew, you really shocked me. Thank God, you're alive, but you could have been killed just as well. If nothing else, you should have considered your parents' suffering... If only I had known, I would have prayed more for you."

"Well, then I saved you all that trouble."

"Andrew, it is not a joking matter. But I guess, it is better I did not know. Worrying about you would have killed me."

Andrew put on a lighthearted front to console her, but he was touched. Sometimes I wonder if she is aware of how beautiful she is, he thought. Driven by this thought, he stood up and kissed her on the lips. "This is for showing how much you care," he said.

"I can imagine what agony your parents went through," Mrs. Erdelyi said.

"Yes, they went through a great deal, especially after George's death," Andrew said. "But I worried about them just as much."

"God was with you and that's the most important thing," Katie said.

Unfortunately, time was running out and Andrew had to leave. As he shook Erdelyi's hand, he felt a new kind of respect in his warm handshake.

"I'm very proud of you, Andrew," he said. "Please take care of yourself and God bless us all."

"Thank you. I believe this freedom will bring new meaning, a new beginning to our lives," Andrew said.

"Let's hope."

"Well, I must go, so long," Andrew said and took a step to kiss Katie good-bye.

"I'll walk with you," she said, "so we can spend a little more time together. Who knows how long this mess will keep us apart."

"It won't be long, sweetheart, but I'd love to walk with you. I sure missed you a lot."

"I missed you more."

Arms around each other's waists, their faces beaming, they clung together as though they never wanted to part. In this happy frame of mind, Katie told him how excited they were during the revolution, wishing for victory, yet afraid to believe in it. But it had happened!

"It sure did, sweetheart. Just imagine: *we made it happen!* Until now, the future was just a pile of dark years, and tomorrow had offered nothing but uncertainty. Although the transition will be scary, yet those tomorrows are offering a light to a happier future. Of course, the future will still depend on a strong and responsible leader, for without that, no freedom can survive. It will also depend on changing our attitude about the work ethic. First of all, we'll have to learn again how to work. It'll be a new world that will require more honesty and less greed. So, the adjustment won't be easy but it will be worth the effort," he said with full of passion.

"Oh, it sounds so interesting, and as a bonus, I'll have my own freedom fighter hero," Katie said enthusiastically. "I'll stand by you come what may because with you, I'm not afraid of anything. I love you so much."

Andrew looked into her glowing eyes and kissed her with love that was almost surprising. "I love you too. Now that we have risen above the dark clouds, the sun will shine upon us. With God's help, we can move mountains and build a bright future without fear and terror."

"Yes, now I can believe it. I wish I could go with you. But for the time being, I must be satisfied just to have you in my heart. Please take care and come as soon as you can."

"You, too, are in my heart and always will be. So till next time just remember, I adore you."

They stood at the edge of the pavement, bathed in the rays of the autumn sun, kissing each other. Then, when the truck approached, Katie turned and walked away gracefully. At the corner, before she disappeared from his view, she waved good-bye once more, sending him a kiss with her hand. She could not imagine anyone being more in love in the world.

Then she was gone.

As Andrew looked after her, the parting had a melancholic quality to it. He couldn't have fathomed how much this moment would haunt him in the years to come. All he felt was a strange, uneasy feeling that perhaps he should not let her out of his sight...

11

BITTER AWAKENING

DURING THE FIRST DAY of November, reports began circulating that Soviet troops had crossed the Hungarian border with hundreds of new tanks and were advancing toward Budapest. To gain time, the Soviet officials in Budapest denied everything, saying the allegations were only a nasty rumor spread by the enemies.

But in spite of all denials, it was apparent that the decision has been made in Moscow to seek revenge with unrelenting ruthlessness. It was because *Khrushchev knew* that America will not help. Mike was right when he said that the retreat was just a temporary bluff; the Russians had always planned to come back and plunge the nation into a deadly pit of despair. Discussing the sad news, Mike stated gloomily, "Well, if it's true, then it is the inevitable fate of a small nation to pay the price for the games of the world powers."

The news was definitely confirmed: *with hundreds of new tanks the Russians surrounded Budapest.*

On November 3, Andrew sat among his compatriots in a dark mood, staring painfully into the dusk. Stunned by the news, rage and horror plead for mercy on his embittered face. His father's suspicion of the Russians occupied his mind. "We must not forget that they're notorious liars and promise-breakers."

The moment of rigid silence was prolonged beyond endurance. Then, on that peaceful Sunday morning, November 4, the Russian tanks returned to Budapest. It was obvious that the Soviets couldn't bear the humiliation of knowing that a handful of determined people had been able to force them out of an unjustly occupied country.

Then, after a foreboding silence, the brutal attack had begun. It was as though two million people had been sleeping on a barrel of gunpowder that suddenly exploded. The Russians started to retake their capital. Heavy guns rumbled in the distance, ominously advancing to the heart of the sleeping city. By the time the sun rose, painting the autumn skyline with a faint pink, the rattle of machine guns and cannons were drilling the horror into their unsuspecting brains. In retrospect, Andrew realized that during those precious few days of victory, the people of Hungary had been dancing around a time bomb.

Then, they heard Imre Nagy's dramatic voice on the radio, repeating the desperate news over and over.

At dawn, the Soviet troops attacked our capital with the obvious purpose of overthrowing the new Hungarian democratic government. Our army is fighting the attack. This is my message to the Hungarian people and to the free world. Help Hungary! Help Hungary! God bless our nation!"

The Hungarian national anthem followed every message. So, once again an embittered nation stood eye-to-eye against one of the world's strongest powers. The most tenacious battles took place at Kilian barracks, the Royal Castle and Csepel. However, it soon have been recognized that this counter-attack was a deadly fight. The Soviets, armed to the teeth, aimed for total annihilation. Every shot by the Hungarians was answered with heavy artillery barrages. Soon the freedom fighters realized that it is suicidal to resist any further. The surrender altered the lives of millions of people forever, including Andrew's.

Even after the fighting was over, the Russian vindictiveness continued. As Andrew was walking home, he saw a jeep driving by a bakery shop and a soldier opened fire into a group of people standing in line for bread.

Budapest looked like a graveyard. No matter which way one turned, his eyes were assaulted by ruins. Savagely mutilated buildings with naked walls and open rooms stared into the air; broken-down balconies dangled above the tangled wreckage, the nauseating stench of dead bodies filled the air. The autumn sun struggled to pierce through a blanket of clouds that threatened the city with mournful rain. Time seemed to stand still. An eerie silence hung in the air and the shocking, senseless destruction underlined the doomsday atmosphere.

It Was Over! A few days later beaten, grief-stricken people roamed the streets aimlessly, carrying their broken dreams. If grief had a physical weight, it would have crushed them. They dragged themselves with leaden legs by the energy of sheer contempt. Fatigue blurred their senses, making it hard to comprehend the destruction. The loss of freedom filled them with bitterness and smoldering anger.

Observing the mood of the people, Andrew could not help remembering the victorious days when the same people had run into each other's arms, delirious with happiness. They believed that they were free. God, what a cruel trick fate had played on them!

As Soviet jeeps were cruising the main arteries, people looked at them with avalanche of hopelessness. Their look reflected the screaming question: *What right these bastards have to dictate how we should live?*

That is also what Andrew wished to know. *What did we do to deserve this wretched fate?* What greed a nation has to think they have the right to suppress others? It became obvious that the Free World watched our struggle against an evil empire with yawning indifference, he thought.

So the powers of evil won. Once again we have lost hope, lost our dream, our future. And again we will be prisoners in our own country, he thought. *Dear God, did George have to die for this?* If there is a God, why does he allow this massacre to happen to innocent people? A shiver ran through Andrew's spine thinking that once again *"Big Brother"* would be watching their every step. *All those idiots who still believe freedom is possible under Communism, should experience life under Soviet rule,* he thought.

While the nation remains in a grief-stricken state, mourning over the death of her heroes, the traitors will put on the malicious smile and celebrate the return of lunacy over this unfortunate people. Then, after the speech, the audience will "cheerfully" clap their hands. Cheating, lying, deceiving and pretending will be the measurement of morality. How they love suppressing people and stripping them of from their dignity!

As he headed home on Great Boulevard, he passed by the

destroyed Kilian barracks. The heroism of the kids crossed his mind. The evil forces may rise to power temporarily but we must keep believe in humanity, and in the strength of decency in people. History is our witness that the evil's destiny always is its downfall. We may not live to see it, but our sons and daughters will enjoy the fruit of our struggle.

* * *

After slaughtering thirty thousand people in Budapest, the next horrifying news came that the Russians started to round up the freedom fighters. Those they caught were deported to Siberia in cattle cars.

Andrew immediately went into hiding, while many of the others took advantage of the confusion and fled the country. The youth, the cream of the nation escaped by the thousands every day, leaving behind their beloved homeland and families.

One night when Andrew risked a visit to his parents, they discussed his inevitable fate: *he must leave the country!* At first he vehemently refused, although he knew a few young men who had been caught and disappeared.

Mike was both sympathetic and angry, but he knew he had to be strong to save his son. "Look, Andrew," he said, "we all have to accept the bitter fact that the revolution is lost. We have already discussed this and came to the conclusion that escape is your only chance to survive."

Andrew shook his head in protest but Mike disregarded it.

"I don't think I have to tell you how heartrending it is for me to advise you to leave this country and us, and immigrate to a strange country. I could never have believed I would be able to do this." His voice trembling, he had to pause to gather some strength."However, since you took part in the fighting and too many people know about it, it's too dangerous for you to stay. Actually it is a miracle the Secret Police has not captured you yet. You're their target and the shadow of death follows your every steps. It's just a matter of time before you will disappear. You have done all you could for your country and we're proud of you. But there is nothing more you can do, except to leave while you still can."

Andrew looked into his father's miserable eyes with a battlefield of emotion. The way the words left his lips, he felt the heaviness of his pain. He was learning that helplessness is the biggest enemy. There was a numbness inside him that restricted his thoughts. The words *escape...refugee* sounded so strange and revolting in this warm, loving home. Yet a voice in the back of his mind kept saying, *"Face the music, man, the dream is over."* He was staring at the naked wall with boiling anger, bombarded by emotion. The inner torture broke through his face thinking life without Katie. They were meant for each other...The pain on his face told more than a million words could.

"Oh, Dad, I don't know. I belong here. Katie, you and Budapest means everything to me. I can't imagine life in a God-forsaken country. What kind of existence would hiding be? How can one survive not even knowing the language?"

"It will be hard, but we're talking about **your life,** son! You're young, have a good head on your shoulders. You know by now that your choices are either to go to Siberia or to a free country. If they capture you, you are dead, period. If you want to be strong and survive, you must learn how to bow to the inevitable."

A turbulent storm raged within him. Everything seemed so absurd yet his father was right. The future looked utterly bleak, and he dreaded facing the morning. Why had he come to this insane situation? Fate had set the trap and he had walked right into it. Never had he felt so frustrated. Bewildered, he sighed and placed his pain-twisted face in his hands. He sat there stoop-shouldered, feeling that he had aged ten years in ten minutes. His chest heaved and he raised his somnolent eyes.

"I just don't know, Dad," he said again, and a twisted smile flashed over his face as the joke they used to share, popped up in his mind. "You see, Dad I just realized, I'm passed the age of knowing everything; I'm over sixteen. My mind agrees with you but my heart is screaming in protest."

Mike nodded, suppressing a smile."We share your pain, Andrew. Even if I know this is the right thing to do, I just hope I'm suggesting the lesser of two evils."

Later, discussing in detail of how he should carry out his escape, their biggest fear was that he might get caught at the Austrian border. But that is a chance Andrew had to take.

Meanwhile, Margie hardly said a word. She felt no comfort in the fact that she had argued against his taking part in the revolution. She just did not have the heart to say: "I told you so." She could only sit there weeping—fear and worry had exhausted her.

Andrew looked at her with a lump in his throat. While the revolution was the vehicle of the misery, but Andrew knew that he caused their pain. Abruptly he went to the window and stared at the scattered stars in the sky, a ponderous sense of defeat descended upon him. As the darkness further symbolized the dark outlook of his future, the tragedy seemed monumental that engulfed Andrew. "This is a nightmare, and God help us all," he sighed. The blow of his own decision was so stunning that it seemed it would take a lifetime to recover. When he turned, between rage and depression he said: "Well, let it be then. I'm sorry for all the pain I've caused you. It seems so..." he made a nervous gesture, "so futile! But I hope that somehow, some day I'll be able to make it up to you."

PART TWO

STRUGGLE AND HOPE FOR MIRACLE

1957 — 1966

12

GOD BLESS YOU, MY SON

GOING TO BED EXHAUSTED, they slept very little. They rose early in the morning, dreading to face the saddest day of their lives. The stress that was gripping their hearts was close to insanity. They moved in a state of stupor, their minds buzzing with fear and worry. In that suffocating daze, it took enormous strength to hold on to their sanity, while silently doing what had to be done.

Whatever they said or touched, everything carried the weight of a lifetime of memory. It was an agonizing reminder that their family unit was breaking up. There was no turning back! Their conversation imbued with fatigue. "I wish we could go with you, but we hope you'll make it and get into a free country," Mike said. "But whatever exprience you go through, please try to learn as much as you can about their rules, for each of us must know how to get along with conventions. Always remember that life is what you make of it.

Andrew nodded. "Yes, Dad," he said, but the stress blocked his capacity to take it all in. "Well, I must go," he said with a heartbreaking finality. "Just remember that I love you both very much. Thanks for all you've done for me. I know I've given you some difficult times ... "

"Oh, don't say that, Andrew. We love you so much," Margie said as the three of them wept. "It was joy having you; you made us very happy, my son." She felt as if a knife were twisting in her heart; she was inconsolable. At the final embrace she held him so tight as if never wanting to part, while a heartrending sob shook her to the border of hysteria as she moaned, "Dear God,.. how I.. want..to... say no! Andrew, don't..go!...But I...I must...let ... you go..."

"Don't worry, Mom, I'll be fine."

Then Mike moved to embrace him. "Good-bye, my son," he said with hoarse, trembling voice, hot tears glistening in his eyes. "Take good care of yourself."

Andrew nodded. "You too," he said, and left.

"My son, please write," Margie said.

Tears rolled down Andrew's face as he stumbled down the dimly lit staircase for the last time. His mind said farewell to the dirty walls that characterized his home, to the familiar street where he grew up. Wiping the tears from his eyes, he glanced back at the old, weather-beaten building and saw his grief-stricken parents leaning out the window. Their hearts went with Andrew as they whispered desperately, "Good-bye, Andrew, and God bless you ..."

Shaking, his composure crumbling, with constricted throat Andrew could not speak. He waved back at them, forming a smile while trying to imprint the last picture of them. He felt a burning ache in his throat as his mind traveled through the narrow path of his carefree youth. He looked around his beloved city with bitter-sweet nostalgia and with crushing heart he mumbled: "Good-bye Katie, Budapest, and good-bye shattered dreams." With terror in his heart, he looked back once more, and the sight of his parents became an imperishable memory. *"Dear God, will I ever see them again?"*

The rising morning sun tinted the horizon with its golden glow while the bright rays caressed the worn, centuries-old buildings. He walked swiftly on the cobblestone street, watching around nervously. He had an eerie feeling walking alone in the silent city of two million people; a silence that had been forced upon them by the brutality of the Soviet tanks. Passing by debris-heaped shopwindows, Budapest was like a ghost town.

Suddenly a yellow leaf caught his eye as it parted from a dried-up tree and fluttered away in the cool autumn breeze. He compared the sight to his own fate: he, too, had been torn away from his family tree, but he had no idea where the breeze of fate would drop him. He was afraid—afraid of the unknown.

Katie came into his mind again, with a heart-wrenching pain. He swallowed to ease his dry throat, as a feverish heat pervaded his body. How will he live without her? The circumstances made it impossible to say good-bye to her, yet the very idea of disappearing from her life tortured his conscience. He felt as if he were committing a crime by disappearing from her life. But what good would it do to see her? He couldn't take her with him. All he could do was hope that she would understand that in order to save his life he must run. "Oh, Katie, please try to understand and forgive me," he pleaded silently, hoping too that *somehow* fate would bring them together again.

Reaching downtown, he suddenly noticed a Russian jeep slowly coming toward him, with machine guns at ready in the soldiers' lap. Nothing could provoke more suspicion than seeing a man alone in this abandoned street. His heart throbbing, a paralyzing terror flooded him. Shivering from cold sweat, he jumped behind a huge advertising pillar and plastered himself to the wall. Fortunately the hazy morning cam e to his rescue, for the jeep passed by without noticing him. He drew a deep breath with a sigh of relief, as if he had just escaped his execution. Slowly the sickening feeling passed, and he scurried away on shaking legs.

He continued walking toward the Southern Railway Station that was located in Buda, a distance of about three miles, which linked the capital to the west side of the border. News has been circulating that in the chaos the control of the border had not been fully restored as yet. Therefore, as soon as the revolution was lost, tens of thousands of people have visited the station. Suddenly they all had "relatives" close to the Austrian border, pretending to be "visiting" them. Getting there, they were virtually within a short hour to the Free World!

By the time he reached the station, he was exhausted. The sight of the huge crowd swarming at the station amazed him.. Mingling anxiously with them, loneliness engulfed him like the autumn fog. If only Katie could be with him! With her by his side, he could be happy anywhere. Then, on the spur of the moment, he decided to write her a letter while he waited for the train. He went to an abandoned corner and wrote:

Dear Katie,

*I'm writing this at the Southern Station. I could have never imagined that there could be a force that strong to make me leave the country and **you**, but it has happened. I think you can imagine the turmoil of fighting with my conscience (and my parents) against this dreadful step. But I know that they were right: life or dead was at stake, period! I must escape to avoid deportation to Siberia. As much* *as I love you, I can't imagine how I will go on living without you. But I want you to know, I'll never give up hoping that one day we'll meet again. Please forgive me for leaving you this way, but I take you with me in my heart. Keep that in mind. Knowing that you love me too, that'll keep me alive. So long my love, till we meet again.*

With all my love, Andrew

*

The immigrant.

On a dark, cloudy November night he found help by some kindhearted people at the border, and Andrew crossed it safely to Austria. As he walked through the field in roaring darkness, occasionally streaks of lightning tore a gash in the dark sky, followed by a mighty crash of thunder. The rain was pelting down, hitting his body like millions of tiny darts. Sometimes searchlights illuminated the field, forcing Andrew to drop into the mud to hide. Soaking wet, he cursed the mud that made each step a struggle.

Some fifteen minutes later he heard a man's voice talking to him in German. He could not understand a word, yet he knew he was an Austrian guard. With great relief, Andrew said something, realizing that he was now a *free man*. To his surprise, the guard was able to say some words in Hungarian, and directed him to a nearby village, telling him to look for a large school building.

On the way, the thought crossed his mind that he ought to be shouting with joy for having made it. Instead, he felt empty, rejected, exiled from the real world to an inconceivable one. Oh, he felt relieved, but it was mixed with the feeling of homelessness, of belonging to no one. He felt as if the earth had suddenly opened up under him and he plunged into a dark abyss.

By the time he found the school, it had stopped raining. As he entered a room, he saw hundreds of refugees milling about, their numbers constantly growing.

A lady from the Red Cross Volunteer Service welcomed him with a warm smile and with the sweet smell of steaming coffee and doughnuts. Andrew thanked her shyly in Hungarian. He felt awkward not knowing whether or not she understood him. Glancing around, he saw weeping children and their mothers crying with them—families who have left their homes and everything behind. They took it very hard. Others wrung their hands in despair, looking ahead with blank faces. One could read from their faces that it was terror that driven them out of their homes. It hurt to see their pain, so Andrew turned away.

However, most of the refugees were young, with completely different attitudes. They were laughing and joking happily at being free. Their carefree faces were shining with optimism, and Andrew wished he could share their attitude. Instead he thought that a nation can be destroyed, thousands of innocent people can be killed, but life still goes on. The world must keep on rolling along with or without us...

Next day the Austrian Refugee Organization took them to a huge camp, close to Vienna. Fifteen to twenty people were put into each room, depending on the number of sleeping decks. The room contained storage for their belongings, with a long table in the middle of the room. Considering the circumstances, it was a decent arrangement. The food was good and plentiful, and they even received thirty shillings as "emergency" allowance. Amazingly, people were able to adjust and find their way around quickly.

In an attempt to ease the fast-growing refugee population, temporary emigration offices were set up on the premises by many countries offering visas, good job-opportunities and a reasonable life to accepted refugees. The process took two to three weeks, and they were on the way to their chosen countries.

Andrew did not have a particular country in mind he planed to go to, though most of the refugees wanted to go to America. "Why not?" said one, shrugging his shoulders. "It's the 'Promised Land', or so they say."

Well, then I'll follow them, Andrew thought. However, by sheer chance, he took some pamphlets from the office about Canada and studied them. He learned that it was a vast country with a small population, economically sound, and he decided that Canada was for him.

While in camp, he wrote his parents a long letter, telling them that he had made it, and soon he would be on his way to Canada. He praised the conditions in the camp to ease their worry. Generally he tried to compose a lighthearted letter, to convey the feeling that the whole ordeal was nothing more than a whimsical adventure. For Katie he sent a postcard only, letting her know that he would write a long letter as soon as he had a permanent address.

*

Two weeks later he was on the ship. The voyage took on the aura of an uncertain dream. Andrew shared a cabin with another refugee, named Ernie. He was thirty-five, and planned to go to Montreal because his brother lived there. Ernie was a good roommate and Andrew was glad to have someone to talk to, but most of the day, he preferred to be alone.

One morning, as he leaned on the railing looking at the vast ocean, it occurred to him that he had seen a movie in which the young protagonist stared at the turbulent ocean with the same grim look on his face. With so much time on his hands, Andrew kept thinking about the past. Although he saw everything vividly, his sense of timing played some tricks on him. It seemed as if those troubled days happened a long time ago. Then a mixture of sounds and pictures began to flash in a crazy, disorderly manner which he was unable to control. The rattle of the machine guns, Katie's laughing, dancing with her on New Year's Eve, happy songs and chanting on October 23rd, marching to the Parliament Buildings with George Pusztai...everything emerged with the present, and he had great difficulty believing that he was actually going to Canada. He swung between pain and rage. How could he forsake his country and Katie, his only love? If he didn't remember the cruel epilogue so vividly, he would be tempted to think of the horror as a bad dream. Tears in his eyes, he struggled with his emotion. As bitterness fanned the fire within him, his senses inflamed. In this frame of mind reality eluded him, and he felt that it was not freedom he was entering, but a prison of his own making.

Other times, leaning on the handrail looking at the ever-receding horizon, he tried to figure out what the future held for him. But all he saw was an empty, aimless, lonely, homeless, friendless life. What was there to live for? All those lofty, patriotic words about freedom, new beginnings, and faith were not only shattered, but the irony of them hit him like a sledgehammer. How could he have believed it was possible? His father knew; he should have listened to him.

As the ship was taking him to his destiny, to passing time he tried to sort out what real happiness is? His motivation to escape was to save his life and to be free. Now he was free, yet he could not be more unhappy. If Katie would be with him, he would be happier, but leaving everything and everybody behind would make both of them unhappy. So the conclusion is, he thought, that one needs home, health, love and friendship, freedom, goal and achievement—all that and more to call yourself *happy*. Hmm, that's a tall order! He remembered discussing this with George one day, and he had said jokingly: "There is no such thing as complete happiness, only contentment. And without challenge no motivation, only compromise....

Then his thought went back to Katie. The bright spot that appeared through the mist was Katie's smiling face. He saw her hand sending him a kiss for the last time. With a faraway look, he swallowed deeply and squeezed his eyes shut to push back the tears. "Oh Katie, what will happen to us?"

Eventually the emotional storm had subsided and he was able to view life in a more rational manner. He realized that the revolution had been unavoidable. And the fact that he had been swept into it was his destiny. He must accept that. The past is over, life must go on, and now he must search for a better tomorrow.

For strength his mind always ended up thinking about Katie. Even in this frame of mind, he tried to conjure up a plan of how to keep their romance alive. The written words could provide a deeper, and a different kind of intimacy. In his thought process, as a conclusion, he was able to visualize that one of his letters would include a ticket for her to join him. They would get married and live together in Canada happily every after ...

Although he realized that it was only a dream, a solemn promise began to unfold in his mind that he would reunite with Katie. He must believe that! But for making his dreams come true, he would willing to work with all his might. An inner light began to shine through his face, as he saw that a new beginning was still a possibility.

*

After a week of sailing across the Atlantic Ocean, the ship reached Halifax. The refugees had no idea of what it would be like arriving at the Canadian port, but the sight unfolding before them was not very attractive. The waterfront seemed too old and shabby, definitely not what one would expect from a free and prosperous country. They stood on the pier in their thin clothes, their bodies shivering, teeth chattering—the pernicious cold piercing right through into the marrow of their bones. The momentary disappointing impression somewhat increased the homesickness that gnawed at their hearts.

"What a dismal sight!" said one.

"What did you expect, my friend? The Riviera?"

Someone brushed the protest aside. "Oh come on, guys. You can't judge the entire country by one of its godforsaken seaports. Besides, appearances aren't everything."

"You're absolutely right! Siberia could be much worse."

After entering a large building, a man appeared from the Immigration Office and greeted them through a translator. He delivered a warm welcome speech, in which he included a few humorous allusions to the inclement Canadian winter. "Just think of the mosquitoes that make life so miserable at south of the border. Nine months of the year, we don't have to worry about them."

After the laughter died down, he wished the refugees good luck in their new country. Following the welcome speech, they entered another room, which was the dining room, where they were served stuffed peppers and fruitcake.

When they were ready, busses were waiting in line that would take them to the railway station. Then, their journey to Winnipeg began.

During the long, tiring trip, Andrew sat at the window of the rumbling carriage. He stared with wide-eyes at the beautiful winter scenery, curious as a newborn baby. This was an unknown world. Suddenly, he let out a short chuckle. So I am in Canada, he mused with a feeling like he had jumped into the arms of a blind fate. What in the world will become of me? "*IT'S YOUR LIFE* we're concerned about," said his father on that fateful night. Indeed, it is!

The refugees noticed the distances between cities with great surprise. It was unusual compared to the crowded European countries. Ernie sat beside Andrew who wanted to go to Montreal and could not understand why he had to go to Winnipeg first...

Winnipeg. It is located in the middle of the vast plain of the Canadian prairie. When arriving, it was a bitter, glacial cold day. Stretching their stiffened bodies, the refugees got off the train. Shivering and chest wheezing, they looked around, blinking, as the reflection of the sharp sun on the white snow blinded them. Their breath produced a frozen cloud before their faces.

"Oh my goodness!" said one with a clownish voice, always

ready for a joke. "I forgot to bring my mink-coat with me. I think I should fly home for it, for if I get cold, my mother will spank me. Well, they told me the Canadian winter was fit only for the Eskimos. Now I know why."

Fortunately, they did not have to wait long. Buses came and took them to their temporary shelter. Driving through the city, they were impressed by the sight of shops and modern buildings. Then, the buses stopped at a curve of a busy street and Andrew looked around. Entering a dormitory, a man in charge showed them their rooms, each with two single beds and a long, narrow cabinet for their clothes. When acquainted with the place, Andrew thought, *well, this is a start.*

*

There was a showroom where they gathered in the days that followed. Many visitors, curious reporters and established Hungarian-Canadians came to see them, eager to help. Because they were the first wave of refugees, the excited Hungarians treated them like heroes.

Observing the mood of the refugees, Andrew's mind played with the thought that the shock over the tragic events was still fresh, and they hadn't yet absorbed the fact that they were here because this country, in fact the whole world, cared and wanted to give them a helping hand. The realization of this, he thought, would come later.

Among the visitors was an older man who watched Andrew rather curiously; it was his serious look that struck him. The changes he had gone through during the last months made him withdrawn, and the uncertainty had a strong affect on him. The compelling picture of being unusually quiet is what made the man finally approach Andrew: he wanted to know him.

"My name is Istvan Pataki," he introduced himself, extending his hand.

"Andrew Dombrady. Pleased to meet you."

"I figured you needed some cheering up and I thought I might give it a try,"

"Thank you. I didn't know it was so obvious."

"Well, I can understand the confusion, for I was not born here either," Pataki said. Then, after a few words, he added, "Listen, we have an empty bedroom and I was wondering, how would you like to come and live with us?"

Surprised by his offer, Andrew stared at him awhile then said, "Well, sure. Thank you. If it wouldn't be too much trouble, why not!"

"That's great!"

Andrew made the necessary steps to the authorities for his departure, then he went with Pataki to his old Ford car. On the way home Pataki explained: "I live with my wife in a bungalow close to downtown, a handy location for one who don't have a car. Since we have no children, I thought why not help you out," he said. "I believe it'll do until you find a better accommodation."

"I'm sure it'll be just fine, Mr. Pataki. I don't know how to thank you."

"Oh, don't mention it. We're glad to help you any way we can."

Pataki stopped at an old weather-beaten house and led him up the stairs. Inside he met Mrs. Pataki, a skinny old woman who was vacuuming the living room.

"Irene, look who is here! I want to introduce you to a fine young man, our first refugee from Hungary."

"Oh, my!" she smiled, stopping the machine immediately, then stretched out her arms. "What a nice surprise. Welcome to Canada."

"Thank you. I'm pleased to meet you," Andrew smiled, making a deep bow while he introduced himself. It was a gesture of love, a warm welcome, and the sudden turn of events deeply touched and confused him. He couldn't have imagined a situation like this.

"I'm so glad I went there," Pataki explained to his wife. "You know it was such an uplifting sight meeting with those bright youngsters. I think they're the heroes of Hungary. So I could not help thinking that the least we can do is to give Andrew a chance to start his new life."

"It was a smart thing to do, Istvan," his wife said. Then turning to Andrew, she added, "I'm glad you have accepted the invitation. I hope you'll like it here; and you're welcome to say as long as you want."

"Thank you, Mrs. Pataki, I feel fortunate to be here."

"Well now, before I fix something to eat, I might as well show you around," she said, taking his arm in a motherly manner. "This will be your bedroom and there is a bathroom next to it."

Andrew looked around with an almost embarrassed feeling. Everything was so new! He had never seen a bathroom beside the bedroom. And they were acting as if he were their lost son. At the dinner table he began to see what a great impression the revolution has made on them.

The Patakis kept on bubbling enthusiastically about the revolution—the version of which the television had introduced them. "But this is different," Pataki said. "Now, we'll hear the real story from one who has been there."

"That's right!" Mrs. Pataki agreed. "We would like to hear exactly how it happened. Ah, my God, how shocking it was what the AVO did. It's hard to believe."

"I believe it," Pataki said. "We saw some of the battles on TV. That took real courage. We were really proud of you kids; you're my heroes. I only wish I could have been there with you."

As Andrew listened to these kind people, he thought that no matter how tragic it was, watching it in their cozy living room, for them it was still entertainment. Nevertheless, their feelings were genuine, and he realized that this was their way of paying homage to the nation's valiant efforts. But he did not say much, until Mrs. Pataki asked him directly, "Andrew how much truth is in it that the Soviets savagely murdered so many innocent people? You were there, what really happened at the Parliament Buildings? How much fighting did you see...?"

When Andrew fled the country, he vowed never to brag about being a freedom fighter. But the Patakis put him on the spot, making it difficult to answer evasively. So he gave them a short account about "those unfortunate days" during which the city had indeed been destroyed. He added, however, that actually it was the AVO that had massacred those innocent people at the Parliament Buildings. "The counterattack was barbaric," he said. But it is important to know that the Hungarian revolution was not only against political terror, but also for humanity and morality."

"Yes, you're right," Pataki agreed.

*

Two days later Pataki came home and shouted with triumph. "I found a job for Andrew!"

"You what? ..."

"It was easy," he explained. "I passed by a nearby hospital and on the spur of the moment I went into the office and explained the situation. They were sympathetic but reluctant. But after some consideration, they decided to give him a chance. Tomorrow we'll go and register you at the Personnel Office."

Surprised, Andrew thanked him. He was happy, of course, yet terrified at the same time. What chance did he have in keeping a job without speaking English? Still, he forced himself to be optimistic. I have no choice, he thought.

"I'll do my best," he promised resolutely.

The next morning Pataki drove him to the hospital. It was a dismal wintry day and frosty air hung over the city. The traffic moved with a sluggish crawl in the grip of freezing weather.

The personnel clerk, a middle-aged lady, smiled at Andrew and awkwardly he smiled back. All went well, and Andrew was given a cleaning job. But because he couldn't speak English, a young man has been assigned to work with him until Andrew was confident enough to do his job alone.

He started the next day, and the poor boy had some problems on his hand in getting his points across. But smiling, he used all kinds of sign-and-body language to make sure Andrew understood. Sometimes it seemed as if he were having fun.

During the first days Andrew's head was spinning. Bewildered, the incomprehensible words that flew around him made him dizzy. Confused, the incongruity of the surroundings drove him crazy! How can they make out anything of this incoherence? He realized, of course, that it was only *his* problem. Nonetheless, he yearned to be *at home* instead!

When Pataki asked him how he was doing, Andrew answered with a wry smile. "If I said terrible, it would be an understatement."

"I'm sure you're doing just fine," he said encouragingly.

Andrew progressed slowly, picking up a few words in the process. The first happy day was when he received his first paycheck. It was hard to believe that he had lasted that long. As he put it to Pataki, he survived because the Canadians are patient people. He received the minimum wage like Jack, which was another surprise to him. Jack should get more, he thought, because he speaks English. Although by now he had learned all there was to know, the job was a little boring, he admitted. "Not that I'm complaining," he added quickly.

When Andrew offered to pay for his rent and food, he received another surprise from the Patakis. They felt that Andrew had added fun to their lives, and were happy to have him. It was a good decision, they thought, for he turned out to be a quiet, serious young man.

"You need it more than we do, Andrew, so don't worry about it," Pataki said. But they accepted a small contribution for food only, for the sake of his pride.

*

As soon as Andrew settled down, the first thing he had done was writing a long letter to his parents and Katie. It was a happy and bragging letter. He described his journey to Canada, his luck with the accommodations then with his job. When he received the first letter from his mother, his hands were shaking with happiness. There was a separate envelope in it, but in his excitement he read his mother's letter first.

"... *You cannot imagine how happy we are that you had chosen Canada," she wrote. God must have listened to our prayers. But we cannot get over your good luck of finding a nice home and a job so quickly...*"

Then as he read it further, the sky fell down on him.

"*Andrew, I'm enclosing the letter you've sent to Katie. It was returned to us because you gave our address. We hope that it is not bad news. Please let us know what this is all about.*"

With trembling hands, he took out the envelope, the same one he had sent to Katie from the Southern Station. It was unopened, and there was an official rubber stamp on it: *OCCUPANT MOVED.*

He stood shocked, rooted to the spot in disbelief. "*Moved away?*" he moaned. It's impossible! His imagination ran wild, and he almost wrecked his mind by trying to figure out what could have happened. She may have been killed. Abducted—anything was possible in this upside down world. The mere thought was staggering. "Oh Katie, my love, how can I go on living without you?" He toyed with the remote possibility that her family also left the country, but knowing how much they loved their home, he could not believe that. Besides, he was convinced she would have written to him, had she been able.

Bewildered, a bone-chilling fear hit him that now he had really lost Katie, and suddenly life lost its meaning. All his dreams and plans about reuniting with her had been shattered. From this day on the nights were an endless blur of nightmares, in which he fought a bitter war with his conscience. I've failed her, he thought. If only he had taken the risk of bringing her to Canada. He could never forgive himself for *not trying*. Now it was too late!

During the following days he went to work like a robot, going through the motions. He tried hard to act normal, not telling even to the Patakis what he was going through. In the evenings he went for long walks. As he walked amongst the faceless crowd, involuntarily Katie's face flashed before him. He heard her lovely voice saying *I could never stop loving you,* her laughter at their kooky little jokes.

We all have a desperate need to belong to someone, and lacking that someone, he was struggling with that huge spiritual and physical emptiness. *But life has to go on*, he thought. Having a stubborn streak in him, it gave him the will to fight against that deadly disease, called depression. "One has to learn how to bow to the inevitable fate that is written for all of us," he quoted his father.

It is the fate of the immigrant that he is condemned to live a lonely life. Even if people surrounded him, they cannot replace the structure of family and loved ones he left behind. He was not a criminal, he argued with his invisible enemy, so why did he have to live as if he were one? What good did it do to survive Siberia if he had to hide like a recluse?

New Year was coming. Never in his life had he felt so alone. For the first time in his life, he witnessed the joyful and noisy preparation for the western style of Christmas. Its commercialized trappings of elaborate Christmas decorations and a multitude of Santa Clauses at large shopping centers with their Ho-Ho-Hoes were a mockery to promote business, he thought. Then he tried to be fair: Maybe he felt this way because he had just lost his homeland, and couldn't see the good side of it...

Lying in bed with his cloistered loneliness, listening to the traffic noise, the sound conveyed the memory of Baross Street. In the mirror of his imagination, he spent some pleasant moments reliving their carefree strolling with Katie on Margaret Island, dancing at the New Year's Eve party. Her favorite song flashed through his mind, '*Should auld acquaintance be forgot...*' How she loved to dance to that song! He could see her glittering dark eyes as she said that their love would last forever. He had promised to protect her, but now he did not even know where she was.

As he was adrift in this nostalgia, the grim reality hit him: a whole year had passed since that happy night. Dear God, how many things had happened during this year! And their future is lain in the ruins of the revolution. As the twilight filtered in, he reached for his valet and took out Katie's picture. With an overwhelming emotion, he looked at her smiling face, and a quiver of physical longing ran through his body—a sensation as if he were kissing her. "Oh, Katie, my love, if only I knew where you are," he whispered. "I wish you *Happy New Year,* wherever you are."

The pain was quickly swelling in his heart and he became murderously angry—angry at the world, at Katie, but mostly at himself. *To hell with Christmas and everything*! he thought. With that current of anger boiling in him, he jumped to his feet, put on his winter coat and went out to get drunk.

13

IT'S A CRUEL WORLD

AFTER THE STUNNING NEWS of the counterattack, the prospect of the returning terror, the horror years of the early fifties gnawed at Joseph Erdelyi's guts. Once again, the world had turned upside down, and he envisioned a hopeless future.

He spent some terrible sleepless nights contemplating what to do. Never did he feel such an overpowering urge to get out of this country, far away from this uncertainty. And now they had a chance! He could dream of places where Communism, the mental and physical torture could never hurt them again. But more than that, it was Katie's future that was at stake. She was young, and deserved more than what the communist system could offer.

Yet the decision to leave everything behind was one of the most difficult things he had ever had to contemplate. It seemed impossible to decide because there was a lifetime of hard work that had to be discarded. And how they loved every corner of their home: the furniture, the garden, and the neighborhood. Even Bokrosh was like a member of the family. What should he do? He knew that they were not young anymore to start a new life. The struggle could be too much. Yet, looking at the senseless, cold-blooded killings, what guarantee was there that they would be able to hang on to what they had..? It was a once-in-a-lifetime chance, and we must take advantage of if!.

"We must go!" Erdelyi said to himself. "I've seen enough terror and fear to last me a lifetime. If nothing else, the revolution has given us the choice wherever we want to live."

He knew that the biggest challenge will be to convince his family. But he believed he could do it. As a rule, they used to listening to him. But when he presented his plan to his wife, she was shocked. Without a word, she went to the window and looked out onto the familiar street. As she turned, her eyes reflected fear and pain. "Oh, Joe, I'm terrified at starting a new life all over again in a strange country where we can't even speak the language," she said. "Aside from losing all this, can you imagine life among strangers, without friends and relatives? After all, we're not spring chickens anymore, you know. We worked so hard for what we have. What a waste it would be!"

"All you say is true, honey. It's scary, I know. Still, stop and think about it. Which fear is more terrifying: to live in Communism or in a strange but free country? -- "

Annie smiled. "Both."

"True enough. But all you have to remember is what we went through before. I, for one, couldn't take it again, thank you. We know what Communism is, so let's choose freedom while we still can. This time it's up to us! I can see some difficulties, sure, but we still could make it."

Annie could not miss the youthful enthusiasm in his eyes.

"The way I see it," Joe continued, "once opportunity is forsaken, it's lost forever. We just can't let this chance pass us by and live to regret it."

Oh, God! Annie thought. Leaving all these treasures behind? we can't! Yet, what value is in them if we have to live in constant fear? Remembering all those troubled years, she said to herself, Joe could be right. "Well, life is too short," she said, "Whatever is left for us, my life is at your side. But if we are going to leave, we must move quickly. However, Katie could give us some problem."

"I'll talk to her. She is a smart girl. I'm sure she'll listen to reason."

But she didn't. When Joe tried to explain diplomatically that they were considering leaving the country, Katie's face turned pale, her sense of decency outraged. She glanced at her parents with complete disbelief.

"*You want me to leave Andrew behind?* **Never!** How can you even suggest that absurdity? You can go, I'm going to stay."

Now Joe put forward the most convincing argument he could to make her see how hopeless it was to stay in a destroyed and subjugated country.

"I'm not going to run away from Andrew."

"Katie," her mother argued, "I know that sometimes we can't see the forest from the trees. Don't you think he would have come *if* he were still in Budapest?"

"Andrew wouldn't leave me just like that," Katie snapped, but unconvinced. She was sure he had taken part in the fighting and he could have been killed. If not, she had heard of the manhunt for the freedom fighters, and God forbid, he might be on the way to Siberia, she thought with a shiver running through her body. But stubbornly she would not reveal her doubts. "Maybe he didn't come because he had no means to do so," she said, her lips trembling.

"Knowing Andrew, I don't think you believe that," Annie said. "We know how you feel, but - "

"*No, you don't!* You can't possibly know how I feel."

Now Joe interrupted. "Katie, my dear, I think you should listen to your mother. Aside from the fact that we're fed up with Communism, we're actually considering your future. You have none here."

"Without Andrew, I have no future anywhere." Katie said softly. But in the end, against her parents' sound logic, her defense began to crumble. Stunned, wordlessly she ran into her room. Her heart swelled with misery until it squeezed the tears into her eyes. Then she started to cry bitterly, envisioning the long road of loneliness and heartache that lay ahead.

How painful it is to prepare for moving out of the security of one's castle called *home*. In the planning stage the mental struggle is not so tragic, because it doesn't seem real. However, at the point when they said good-bye to their treasures, the full impact hit them with lightning force, and the iron grips squeezed their hearts.

It was impossible not to look back when even Bokrosh was howling so painfully, it tore at their hearts. How smart a dog can be, Joe thought with quivering lips. They used to leave him in the backyard many times, sometimes for the whole day, but he took it naturally because he knew they would be back. But this time, somehow he must have sensed that they were leaving him for good, and all the patting in the world could not console him.

* * *

A cold darkness gripped the countryside. Chill penetrated their coats as the Erdelyis stumbled along silently across the frozen field, near the Austrian border, each carrying a suitcase. They were running away from the terror to an unknown, mysterious future. Regardless of the reassurances of friends that thousands of people were crossing the border, the eerie silence still gave them the shivers.

From time to time, the silvery moon peeked through the slowly moving clouds and lit their way toward the free world, allowing Katie to see their dim shadows. She saw a ghost of a slender girl dragging her feet as if some unseen force were pulling her down. As she listened to her steps, the sound pierced through her brain like a painful echo. She felt as if life had left her body and she was going to her own funeral.

Finally they reached the border, and with the help of some kind Austrians, ended up in a large refugee camp located in Simmering, at the outskirts of Vienna. Although Andrew landed in another camp, the Erdelyis' escape took place only two days after Andrew's.

In the camp, living together with four strange families without any privacy, a terrifying mystery of life was enfolding before her. She felt living in the wilderness and had a terrible time to adjust to the rootless life. The empty loneliness was too much for Katie's tender age. The horror of it overwhelmed her. She knew but did not care to accept that it was only a temporary situation. The future was bleak and utterly hopeless.

To ease the boredom, she was mingling with the refugees. But seeing the mass of depressing humanity was so painful that to suppress it, she tried to adopt the mental evasion of looking without seeing; being adrift in the sea of moving shadows. The world as she knew it crumbled down around her, and the silent suffering ate away at her will. Since she believed that *she had* abandoned Andrew, she begged for his forgiveness. *No one understands me*, she thought. Without Andrew I'm dead. Her feelings were genuine, but she could not help dramatizing them. She felt that the world around her was a hostile place she did not belong, and she cried herself into a nightmarish, consuming darkness...

It was bad enough that she did not know what had happened to Andrew, but in addition she could not write to him. It seemed incredible but she did not know his address. Whenever she had visited him, Andrew was always with her, so she never needed to write the address down. And who could have predicted such a turn of events? So, unless some miracle happened, she would never be able to get in touch with him. Each time the thought emerged, it brought bitter tears into her eyes.

However, as the days passed, she slowly began to realize that tears wouldn't help and wouldn't solve anything. Instead she must concentrate on finding a way to locate Andrew. The challenge brought her some peace of mind.

Katie's suffering remained Joe's biggest concern. Watching her silent struggle made him question the wisdom of leaving the country. What good would it do to have their freedom if they lost Katie? Finally he admitted that he had not considered enough the most delicate feeling: love. Well, it was too late to do anything about it now—they could not turn back. So they would have to do their best to help her.

* * *

While in the camp, they were free to go out and see the city. In an attempt to cheer Katie up, Joe took his family for sightseeing tours in Vienna. They saw many historical buildings, magnificent churches, parks and statues. It was a roaring, lively city; so refreshingly different from the ruined and smoked-out city of Budapest. The feeling of freedom vibrated in the air. One day they even went to see the beautiful Schonbrunn Palace. But they did not have much time to explore Vienna because they had already registered with the Australian Emigration Office.

It is interesting how fate brings people together. While waiting in line to register, they met the Beresh family with a fourteen-year-old daughter, Marika. And amongst many similarities, the two families became good friends. To Joe's great amusement, Beresh told him that one of their reasons for choosing Australia was because they have heard about the shortage they have in girls. So their daughter would have a greater opportunity to find a rich husband.

"Mind you this is not the only reason, but as a father of a teenage girl, I would be a fool to pass up such golden opportunity."

Joe smiled, but made no comment. Thoughts like this was the furthest from their minds when they chosen Australia. Rather it was because they had learned that Australia was a free and prosperous country with excellent opportunities for people like himself. Besides, he knew that for Katie, the subject of marriage was out of the question—for a while. It was still a welcomed chance to have someone to spend the time during their long journey...

* * *

After the registration everything happened quickly. Within two weeks they were on a train headed for Geneva where a Spanish ship awaited them. The next day they sailed into the Red Sea with hundreds of other Hungarian refugees.

The ship's flamboyant appearance carried an aura of luxury these people had never experienced. They observed the ship with child-like fascination—the cruise promised an exciting adventure of a lifetime. Even Katie was cheered up by it.

Not having any experience in such luxurious traveling, the accommodations was excellent, the food rich and plentiful. The crew-members exceptionally kind; it was amusing how quickly they broke through the language barrier. The servants would make humorous expressions with their smiling faces, and their exaggerated gestures became a game of charades.

At Port Said the ship stopped for an hour. Within minutes a multitude of small boats surrounded the ship. People were standing at the handrails, curiously listening as the Arabians shouting, offering their dazzling handmade merchandise. Fascinated by the unusually enticing sight, Joe bought a fancy handbag for Katie as a souvenir.

Passing through the Suez Canal, the heat was intolerable and the humidity swirled like a hazy cloud above the burned-out land. The sight of the poor Arab workers along the shore astonished the Erdelyis. Their emaciated and stooped figures were stark testimony to their poverty. Under the torturing heat their faces were like pieces of dark, crinkled rubber; and the indelible lines made it impossible to even guess their ages.

As the ship reached the equator, Katie was hit by a bout of seasickness. The hellish blistering heat added to her sickness, and she had to stay in bed for two days.

The Erdelyis and Bereshes developed a warm friendship. It was an ideal situation: while the men played the game of chess, the wives chatted. Other times both families sat together and talked about the past, their work and the experiences they had gone through.

Ernie Beresh was a broad-shouldered, army-type man with a candid aristocratic face. His square jaw gave him a commanding look. One day Beresh told them how they had been deported to a godforsaken *kolhoz* (collective farming) in 1951. They were forced to work on the field from sunrise to sunset for more than two years amid disgusting living conditions.

"Ah, it was awful! We lost everything!" Beresh said. Rakosi had deported them because Beresh was a captain who fought against the Russians during the Second World War. Being a high-ranking army officer was his "crime".

"So you actually went through that tragedy?" Joe said. "We were on that deportation list to report to Csongrad, but at the last minute for some miraculous reason we received a letter that a mistake had been made. So we were spared from that hell."

"You don't know how lucky you were."

Meantime Marika struck up a friendship with Katie. Although she was not a stunning beauty, she was pretty. Her heart-shaped baby face and blue eyes gave her an air of innocence. However, her precociously mature body made her looks older than her fourteen years. From the start, she was overwhelmed by Katie's beauty. She had admired and looked up to her with great respect. It seemed to her that Katie had a graceful, worldly manner, and Marika believed she knew all about love and romance.

By this time they got used to the monotone drone of the ship. It was a lovely, nostalgic day when the sunlight was dancing on the water. They stood against the handrail, smelling the salty air and gazing at the vast, softly rippling ocean. The gulls were circulating above them in their never-ending search for food. The two girls found their funny crackling voices amusing.

When they were together, Katie was usually reserved, and avoided talking about any personal subjects. Marika misunderstood her silence, thinking that Katie too was dreaming about her future love and romances in their new country. She was full of life, a poetic soul, who was fascinated by the color of the brilliant sunset over the ocean, or the amazing clarity of the blue sky.

On this day Marika could not resist asking questions about love, like did she have any personal experience kissing a boy passionately on the lips? How did it feel?

Katie was in a mischievous mood and laughed at Marika's

curiosity. She was also amused by the assumption that she must have had those experiences. So she decided to shock her with exaggerated accounts.

"Well, I can tell you that when a boy you love kisses you, it feels like you're in heaven. And if you really love the guy, he can make you feel electricity running up and down your spine that makes you shiver, and oooh, you feel a hot liquid pleasure flooding your body."

Marika turned her blushing face away, flustered, and stopped asking.

Later the girls walked through the room where their fathers were playing chess. Beresh looked up at the girls and he remarked, "You know, Joe, you've an exceptionally beautiful daughter. I can predict right now that she won't have any problem finding a rich husband."

Erdelyi smiled. "Thanks for the compliment. To be honest, although it helps, I don't believe that money is more important than true love. By the way, it goes without saying that you too have a lovely girl. I'd rather wish them both happiness over wealth."

The New Year reached them on the ship. For celebration they gathered in the large ballroom. One of the refugees took the microphone and made a patriotic speech. "Dear fellow countrymen! The historical events we have witnessed in the past few months will bring about an avalanche of irreversible changes in our country and in Europe for many years to come. And rightfully, we're very proud that we had the guts to reveal the corruption that crippled us. We must never forget that 30,000 fallen heroes gave their lives for our freedom. Throughout their sacrifices we have the chance to choose between freedom and slavery. *When you pray, say a pray for them, and when you cry, shed a tear for them. God bless our nation.*"

Then he entreated them to sing the Hungarian national anthem.

People stood, their heads proudly erect as they sang. When they reached the words, *"This nation already had suffered for the past and for the future..."* many of them could not continue. Their lips quivered and painful sobs replaced the song.

Katie thought about Andrew and the last New Year's Eve party. They had wished happiness to each other, and he wanted to give her the whole world on a silver platter. Now she didn't even know whether he was alive or dead. With Andrew by her side, this trip would have been paradise, without him, it was but a dull journey into an empty darkness. Dear God, what am I doing here? she thought. She had a sinking sensation in the pit of her stomach. Tears blinded her, and she was unable to stand any longer.

She ran out to the deserted deck, bent over the handrail and looked down into the dark water. Pictures from Lake Balaton were filled her head, as she sat beside Andrew. They had dreams then about their future that threw no shadow over their happiness. The world and all the golden years were hanging before them like ripened fruit, waiting to be grabbed whenever they were ready to take them. Life had never looked more beautiful, their love more encouraging and hopeful. "With God's help we can move mountains," he said. And now she was sailing to Australia—without him! What kind of cruel fate is playing games with their lives that would put the whole world between them.

"*Oh Andrew, what's happening to us?*" she cried out to the darkness.

14

ALL ALONE

TWO MONTHS HAVE PASSED since Andrew started to work at the hospital. Because he really wanted to succeed, he did, and was proud of it. By now he began to feel comfortable around people. He was eager to learn the language, too. His pocket dictionary was always at hand and struggled with it every day for hours, trying to form sentences from single words. Talking about frustration, he has had it! So much so that sometimes he threw the book to the floor. The most difficult aspect of the language for him was the pronunciation. Once at the coffee break he wanted to use the word 'therefore', which he pronounced by each syllable: *"de-re-fo-re"*.

Surprised, his workmates frowned, and then burst into laughter, for which they apologized later good-naturedly.

Among his co-workers was a young woman named Betty, who used to sit beside him at break times. She was a Japanese-Canadian who liked Andrew from the beginning. She was fascinated by his European accent, and sometimes she even imitated him. After this incident, she reached over and stroked his face, "Now that was very cute, wasn't it?" she said, trying to ease his embarrassment.

Moments like this made him feel he would never be able to learn English. But he persevered. When he was in the mood and wanted to carry on a "conversation", Betty was always a willing partner to help. Actually, most of what he learned was from her. Therefore she was the only person he felt comfortable with. It did not bother him that others chatted among themselves, seemingly ignoring him, because Andrew knew that he could not contribute anything to their conversation anyway. Nevertheless, he loved to listen to them, for it was like being in school—a chance to learn. And he learned.

However, human nature being what it is, Andrew noticed some hostility toward him. It came particularly from a young man they called Bill. He was a ragged-faced youth with watery gray eyes and a messy hairstyle. Andrew did not mind that Bill was not friendly with him, but he didn't like the contempt in his glances, for it trans-mitted his hatred conspicuously. He certainly knew prejudice and discrimination by the communists, but he had not expected such gut-wrenching experience here. He remembered his father talking about it, but he thought that he *had to do* something to trigger it.

At the beginning he would put on a token unconcerned appearance, although it was hard. Bill was careful never to mention Andrew's name, figuring that this way he wouldn't understand whom he was talking about. Yet, even if he did not want to fall into making a regrettable mistake, Bill was so openly obnoxious, that Andrew did not need to understand the words—he knew that Bill was talking about him. But since he didn't know enough English to retort, Andrew kept silent, pretending not to understand.

During their next coffee break, Bill went as far as saying, "These assholes can't even speak English and take away the jobs from us," spitting the words out between clenched teeth.

Betty could not let him get away with it. "Oh, come on, Bill, how would you like if you would be treated like this? Besides, this is a free country, you know. If you don't like the system, I think you should go back where you came from."

Some of the men laughed and nodded, which encouraged her, "Yes, I think you are the ignorant asshole. You talk like this because you think he doesn't understand. Besides, except for the Indians, we're all immigrants. Did it ever occur to you that your parents came from Ireland?"

'Betty, better if you keep out of this," Bill mumbled under his breath. "What are you anyway, his guardian?"

"If I am, it's still more decent than your sneaky swaggering. Would you feel better if he lived on welfare?"

"They should stay in that bloody country from where they came from," he said, laughing, nudging his workmate in the ribs, as if he were being clever.

Betty looked at him sharply. "Oh, bite your tongue! That idea could also have applied to your and my parents as well."

Even though he didn't understand many of the words, from their argument it became increasingly obvious that he was at the center of it. His father's words flashed through his mind: "There are people who can hate you without knowing you".

When the coffee break was over, Jack, the young Canadian stood and indicated to Andrew that he was going to wash the corridor. It was a job that Andrew shared with him—an agreed shift between the two of them. And this time it was Jack's turn. As he passed Bill, he grabbed Jack's arm and muttered through his teeth, "Let that bloody D.P. do that dirty job!"

Andrew heard and saw the contempt on his face that stung him. He had heard the expression before, and Pataki explained to him that "D.P." meant (*Deported Prisoner*"), which they used to insult new immigrants. The accumulated insults finally made his blood boil, and with a spasm of rage he jumped and grabbed Bill's collar and demanded that he repeat the words again.

He did, and at the same time he swung his fist. But Andrew, a trained boxer, was prepared and had no problem counter-attacking. With a quick sideways move, he landed a powerful right that exploded on Bill's jaw. He sprawled against the wall and slid to the floor. His legs apart, Andrew defiantly stood over him, ready to fight.

"You want more?" he flared, glancing around resolutely to see if anyone sided with Bill. But all he saw was a stunned audience.

Nursing his wound, the surprised Bill decided not to fight back. He knew that to continue would mean losing his job. He rose to his feet and muttered, "You'll pay for this."

Andrew did not care, and with a shrug he returned to his work. But when he passed by Betty, she nodded and smiled at him with satisfaction.

By nature, Andrew was not a paranoid person. But the circumstances of the past few months made him overly sensitive. He tried to mind his own business, but he found it difficult to adjust. What else could he have done? He could not let Bill get away with it, he thought. His youthful blood was boiling with resentment toward the world. The easy humor and laughter that had filled his life just a year ago was gone. Now his mood would change drastically from one moment to the next. Frustrated by a minor irritation, once he smashed his fist into a brick wall. Nursing his fist later, he smiled, remembering his father's advice, "Sometimes you need to express your anger to vent your frustration".

At night, lying in bed and staring at the ceiling, a strange fear came over him. He was afraid that he was losing the little he had gained by leaving his country. His dream of becoming an electric technician was gone, and it seemed that he was wasting his time. There were moments when he remembered that had he stayed in Hungary, he could be rotting somewhere in Siberia, freezing and starving to death. That reminder has helped a little, but what he had did not make him happy either.

* * *

Meanwhile, Bill had reported the fight and got his revenge: with one week's notice, Andrew was dismissed.

Walking home dejectedly, he mumbled to himself, "I'm my own worst enemy." Until this day, Andrew kept his personal problems a secret from the Patakis. They could not help him, he reasoned, so what purpose would it serve to complain? But sometimes the temptation was strong, because he knew that sharing things with someone had a therapeutic effect. This, however, he could not keep it a secret. He was embarrassed, for it was Pataki who had gone into the trouble in finding the job for him.

By now Andrew knew that Pataki was sixty-two years old. He has been a construction worker, and now he was living on a disability pension.

Arriving home, he explained to Pataki with an apologetic tone that he had lost his job. "He challenged me and I just could not let him get away with it," he said, shrugging his shoulders.

Pataki nodded, "I understand what you mean, Andrew, I've been there."

"Well, this is unfortunate, of course," Mrs. Pataki said, "But things will get better. Let's just put this behind us."

"That's right!" Pataki said. "You know, Andrew, we're living under the heavy clouds of prejudice," He continued. "But ignorant people can be found anywhere. They're the kind of people who say 'I like humanity, but I hate people'. One of the saddest part in life is that sometimes we are being hurt by complete strangers. They seem to have conveniently forgot that their parents too were immigrants. This reminds me of a comedian who said, 'I'm free from prejudice; I hate them all equally'. Fighting these people physically may be satisfying, but in the long run it doesn't solve a damn thing."

Andrew laughed.

Then later, after a moment of silence, Pataki patted Andrew's shoulder cheerfully. "Don't worry about it Andrew. We'll find you another job sooner or later."

But this time it was Andrew who found the next job. As he was walking on Main Street the next day, he met John Meszaros, the butcher. Andrew knew him from the hospital, as he had been hospitalized for a few days with a minor ailment. He was about forty years old. By chance, he had seen his typical Hungarian name, which was displayed at the end of his bed. Well, this man certainly cannot deny his nationality, he thought. Happy for the chance of having someone to talk to, he had greeted him in Hungarian.

When he learned that Meszaros was a butcher, Andrew laughed."Well, my friend, you certainly couldn't have picked a more appropriate occupation." ("Meszaros" means butcher in Hungarian.)

When Andrew recognized him on the street, he greeted him cheerfully. "Hi, Mr. Meszaros, nice to see you. How are you.?"

"Oh hi, Andrew. Do you have a day off or something?"

"No, no. I'm not working at the hospital anymore. As a matter of fact, I'm looking for a job right now."

"Is that right?" he exclaimed, as if he was glad to hear it. "Then we met just in the right time. I think I can get you one. If you have the time, why don't you come with me?"

They went to the butcher shop where he was working. In the office Meszaros introduced Andrew to a huge man, the Boss. For a few seconds, he studied Andrew as if measuring him up. For the position he definitely needed a strong man. They have exchanged a few words and he gave Andrew a form to fill out.

Meszaros helped him and when he had finished, the boss said, "All right, Andrew, you can start tomorrow morning."

The next morning Andrew was given a greasy bloodstained pair of overalls that were too big for him, and was assigned to operate a high-powered bone-cutting machine. A foreman showed him how to cut through the hard bones like butter. The job was not difficult, but dirty and dangerous. He had to cut the bones into certain sizes and throw them into a huge plastic container. For this the pay was seventy-five cents per hour.

Working with Meszaros had some advantage. Besides helping out as a translator when needed, he showed him a few tricks of the trade, like how to hold the slippery bones safely under the cutter.

But despite all the precautions, the blasted tricky blade once wrenched a large bone out of his hands and smashed it against the door of a thin cabinet with such a tremendous force, it sounded as if a bomb had exploded. Fortunately, no one was hurt, but it left a huge dent on the door. Shaken, Andrew apologized for his clumsiness, grateful for the luck that he had not been hurt.

As his job-searching problem solved, Andrew continued writing to his parents. Even in his gloomy days, he always painted a bright picture, never burdening them with any complaints. The only burden he felt putting on them was that he kept asking about Katie, wondering whether they have heard anything what had happened to her. When there was no good news, the haunting fear of never going to see her again grew deeper and deeper. He dreaded the thought that he was trapped forever in his lonely existence.

Yet, he tried to keep his spirit up. Her beautiful face was still as vivid in his memory as ever, dreaming about her often.

Her mother's letters dealt only with family matters.

Dear Son,

Somehow we are holding on to the thread of life however sad it is without you. Naturally we live only for your letters, and you have no idea how happy it makes us when they arrive. Our hands shake when we open and read them. Of course, I hardly dare tell you that as I am writing this letter, I hold the pen in one hand, and a handkerchief in the other. Your father does not like me to tell you this, but when he reads your letter, tears come into his eyes, too. Just make sure to put on plenty of warm clothes, so you won't get cold in that terrible winter....

Her heart-rending letters, overflowing with love, always touched him deeply. Feeling emotional at times, he was glad to read them alone in his room. These letters were an important link with his homeland, because even from a distance of ten thousand kilometers, in soul he was still in Budapest. He was learning the hard way that it requires many year of absence before one can actually lose identity with one's native land.

From her letters he learned with great relief that his parents had not been harassed by the secret police. It was only natural that she never mentioned anything of political nature. Cautiously she mentioned only once that most of the ruins had been carted away, and things were slowly getting back to normal.

The rest of the information he received was from the local Hungarian-Canadian newspaper, subscribed by the Patakis. He learned that actually over two hundred thousand Hungarians had fled the country. This information suggested again that the Erdelyis might have been amongst the refugees somewhere, although it was hard for him to imagine that.

After the revolution, Janos Kadar became the new Prime Minister. It was known that Kadar had been a member of the Imre Nagy's cabinet during the victorious days, but in the wake of the Soviet counterattack, he betrayed Nagy and secretly formed a so-called "rebel" government. Then, under the shadow of the Soviet tanks, Khrushchev rewarded him with the leadership.

Despite Khrushchev's promise for their safety, Imre Nagy and Colonel Pal Maleter, commander of the Kilian Barracks, were trapped and captured by the Soviet KGB. (*).

Reading this news, Andrew came to hate politics! During the Second World War the Nazi Gestapo, later the AVO communists —all greedy fanatics—were marching on the shoulders of the nation, claiming to be *the true saviors!* With the same ideology, all maintained the tradition of sending millions of innocent people to their untimely deaths. In their ivory-tower mentality that was based upon dripping hatred, they were incapable of realizing how insane they really were. Far too many deranged lunatics are walking the streets who should be behind bars, Andrew thought.

On the same thought process he learned from TV programs in Canada, that the same things are going on in America by the Ku Klux Klan...With their bankrupt minds, they are hopeless non-achievers, living in a day-to-day existence without decent goals in their lives; freeloaders, drifting whichever way the wind blows them, always blaming others for their misery. And when the opportunity

(* Imre Nagy was executed in 1958, and buried in an animal cemetery. But in June, 1989, he was given an honorary funeral by the newly reformed Communist Party, and credited for his efforts to free Hungary in 1956.)

arrives, they vent their vengeance on successful people, claiming their share by robbing and murdering them to get even. The German Nazis did it with the Jews, and Stalin with everybody.

"True saviors, indeed!" He did not pretend to be a moralist, but rather a humanist. He knew the graveyard they create too well. He had just left one behind. Here in the Free World, as he had learned what the Ku Klux Klan is stands for, outraged him. Their goal of destroying a race is *well known*, yet the law is punishing them *only* when (too late by then) they have executed the crime. Does that make any sense? Andrew just could not get it.

"One day you'll learn that politics is the dirtiest business there is," his father told him once. How right he was!

In his suffocating loneliness he maintained his long walks in the downtown streets. Having a nonexistent social life, walking was a safety valve. He missed all those small youthful pleasures that make up the fabric of an ordinary life. As he looked at the city traffic, the neon signs and brightly lit windows, he could not help comparing this uncongenial city with Budapest. But doing that was unfair, he knew. The magnetic power that pulled his heart to Budapest, the romantic charm and the thousand-year history —there was nothing to compare.

It was Saturday. Late strollers, young lovers past him, holding hands, occasionally kissing and laughing. By their smiling faces it seemed as if a sense of carefree childhood still clung to them. It was painful to see, and sometimes he looked the other way. Naturally Katie's image crept into the forefront of his mind. In his imagination he was in Budapest, and bittersweet thoughts were lingering on his mind, reliving many pleasant moments again and again like a vicious circle that pressed his chest like a giant stone. At times it seemed like a fairy tale, other times it was a mental torture. He yearned to hold her hands, to share his feelings, open his heart to her... He could not imagine a worse curse on earth than loneliness. "Oh, Katie, if I only knew where you are," he sighed.

Roaming around in his melancholy mood, Andrew realized that it was getting late. He stood hesitantly at the corner of an intersection and looked up at the majestic sky as if searching for some consolation. The moon had already appeared in its cold silvery glow, and the twinkling stars sparkled brilliantly in the frozen sky. The night wrapped around him like a blanket. Then that lost feeling he knew so well engulfed him once again. His eyes and body begged for sleep, so he turned up his collar and buried his head in. He began to walk briskly down the windswept street as if trying to increase his blood circulation.

*

The weeks turned into months at the butcher shop. He was just getting used to his job when fate caught up with him again.

There was a large separate room, which served as a freezer where all the boxed goods were kept. It was a biting cold place, and the workers hated to go into the "*ice-cave*" as they called it. Whenever its door opened, they could hardly see through the cold steam, and the boxes themselves were like blocks of ice. When they brought out the crates of frozen meat, the boxes stuck to their coats like magnets. So going in was a hateful chore, but it had to be done if one needed a box out of the freezer. Nobody would do it for anyone else, unless it was a special favor.

At the beginning, when Andrew was new, some of the butchers took advantage of him and asked in a friendly manner to bring out a box, although it was not his job. However, when he became wiser, he was selective about to whom he would do the favor. Usually he did it gladly for older men for they had genuine complaints about their rheumatic pain.

But there was one butcher among them, Otto, a fat early-forties man who regularly sent him to the freezer. It was his tone of *telling* instead of asking that began to irritate Andrew, and one day he said, "Go and get it yourself, you're not my boss."

Andrew's response took him by surprise, and with a purple face, he shouted indignantly in his German accent, "All right you little Hungarian bastard, I'll show you who is..."

Unfortunately, Andrew had his code to live by, that together with stubbornness and pride would not let him listen to wisdom. Of all that Otto said, he heard only the slur insulting his nationality. His temper flared, and without waiting for him to finish the sentence, he jumped at him with a wild fury and beat him to the floor.

Meszaros looked at them with horror. "*Good God, Andrew! Andrew! Are you crazy?*" he shouted and tried to pull him off.

The voice of his friend brought him to his senses. He straightened out his coat and looked at him apologetically.

"There is a limit to everything, including my patience," Andrew told him in Hungarian. "Just because I'm young and Hungarian, it doesn't mean this boorish bigot can bully me."

"Still, you shouldn't do a thing like that. You must learn to control your temper," Meszaros said. He was convinced that this was going to be Andrew's last day of work here.

Otto got up, heaving and trembling, his face twisted into an ugly mask of hate. As he passed Andrew, his eyes were spitting fire at him. "This is a mad dog!" he hissed, and went straight into the office. Andrew went back to his machine, but a few minutes later he was called into the office.

The Boss, sitting across from Andrew, pretended to be calm. "Please, sit down, Andrew, and tell me *your* side of the story. What happened?"

Andrew cleared his throat and tried to describe in his muddled English what had happened. But he had a hard time putting the words together.

The boss listened patiently and occasionally nodded that he understood. Then he said that although he had sympathized with him, but he was sorry, he could not tolerate fighting in his shop.

He gave him his paycheck and dismissed him. Andrew's fist clenched but he smiled.

"Thank you," he said, then turned and left the office, wondering how in the hell could a man like him ever understand.

"I'm out of work again," he told Meszaros without any regret. They shook hands and Andrew was gone.

15

UNDER AUSTRALIAN SKY

FINALLY THE SHIP ARRIVED at the Melbourne harbor and the month-long voyage was over. Living on the constantly swaying boat for so long, the refugees felt a strange sensation walking on solid ground again. At first, they tottered like drunks.

"Hey, damn it! What's wrong with me?" shouted someone in the crowd. "Did I forget how to walk, or what?"

"Well, I've enough of ship traveling to last me a lifetime," Katie said. The reason she felt this way was mainly because of what they went through in the last week. They sailed into a large wave-zone, which threatened to overturn the ship. Anything that was not fastened to the floor slid from wall to wall. At the beginning it was amusing, and some youngsters sat on the floor in the dining room for a slide. But then the ship swayed dangerously like a toy—it was dreadful.

Now, safely off the ship, they hugged each other happily, thanking God for their safe landing. It was January and a terribly hot day.

"In Hungary this is the coldest month of the year, but here, boy is it ever hot!" Joe said, wiping his forehead and looking up at the burning blue sky. "I feel like we've jumped out of the freezer into the frying pan."

Beresh laughed. "Yes, but consider the great advantage! We will save a lot on heating bills and winter clothes."

Having collecting themselves, a brief official greeting followed and they were taken to the railway station. Then after many hours of idle waiting, finally they boarded the train. Having settled into the oven-hot compartments, the train slowly began to roll through the green, gently sloping Victoria landscape—to their destination.

Watching the vast countryside from the rumbling train, they could recognize some similarity to Europe. However, as they advanced toward New South Wales, the landscape began to turn rocky, gray and barren.

The sun was beating on them mercilessly, and they could see the heat waves dancing in the windless air. Perspiration dampened the shirts that clung to their clammy skin. Their throats felt parched, so they gulped water constantly to relieve the thirst. Looking at the changing landscape, they saw burned-out hillsides with only a few scattered silver-colored skinny trees. The scarce, dried-up leaves rustled in the faint breeze that feebly brushed through the spiky grass. "This must be one of the most sunbaked country in the world," remarked someone.

But Beresh tried to keep their spirits alive by saying, "Since this is kangaroo country, they should come out and greet us."

"You didn't make an appointment with them," came from someone else. "They're probably hiding somewhere in a shade—if there is such a thing in this damned desert."

Then, to their great relief, finally the train stopped at a small station. As they got off they saw the buses, which took them to their new camp. In the withering heat, their moist bodies moved in soggy silence. How they yearned for cool air! But they did not feel even a whisper of breeze.

The camp was located at Bonegilla. Upon arrival, every family was assigned to a cabin, according to the family size. There was no kitchen or running water in the rooms, only public pumps outside which they shared, but at least they had some privacy. There was a large community kitchen where they lined up for their meals, which they could take to their rooms if they wanted to. It was a strange feeling living in the middle of nowhere, as though they were hiding from the world. The huge distance renewed Katie's terror. Realizing how far she was from Andrew, the nightmare of losing him consumed her. The lust for life and happy smile had long gone from her black eyes, washed away by the mourning tears for Andrew. Feeling utterly lonely, she fell into the habit of sitting on the step in front of their room, her arms hugging her knees, gazing at the millions of dazzling stars in the southern sky. She was wondering about her future...

Not knowing how long they would have to stay here, the restlessness was getting to Joe too. As independence lost, the uncertainty was affecting his nerves. In edition they were not getting any encouragement about job opportunities either...

The sun continued burning the land so fiercely that a man would almost feel faint. Even the feeble breeze was too hot to offer any relief. They tried to hide from the ravages of the roasting sun, while fighting a hopeless battle against those stubborn flies.

When one day the Erdelyis washed their dishes at the water pump, Erdelyi remarked to his family, "It's funny how one can get used to almost anything to survive. With time the most unusual thing becomes natural."

Remarks like these would make Katie explode. "For me, life here is neither funny nor natural. I could well live without it, thank you!"

"Katie, please!" her mother exclaimed.

But she was past the point of being reasonable. "It's true!" she burst out. "Why did we have to come here to this...this wilderness? I hate it, I can't stand it!" she cried.

Sadness darkened Erdelyi's eyes. He knew that Katie was taking every opportunity to voice her resentment by lashing out at them. It was depressing to see that she could not, and probably never would, overcome her resentment about leaving Hungary. And her 'who cares' attitude was written all over her face. What he would have given to share Beresh's peace of mind.

In the camp, they were given cigarettes and pocket money. Since Joe did not smoke, and cigarettes were extremely expensive in Australia, he sold them and was able to save some money.

Then, after living there for four weeks, an unexpected announcement came from the office that they were free to go anywhere at any time. Their fate lay entirely in their own hands.

"Hmmm, just like that!" Beresh remarked.

Now the time has come to think of how to go about starting a new life, Joe thought. There was a large map on the wall in the office, and he began studying it. Canberra and Sydney attracted him the most. However, one of the office workers informed him through a translator that the population of Canberra was about 35-40,000, indeed a small town for being the nation's capital. He did not see much opportunity to go there.

The solution to his dilemma came unexpectedly when a small group of men came to the camp from Sydney, representing the Hungarian Volunteer Association. They were recruiting tradesmen for whom they could guarantee jobs in Sydney.

Joe immediately approached one of them and started a conversation. When he mentioned that he was a house painter, the man's eyes widened and exclaimed, "Well, my friend, if you're ready to work, I can guarantee you plenty of jobs in Sydney." He extended his hand and introduced himself, "My name is Imre Mezei."

"Joseph Erdelyi. And this is my wife and my daughter, Katie."

After the introduction, Joe continued, "Mr. Mezei, you've asked me if I'm ready to work. I can tell you, the idleness of camp life has just about driven me crazy. I'm sick of doing nothing."

"That's great! I mean you've got yourself a job," Mezei laughed. With that, he quickly scribbled down their cabin number and set the time to be ready to leave early in the morning. "I'll pick you up at seven."

Joe felt as if he were in heaven. That evening, during their packing, he was as excited and happy as a child. With this unexpected luck, he felt that the door had opened up for them for a new and prosperous life.

"From now on, everything is going to be all right, you'll see, my two lovely ladies," he said, hugging them. "I feel our lucky star has shone down on us, and I'll do everything in my power to make you happy. That's a promise!"

Joe's renewed optimism created an exciting atmosphere, which rubbed off onto his family. Even Katie showed some enthusiasm. So they went to bed with eager anticipation. Joe believed that by this luck he had just received a new lease on life that promised them a free and contented life.

* * *

Since Beresh did not have a particular trade, (he has been an office worker in all his life), he had not made up his mind yet as to which way he wanted to go. So the next morning the two families said good-bye to each other with a warm embrace.

"You lucky son-of-a-gun, I wish you good luck, and take care," Beresh said.

"All the best wishes from me, Ernie. You, too, take care."

Mezei had a cream-colored Holden station wagon, which

was very roomy. With their belongings in the trunk, Joe sat in front with Mezei while the two women made themselves comfortable on the back seat. Then they were on the road.

After Joe answered a few questions about the revolution and their long journey, it was Mezei who carried the conversation. He seemed like a likeable man who volunteered to give as much information about Australia as he could. From the tone of his voice, it was obvious he was happy with his life in Australia. "Presently Australia *is* the true 'Promised Land'," he said. "This is a fairly new country, vast, rich, and most of all unexplored, which means there are all kinds of opportunities. Unemployment is virtually unknown, especially in the building industry.

"Naturally, there are lots of new things that you'll have to get used to. First, the unusual climate with its upside-down seasons; the coldest month is July, and the hottest is January, as you're witnessing right now. This is a commercial world where money is worshiped like a religion. It's a sad comment, but in this kind of world, it's easy to lose your inner self. Then another thing: don't be surprised if you bump into some good old-fashioned British prejudices. To some of them, we're the un-welcomed *'bloody new Australians'.* Yet in all fairness, as soon as they get to know you, they're friendly. Basically they know that we're the same human beings with the same purpose in life."

He paused then added, "As you know, just like every country, Australia, too, has its drawbacks. The most serious one is the summer drought. This is indeed a dry and water-poor country. We have summers when we have no rain for 4-5 months! But of course the winter months more than make up for it."

Listening with great interest, Joe shook his head. "My God, that must be dreadful. I can imagine the havoc it plays with the price of food."

"Oh it does. But we have to accept it as part of the Australian way of life." Just then a fly landed on Mezei's forehead. "Likewise these omnipresent flies!" he waved his hand chasing it away. "A more impudent pest you could never find anywhere."

When they reached Goulburn, Mezei said that the engine was "thirsty" and he was hungry. He stopped at the gas station, refilled the tank then drove off looking for a restaurant.

After a full day of driving, they reached the outskirts of

Sydney. Scanning the streets with great curiosity, the Erdelyis found an imposing and thriving metropolis. They drove on a six-lane street, with the traffic growing heavier by the minute. The frequent traffic lights reminded Joe of the days when he was a traffic controller in Budapest. But here in this modern world, there was no such thing as a policeman standing in the middle of the intersection, unless there was an emergency.

When the traffic got more hectic, Joe exclaimed, "This is crazy! You really have to watch the road if you don't want to be killed."

"Oh you get used to it, just like anything else," Mezei said. Soon he took a sharp turn into a side street and stopped in front of a beautiful red brick house, landscaped high on the rolling terrain. The garage was cut into the slight hillside, above which was a large terrace with white, fancy wrought-iron railings. Behind the terrace was a huge sitting room, and on the other side were two bedrooms. But the most impressive feature was the large windows.

"Well, this is my home," Mezei said proudly.

"It's beautiful," Erdelyi said. "It must have been cost you a fortune to build a dream house like this one."

"Oh not really. With a little effort and perseverance, plus some government loan at 4% interest rate, you could have the same within a few years."

They went up the steps then Mezei opened the door and led them into the house. In the sitting room sat an overweight woman who stood up to greet her husband and the visitors.

"This is my wife, Elizabeth," he said, then switching to English, he introduced their guests from Hungary.

"Oh? Hello! Welcome to Sydney," she said, confused. "I'm sorry,"she apologized, "but I can't speak Hungarian." From her accent it was obvious that she had been born in Australia.

"That's quite all right, Liza, "Mezei said. "I'll translate for you. Now, please sit down and make yourself comfortable. It's time to celebrate your arrival to our fair city."

He walked to a handsome glass cabinet and took out some liquor while explaining to his wife that the Erdelyis were refugees from the revolution.

She made a sad face. "Oh you poor people, we were so sorry seeing in the news what you had to endure in those horrible days.

We really felt for you."

It was obvious that the language barrier made the Erdelyis uneasy. So Mezei told them with a mix of humor, "Don't let it bother you because I assure you, for them it is a lot harder to learn Hungarian than for us to learn English."

They smiled good-naturedly. Then Mezei lifted his glass and proposed a toast to the Erdelyis' health, wishing them the best of luck in their new country.

During supper, Mezei told them that he came to Australia in the late forties. As a soldier, the Americans in Germany captured him after the war in 1945. When freed, he had chosen Australia rather than return to the Soviet-occupied Hungary. Besides German, he had learned some English in school and was able to practice it in the prison camp. The Americans treated them fairly, he said, as long as the prisoners were willing to work.

"As you will see, when we arrived here, it was more difficult to start in Australia, because we had moving restrictions for a year. After that I was able to get a job in Sydney as an architect at a large building company. However, I don't want to bore you with my life, for it wasn't that bad really."

"Oh no, no, I find it very interesting," Erdelyi interrupted.

"Well, I'd rather hear some more about your life in Hungary, since I never wished to visit Hungary and help the communists with my money."

So Joe made an effort to talk about the most tragic events, especially in the early fifties. Then, all of them gave a brief account of the events that led to the revolution.

Mezei nodded. "You know, when one hears these things from people who had been there, it is more believable. Because there were times, I admit, that when we were reading some horror stories, it seemed to be pure anticommunist propaganda. But now I can see that we were wrong."

"Oh, yes, the communists had learned and played cleverly into this philosophy that the bigger the crime the less people are willing to believe that it really happened."

"Hmmm, sounds like an excellent axiom."

It was getting late, so Mezei suggested they turn in for the night. He showed them a large bedroom with two king-sized beds. "This is your room. And please remember, if you need anything, just ask, and it'll be there."

A warm feeling overcame the Erdelyis. Leaving a cruel and miserable system behind, suddenly facing up to so much kindness, it moved them beyond words.

"Thank you very much," they said. Then, trying to please Mrs. Mezei, they said good night in English.

* * *

The next morning Mezei greeted Joe with a smile and told him casually, "Take your time and have some more rest if you want. No need to rush. When you feel ready to go, just say the word ..."

Joe frowned. "Take more rest? Mr. Mezei, since the day we crossed the border, I've done nothing but rest. I'm tired of resting."

Mezei laughed. "Joe, from now on it is Imre. Let's go then."

A few minutes later, they were in the car. While Imre drove along, he told Joe that there were many Hungarians in Sydney. "In fact, I'm taking you to a real estate company owned by Hungarians. So you don't have to worry about speaking English in a hurry. That gives you time to catch up."

"That's a definite bonus already," Joe said.

They traveled on the same main road they came to Sydney, which led them into the city center. While Erdelyi gazed curiously at the rows of shops, he thought about his miraculous luck in finding these people, his own kind. He felt a sense of security, an innate reassurance that even if Hungarians were spread all over the world, they were not alone.

Imre stopped in front of an office building, above which the board displayed a name that could be nothing else but Hungarian:

JOHN NAGY
BUILDING CO. & REAL ESTATE LTD.

"This is it," Mezei said. When they entered, he greeted a big man in his fifties sitting behind a large desk.

"Hi John. I've brought you a man I think you'll be glad to see. This is Joseph Erdelyi, fresh from Hungary, and he is in the building trade."

They shook hands, and Nagy welcomed him with a friendly smile. He expressed his condolence for the tragedy the Hungarian people had gone through. "Let's hope one day some good will come out of their efforts," he said. Then Imre gave him some more information.

Hearing that Joe was a painter, John's face lit up. "That's great! You're right, Imre, he is just what I need. Well, my friend, one thing is sure, if you want to work, I've got plenty for you."

The rest of the conversation turned strictly into business. John told him that until he was able to determine Joe's skill, he could pay him only eighteen pounds a week. "However, if you are really good at it, you could earn even double that. Another thing, since you don't have a car yet, I'll make arrangements with one of my men—also Hungarian—to pick you up in the morning and take you home after work."

It sounded almost too good, so Joe had asked if it would not be too much trouble?

"No, no, don't worry about it," John waved his hand. "After all, what are friends for? Besides, we all have been there, right, Imre? So we know what it's like to start a new life."

"I'm very grateful, thank you very much."

After this auspicious beginning, they made the final agreement and left. On the way home, Joe was in a daze. "I can't believe my luck," he told Imre.

"I'm glad it worked out," Imre said, "but actually I expected this. You know, I've known John for a long time. He is a strict man, but I can assure you he is an honest guy. If you're good at your job, he'll appreciate it and will keep his word. I think he'll give you all the chances you need. But I warn you, don't you ever try to cross him. That he would not forgive you. As far as your pay is concerned, since you don't know much about the value of the pound, eighteen pounds for a week isn't the best pay, but it is above the average."

"It sounds fair to me."

Then for a short while they became quiet, watching the traffic. But even in silence the mind does not stop working. Musing over what was happening to him, something hit Joe's mind. What was it that brought these people into his life? Was it fate or luck? For he could never imagine that strange people would act like this. Well, these people *are* real! he thought. Writers are always portraying the other side of life where we are supposed to be running into greedy characters who have nothing else in their minds but *how to take advantage of us.* Anything could happen, of course, but in real life, most of us are decent, honest people. What is so "entertaining" about portraying the cold-blooded vicious side of life as if it were the norm? For the life of him, Joe could not understand it. Curiosity forced him to discus the matter with Imre. Thinking about it, his answer was right to the point.

"You know, we believe what we want to believe, but I think you can always find some weird or sick individuals. Let's face it, they're out there, no question. Though I find it interesting that you brought this up. It reminds me of something that I thought I had forgotten. As I told you, I was fighting against Russia in World War II, winding up in Germany. By sheer chance, I had seen once what the Nazi SS did with the Jews in one of the concentration death-camps. Seeing those starved-to-the-bone, mass-murdered people—children, young and old, dumped into their mass graves, turned my stomach. I was truly convinced then—and I still believe it—that *there are people in this world who are **born** evil.* They sank into the lowest level of mindless animals. But I believe also, that the chances of finding good and decent people are still very good."

* * *

The Erdelyi family was happy with the fine turn of events. In the privacy of their bedroom, they took the pen and paper out, and began to plan their future. At this moment they looked at life through rose-colored glasses, and could see the possibility of owning a house again. Joe could not pretend that he did not miss all he had left behind, but he was able to let the past rest. He was grateful for his good health, and for the opportunity he had been given, and he looked forward to taking the challenge. At forty-two, he was still young enough to build a future. He felt that fate had handed him the key to a treasure chest, and all he had to do was to dig it up.

Since Joe was mentally and physically ready, entering the workforce was a smooth transition. He was a conscientious worker so it was just a matter of time before the routine took over.

Meantime, Katie picked up a new habit. With the help of the dictionary, she tried to read the papers. As a result she became the most advanced in English language, therefore her mother insisted on accompanying her.

One day as they walked in a nearby shopping center, an elderly woman heard them speaking Hungarian, and she had approached them apologetically. "Excuse me for intruding, but I could not help hearing you speaking Hungarian."

"Oh yes, our mouths are a giveaway," Katie smiled.

"How long are you living here?"

"Three weeks."

"Oh, new arrivals? Well, in case you are looking for some work, I think I could help. I know an old well-to-do couple who is looking for help…"

That is how Mrs. Erdelyi got a job as a house cleaner. It paid two pounds a day plus lunch.

Katie also could have found some work, but Joe had a better idea. "Now that the two of us are working, there is no need for you to rush into just *any* job," he said. "Better if you work on your English first."

Yes, Katie wanted to learn English, the only subject in which she had shown any interest. Reading the papers, it turned out to be useful: one day she found a suitable accommodation in the ads. It was an older house not too far, so they walked over to see it.

A smiling retired couple greeted them. In their friendly conversation, the first thing they learned was their nationality: they were Lithuanians. Communication was difficult but they managed. The Erdelyis inspected the two bedrooms, the kitchen and bathroom that they would share. The rent would be three pounds per week. For privacy, it had one big advantage: they had a separate entrance, which pleased them.

"It will be just fine; we'll take it," Katie told the Lithuanians.

"The smaller room will be just fine for Katie," Annie said.

Joe was exuberant. "Now that's what I call good teamwork!" he said. Then, to boost Katie's ego, he added, "Of course, the credit belongs to Katie, our clever negotiator."

Katie smiled modestly. "Oh, come on Daddy."

"Anyway, it'll be fine until we're able to move into our own house."

16

THE WANDERER

ANDREW'S STAY IN WINNIPEG lasted for five months. With the winter over, he was convinced that Winnipeg was the coldest city in Canada. He was fed up with the towering snow-banks, the intense, numbing cold, the vicious blizzards blasting across the prairie—for which the city was called: "Windypeg."

Although lately Andrew was not in a joking mood, but on one of a particularly freezing day he asked Pataki if summer ever came to Winnipeg. If so, it must be by accident.

Pataki looked at him as if offended. "Oh, come on, Andrew, there is no need to be sarcastic. Remember Hungary was not exactly a Hawaiian paradise either." Pataki never criticized him openly, but his tone was accusatory and disappointing over his inability to hold onto a job.

Andrew's eyes darkened, like the sky when the clouds move through. He truly loved the Patakis and tried to show his appreciation for being there when he needed them. But after this, he was more careful and uncomfortable with him.

"Istvan, please, now why did you have to say that?" Mrs. Pataki said. "Have you already forgotten how many times *you* have complained over the years how dirty cold Winnipeg was?"

The difference of opinion is the lubricant of progress, Andrew thought, so he decided to mollify things. "Well, it's true, we tend to forget things,' he said. "I remember that my Dad had volunteered to shovel the snow in 1940, because the snow was so high that the traffic came to a complete halt."

It appeared that Pataki understood Andrew's intention, and

regretted his remark. But without apologizing, his attitude changed.

"Oh yes, I sure remember that year very well," he said.

Slowly but surely spring arrived. Since Andrew was out of work, there was nothing to keep him there any longer— it was time to say good-bye. He thanked the Patakis for their generosity, saying that he would never forget how they had been like parents to him, which made it easier for him to start his new life.

In return, the Patakis expressed their deep regret at his leaving them. "I'm sorry if I was harsh with you at times, Andrew," Pataki said, "but remember you enriched our lives. We know that good-byes are a part of life, but we hope you'll remember us. Good luck on your way and Godspeed."

After kissing the crying Mrs. Pataki, he threw his scarf around his neck with casual elegance, picked up his suitcase and headed for the railway station. Violets spread their purple clusters and renewed life was visible everywhere. Dew sparkled on leaves like glass droplets; the air he breathed deep into his lungs was fresh and heady with the fragrance of spring.

Andrew had learned that Ontario's climate was a little better, so his destiny was Toronto. As he looked around while waiting for the train, he felt an inexplicable sense of relief in leaving Winnipeg. It could have been spring fever, for he felt an exuberant sense of freedom. It was as if he were escaping from his troubled past.

Once in Toronto, he stared at the gleaming buildings that soared high into the sky and looked around hesitantly at the swiftly moving, noisy traffic. A sudden feeling of unease mixed in with his excitement. What now?

No matter how desirable it seemed to be leaving Winnipeg, he missed the security he had left behind, and the supportive atmosphere of the Patakis. It was almost like a repeat of leaving his country.

As he stood there hesitantly, he decided to board one of the many buses that were coming his way, even though he had no idea where he was or where the bus would take him. After riding for half an hour, Andrew impulsively got off in the suburb of Willowdale. Suitcase in hand, he wandered aimlessly until he spotted a motel and took a cheap room for two nights.

The next morning he went for a walk, thinking what could be worse than hardly speaking English, and having no idea of how to go about finding a job? Feeling lost, he did the only thing desperate people do: he kept walking as if some higher authority programmed his feet. Suddenly, he spotted a car wash place where he saw young people working busily. Poverty is a good incentive. Impulsively, he decided to go in and apply for a job. At least he knew enough words to make himself understood. And just as luck would have it, he was hired on the spot. The next day he started to work.

There was not much to learn and his work quickly turned into a mechanical routine.

As the days passed, Andrew extended his stay in the motel, making a deal with them to pay on a weekly basis, $10.00 a week. He wrote his parents a quick letter, letting them know that he had moved to Toronto. Although he put the motel' address on the envelope, he asked them not to write until he sent them a fixed address.

At least one good thing came out of working there: Out of necessity, Andrew learned how to drive a car. As the setup was, one of his duties should have been to take the car from the customer and drive it to the hauler. But because he did not have a driver's license, someone had to do it for him.

Fortunately there was a young man, Stan Mackay, who was more than willing to help him. He was a freckle-faced, wiry young fellow whose veins streaked the skin on his muscular arms and neck. His hands were rough and knobby, a sharp contrast to his open, friendly disposition. There were many things about him that Andrew liked from the beginning, but mostly it was his remarkable sense of humor.

Stan already knew that Andrew was new in Toronto and lived in a motel. Watching him, from his mood he could read the loneliness, along with the mysterious sadness that seemed to shadow his face. He did his job well but worked like a robot. He spoke very poor English and he only spoke when it was absolutely necessary. Stan felt sorry for him, so he decided to cheer him up. He had the ability to melt the icy wrapping off that was surrounded Andrew.

One day, sitting beside him on a bench with a sandwich in his hand, he said, "Look, Andrew, you have to learn to drive a car. You can't deny that you need a license in this job."

Andrew glanced at him, as if he lost his mind. "Oh, sure!" he said with a smile, taking it as a joke. "But me no car,...no money for..." and he made his usual impatient motion with his hand when he searched for the right word... "lessons."

"That's no problem. I'll teach you. My car may be a piece of junk but it'll do. Next Sunday afternoon I'll come and take you to a large shopping center's parking lot. There'll be plenty of room for practice, okay?"

Andrew stared at him in amazement. It was as if he were looking at him for the first time. In Andrew's eyes, a car had a huge value, certainly not a toy to fool around with. And yet, here he was, a complete stranger, acting in a generous manner, willing to help him as if he wanted to save his life. It was incredible!

"You think I...learn...drive one day?"

"You might. But if not, we'll keep working at it until my car falls apart. You might end up having to buy me a new car. How about that for a good deal, hah? What do you say?"

Andrew shook his head. "That car...cost...too much money. I do not know."

"You don't have to know," Stan smiled.

Stan kept his promise, and the following Sunday afternoon he went to the motel.

"Are you ready?"

"No, but we can go."

Stan drove him to an empty parking lot and the lesson began. "Now listen, Andrew, and watch carefully. I'll explain everything but if you don't understand, I'll try again, okay?" Starting with the ignition, he showed and explained every move.

"Stan,...slow down...I..."

"All right, I'm sorry." They made a few rounds together, Andrew watching him with in a dizzy state of mind. When Stan made him to take over the wheel, the car jumped forward like an unbroken bronco, and stalled. The darn old Dodge had a manual transmission. Stan realized that Andrew did not understand half of what he had said, but he was patient. He explained it over and over again. As soon as he showed some progress, Stan praised him like he was a genius. After a few hours of practice, Stan decided to teach him how to park. He placed a big stone next to a lamppost and showed him a few times how to back up without touching the stone

"Oh, no! I'll break your car," Andrew groaned.

"So what?" Stan shrugged. "The car is insured. Besides, I'm still counting on a new car out of this overtime, remember?"

The next Sunday, they repeated everything all over again. Things went a little smoother; progress showing. When Stan thought that Andrew was ready, he took the car to an almost deserted street for practice. Andrew was terrified. "I'm not ready ...yet...for...that..!"

But Stan was stubborn. "I knew you'd say that. If it were up to you, you'd never be ready. Listen, I'll tell you everything, just do what I say. You're doing just fine. Take it easy and the rest will come naturally. After all, we're not in rush hour traffic, for God's sake."

Trembling and his heart beating in his throat, Andrew reluctantly pulled out into the street. He was holding the steering wheel as if his life had depended on it, perspiration trickling down his back. It seemed like an insurmountable task to drive the car and, at the same time had to watch the traffic lights, stop signs and pedestrians....

When Stan finally took over, Andrew was as relieved as if he were saved from a death sentence.

They did this for a few more weekends, then Stan gave him a driver's manual, so he could learn all the rules. "I'm sorry, sir," Stan smiled, "but I couldn't get it for you in the Hungarian edition. So you will have to sweat it out in English."

The shock on Andrew's face indicated that he was not sure which was more terrifying: reading the book, or driving. "Oh, Jesus!" he moaned, frustration tearing him to pieces. But Stan was there to help him through this too. Gradually, the blur of lines started to make sense and with understanding, his confidence grew. As he learned the rudiments, he was amazed by its simplicity.

For the test, Stan went with him and let him use his car. Andrew failed the first time and went home disappointed. But two weeks later he went back and received his license. When he put it in his pocket, he felt true happiness, perhaps for the first time in Canada. At last, he had achieved something he could be proud of. How happy Katie would be could she share this with him!

Andrew stood before Stan with an ecstatic smile and he said proudly in broken English: "Stan, I thank you very much for your big help. Now I have my driver's license."

"That's great, Andrew, congratulations!" Stan beamed. "Welcome to the club! I knew you could do it and I'm proud of you."

"Thank you. One more thing, Stan. To show my appreciation, I would like to invite you to the corner restaurant for a dinner." Then he added sheepishly, "but sorry, I cannot buy you a new car."

Stan laughed. "That's all right, buddy, that can wait. But thanks for the invitation."

When he arrived home, the motel owner gave him a letter. He immediately recognized his mother's handwriting. Hmm, he thought, I told them not to write here. But his mother couldn't wait. Her letter was short and angry. With outrage, she asked why did he have to leave Winnipeg where everything was going so right? Had he lost his mind? What kind of gypsy lifestyle was he getting into?

The situation epitomized his exile. On one hand, the license in his pocket gave him a happy smile. On the other hand, his mother's scolding letter destroyed it. Forgive me, Mother, he thought, but you wouldn't understand it anyway.

* * *

As they sat at a table in the restaurant, quietly waiting to be served, Andrew looked upon Stan as one of his best friends. By now Andrew felt a sense of kinship, as Stan had demonstrated qualities on which true friendship is built. Only a few months ago they had been complete strangers, thrown together by chance. Yet, after losing George, he felt that this was a friendship that would stand the test of time. He realized that in this shrinking world it is irrelevant where we born because, except for language differences, basically *we're all the same!*. We all strive for love, happiness and financial success. That is the mystic bond of brotherhood.

He was convinced that Stan had his dreams just as he had. How lucky they are to born into a free country where the possibilities are endless...What a priceless gift! Andrew thought that because of the circumstances he appreciated it more. But it is human nature that we tend to take things for granted. It could be dangerous, he knew. Too bad that he could not discuss this with Stan so while they ate he said, "Stan, you..missed your...vocation. with your..teaching skill, you...should open a...what is that?...a driving school. You...could be a....rich man."

Stan smiled, and with a shrug he said, "Thanks for the vote of confidence. Teaching you was fun."

* * *

Now that Andrew could drive, he was anxious to have his

own car. He realized that the automobile was more than just a necessity— it was a status symbol. Just imagine, *I could have a car!* —The first one in my life!

A few days later he could not resist looking around for a second-hand car. He didn't know much about cars, so he needed Stan's help again. Examining a few, Stan recommended an old Ford that was within Andrew's price range. They took it out for a test drive, which was another source of surprise to Andrew. They let you take it out before paying for it? He bought it on the same day. What a royal feeling it was driving around *in his own car!* It brought a new restlessness with it. Not only did he feel that he had washed enough cars to last him a lifetime, but he was still gripped by the idea of becoming an electric technician. In the deep recesses of his mind he kept his dreams alive.

He was aware of the annoying lack of English, which kept him from achieving his goal. Yet he couldn't help chasing this seemingly unattainable old dream, sustained by the fierce determination and burning desire—even if he hadn't the faintest idea of how to overcome those barriers. But he had to put his best foot forward, or he would fritter away his chances of ever becoming one. He just couldn't give up! "Perhaps, I'm crazy and obsessed," he mused, "but whatever it takes, I'll hang on to that idea...."

He resigned from his job and two weeks later Andrew said good-bye to Stan with a warm embrace.

"Good luck, Andrew," Stan said dejectedly.

* * *

While in Toronto, Andrew heard that if he wanted to earn good money, he should go to Delhi to pick tobacco. So now Delhi was his destination. Driving along on an unpaved road between huge fields of tobacco plants, suddenly he noticed a crooked letter box in front of a farmhouse. On it a familiar name hit his eyes: Stephan Szollosy. "He is another Hungarian, if I ever seen one," Andrew muttered and turned in.

He found Szollosy in the backyard, feeding the chickens. He was a big man in his sixties with a typical up-curled Hungarian moustache. Andrew greeted him in Hungarian, saying he was looking for work.

Szollosy looked him over. "As a matter of fact, I'm just hiring some casual workers," he said. "Have you ever done this kind of work before?"

"No."

"Well, I don't want to scare you away, son but you might find the going a little rough. So, be prepared, though you seem to be in good shape."

Andrew nodded, noting that Szollosy came right to the point. "I'll do my best."

Szollosy led him to a building and showed where he would sleep. He told him that his pay would be 80 cents per hour, plus room and board.

The building that was now empty, was a barn, which had been converted into a dormitory for part-time workers. It looked much like an army barrack. Szollosy pointed to a bed. "That'll be your bunk and the dresser beside it. The building over there," he pointed outside through the window, "is where everybody eats."

In the evening Andrew met all the workers. They represented many nationalities, among them one Hungarian, John Pasztor. They were friendly, but the information he gathered regarding the work was not encouraging at all.

"If you survive the first week, you're okay."

The work began at seven in the morning. A foreman told Andrew how to pick the tobacco leaves two rows at a time and how carefully he must handle them.

Andrew nodded and started vigorously, glancing at the man next to him, hoping to learn ways to pick it faster. But what he soon learned was what Szollosy meant by the work being rough. It was backbreaking! Never in his life had he worked so hard. Bending under the hot sun all day was exhausting. By the end of the day his muscles were sore, and every move was agony. Nine hours on the field had drained him of all desires except to eat and sleep. But even that seemed difficult, for he tossed and turned like a man delirious with fever.

To divert his mind from the pain, he tried to thinking about Katie. But it did not work and he was amazed at how a man's body and spirit could function at all under such adverse conditions.

It took him a week to get used to the grueling regime and he needed all his willpower to carry on. But carry on he did for three weeks. Then the work was done. Szollosy was satisfied with his work and he wanted to recommend him to another farmer. Andrew was pleased by his offer but he was too relieved the work was done that he said, thanks but no thanks. He did not want to pick tobacco ever again.

The next move was to the Niagara Peninsula's fruit farms to pick apples. While driving, he wondered bitterly if he would be drifting aimlessly from one place to the next, like a bum, for the rest of his life.

Picking apples was much less demanding and the pay was the same. He worked for another two weeks and he went to see Niagara Falls.

He has heard so much about the world famous tourist sight that he could hardly wait to see it. When he arrived, the scene that unfolded before him was breathtaking. After parking his car, he walked through the crowd to the Horseshoe Falls. He stared at the half-circle cataract in silent amazement; the sight was beyond his imagination. Thousands of gallons of water rushed over the shiny stones like an endless carpet, plunging down thunderously in a brilliant turquoise-green color. Deep below the roaring water spewed forth a constantly accumulating mist, which grew into a swirling cloud, producing a fine mist of spray that sprayed the sightseers, like dew covers the flower petals.

In the heart of all of us resides a desire to share beauty and joy. Andrew thought about Katie; what he would have given to share this eternal grace of mighty wonder with her.

As he lifted his head, he saw a beautiful rainbow arching over the Niagara River. In his nostalgic mood, a deep sigh escaped from his chest, for the rainbow reminded him of Judy Garland's song, *Somewhere Over the Rainbow...*

Reluctantly, he returned to his car. As he drove slowly through the main tourist section, he realized why this place was called the Honeymoon Capital of the World. Never had he seen so many motels in one city.

Although the tourist season was almost over, he decided to stay. Up until now, he had been drifting around, searching for a place to put down some roots and he felt that this was the place. He liked the city. He drove toward the outskirts, looking for a decent but cheap motel. Randomly he had chosen one on Lundy's Lane, named **MOTEL OHIO**. It was not too fancy but clean, so he drove in. Stepping in the office an older, stubby little man leaned on the counter and greeted him with a smile.

"What can I do for you, young man?"

"I like to...have...a room," Andrew said, haltingly.

"Sure, I have a room for you. Welcome to Niagara Falls," the man answered in Hungarian. "My name is Stephan Balogh."

Andrew frowned. "How in the hell did you know I was Hungarian?"

Balogh laughed. "Young man, after working in this business for all these years, I've some experience in judging people. Besides, your accent was a dead giveaway. As for the weekly rates, I charge ten dollars but as the season is over, you can have it for nine dollars."

"Thank you. I sure appreciate it."

Balogh showed him two rooms to choose from.

"I'll take this one," Andrew said, taking the one with the TV in it.

The next day Andrew went to the unemployment office in the hope they could offer him a job. Since the tourist season was over, he knew that there was not much work around. He knew also that he could apply for unemployment benefits, but he did not want that. His English was still poor, so he would not be choosy.

After some waiting, a man greeted him and invited in the office. The first thing he noticed was Andrew's poor English. He looked at him for a moment, then asked Andrew point-blank what his nationality was.

"Hungarian."

"Oh, another one," slipped out. Then he smiled. "Not that it makes any difference," he added quickly. "It's just that I've met so many lately. Anyway, as you probably know by now, there is no job around here that I could offer you right now. You do qualify for unemployment of course, but I think I have something better to offer that might interest you. If you are willing to go to school for the next ten months, you'll be paid to learn English. Let's see..." he began riffling through some papers. "Yes, as a single person, you'd receive thirty dollars a week."

Andrew could not believe he had heard it right. *"You mean I get paid to learn English?"*

"Exactly! You see, the purpose of this program is to help new Canadians to become more valuable citizens in the work force. That way they can produce more, become better taxpayers and hopefully better members of our society. Do you understand what I'm saying?"

Andrew nodded. He understood more than he could say.

"In this way the government would get back the cost of your training. Actually, it is an investment in you and in Canada's future. By the way, I hope you have a car because the classes are given in St. Catharines."

After this the clerk helped him to fill out the form, and gave him the address.

Andrew thanked him and walked out of the office, his head reeling. On the way in his daring adventure, slowly he began to realize that fate was smiling on him today: his lucky star had guided him to Niagara Falls. Suddenly a moment of sparkling light came to life in his mind. Hunted by a lawless, evil regime, here he was in this freedom of paradise, which is a continual testimony that with God's help he had made a good choice. He could hardly contain his joy. *"Can you believe it?"* he asked himself. "I'll get **paid** to learn English! Incredible!"

His heart was swelling with emotion as he thanked Canada for her generosity. Then he made a pledge that he would do everything to keep his side of the bargain.

17

NIAGARA FALLS

ST. CATHARINES, THE GARDEN CITY, is located on the bank of Lake Ontario. With a map at hand, he found the school without difficulty. It was located at the bank of a small river.

As he parked his car in the schoolyard, he could not help but notice the hundreds of cars, presumably owned by non-working people. Coming from an economically ruined country, Andrew picked up things like this because such a sight was unthinkable in Hungary — working or not.

Inside the building hundreds of people were assembled, most of them new Canadians, eager to learn English. Andrew was assigned to Mrs. Wilson's class.

Mrs. Wilson was a pretty, middle-aged woman with a charming, friendly smile. That is what Andrew had noticed first. She started by reading the names of her students. As Andrew listened, soon a familiar name hit his ears: Mrs. Margaret Szabo. Looking at the direction where the answer came from, he saw an attractive woman of about thirty, with blond hair. She had a charming, movie star face with cute dimples. Their eyes met as she glanced at him, probably for the same reason: both their names were unmistakably Hungarian. Soon as he had a chance, it was only natural that he went to her and introduced himself.

"It's a great pleasure to know that I'll be in a class with a pretty Hungarian woman." Andrew said.

"I'm pleased to meet you for the same reason," Margaret said. "It's amazing how many Hungarians are in Canada, isn't it?"

"Yes, the force of evil threw us all around."

"Well, I hope I'll be smarter a year from now," she said. "My English is horrible. To be honest, I felt a little uneasy about coming here and being with all these strangers."

"We all feel that but I, for one, am kind of getting used to being a little dumb when it comes to talking."

Margaret laughed. "Welcome to the club."

"Anyway, it will help to stretch our brains together, Mrs. Szabo."

"Please call me Margaret."

"With pleasure, if you'll call me Andrew."

When seated, unfortunately Andrew sat far from Margaret, so he gathered some courage and asked Mrs. Wilson to let him sit beside Margaret. "She is very shy," he reasoned.

'Well, since you're the same nationality, I don't think it's a good idea but if it helps, I guess it's all right."

The first hour went by distributing pencils, brochures and some exercise books. In the first ten-minute recess Andrew invited Margaret for a walk. They passed through the crowd then Andrew asked, "Did you say you came from Budapest too?"

"Yes, we lived in the eighth district in Nepszinhaz Street, close to the Republic Square, where the AVO headquarters were. During the revolution, we were in the country, visiting my parents. When we returned, our apartment was quite damaged. They said there were some big fights with the AVO."

"I know," Andrew said, "I was there."

"Really? Anyway, everything looked so doomed, we simply didn't have the strength to start all over again."

"I don't blame you."

"When it was over, my husband said that if we're to invest our time and energy again, we might as well do it in a free country. At least we wouldn't have to worry about Soviet oppression. He is a carpenter and makes good money. And since we don't have children, I plan to get a job soon. Our intention is to buy a piece of land and build a house later."

"That's a very wise plan. I wish you good luck."

"Thanks. So since you know a little about me, what about you?"

There was a musing look on Andrew's face. "Ever since I can remember I always wanted to be an electric technician. I started to learn the trade before the revolution. But it seems like it was hundred years ago and I was dreaming about an impossible future," Andrew said with a wry smile.

"Yes, but now the possibilities are opened up again, don't you think?"

"I hope so."

The recess has ended and they went back into the classroom. Observing people, Andrew learned with surprise that among many nationalities there were two French-speaking Canadians in the program. They had moved to Ontario from the province of Quebec and spoke very little English. He knew that Canada had two founding cultures, yet he could not imagine how anyone could survive in Canada without speaking English. They told him later that in the province of Quebec, most people speak mainly French.

The program was designed to introduce grammar in the simplest terms. It was a heady experience and Andrew plunged into it with enthusiasm. He noted with surprise that no matter how proficient one would become in another language, working with numbers would always come to his mind in his mother's tongue. However, it did not take long to realize once again how much difficulty they were facing.

Life is a constant repetition, Andrew thought. He studied until eleven o'clock every night, trying to make sense out of sentence structures. His biggest stumbling block was syntax; arranging the words into the correct sequence. As he toiled over this formidable task, he tore the work into pieces and rearranged the words again, cursing his inadequacies. He often felt as if a storm were sweeping through his brain.

Yet, as time passed, he absorbed into studying with blind diligence, and his knowledge expanded. He started to lose his insecurity, by which gradually he gained back his self-confidence. He always loved playing with words, and began to enjoy this crazy, exciting language as a new toy.

In school Andrew always discussed the homework with Margaret. He seemed to learn a little faster, and was eager to help her. However, she was an excellent cook, and in appreciation she shared her delicious home-made cakes with him, which prompted Andrew to say, "You know, Margaret, if you were a single lady, I'd ask you out for a date."

"For myself or for my cookies?" she asked jokingly.

"For yourself, of course. I must admit I find you a very beautiful woman. But obviously, I'm not the only one."

A slight flush crept up in her cheek. "Oh, thank you." Then, as they sauntered along the bank of the river, she glanced at him. "You know, just the other day the thought flashed through my mind that if I were single, you're the type of man I'd fall in love with." She flushed again. "Oh, I'm jumping into deep water without a lifesaver," she said. "What I meant was that I believe we should be completely honest in our friendship. That is to say that while I love my husband dearly, at the same time I like you as a person. Does it make any sense to you?"

"Yes, it does. Your honesty is commendable and I thank you. Naturally, it is possible to like someone without being in love with him or her. Of course, I'd rather be loved than liked, but without going too far, I would say that I like you and love you just the same."

"Well, let's change the subject," Margaret suggested with a smile. "In the years I found it interesting how many ways a person can be beautiful and loveable. One can be loved for one's mind, for one's kindness, or for one's personality. Others for their shape of bodies, the color of their hair, their smile. I personally prefer to be loved for my mind and my inner beauty."

Andrew came alive. "I couldn't agree with you more. I can attest to it that you certainly qualify to be loved for all. But I want to play the devil's advocate. Regardless of the rules, isn't it too bad that people should be denied happiness because of that piece of paper?"

Margaret laughed. "Oh, you men! You're presenting the sentiment of a selfish pleasure-seeker. There is more to a good marriage than sex. What about commitment? People should keep in mind that there is always a price to be paid for everything."

Andrew not only agreed but he felt a new respect for her and began to look at her in a different light.

"Let's suppose I agree to make you 'happy', Margaret said. That means I'd have to make my husband unhappy. And don't tell me he wouldn't have to know. It just doesn't work that way. And since he is a good man, he wouldn't deserve it. You can't play games with a good marriage."

"What if he deserved it?"

"In that case, I'd no longer be his wife—as simple as that.

Maybe I'm out of step with the today's trend, but I wouldn't tolerate unfaithfulness or abuse of any kind. So, if I expect him to be faithful, then I must be as well. Otherwise, why bother to get married?"

"Well, Margaret, I provoked you on the basis that people are made of flesh and blood and temptation is quite a force in human nature, but you stood the test. I take my hat off. I hope that when I have a wife, she will be like you. You should teach lessons on fidelity."

"I think that fidelity in marriage is subordinated to decency and morality. Why, if you had a wife you loved, could you be unfaithful to her?"

"With a wife like you, I wouldn't take the risk of losing her."

* * *

Living in Balogh's motel was a satisfying arrangement for Andrew. Through their daily life a certain friendship developed between them. Sometimes Balogh came to Andrew to talk, or watch a hockey game with him. He told Andrew that he was a widower and was planning to retire soon. Aside from having a lot in common, loneliness seemed to be another strong bond that linked them together.

Circumstances like his, and frequent moving around, made it easier for Andrew to fall into a solitary lifestyle. Because he was lonely, it made his longing for Katie even stronger, but he did not feel the desire to go out of his way and replace her. Oh, it crossed his mind how much better it would be to share his days, but he did not want to betray her memory. It just gave him more reason to devote his energy to his studying.

In his spare time he loved to go for a walk in the beautiful Niagara Park. This park presented an enchanting sight with its old trees and well manicured gardens—a place of luxurious tranquility. He never got tired of looking at the falls, the Rainbow Bridge and the American side of Niagara Falls.

During these walks positive thoughts occupied his mind. He re-established his correspondence with his parents. Since he was fascinated with the place, he wrote enthusiastic letters to them about Niagara Falls and his English class. Their replies told him they couldn't have been happier and prouder of their son.

He also wrote to the Patakis, telling them what had happened to him, and his great luck in Niagara Falls. It was only Katie with whom he could not share his happiness, he thought bitterly.

In retrospect, Andrew was able to smile about an incident that had shocked him a few days ago. Approaching a large department store in St. Catharines, he saw a young girl standing at the window, daydreaming. She had beautiful black wavy hair, full breasts and a slender figure. But it was her profile that knocked the breath out of him: **It was Katie!** He ran to surprise her with a kiss. Just as he was about to greet her and fling his arms around her, he froze as the terrified girl was glaring at him. Stunned, he mumbled an embarrassed apology and ashen-faced, he walked away, shaken by the realization that it was only wishful thinking. He was so sure! He scratched his head wondering how in the world could two people look so much alike? He continued his walk with his startled thoughts for company.

The avalanche of beautiful colors, which the fall lavishly stored up, was an accumulated gift of summer. Then when the winter months arrived, another wonderful transition took place. The frozen snow replaced the once delightfully manicured landscape and rustling leaves with its glitter under the bright sun. It was like millions of sparkling diamonds, creating a dazzling fairyland.

The trees were scintillating in their snowy pageantry, while the branches were wrapped in white coats of frozen mist, hanging heavily like huge icicles. The same mist was sprinkled on the lampposts, rim-coating them to double their sizes. They looked like rows of giant candlesticks. Walking in the park and admiring its beauty, Andrew thought that only nature was capable of creating such a wondrous picture.

At night, soft-colored lights illuminated the trees, adding yet another dimension to the fairytale scene. Strolling along in silence, he believed that nothing could have provided a more picturesque scene than this park at Christmas time. From the speakers, concealed between the branches, came the hauntingly beautiful strains of music like *Silent Night* by Bing Crosby, radiating softly in this mystical calmness.

Listening to this beautiful song, the frosty air seared his throat as he took a deep breath. Captivated by the spirit of Christmas, a warm feeling came over him and he decided to buy some Christmas cards. He wanted to share his feelings with those he loved most. It was only Katie who remained a painful spot in his heart. By now it became clear that she had disappeared, as though she had been wiped from the face of the earth.

When he came out from the store to drop the cards into the mailbox, the snow was beginning to fall in huge flakes, swirling in the glittering lights. The city itself looked like a giant Christmas card.

He celebrated New Year's Eve with Mr. Balogh, playing cards, drinking and singing nostalgic Hungarian songs. The TV was broadcasting Guy Lombardo's New Year's Eve program and at midnight, the orchestra began to play: *Should auld acquaintance be forgot...*

The year of 1958 had begun.

Andrew was not sober, but the music rang through his mind like a golden memory. He squeezed his eyes to suppress a hint of tears as he looked away. *"God bless you, Katie,"* he mumbled, lifting up his glass to her image.

Balogh stared at him blankly, then they were embracing one another and wishing a very happy New Year.

18

NEW HOPE

THE ERDELYIS SLOWLY SETTLED into their new lifestyle. In this foreign world, the transition was smooth but not without pain. New friends became highly treasured, almost as if they were close relatives. The strange surroundings were a bitter reminder of how much their lives had changed. They discovered how large a city of Sydney was, and by now they learned the new monetary system in which a *"bob"* was one shilling, 20 shillings one pound, and one guinea was 21 shillings. It did not take long before Nagy and Mezei became the Erdelyi's good friends, and in turn, they took them to sightseeing. They visited the Toronga Park zoo, drove over the Harbour Bridge, which was the symbol of Sydney, and walked in the famous business section in Kings Cross, in the heart of Sydney.

On the national scene, there was a heated debate whether to build a new opera house in Sydney or not. After all the pros and cons were widely discussed, the government established a fund-raising scheme: the SYDNEY OPERA HOUSE LOTTERY. It was an excellent source of revenue with which to build that magnificent structure. On one of Joe's paydays, John persuaded him to buy a ticket every month just for the fun of it.

"Why not?" Joe agreed. "I don't smoke and rarely drink, so considering what I save on those luxury items, I think I can indulge myself in a little bit of gambling."

"That's the spirit!" Nagy said and they bought the ticket faithfully. But luck did not seem to come their way.

However, among the happy winners was a family in Sydney whose heartbreaking tragedy shook the world. One of the jackpot winners was a couple that had an eleven year-old son. A few days after their winning was published, their son was kidnaped on his way to school. This was the first huge crime scene since the Erdelyis had arrived, and the shocking event became part of their lives, deeply touching them.

Soon a ransom demand came for 100,000 pounds. The kidnappers tried to divert the suspicion from themselves by pretending a moving to a new address on the same day. But for some reasons they smelled the danger, and had murdered the boy.

After many months of intensive investigation, in which even the Scotland Yard had been involved, the guilty couple was arrested on a ship in the middle of the ocean. They were trying to escape to Europe.(*)

* * *

Time has a way of healing wounds, but sad events can easily reopen them. As the Erdelyis were slowly settling down, a letter from Joe's brother, Bela, arrived. Joe had written to him both from Vienna and from Australia, so this reply was long overdue. Bela was a careless writer probably because the two brothers' relationship never had been a close one. Nevertheless, because Bela was the closest relative, Joe left the house—and everything—to Bela, instead of leaving them to the government.

Although it took a month for Bela to move into the house, but he had checked the mail for the Erdelyi's regularly.(The fate of Andrew's letter to Katie plays a role here.) There was a time when Andrew had the misfortune to visit Katie when Bela was present. Andrew had been discussing the subject of Soviet oppression with Joe, and Bela interrupted, siding with the Russians for freeing Hungary from the German Nazis. A heated argument had erupted, and Andrew called him a fanatic Stalinist. Since that day they hated each other. And seeing Andrew's letter to Katie, he made sure she would never receive it.

Now Bela finally wrote. Between the lines he casually mentioned that Bokrosh had passed away. He went into detail explaining how the dog howled day and night, refusing to calm down. The neighbors told him that the dog is becoming a nuisance, and were considering poisoning him. But somehow, one night he freed himself and disappeared. Later he learned that in the pro-

(*This is a true story, it really had happened.)

cess of searching for his masters, Bokrosh went to the city and was killed by a truck.

After reading the letter, Katie sobbed bitterly. "Even Bokrosh was a victim of the revolution," she cried.

Joe put down the letter and went outside to hide his emotion.

* * *

Although Katie made herself useful around the house, she was desperately lonely. While dusting the furniture, she heard in the radio that the Immigration Department was offering a correspondence course for new Australians to learn English. She grabbed the opportunity and wrote for the registration form. Katie had an ear for language and picked up quickly. In her youthful attitude she always believed that knowledge is power. One of the big advantages was that she would be able to learn English at home. In the evening she told her parents about it and convinced them to take the course.

"Sure, I'm game," Joe said. "We have decided to live in this country, so it's our duty to learn English. It could do no harm."

"That's true," Annie said, supporting her husband. "I say let's give it a try. All we can lose is our pride if we flunk. I'm afraid our brains are a little rusty for this sort of thing, but for Katie, it'll be perfect."

"Sure you can learn," Katie said. "And I'll help you as much as I can."

The first envelope arrived within two weeks. The pages contained many questions but they were easy. They answered them and mailed it back.

The rest of the material came in time, but the subject matter became harder and harder. The booklets provided some explanations but it was too sketchy for them to understand. The Hungarian way of thinking with its different rules and structures got so much in the way to contradict the English syntax. With its reverse ways it just did not seem to make sense. It was too hard to grasp the idiomatic or colloquial phrases.

Sometimes Joe called Imre on the phone asking for help. Occasionally, they would get into quite a heated argument over the seemingly preposterous rules of the English.

"Just listen to this," Joe would say, "the English says '*I live* in Sydney' but 'I'm *alive*'...Now why in the hell do they pronounce it differently?"

Imre laughed. "Look, Joe, all I know is that *this is English!* Every language has its own rules." Then they would switch the conversation to something else and would end up with both men laughing hysterically.

Katie, however, loved it and found the lessons fun. To her, the English language was challenging but beautiful. This was the first time she actually had shown some ambition. Whenever something became clear to her, she would eagerly explain it to her parents. Her efforts had an inspiring effect and under her tutelage they made progress.

The course lasted for six months and after the written test, they received their diplomas.

* * *

Living a fairly modest lifestyle, the Erdelyi's financial situation steadily improved. While Annie's salary covered the cost of food and rent, Joe's earnings were scrupulously deposited into a saving account. Making the necessary compromise, they lived with the Lithuanians in comfortable harmony for over two years. Then one day, as Joe was having his coffee after supper, he went over their financial checking and his face brightened.

"Annie, listen to this!" he exclaimed. "Would you believe if I say, should we really want it, we could have our own home soon."

"You're kidding!" Annie said, sitting beside him excitedly.

"The way I figure it, we have almost 3,000 pounds, more than enough for a good down payment. Now, wouldn't it be nice to live in our own house again?"

Annie let out a deep sigh. "Ohhh, Joe, that would be wonderful! You really think we could?"

"You bet!" Joe said, and in his happy mood, he started to draw the base of a house, explaining, "This would be the main entrance where my lovely wife and daughter would enter with a bag of groceries. Then, they would go to the kitchen here and discuss what to cook for supper for their tired old man..."

"Oh, come on, Joe, you're dreaming," Annie teased him lovingly, happy tears glistening in her eyes.

But as soon as the thought took root in their heads, they could talk about nothing else. So one day Joe went to John and they talked about the prospect of finding a suitable property.

"But John," Joe said, "keep in mind that the matter is not urgent. We can wait until the right thing comes along."

"Sure, I understand, Joe. By the way," John said, "in my opinion, you're the type of man who really should have a house because you could take a shed and make it into a castle."

Joe laughed. "Oh, I don't know about that but thanks for the vote of confidence."

* * *

About a month later John called Joe into his office and welcomed him with a satisfied smile. He held out three photographs and gave them to him.

"Take a look at these houses, Joe. I've already inspected them inside and out. Now it's up to you to decide which one you like best." Pointing to the first picture, "I can tell you that this is in Hurstwill. It's in tip-top shape but it's a little far out. The second one is in Canterbury. The house itself is not bad but it has no backyard. The third one...Well, I don't know. I'm reluctant to recommend it because it has been neglected. It would require a great deal of work. However, it's basically a well-built house, located in Burwood and it has a large fenced yard. I think I could get you a good bargain on that."

Erdelyi considered them for a minute. "I don't know," he said, "but from the pictures I like the second one best. But of course, I'll have to drive out with my family and see them."

"That's only natural. Take your time, Joe, and good luck."

The next day the Erdelyis sat in the old Holden car they had bought just a year ago and off they went on their exciting home-buying excursion. As John said, there was *something* wrong with each of them, and off they went to the next address. At the end they preferred the third one—not the house but the location. The house was on a quiet street and it stood out among the tidy homes like a derelict eyesore. The white paint, which had yellowed with age, was peeling from the window frames. The garden was unkempt and the yard was a mess.

On the inside neglect was everywhere. Water-stained, faded wallpapered rooms greeted them; a thin film of dust covered everything, that even the sunshine, seeping into the house, could not make inviting.

Annie was apprehensive. "I don't know, Joe. It would need

an awful lot of cleaning and fixing up to do before it could be livable."

Joe agreed. But at the same time, he could see that with some effort it could be made into an attractive home. The floor plan was good, hardly needed any changes.

"The work doesn't matter, sweetheart," he said. "The structure is good and if we apply some wood paneling and all the painting it needs, that would take care of most of the shortcomings. To be honest, I see some excellent possibilities."

So far Katie listened quietly, but she agreed with her father. "What I like most here is the peace and quiet," she said. "Yet, we're close to everything."

That was the deciding factor. Whatever Katie liked, Joe appreciated, and respected her opinion.

The next day Joe marched into John's office and made a happy announcement. "You were right, John. We've chosen the third one."

"Good for you. I kind of thought you would. Now, let me work on it. The owner is an old man, desperate to sell. And if we give him a sizeable deposit with an offer, I'm sure he'll accept it."

"All right then," Joe said, "I offer 5,000 with half deposit," and gave him the check.

"Good. I assure you I'll do my best."

The next day the deed was signed and their enthusiasm transformed them into explorers. Joe took a few weeks holiday and the next day, armed with brushes, mops, buckets of detergent, paints, plywood and all the necessary tools, they sprang into action.

When they put on their working clothes, Katie started to laugh. "Dad, you look like a genuine construction worker."

"That's what I am, my little girl."

"I saw a documentary film on TV about Russian laborers in the concentration camp. I feel like I'm one of them," Annie said, looking herself over.

"But I'm sure they would have changed condition with you any day," Katie remarked. Joe took care of the carpentry work and the painting, while Katie and Annie spent days scrubbing and cleaning. But they were smiling, humming and joking along the way. It was an invigorating experience, fueled by the vision of having their own home again.

Joe's heart swelled with happiness as he watched his family work. He inspected one room they had just finished and praised them.

"Well, isn't it coming along nicely? That's beautiful! I sure am blessed with a wonderful wife and daughter."

"So are we," Annie said, pleased, "for having you. We're a great team because we have a great organizer."

After three weeks of relentless effort, working ten-twelve hours every day, the old house was reborn. They surprised not only themselves but also the neighbors. They were amazed by the changes. One neighbor brought them a hot meal as a welcoming gesture, which was a pleasant surprise to them.

The inside was completely redecorated. And because of the freshly painted walls, the rooms seemed larger than before. The new furniture dramatically transformed the rooms into cozy living spaces. They have dreamed of this for so long and they had risen to the occasion.

When they moved in and felt ready, they invited the Nagy and Mezei families for a housewarming party. For this special occasion, John brought not only his wife but also their son, Frank too. Joe saw him only once for a minute, so he barely knew him.

Katie stood in the living room in her velvet dress, with the scarlet belt around her delicate waist that emphasized the thrust of her round breasts. Frank made an involuntary gasp, as it took him but a second to see that Katie had something money can't buy: beauty and good disposition. He saw a pair of dark eyes, black wavy hair that swirled around her shoulders; everything about her was charming and unblemished. Indeed no woman had ever left such a powerful impression on him: her beauty bewitched him.

When Katie saw him, Frank also made a surprising impression. He was a handsome young man of twenty-six, tall with wavy brown hair. His suit identified him as one who belonged to the upper class. She couldn't put a finger on it why, but she was sure that Frank worked in an office, and wore a necktie all the time.

At the introduction, Frank's polite manner surprised her further when he bowed and kissed her hand. In Hungary, it was customary, but here she was unprepared. She said her name with a charming smile.

Mrs. Erdelyi was the most impressed by Frank, making a

mental consideration for Katie's future. Some pleasant courtship in mind, she deliberately managed to sit him opposite to Katie. She, however, was not too pleased with the situation, for Frank's staring made her feel uneasy.

Frank noticed it and tried to calm his thundering heart with polite conversation. From information he had learned from his father, he also acknowledged the Erdelyis' tremendous efforts in bringing the house back to such a lovely condition.

Katie's response was polite. "Thank you. It was hard work, but we love it..." Then, to conceal her uneasiness, she talked about the difficulty in adjusting to the Australian way of life. "But I'm getting there," she said.

"Oh, it could not have been that bad," he said. "I bet you haven't even seen an Australian aborigine yet."

"Only in pictures. I hope they are not dangerous."

"Oh, no! It's just that they have their own way of life."

When the supper was over, Frank suggested going for a walk. Katie agreed, hoping to shake off her discomfort before she spoiled her chances of developing a friendship with him. They excused themselves and a minute later, they were walking along the pathway.

It was a warm, pleasant evening. The streetlights shone, and only an occasionally barking dog disturbed the quietness.

"I'm really happy for the chance to meet you," Frank said. My only regret is that it didn't happen much earlier."

"Well, as the saying goes, better late than never," Katie said.

"It's true. I knew that a Hungarian refugee was working for my father, but I had no idea he had such a beautiful daughter."

Katie blushed. "Thank you." Sometimes I feel ugly, she thought. "It's no wonder we haven't met because I don't go out much," she said, feeling dreadfully out of practice in socializing with a man.

"Oh, that's a shame! I mean a lovely girl like you should not hide behind four walls. I'd be honored if you would give me a chance to remedy the situation."

Katie was silent, so Frank continued, "Well, maybe I'm coming on a little too strong, since we've known each other only a few hours. My only hope is that you'll consider my offer. I also admit, I've never been more grateful to my parents for insisting that I speak Hungarian. There were times, you know, when I couldn't see the point in learning it. But I was wrong, for now I could not converse with you."

"Oh, I think you speak well in Hungarian. At the same time I'm learning English diligently, so you could not really 'sell me' in English as we used to say."

Frank smiled, "That's a funny way to put it, but I'd rather 'buy' you then 'sell'. From what you've told me, I assume you don't have a job yet."

"No, I don't. And I think it's just about time to start to look for one, because with this new house, I feel I should contribute to the cost of living."

Frank nodded approvingly. For a while they walked silently, immersed in their thoughts. It flashed through Frank's mind that he was always proud of his heritage. He was nine years old when his parents sensed the disastrous political direction Hungary was heading. Pretending to go for a vacation, they left the country in 1942. During the war years, they lived in Salzburg, Austria, and then after the war, they immigrated to Australia. His father told him that when the immigration officer asked him why had he chosen Australia, he said, 'Europe is a firetrap— the further away the better.'

Frank had a sheltered life. The hard times at the beginning fell solely on the shoulders of his parents. Then, through the prosperous years, the only thing that worried his father was that his son's easy life might prevent him from being prepared for the tough life that might awaits him. So with loving strictness, they were able to instill in him the discipline he needed. They wanted to be proud of him, and they were not disappointed. Frank was an excellent student.

By nature Frank was a mild-mannered, gentle youth. He was a spiritually inclined individual, rather than sporty or physically aggressive one. He preferred books to sports, except playing chess. Beside Hungarian, he spoke German as well as English. Being successful in the real estate business, his parents hoped that Frank would follow suit. But it was not meant to happen, for Frank had no desire at all to follow his father's footsteps. Instead, he pursued his education in economics. That was a subject he loved most and it landed him a good job at one of the largest banks in Australia. His ambition and hard work had paid off and he received a promotion as manager at one of the downtown branches. Now, contemplating whether he should offer a position for Katie, he looked at her curiously.

"Tell me, Katie, just how good is your English?"

Katie shrugged and muttered, "It depends.... ."

"All right, if you don't mind, I'd like to find out. Will you be a good sport and have a conversation with me in English?"

"Sure, but I warn you, the fun will be yours, not mine."

"Oh, I won't be too hard on you," Frank reassured her. Then he carefully selected some words from an everyday conversation, pretending that he was a bank teller.

At first Katie was nervous, but other than a little mixing up the order of the words, she did well. Frank was delighted.

"Katie, that's not bad. Listen, I'm the manager of the Bank of New South Wales at the Kings Cross branch. How would you like to work there as an office clerk? In other words, I'm offering you a job.

Katie could not describe how she felt. She was pleased, yet horrified.

"Oh, no!" she protested. "Mr. Nagy, I could not possibly handle a job like that. It would be an embarrassment for both of us."

Frank smiled and dismissed it with a wave of his hand. "Let me be the judge of that. And please, call me Frank. To begin with, you wouldn't work with the public. There are many kinds of jobs that you could do, I'm sure."

"Well, you probably know best, Frank." She said. "Only, I don't want you to get into any trouble on my account."

"No, I won't. First, you'll go through a good training, so there is nothing to worry about. Now, getting back to your job, you have a good bus service from here. You won't even have to get a transfer."

Katie laughed, "You're talking as if I already have a job."

"That's true. But it is because I'm the boss, and it's up to me to decide. Anyway, I'll let you know in a day or two."

Having settled that, Frank felt good and he started to talk about Sydney, describing his favorite places for entertainment and restaurants that he would like to take Katie in the near future. He spoke eagerly about his hobbies, like collecting stamps, playing chess and his love of good books.

Katie's head was buzzing with this sudden development. On one hand, she was pleased with the outcome, but at the same time, she was curious as to how far she should go in appreciating it. She responded to his enthusiasm with caution, revealing very little about her life in Hungary. She certainly did not wish to talk about Andrew. But she would talk gladly about the love of reading good books, which she preferred over television any time...

An hour later they turned and went back. Frank assured her that he would get back, concerning her job.

* * *

The following evening Frank stopped by the Erdelyis' home and ran up to the front door in a happy frame of mind. Surprised at seeing him so soon, Mrs. Erdelyi showed him to the sitting room where Katie was reading. After a friendly greeting, Frank told her that she had a job at the bank as an office clerk.

Katie's face lit up. "Oh, really? Frank, thank you," she said happily, and on the spur of the moment, she kissed him on the cheek.

"You are welcome," he said, pleasantly surprised. Then while explaining the work in detail, a beautiful vision of their being together danced through his mind.

Knowing nothing about it, the Erdelyis were surprised. It was a job that was worth waiting for, and Katie deserved it. Especially Annie had a reason to be happy. Frank was a good looking, smart man with a good future, and she saw him as an excellent prospect for a husband. As far as she was concerned, Katie could not hope for a better man. And one would be blind not to see that Frank was smitten with her.

The only thing she feared was that Katie was still carrying a torch for Andrew. She watched silently how Katie was suffering; the way she was still dreaming, waiting for a miracle. It was sheer craziness, but at times it seemed as though she had expected to bump into him on the street. She simply could not shake off the idea of losing Andrew. A few times Annie tried to convince Katie that the past was gone and done with, and her attitude was unreasonable. She would not listen. In their heated arguments, Katie always put forth such a stubborn, defying front.

"Just because I deserted Andrew, my feelings for him will never change," she would say. "As far as I'm concerned, he is still alive. And I know he loves me as much as I love him."

To get through to her seemed hopeless. So in that frame of mind, Annie had resigned herself to the hope that only time would cure her.

But now, as if God-sent, Frank had come into her life with this unexpected offer. It gave her a renewed hope that he might be able to jolt Katie out of her obsession. It was high time for her to live a normal life.

19

IF THERE IS WILL . . .

WHEN THE ENGLISH COURSE HAS ENDED in St. Catharines, the students received their diplomas at an elaborate ceremony. Having been together for almost a year, the students came to feel like one big family. On the basis of equality, friendships were formed among strangers, therefore the parting was a certain mix of sadness, and a sigh of relief.

It became natural for Andrew and Margaret to sit beside each other, helping and laughing—making life so much easier. They really enjoyed each other's company. So when Andrew came to Margaret to say good-bye, the parting was a sad one.

"Well, Margaret, I think we're both glad the course is over, but on a personal level, I'm truly sorry that we have to part. What makes it more painful is that I always looked forward to coming to this class, knowing that you would be here. I'm going to miss you a great deal."

"I'm going to miss you, too. Without you, I'm sure I'd have had a miserable time. But your friendship made this struggle a more pleasant experience. Thanks for your help."

"It was my pleasure." Then with a searching look in his eyes, he said, "Good luck in building your home." They kissed each other and he jumped into his car. After putting it in gear, he waved at her through the open window, and drove off.

During the course one of his French classmates told Andrew that he should go to Elliot Lake, because there are rich uranium mines with plenty of good-paying jobs.

Since I know your goal, that is what you should do."

Although drifting from place to place was not his idea of living, armed with much improved English, Andrew decided that Elliot Lake would be his next move. A man has to go where the job possibilities are. The following day he told Mr. Balogh that it was time to move on.

Somewhat surprised, Balogh turned his head. "Well, I guess it was wishful thinking that you would stay, but I wish you good luck, Andrew," Balogh said.

Andrew was touched. "Well, it was nice while it lasted. I'll always remember you with great affection. Thanks for everything, and have an enjoyable retirement," he said, then, after a warm handshake, he was gone. With an Ontario map spread out on the seat, his adventure to Northern Ontario's rolling landscape had begun.

It was late afternoon when he arrived. The first thing he had to do was to find a motel. He smiled at the thought of how his life became connected to motels. After taking a room, he wanted to look around and get acquainted with the city. He was not particularly impressed with its appearance, but it will do for a while, he thought.

In the morning, before he went job-hunting, he went to the coffee shop across the street for breakfast. When he approached the first mining company, luck was on his side and was offered a job as a laborer. The clerk told him that the job will be hard, but the salary would be $1.25 per hour. Andrew was impressed with that, as it was the highest he had received so far.

"That's fine," Andrew said.

Another clerk showed him around, explaining to Andrew that those rows of bunkhouses were for the workers, and a few days later he will get a room, too. There was a central canteen where the workers could eat or take out a meal.

This time his tools were pick and shovel, and the work was hard indeed. Although Andrew exercised every morning in Niagara Falls, he felt the miss of physical work. Also, with the summer heat and humidity, this work had also had a way to take its toll on him. After the day was over, he was exhausted.

But being alert, it did not take long to have acquainted with the place. He soon visited the electrical installation department. Finding the supervisor, Andrew explained that he had some experience in the electrical field, and asked if he could be transferred to this section.

Rubbing his forehead, the supervisor looked at him doubtfully. "I'll tell you something, young man. The kind of jobs we're handling here are quite different from what you've been doing," he said. "But I'll see if I can find something here for you, and I'll get back to you." He took down Andrew's name and the section in which he was working. It did not look promising, but Andrew thanked him politely and left.

To his great surprise, Andrew did not have to wait long. Several days later he received a notification to come to the office, for he had been transferred to the electrical department, as an assistant.

Andrew could not have been happier. He was not only getting rid of the pick and shovel, but his pay had increased also. And along with it was some opportunity for working overtime.

After the transfer, he worked under the guidance of a man in his fifties, named Ernie Golding. He was not much of a talker, but a decent man, and he liked Andrew for his diligence. One day, when they were on recess, Andrew told him how much he wanted to become an electrical technician. Ernie listened quietly, then he said that if he wanted it so badly, he should go to Ottawa and enroll for the course at Algonquin College.

"Really?" Andrew said, storing his advice in the back of his mind. This gave him an incentive for saving as much money as he could, so he would be self-supporting while learning his trade. Because he had no doubts about it, this is what he was going to do. He already had some savings, but the overtime helped him greatly to reach his financial goal.

However, there was one drawback at this place that annoyed him. There was a very mixed ethnic group of people working there. That alone would not bother him, except that their diversity resulted in ill feelings, jealousy and prejudices. And the hostilities had been manifested in drunken fights, especially on the weekends. After an evening of drinking, rambunctious fights were sparked at the drop of a hat.

Knowing the trouble that fighting had got him into before, Andrew had no desire to get involved in another one. He drank moderately, and made every effort to keep away from such gatherings.

Yet, because of his moderate lifestyle, some workers criticized him. Once he heard that he was called a "snobbish"

Hungarian. He just ignored it.

By now Andrew had another good friend, Istvan Lovas. They met by accident in the canteen. As Lovas carried his food to his table, someone hit his elbow by accident and he spilled his coffee. The man apologized, but Lovas muttered an obscenity in Hungarian, which Andrew overhead.

"Hey buddy, I wouldn't advise you to repeat those words in English," Andrew laughed.

Surprised that his Hungarian had been understood, Lovas looked at him and started to laugh. Then he sat down beside Andrew. They were about the same age. The next pleasant surprise was that he also came from Budapest. When they found out that both of them had been freedom fighters, they hit it off.

Having so much in common, their past was a priceless bond. They spent many evenings in Lovas' room, talking or playing chess, while reminiscing those troubled days. Lovas told him that he had been fighting in Buda..

"I was there at the Moricz Zsigmond Square fighting with the students against the Russians. Then we moved to defend the Castle Hill But you know, we don't mention it often enough that girls fought with us. I couldn't believe the heroism some of them displayed."

Andrew agreed. By analyzing the revolution, they realized that it had to happen. "We, who have lived and suffered beneath the heavy foot of Soviet Communism, did our part to slow down their spreading lies about how free we were. Just imagine, two hundred thousand Hungarian refugees will be reporting all over the world what Communism is like. Living in a free country, we have learned what freedom means. And if life had taught us anything, it was that we have to fight evil —*all evils.*

* * *

Although the Hungarian revolution was a thing of the past, news about it still appeared occasionally in the newspapers. One day Andrew was standing in line in the canteen, waiting at the cashier to pay for his supper. Behind him two young Canadian were discussing a familiar subject—the concept of a freedom fighter. One of them held a newspaper, which dealt with the anniversary of the Hungarian revolution, showing a Soviet tank that was captured by the freedom fighters in 1956.

"I get a kick out of this word, *freedom fighter*," said one of them. "What does that mean? As far as I can see, they lost the war to the Soviets so they were there rightfully. Then some rebels decided to start a revolution because they disagreed with the rulings of their government. Based on that, we could have a revolution here any day, ha-ha-ha."

"You can say that again," said his friend, also laughing.

"Look here, it says, thousands and thousands of people were killed for trying to overturn the government. But had they won the revolution, I bet they would probably have done the same dirty work they had been rebelling against. And they called themselves 'freedom fighters'."

What can one say to stupidity? Andrew thought. What do they know about the fate of Peter Kardos, George and the thousands of kids the AVO had slaughtered? They haven't got the faintest idea of what it would take to convince them that they are blind? Forgetting that he could get himself into trouble, he turned and faced them.

"Well, my friends," he said, "it seems you think you know what you're talking about. But since I was one of those freedom-fighters, I hate to say it but you're not only ignorant about the subject, but badly informed."

"Oh really?" one said provokingly, with piercing black eyes.

"Really. But let me tell you this. In this country where you have the means to fight back by free election, you could not possibly know the meaning of oppression. And yes, we were willing to die for the same freedom you are enjoying here. However, I wonder if you'd be willing to do the same."

"Now just a minute," said the black-eyed man angrily, but his friend calmed him down with a wave of his hand.

"Listen, I don't want to argue with you," Andrew said amicably, "but I could not help hearing what you just said. All I meant to say was that you should count your blessings, for unlike in my country, you have the freedom to express your opinion without fear. So have a good day," he said with a smile, then turned and left.

* * *

It was a murky, rainy Friday evening in November when Andrew left Lovas and went to the canteen. By the time he finished his supper, the rain had finally ceased, giving way to a sullen grey sky. On his way back, Andrew saw two young miners approaching him, each holding a bottle of beer. Their loud voices and swaying ways of walking indicated that they were drunk.

Andrew stayed on the side of the muddy footpath trying to give them enough room to pass, but he saw that the two men's intention was to walk deliberately into him, attempting to force him off the path. Andrew could have stepped aside, but their insolent manner infuriated him. It was obvious they wanted to provoke a fight, and it just was not in Andrew's nature to let anyone pushing him around. One of them shouted in a besotted voice, "Get out of the way, you dumb bastard," lifting his bottle to hit Andrew.

So no matter how much he had feared this might happen, the fickle finger of fate made it impossible for him to avoid the fight. Andrew jumped out of his reach, at the same time punching him in the stomach. The man gasped, his mouth wide open as though he was suffocating, then lunged forward and fell to the ground. But Andrew did not have the chance to stop the other hitting him from behind on the skull.

Andrew was dazed for a moment, then recovered enough to grab him and they started wrestling in the mud. During their struggle the other one regained his strength and inflicted a nasty kick to Andrew's head. The blow knocked him unconscious, and his attackers disappeared into the night. He didn't know how long he lay there, but when he regained consciousness, there was a roaring buzz in his throbbing head. As he was struggling to get up, Lovas came running to him, uttering a cry of fury. He helped Andrew to his feet and led him to his room.

"Do you know who did this?" Lovas asked him, while he cleaned his wound.

"Yeah, I recognized one of them," Andrew said, wincing.

"Don't worry, we'll get the bastards," Lovas said, as he applied a cold pack to the wound.

20

IN SCHOOL AGAIN

FORTUNATELY THE INCIDENT OCCURRED on the weekend, so Andrew missed only one day of work. When he was well again, the two friends worked on their plan carefully for weeks, quietly studying the attackers' every move and habits. It was important not to arouse suspicion in the two miners. They even worked out a good alibi, just in case, then one night they surprised them. It was a bloody fight, and Andrew hoped it would be his very last one. The two miners needed a few days to get back to work.

Spring arrived swiftly. The snow had already melted, exposing the gray grass, and in the warmer places a mild thaw set in. Andrew felt that he have saved enough money and decided to move on. He resigned and he was on his way to Ottawa. The sky was bright blue with scattered drifting clouds. Light warm breezes wafting in from the south, swaying the multi-colored wildflowers and violets on the hillside. On the branches of the trees, which not long ago were covered with heavy snow, singing birds were celebrating the season. It was obvious that spring was fighting successfully for possession of the earth.

Andrew drove leisurely, enjoying the country-sight. The road was bordered by freshly blooming trees, and he was passing by brilliant sky-tinted lakes that reminded him of Lake Balaton. What could be more beautiful than spring, he thought.

Arriving in Ottawa, the place gave him the impression of a charming, peaceful town with plenty of breathing space. The Ottawa River ran between Ottawa and Hull, dividing the two provinces Ontario and Quebec. He liked the Parliament Buildings, but shocked by the ugly paper factory across the river. It was an eyesore!

Once again he was grateful for the motel system in Canada; a constant reminder how unknown this lifestyle was in Hungary. He turned into one at the West End.

The next day he went to the college to find out what his chances were of taking the electrical course. Problems arose immediately. The registrar told him that his Hungarian diploma was not recognized by the Canadian school system, and if he wanted to attend college, he would have to take a high school equivalency course in mathematics, physics and chemistry first.

"If you have the basic knowledge of these subjects, you could probably finish the course within six months. The main purpose of the course is to determine whether you have the aptitude for the field you want to enter. The English course you've taken will be valuable, I'm sure."

Andrew was taken aback. Mumbling a confused thank you, he left the office. When on the way to Ottawa, he had some nagging fear that certain problems might arise, but he was not prepared for this. An unsure feeling of what to do next hung over him like a dark cloud.

Driving back to the motel, he thought grimly, now I'm back to square one! As he passed by those beautiful suburban homes, he watched with envy as contented-looking owners watered their lawns. He felt as if he were in a dark tunnel; but there must be a light at the other end. And he would get there! The challenge intrigued his pride. *The greatest failure is to fail to try*, he had read some-where. He bit his lips with stubborn determination. Well, if he had got this far, he was not going to take the back seat! He would not let any wretched hindrance impede his progress.

The next day he went back to the office and filled out the application for the course. That being done, he bought a map, the **Ottawa Journal,** and looked for a cheap apartment. He found one in the Britannia area. After moving in, he studied the ads in the paper, searching for odd jobs to consolidate his financial position. He was not sure how long he would have to wait for his acceptance. So he mowed lawns, cleaned windows, gardened—anything that came his way. But instead of charging by the hour, he became a contractor. If he charged $10.00 for a three-four hours job, he could make $3.00 an hour! So the money was much better this way.

Then one day when he returned home from a grueling day of work clipping hedges in the Rockcliffe Park area, he found an official letter in the mailbox. It was the acceptance of his application for a six-month course that would begin in September.

He jumped in the air triumphantly. "I've got it!" he shouted.

So he found himself in school once again. As part of his spiritual preparedness, he decided to go to a nearby library. Since he was now able to read English, it enriched his life. He was fascinated by this unknown world of English literature and became an avid visitor to the library. Among so many, he loved reading books by A.J. Cronin and Howard Fast.

Meantime, he discovered that Ottawa was a typical government town with its large office buildings filled with civil servants. Having worked for those well-to-do civil servants before entering school, one retired civil servant told him jokingly: Ottawa was a city of the spoiled and the privileged, where people were living *"high on the hog."* It is a foregone conclusion that the government provides them a lifetime of financial security. Andrew laughed when he said: "In our youth, we step into the government office with our right foot, and 35 years later we step out with the left foot—as a have-it-made, proud retired Civil Servant."

* * *

Andrew successfully finished the evening course. And with the diploma in his hand, he was accepted for the electro-technician course at Algonquin College. The joy overwhelmed him, as he felt that this new world had lifted him out of the dark days into paradise.

They had highly qualified teachers, and the students had their theoretical sessions where they have learned the basics of reading diagrams. Although the mental preparation was a very important part, they also had a well-equipped workshop with the necessary electrical appliances, where students could go and learn the practical applications of their subjects. This was the room Andrew loved the most and felt at home in it.

He took his studying seriously, and hardly noticed that it was spring again. During the summer break he did not want to waste time, and he found temporary employment in a radio and television store as an assistant technician. He was so happy to have found a job in this field that he did not care if he was paid or not. He would have been happy to work for nothing, just to have an opportunity to practice.

* * *

There was a restaurant close to Andrew's apartment that was famous for its pizza. Andrew dropped in once in awhile when he got tired of eating sandwiches. Among the many waitresses, one caught his attention. He had seen her before, but this was the first time he sat in her section. Her accent revealed her European background and Andrew thought that she might even be Hungarian. In her black-and-red uniform she looked exceedingly pretty. She was also perky and witty. When she talked to a customer, her easygoing manner and her sense of humor cast a magic spell. But what made an indelible impression on him were her teasing, sparkling, eyes—a roguish quality, a sure sign that she liked mixing business with pleasure. As she moved confidently between the tables, her provokingly out-thrusting breasts made her look like she had a million-dollar body.

"What an interesting pretty girl!" Andrew murmured to himself as he sat in the dim, smoke-filled corner, waiting to be served. When she finally came to his table and asked him in a charming voice what this gentleman would like to order.

Using the teasing voice of his own, Andrew said: "Before I eat, I'd like to know if you're married, whether or not I could have a date with you, and what's your nationality?"

Surprised, she burst into laughter. "Whaaw! Hold on just a minute, mister. That much curiosity could get you into the slammer. This is not a private information service, but are you sure you need to know all this?"

"Yes, I'm sure. But if it's a crime in wanting to know you, I withdraw before you sue me. Although I hope my lucky star will rescue me."

Pen and ordering pad in hand, she glanced around, checking how busy things were.

"Look, sir," she said decidedly, "since this **is** a free country, you committed no crime. I certainly don't want to disappoint your lucky star, but I'm too busy to talk right now. So why don't you come back after nine o'clock? (Now she switched to Hungarian.) Then I'll tell you all you want to know in Hungarian."

"That's what I thought," Andrew said without surprise. "I'll be back, but for now, I'd like to have a small pizza, please."

When Andrew was ready to leave, he left a generous tip. On

the way out their eyes met and he lifted his finger with a *"see you later"* motion, and she nodded, smiling.

*

Andrew was walking up and down in front of the restaurant and at one turn he almost collided with her.

"Ooops, good evening, curious man," she greeted him.

"Oh good evening." Andrew said, surprised. "Without the uniform you're even more beautiful. I could hardly recognize you."

"Thank you. I hope you were not waited long."

"No, no." Andrew said, falling into step with her. "Well, for a proper start, my name is Andrew Dombrady."

"Catherine Foldesy," she said, "but people usually call me Cathy."

The name hit Andrew like a bolt of lightning, and he stopped walking. **"Ca...thy?"** he said in disbelief.

"Yes, why? Did I evoke some ghost from your memory?"

Andrew kept shaking his head. "You sure did. It's unbelievable! Oh not your name, but the coincidence. Would you believe that I had a girlfriend in Budapest whose name was also Katie. Of course it wasn't spelled 'Cathy' like they call you here."

"In Budapest—I was born there too—my name was also Katie, but I changed it when I came to Canada. For some reason, I like it better, maybe because it gives me a new identity. I don't know. Anyway, enough of this," Cathy said, looking at him searchingly. "Now with your surprise you made me curious, Andr... can I call you Andrew?"

"I insist."

"Did I strike a raw nerve? Is she your...sweetheart?"

"Let's just say she was. I had to leave the country in a hurry and I couldn't say goodbye to her. I wrote her but the letter came back unanswered. And I haven't heard from her since; I have no idea what happened to her. And it seems I will never know." God, how it hurt to say it, he thought. "For all I know, she might be married by now. Anyway, as you see, my fate seems to be chained to Katies. Perhaps it is because they're so beautiful, like you."

"Thanks again. It's nice to know that in some ways I measure up to competition."

"Well, if you want to compete, it indicates that this is my lucky day; it gives me some hope."

"Perhaps, but I detect you still love her."

"I'd be lying if I deny it. She was the loveliest girl I've ever known. But that's irrelevant. One can't live on memories forever. Right now I want to know you. So let's talk about you."

"Life is interesting," Cathy said, as if talking to herself. "Take dreams and realities, for example. Usually they proceed in different directions. By the way, what are you doing in Ottawa?"

"I'm in school, studying to be a radio and television technician. But you have a way of evading my question. I still don't know if you are married or single."

"I'm single. I had a boyfriend, but we broke up a few months ago. I hope that answers your question. As for talking about myself, I either say too much or nothing. I prefer the nothing."

"I would be pleased if you would choose the *'too much'*."

"Ah, I know, you're the curious type," Cathy said with a wry smile. "Well, I don't even know where to start. Unfortunately, both my parents are dead."

"Accept my deepest condolences."

"Thank you. My father was abducted by the AVO one night in 1951. When the nationwide deportation was going on to work on the farm, he was furious because one of his best friends was on the deportation list. A communist worker overhead him cursing Rakosi and that was the last evening we saw him alive. Two plainclothes secret police came for him in the middle of the night. I'm sure you remember those terrible years when the midnight abductions hung over our heads. We used to call it *bellfright*."

"I sure do."

"Well, danger is the currency of living, and some of us pay for it more than others. It was not enough that we lost him, but being a daughter of a man who was considered an enemy of the Communist System, you can imagine the fate that awaited us. My poor mother couldn't cope with the tragedy, the grief killed her two years later. As a young girl, my heart was torn by pain, too deep for words. I'm happy I was able to leave the country."

"Oh, dear God, another tragic story out of the millions."

"That's right. This is why the words *earth shattering* or *shocking* are meaningless; nothing can surprise me anymore. The wounds will heal in time, but you can see why I'm reluctant to discuss the past, it's too painful."

Andrew nodded. Poor girl, he thought, what a dreadful burden she is carrying in her heart!

Just as if she read his mind, Cathy continued, "From all those bitter experiences, I've learned that there is no sense of taking life too seriously. After all, no one walks out of it alive."

Andrew laughed. "That's an interesting philosophy. It reminds me of an anecdote. When a millionaire was asked why he would want to make more millions, he couldn't take it with him. He thought for a moment then said, 'Then I won't go there'."

Cathy laughed. "Wouldn't it be nice if it were up to us to decide how long we want to live?"

"It would be nice only if we could stay young and healthy."

This subject seemed to fascinate them, and they began to dream a little on what life would be like if they were millionaires.

"Oh, I don't know if I really would like to be a millionaire," Cathy said. "To me, the main purpose of having lots of money is to keep you from having to do a job you really hate."

"I could think up many worthy reasons why money could make me happier," Andrew said. Then they speculated on how they would live if money did not matter. They would travel around the world and see every corner of the universe. "Life would be a continuous holiday. But it would make me happy to help my loved ones. I truly believe that money would not "spoil" me.

"Oh, yes, but the statistics say that somehow you would have more enemies than true friends," Cathy said.

"Could be. However, it's easy to say all this, for we know that we will never have a chance to prove it."

"How true. Well, it was nice to float in a dream-world over the rainbow where you can reach for the stars, pretending to be whatever you wished. There is a saying that what you never had you can't miss. We've just proved that it is not true. But having been in heaven and landed safely back in the real world, I'd like to invite you for Sunday dinner."

"Cathy, that's a wonderful idea! Thank you."

* * *

The following Sunday at six o'clock, Andrew stood at Cathy's doorstep holding a bouquet of roses and a bottle of wine. After ringing the bell, Cathy greeted him with her charming smile.

"Hi, Andrew, come in."

"Hi, Cathy. Here is my token appreciation for the invitation, and also my modest contribution toward the meal," he grinned, handing her the roses and the wine.

"Oh, thank you, Andrew, they're beautiful. But you should not go into so much trouble, you know."

"It was no trouble at all."

"Well, it just shows that you know how to please a woman," she said, kissing him on the cheek.

Cathy's inviting words brought back pleasant memories. After those long, wandering years of struggle to survive, somehow he felt "out of touch" with socializing. It was a wonderful feeling to belong to someone again, and he felt alive.

"The supper will be ready soon. So while I put on the finishing touch, why don't you make yourself comfortable in the living room? You may turn on the TV or read some of the magazines if you like."

Andrew thanked her and looked around. He observed how clean and tidy the place was. The living room smelled fresh and inviting. The furniture and the pictures on the wall struck a note of enticing coziness. In one corner, beside the TV and a rack of records, there was a stereo with a turntable.

"My compliment to the host." Andrew said. "You work so hard and yet you keep this place so neat and spotless."

"Oh it's nothing, really, "Cathy said, pleased. "This is such a small place, as you can see. Besides, there are no children to mess it up."

Then she left him with his thoughts. Andrew picked up a magazine, but he hardly had time to leaf through it when Cathy was back.

"If you're ready, the supper is on the table."

The roast chicken with baked potatoes and French salad was expertly served.

"Hmmm, this is delicious," Andrew complimented.

"I hoped you would like it. You know, I have never met anybody yet who didn't like roast chicken."

"I believe you. This is one of the things I was missing in exile: my mother's Hungarian cooking. She was great at it."

"I can imagine."

The wine went well with the good food, and it contributed to the mellowing of the atmosphere between them.

"And now I wish to drink a toast to our friendship," Andrew said, lifting his glass. "Hopefully a lasting one."

"Hopefully," Cathy said. "Also to your success. Cheers!"

After the drink Andrew said, "You know, it just crossed my mind that coming from the same city makes a great difference."

"It sure does. Not only that, but we share the same language and the same loneliness, everything..."

It was exciting to reminisce their lives in Budapest, recalling places they both used to go. Cathy said she used to love to go to the Gellert public bath, and walk up the hill enjoying the lovely view of the city.

"Yes, I liked that, too. But one of my fondest memories was going to the People's Stadium to watch some of those great soccer games. Next to that, good movies, the unreachable glitters were my great passion. Besides some good Hungarians, the Piccadilly, some great James Cagney gangster movies and Charles Boyer with Diane Durbin stand out in my memory..."

"Ah, yes, they were great fun." Cathy said nostalgically.

From the living room soft music filtered into the dining room and Cathy suggested moving there. Seeing those records again, Andrew wanted to know what kind of music she liked.

"Oh, I love all kinds of music, as long as it **is *music*** and not just noise. Naturally I love the old Hungarian tunes too. My favorites are those good old hits from Katie Karady."

"But besides those great nostalgic songs, Janos Sardy, Imre Laszlo and Hanna Honti were my favorites, the biggest Hungarian stars," Andrew said.

Suddenly Cathy stood up and put one of Karady's records on the turntable.

"It's useless to run from your fate..." Karady sang in her seductive voice. Andrew was a teenager when those songs were new but he remembered them well. They listened for a few minutes, then Cathy glanced at Andrew flirtatiously and asked if he would like to dance.

"Sure," Andrew said, and he took her eagerly in his arms. Cathy edged close to him, her arm around his neck, moving gracefully to the rhythm of the tango. Meantime, the song changed.

"Accept me darling just the way I am,

It's the best advice I can recommend..."

It was an enticing song, and Cathy sang along with the record. Whispering the melody, Cathy's soft lips were almost touched his face. As their bodies pressed together, the sense of contact was electrifying, pure delight. Inevitably their burning lips met and pressed together hungrily as their bodies drew closer and closer. Feeling Andrew's hardened manhood heightened Cathy's pleasure. She moaned with a delicate shudder that drove Andrew to something so explosive that he couldn't stand it any longer. He had never wanted a woman more in his life. It was impossible to continue dancing.

He gazed into her glowing eyes and groaned, "Oh Cathy, I want you so!"

Cathy's feverish glance issued a tacit invitation. As she led him to the bedroom, Andrew stole a sideward glance at her. He found it hard to believe that it was really happening. Blushing with embarrassment, he confessed that he had never slept with a woman before.

A pleasant surprise flashed across Cathy's face and gave him an intimate smile. "Oh that doesn't matter a bit," she said as they turned into the bedroom.

21

STRUGGLE OF THE SOUL

KATIE WAS WORKING AT the bank from nine to five, and she loved her job. At the beginning she had been timid and shy, but to her surprise her colleagues went out of their way to help her. Naturally, it did not take much to figure out that Frank must have had something to do with it. Soon she felt at ease, and was happy for earning her living. At the same time it filled a valuable void: it was a pleasant substitute for socializing.

Naturally Frank stopped at her desk occasionally, always making the appearance that the visits were for official reasons. It was with the highest reverence that he hides the obvious, indicating his concern whether everything was going all right...Although Katie appreciated his "playing it cool," but his attitude did not fool her a bit. Should he came on more strongly, she was not sure how she would handle him. Because even though so much time had past, it did not make any difference, she was still longing for Andrew as much as ever. The power of love kept her going.

However, sometimes she wished that she wouldn't think about him so much, but how could she not, when her memories were so vivid. She was obsessed—feeling that her heart was chained to Andrew's and was unable to break it.

Without Andrew, the surroundings, the city of Sydney, everything around her was still alien to her. People were only moving objects that meant little to her; she could not relate to them. Subconsciously she knew what the solution should be: to integrate, accept reality. But she stubbornly clung to her hopeless dreams. How she wanted to believe that after the rain the sun is always shines...

Her favorite pastime remained sitting on the step of her house, her arms clasped around her knees in the pure, calm silent nights, looking at the flickering stars. Since with her mental power she could bring back the past, oh, what a bittersweet pleasure it was to relive those memories! In her imagination she would be walking with Andrew on Great Boulevard, wrapped up in the corner of their own world, laughing like carefree youngsters. Then, with a moan, she would close her eyes, desperately trying to dispel the longing that was tearing her very soul apart.

A few years ago Katie made another attempt to write to Andrew. She knew the chances of getting there was slim because the Baross Street was a long one. The letter came back with a rubber stamp: **ADDRESS INCOMPLETE**. At times the uncertainty planted the terrifying fear into her mind that she would never have a life with Andrew. Life is so cruel, she mused. She remembered the New Year's Eve party when Andrew talked about a *two-year plan to get married*. How time flies! Two years...and poor Andrew wondered if they could wait *that long*. Hah! Fate has its way of altering people's plans. Meanwhile, instead of marriage, she had learned how to cry without tears. Loneliness stripped away the last vestige of self-confidence; she felt that the past image of herself no longer existed. It was with the passing time that she felt she had become someone else, she had yet to discover and learn to know. Some of her dark moments were conducive to question of God's existence. Then the thoughts terrified her as being unfaithful. She must not lose faith and hope!

Living in a free world where the lifestyle was so different from that of Hungary, she was surprised to see in magazines and in television how *open* sex was. The movies were constantly highlighting human sexuality. Being young with a healthy desire for the opposite sex, naturally she was aware of her sexuality. She had long discovered the pleasure of touching herself in the bathtub, and she had difficulty suppressing the agonizing fire. So she turned to her secret touching to release her frustrations.

She did not look deliberately for movies with explicit love-scenes, but when she saw some heated love plays, she fantasized that she was making love with Andrew. It drove her to a painful physical craving, and she could not stop the dampness she felt in her crotch. "Ohhh Andrew," she sighed longingly.

As the months and years passed, the thought of getting old made her fearful that she was missing out a lot on life. After all we're young only once, she thought. Most of the girls her age were married by now and had children. There were times when she had played with the idea of taking what life is offering her, no matter how she felt, because, brokenhearted or not, life has to go on. Thoughts like these led her to the idea that maybe she should give Frank a chance. But the next moment, because she had a strict moral belief that having an affair was unforgivable, she rebelled, for at heart she was a hopeless romantic.

* * *

Frank soon asked her out for a date, and she had no reason to refuse because they were friends. She could not deny that Frank had a pleasant personality. Her only problem was that she knew Frank was in love with her, but she was not in love with him. Oh, she absent, musing look. Sometimes there was a faraway look on her face, as she immersed in her thoughts, and let out a deep sight. He noticed that when talking to her, occasionally she did not hear him, and asked what he had said. There was a confused, even hurt look in her eyes, almost like grief; something that indicated some inward suffering. He didn't dwell on it, although he was tempted to ask her about it. He had seen already that Katie could be charming and laughing one minute, and burst into tears in the next, for no apparent reason. But if she did not want to talk about it, he understood. Being uprooted from her familiar environment and thrown into a strange world, could leave a lasting scar in her heart. It only made him more considerate.

. Naturally he would have been happier if she shared her problems, for he would know if he could help her. First, he would be an interested listener, but most of all, he would try to make her feel more at home in Sydney. He wished more than anything that Katie was in love with him, but he did not for a moment pretend that this was the case. It hurt somewhat, but he was determined to win her heart. And when that day comes, my God, it would be a wonderful payment for his patience—a dream come through. In the meantime, he would give her all the support and encouragement she needed, because just being with her was all worth it.

* * *

Because Frank had a car and knew the city well, Katie let him decide where they would go. They had already been to Lavender Bay, which was a nice place to stroll around. It had a good view to the city and the Harbour Bridge. But when the summer heat was upon them, they headed for Bondi Beach. It was a popular and beautiful beach with its long sandy shores, and so close to the city. In the near distance luxurious villas mushroomed, set against the backdrop of the city.

It was a marvelous sunny day, and the huge crowd of sunbathers had already overrun the shore. The beach shimmered in the golden rays of the late morning sun, under which the sand glittered like millions of dazzling diamonds.

Katie and Frank plopped down at the far end of the crowd to their favorite spot where they liked to sunbathe. With a portable garden chair in hand, Katie settled down with a book to read, while Frank went swimming. But before she started to read, with an air of detachment, she let her eyes wander over the crowd. Then, as she read for a while, she heard some soft sounds of moaning and chuckling. Driven by curiosity, she looked over the sea of sunbathers until she saw a young couple entwined on a blanket, kissing passionately, blissfully oblivious to the people around them.

The scene brought back tender moments of intimacy with Andrew at Lake Balaton. But that was at night with only the stars watching them. She concluded that what could be a beautiful thing between two people in private, was an obscene act in public. To her, intimacy was a private matter and not for public display. However, despite how she felt, she could not help glancing furtively toward them, like a thief in a jewelry store.

A while after, Frank came out of the water and looked at Katie with silent admiration. He loved to watch her beautiful figure, her bright, jet-black hair on which the sun glittered playfully; her long black eyelashes blinking against the sun. She smiled at him as he was teasing her for not going to swim with him.

"Too much sun could turn you into a wrinkled prune, sweetheart," he said. Then he noticed the kissing couple and glanced back at them longingly. "How I envy them," he muttered with an obvious hint. But Katie pretended not to hear it. Hesitating over whether to settle down or not, Frank decided to propose a walk along the beach.

Katie agreed eagerly. As they strolled along slowly on the soft warm sand, they heard music drifting from a portable radio. It was playing a popular song that was one of Frank's favorite tunes.

"*Look, look, my heart is an open book...*"

Somehow everything around him was a reminder of what was missing between them. "Yes," Frank sighed wishfully. "My heart, too, is an open book. How happy I would be to hear the same thing from you."

Katie took a deep breath. "All I can say is that my book is a confused mess, figuratively speaking. And somehow I can't seem to put it in order. I'm sorry if I'm disappointing you." She did not wish to explain further. The song, however, brought back the memory of Lake Balaton, when Andrew had opened his heart to her. Seeing him in her mind, a smile flashed across her face. Comparing Andrew's eloquent prose to Frank's confession, Frank's was a colorless imitation.

"How I wish you to give me a chance to help you sort out your mysterious confusion, whatever it is."

But all Frank's voice did was to ruffle the surface of her secret pool of thoughts, and her daydreaming was broken. Glancing at him with a sad face, she repeated what she already had told him.

"Forgive me, Frank, but I can't help it... I thought that I'd have gotten over the past by now, but my heart is still in Budapest... But I like being with you, honest ... "

Her stammering voice broke off, as she knew that actually it was Andrew she was talking about. Nevertheless, she thought that he is right. Instead of spraying dust into his eyes, she should be more honest with him.

A flicker of painful emotion rushed through Frank anyway. He expected more than just a lukewarm "I like you" reply. He was contemplating whether or not he should pursue the matter. But Katie's gloomy face wilted his confidence, and he decided that this was not the right moment.

They continued walking, and by the time they left the crowd behind, Frank was able to change her mood. He was good at finding something to talk about, and Katie seemed to enjoy his easy bantering. This time he had a witty story about what happened in the staff dining room.

"Just imagine, Katie, when that big-bellied Mike carried his hot soup on the tray and collided with a secretary. All the soup spilled onto his pants."

Katie, widening her cherry-red mouth that crinkled her pretty nose and burst into laughter. "Oh, that poor man. I can imagine the horror on his face."

Frank loved when Katie laughed. She had regained her easy, carefree frame of mind and seemed relaxed. This was the moment he had waited for. He was bursting with desire and just couldn't wait any longer to confess. He stopped suddenly, and against his own pledge of being content just to see her, looked at her with yearning. Then he committed the blunder of swooping her feverishly into his arms.

"Oh, Katie, by now you must know how much I love you," and he kissed her passionately before she could utter a word.

Trembling, and without responding to his kisses, she stared at him frozen, struggling to free herself. It seemed as if she were fighting off an unsavory attack. She finally freed herself and started to cry. They had exchanged casual goodnight kiss before, but never like this. And she was no good in acting.

Frank stood there with a look of sheer disbelief on his ashen face. Awkward as it was, he did not think he had gone too far, yet Katie managed to convey the feeling that Frank's behavior was out of line. He had the crushing feeling of being ridiculous. He just could not understand what the hell was wrong with kissing her? If she couldn't stand him, she should say so. He was so hurt that deep in his mind he wished to shake her and demand that she be more honest with him. Driven by a wave of anger, he grabbed her arms and shook her roughly.

"What in hell is the matter with you?" he shouted. "What is wrong in wanting to kiss you? What are you hiding? Are you a man-hater?"

Katie suppressed a laugh at his suggestion. "Frank stop it, you're hurting me!" she cried with dismay.

"That's not what I want to hear. You're treating me like a common criminal. If you don't love me, why the hell do you keep going out with me?"

"I don't know," she snapped. But she knew, of course. Her heart overflowing with secrets untold, her bosom heaved from feelings that she could not confess...That it was a duty bound affair—but she could not tell him that. Frank's words, however, made her feel as if she had been x-rayed. She never felt so cornered, and grabbed the only excuse she could think of.

"Please, Frank, take me home. I have a headache."

Frank's anger melted a little and felt embarrassed. "All right, Katie, then we go. I'm sorry for behaving like this, please forgive me. Katie dried her eyes and looked at him with a charming, conciliatory smile on her face. "I'm sorry too. But please don't rush me, for I'm not sure how I feel. I know it seems unreasonable, but I need more time and patience."

Frank sighed. Even in her sadness, all he could see was her irresistible beauty. Her beseeching smile diminished his anger and melted his heart. It enveloped him like a warm healing cloak and rekindled his love for her. What happened may have hurt him, but in his adoration, he always found the most incredible excuses to forgive her. Picking up the dangling thread of conversation, he said gently, "Well, being close to you, patience is the hardest thing you could ask. But I'll try. However, it saddens me that you have erected a wall around yourself, making it impossible to approach you. Your attitude radiates a silent message that says, 'don't touch me!' I'm sure you're holding back something; and I would like to figure out why. I wish I knew what it is that I'm up against. I never thought that I would say this, but whatever it is, I think you should pour out your heart. Trust and good communication is the key for a better understanding."

Listening to him, Katie looked into herself. She was amazed how close Frank was getting to the truth. He is right, she told herself. I must tell him my secret even if it may end our friendship. He has the right to know.

"All right, Frank," Katie said, taking a deep breath. "I've just realized how right you are. Yes, I have a secret, and I feel it would be a further insult if I keep holding it back. So I have a confession to make, but I'm not sure you'll want to hear it."

Oh my God, Frank thought, she is married already. "Go ahead."

"I hope you'll realize that what I have to confess, it is hard for me to talk about." She paused, looking into the distance while gathering her strength. "I'm sure you know that I've never led you to believe that I'm in love with you."

Frank smiled wryly, "God is my witness, you haven't."

"Well, what I'm about to say is that although I like to go out with you, I'm not ready for an intimate relationship, and marriage is not in my plan at all in the near future."

"Ohhh?...Why, are you already married or in love with someone else?"

"Not married, but yes, I am in love with someone else. I had a man in Budapest and we were very much in love. Before the revolution, we planned to get married, but what happened turned everything upside down. He took part in the fighting and I don't know what happened to him—whether he is still alive, or not. He could be dead or in Siberia, or anywhere in the world, for all I know. That is why it's so hard for me to talk about him. It seems so hopeless."

Frank looked at her, speechless.

"Good God in heaven! How can you stick to a ghost? And

how come you couldn't find out where he is, or anything?"

"It is hard to explain. Budapest lain in ruins and we had to rush to get out of the country. But what is most unbelievable is that I don't know his exact address."

"Katie, I don't mean to be harsh with you, but I'm speechless. You're chasing the rainbow. It is crazy! Still, I sure would have appreciated if you were more honest from the beginning."

"I agree, and I'm sorry that I didn't have the courage."

"You must have loved him terribly."

Whenever Andrew occupied her mind, a switch from her soul lit up her face and a familiar secret pleasure was lurking in the corner of her mouth that Frank simply could not ignore.

"Yes, and I still do."

"But you can't wait for him forever. What kind of future is there for you? None, as far as I am concerned."

"Well, it seems silly after all those years, but time will tell."

"That's not only insane, it's ridiculous."

"Probably. Still, what I'm trying to say is that it would be a great injustice to give you false hope and let you waste your time by waiting for me. I wish I could promise you more, but if you can get into a more meaningful relationship, I would not only understand, but I would recommend it. Otherwise, you'd have to accept me only as a *good friend*, without any strings attached."

Now, receiving all the answers to his puzzle, finally Frank had the picture, and he did not like it a bit. What made it worse was that Katie had shifted the responsibility on to his shoulders. He was not sure whether he gained anything by her confession. Now the decision was up to him. Then the idea began to form in his mind. He rationalized that since Andrew was a ghost of the past, he could not see any threatening danger. As long as she was willing to put up with him, he was willing to wait. He was confident that she would change her mind; she had no choice. Time was on his side. What he did not realize was that Katie's beauty pulled a rainbow-colored curtain over his eyes, and fogged up his judgment.

"Hmmm. *Friendship* only, huh?" Frank asked finally, rubbing his chin. "All right, Katie, I hear you clearly and I appreciate your frankness. Considering everything, I've decided that however hard it might be, I'm willing to take my chances. I feel that I'm not a fool in figuring out that I don't have to worry about Andrew. After this length of time there is no sense in waiting for him. In the meantime, our friendship will give us more time, during which I'll convince you how futile a dream it is to chase a ghost of the past."

"I don't know if I deserve your generosity, but thanks," she said. "I feel better knowing that I have told you the truth."

"I guess, generosity is my trademark," Frank said.

Listening to Frank, Katie suddenly felt uneasy. She did not like *his* confidence, his down-to-earth reasoning. It shook the foundation of *her confidence*. It made her wonder who was the bigger fool—whose wish fate would fulfill. She knew for sure that Frank's friendship would never supersede Andrew's love. So the dream that she must find Andrew kept persisting, and it seemed more than an obsession. "*I must be stalling for time! I must!*"

22

LOVE AFFAIR

ONCE THEIR AFFAIR STARTED, Andrew became a frequent visitor to Cathy's apartment. He could have moved in with her, but some instinct told him not to. They liked each other spiritually as well as physically, but Andrew could not say that he was in love with her. Still, enjoying their sexual compatibility made them very happy.

While both of them benefited greatly from Andrew's eagerness for sex, it became evident that Cathy was more than just a sex partner. With her skill and experience in bed, she was quite an education. She was a passionate lover, always ready, displaying her sexual desire freely, holding back nothing. She enjoyed the gift of giving as much as receiving.

The affair certainly brought a new zest into Andrew's life—like an elixir, it invigorated him physically and mentally. He will never forget the fantastic pleasure as the soft walls of her hot vagina swallowed him. He smiled at his discovery that for a man's well being, sex is as essential as breathing, realizing that sex has to be part-and-parcel of an intimate relationship. However, this convinced him further that he had to *like* his partner's personality first before he could have any physical intimacy with her. That was the main reason why he never wished to approach a prostitute: the physical act alone with a complete stranger did not appeal to him.

One day, after lovemaking he discussed the subject with Cathy, adding that now…"I just can't get enough of you."

Cathy laughed, pleased. Although she would never embarrass him by saying it, she smiled at the thought of his embarrassed apology for his clumsiness of climaxing seconds after entering her. But he had more than made up for it later.

"Well, that's wonderful news, lover," she said. "I always knew that it's true what they say, 'when you get the taste of it, you're craving for more! You're hooked. But I also agree with the rest of what you said. I, too, have to like the guy first, or I wouldn't go to bed with him. Anyway, if you're happy, then I'm the real winner here. Because while I introduced you to paradise on earth, in exchange, I've gained a sex maniac. And if the pun can be forgiven, it's just what the doctor ordered for me."

Andrew laughed, "Oh, my! You're painting me a monster."

"Having nothing to complain about, it is better if I don't boost your ego more than I already have."

In their free time they went to the Ottawa River Parkway for a leisurely stroll in one of the city's beautiful promenades. Since all the inhibitions had vanished between them, they would discuss any subject under the sun. Cathy's liberated opinion, however, sometimes surprised Andrew. She was two years older than he, but with her outlook she seemed to be way ahead of her time. One of her favorite subjects was "progressive thinking".

"You know, if two people love each other," she said, "contrary to what our grandparents wanted us to believe, an active sex life is nothing to be ashamed of. I still feel some resentment when I remember how they tried to instill guilty feelings. I don't know what it is with old age, but when they had it all; suddenly it was 'degrading' to have a sex life. It seems to me that time erases from their memories that God gave us a sex drive for two reasons: to enjoy it and to keep up the human race."

"Holy smoking catfish! What an earful you're giving me," Andrew exclaimed. "My brain wants to burst. Are you sure we came from the same country?"

Cathy laughed. "You bet. But what's that has got to do with anything?"

"Well, I can't speak for old people, for I'm sure they're enjoying sex as much as we do, providing they are healthy. But you can't belittle maturity. You even make me feel as if I'm living in the Dark Ages. You mean to say that we should have a sex life as soon as our sexual desire is aroused? In that case, I should have had it at the age of ten, at least."

"No, I'm not saying that at all," Cathy laughed, "What I'm saying is that it's okay to be sexually active as long as you're capable of taking responsibility for your actions. In other words, it shouldn't be a shame or a taboo, as if it were a sin to enjoy it *without* being married."

Suddenly Andrew started to laugh.

"What is so funny?"

"Just that I know there are people who strongly believe that sex belongs to married couples only. What would you tell them?"

"I say that's bull!" Then she smiled. "I hope you are not complaining. Anyway, to tell you the truth, I don't care much about those views. What if I don't want to get married?"

"Being a Catholic, I think the Pope would crucify you."

"Well, if you ask me, I believe in God, but I have my reasons for saying that organized religion disgusts me. Starting with wars fought on religious ground, it's loaded with conflict of interest."

"Hmmm ...I have some mixed feelings about that, too, but I better leave that subject alone," Andrew said.

"All right, but going back to the moral values, they are constantly changing. Take the style of dressing, or the use of foul language that seeping in. What was offensive fifty years ago, it is becoming the norm of today. For example, did you know, that in 1906 it was illegal for a woman to smoke in public? "

"I didn't know that, but I sure would have kept that one in the book."

"I think that for sweep out the hypocrisy and double standards, every generation should question the moral code of yesterday. My pet peeve is: why should the Creator have bothered to equip us with a strong desire for sex if we're supposed to suppress it?"

"I think suppress is a wrong word. What you need is control. There must be some code of ethics to live by. It is one thing to have desire, and quite another to act it out like mindless animals. Just because we are born naked, it does not mean we should walk around in the nude."

"You have a point there. But I want to go back to the code of ethics. I wonder what kind of people would make up those rules."

Andrew chuckled. "I would like to think that code of ethics evolve around common decency. Everything is subordinated to morality. It seems that I'm the product of old fashioned conditioning because I feel that should there be complete openness, the subject of desire would lose much of its mystique. Curiosity gone, the beauty of sex would sink into a 'take it or leave it' dullness. There must be something that is left for the imagination. Are you saying that you are agreeing with the current sexual revolution?"

"Generally I sympathize with them for getting rid of some outdated rules. For example, there are countries where it is still a crime to kiss on the street, or for women to put on any makeup, let alone to show their faces. Can you imagine? In the last century people would be horrified if a woman showed her ankles on the street, for heaven's sake. Wearing a blindfold won't help you to see the light. Progress, sweetheart, like it or not, is inevitable," Cathy said.

"Oh, yes. But we pay a heavy price for some of the results. Just because there is a grain of truth in everything, it does not mean you have to throw the baby out with the bath water. It is one thing to question the moral code, but the trouble with this new "freedom" is that in the meantime the concept of human decency is swept into the gutter. I think there is too much dirt whirling around us and blocking our clear vision of thinking. Take the morbid interest in drugs, for example. It drives people into impaired-minded, sub-human zombies. Those idiots are using it for a crutch, pretending that they're *'having fun'* while killing themselves —and us."

"Well, well, I can see that I have a philosopher at my hand. But don't you have any weakness?"

"Oh, I have some. For example, ignorance is fine with me as long as someone doesn't want to *prove* that two and two is five, like... the KKK. Also, I am the most impatient with stupidity; and with habitual liars. But what concerns me the most is that while the human mind is inexhaustible, unfortunately, there are people in responsible positions who are twisting the new generation's minds into moral bankruptcy. Now I'm talking mainly about the TV that pumping all the cruelty into this gun-crazed society. It would be very interesting to see where the crime rate will sink by the end of this century. But so much for my two-cents worth of philosophy."

Cathy nodded. "I agree. As far as guns go, thanks to some greedy or bleeding-heart politicians, the picture is alarming."

As they walked toward the Parliament Buildings, enjoying the scenery of the hilly Quebec side, people around them were talking and laughing, enjoying the lovely Sunday afternoon.

"Now we could talk about marriage," Cathy suggested.

"Oh-oh," said Andrew, "here comes trouble."

"Now come on, Andrew, I don't mean about us. I mean that in my opinion the beauty withers when it is not shared with someone we love. I can't imagine being happy by living a life alone. Though I know that routine in marriage is a deadly weapon that creates a colorless way of life. When the excitement ends, the zest for life is over, and boredom sets it. I know marriage breakups that were based upon the 'yes darling', 'no darling' syndrome. God knows where the passion goes over the years."

"I suppose everything has a way of running its course into routine. If there is true love at the beginning, people compromise and outgrow a lot of preconceived ideas from their youth. But until we acquire personal experience, we have to go by the examples we grew up with. I don't know about your parents, but I know mine still love each other. They lead a simple life, and I don't think they ever dreamed of analyzing their sentiments, or taking the trouble to clinically examine their lives together. They loved each other and that was that. Sure, they had their ups and downs, but they took them in stride," Andrew said, throwing a stone into the river.

"Seems like you had a happy childhood."

Spotlights of his childhood memories rushed back that for a moment moved him. "Yes, I had. But I'm wondering what *your parents* would think, should they be in a position to hear you."

Seeing his point, Cathy laughed. "You could be right. Yet, even if I may not set a good example, I hope I'm not past praying for. I think my heart is still in the right place. Don't forget that there always will be a generation gap which creates disagreements."

"Who could argue with that?"

"All I hope is that even if I change, I won't turn out to be one of those people that I'm rebelling against." Cathy said.

They stopped at one of the lookout spots and sat on the bench for awhile. Andrew derived some pleasure by watching cars passing by, ladies walking their dogs, children running around noisily. Ten minutes later, they decided to move along. The sun, like a huge disk of vermilion, slowly sank behind the horizon. From the mountains soft breeze whisked through the valley like a breath blown from the clouds. It rippled along the surface of the river, flecked it with white crests, and ruffled the grass.

Cathy snuggled up to Andrew like a fragile little girl, seeking warmth and comfort against the cooling evening. It was getting late, so they turned around and headed for home.

* * *

In June 1962, Andrew successfully completed the examination and received his diploma as a radio and television technician. A glow of triumph filled him. During his long years of studying, there were times of fear from failing, fear of only chasing rainbows... But he believed in himself, and he had that oxygen of hope and stubborn perseverance that kept him going. And now a glorious relief and pride swept through him: it was victory over incredible odds! Suddenly, looking at his diploma, the image of his parents appeared in his mind, and hot emotion brought moisture into his eyes. "This is for you Dad and Mom," he whispered. Then, with renewed energy, he rushed to Cathy to share the good news.

He dashed into her apartment and swept Cathy into his arms, kissing her deliriously.

"Sweetheart, I've done it! Look, I've got my diploma. Let's celebrate!" he shouted with excitement.

"Oh, Andrew, that's wonderful. Congratulations! But I'll tell you this, my clever love. I've never doubted it, because I knew how badly you wanted it. So I'm not surprised. Although you'll still need a little luck raking up a job."

"Don't worry about it, I'll find one. The field is wide open. Now it is you I want to explore."

From the next day on Andrew began to scrutinize the papers to see what his chances were of finding a job in Ottawa. But it turned out to be a fairly small town, and the chances were limited. Even if he found a place where they needed a technician, they wanted someone with experience. So he started to buy the Toronto Globe and Mail, although he did not cherish the idea of leaving Ottawa. His hunch for a better chance was right. A few days later an ad caught his eye that seemed just what he was looking for:

RADIO AND TV REPAIRMAN, NO EXPERIENCE REQUIRED.
IF EAGER, WE'LL ASSIST YOU.

There was no address, only a phone number. Andrew dialed promptly and asked if the job was still available. The man said it was.

"That's great!" Andrew exclaimed. Then quickly explained that he was calling from Ottawa and asked if he could hold the position until the next day.

"Well, since I don't know you, I don't hire over the phone."

"Of course, I understand. What I meant was, could you hold it until tomorrow. I'll be there early afternoon."

"All right. I'll make an exception."

"Thank you," and quickly scribbled down the address. "See you tomorrow then."

"Fine. But hold on a minute," the man said quickly. "Do I detect a European accent?"

"Yes. I'm Hungarian."

"Well, how about that for a coincident?" the man said in Hungarian. "Drive carefully and have a good trip."

"Thank you." Putting down the receiver, Andrew mumbled, "Now wasn't that weird? He looked forward anxiously to seeing the place. The only thing that bothered him was Cathy. He knew that she would be upset about his moving, but there was nothing he could do. Andrew started to make the necessary arrangement that had to be done, like giving a note to the manager of his moving out.

When he stepped in to Cathy's apartment, he put on a cheerful front.

"Well, how about it, sweetheart? Imagine, I have a job."

"Oh really? Andrew, you're a genius! Congratulations!"

"Thanks, honey, but there is a catch: the job is in Toronto. I'm sorry, honey but we have to part. I must leave early in the morning."

Cathy's heart sank, and a veil of sadness shadowed her downcast face. Then she blinked and bravely forced a smile.

"I'm sorry, too, but at the same time I'm happy for you. Right now it is your future that is most important. Besides, Toronto is not exactly at the end of the world, is it?"

"That's the spirit, sweetheart. Though to tell you the truth, the thought crossed my mind to stay if that's what you wanted."

"Oh no, no! Not if the price is to give up a job!" Cathy protested. "You should never ever play with fate."

Andrew kissed her. "We will keep in touch," he said. "Not as often as before, but it'll be just as sweet."

"You bet we will!" she said bravely. Nevertheless a touch of uneasiness crept into the conversation. When Andrew felt he has to go, Cathy insisted of going with him. "I want to help...A woman's touch makes the difference, you know...."

"It was nice to be close to you," Andrew said. "I'm going to miss you."

"I miss you already," Cathy said, and tears filled her eyes. After all those clowning about her feelings, this was the first time she had shown some genuine emotion about how much she loved him.

When they made love, there was a quality of desperation in it. Then early in the morning Cathy stood beside the car, kissing Andrew once more, and they waved good-bye.

23

ALEX'S STORE

AFTER FIVE HOURS OF driving on the 401, it was two o'clock in the afternoon when Andrew arrived in Toronto. It was exciting to see the city again. As he leisurely drove through the city, the memory of Stan Mackay came to mind, and he wondered whether he was still washing cars somewhere.

The shop was on Bloor Street and he had no trouble finding it. Then he saw the sign:
ALEX'S RADIO AND TV SALES AND SERVICES.

When he stepped into the store, he saw a man standing in front of a shelf, busily readjusting some small appliances. He turned around swiftly and greeted Andrew with respect due to customers. He was in his early fifties, tall and still handsome, with wavy black hair that was graying at the temples. The age-defying resilience in his move struck Andrew's attention first. His reassuring manner went with his disarming smile.

"Good afternoon, young man, what can I do for you?"

"My name is Andrew Dombrady," he introduced himself in Hungarian. "The man who phoned you from Ottawa."

"Oh, yes, yes. Welcome to Toronto." He cleaned his hands from the dust then extended his hand, "My name is Alex Kerekes. Pleased to meet you."

"Pleased to meet you too."

"I appreciate your showing up on time," Alex said. "I always say that punctuality is not only a courtesy but a very important asset in the business world."

Andrew nodded. "It is worth to remember."

"Now, if I remember correctly, you said you've just received your diploma."

"That's right, sir. Although during the summer break I was working in a similar shop like this one. It gave me some experience."

"So much the better. Okay then, Andrew, let me show you around, so you can get some idea of what the shop is all about. As you can see, this is the storeroom, and that is the workshop. Most of the repair work comes from servicing the Japanese-made radios and televisions, which are covered by a one-year factory warranty. Generally, we have a steady flow of work."

Andrew was impressed by the well-organized place, and Alex seemed to read his mind.

"Your predecessor was a German fellow, a really good worker. We've worked together for the last two years. But unfortunately, he received some bad news from home and he had to return to Munich. He was not sure if he would return ."

"Yes, these things can happen," Andrew said. "Well, as far as I'm concerned, I like the place, Mr. Kerekes. So if you'd give me the chance, I'd like to prove my worth."

Alex was impressed with Andrew's attitude. "The job is yours. But for the sake of starting right, let's get rid of the formalities. I prefer you call me Alex. Now, as far as your salary is concerned, it will depend on your skill, of course. But for the start I can pay you sixty-five dollars a week, then we'll see. Unless you have a better idea?"

"No, it's perfectly fine with me," Andrew said.

"Well, then, when can you start?"

"Hmmm, I could start by tomorrow, but first I have to solve a little problem, Alex. And that is, I must find an accommodation around the area. Could you carry on for an extra day or two?"

"Yes, of course. I don't think you'll have much problem finding a good apartment at the nearby high-rises. Just go and check around."

Alex was right. Andrew found a modern one-bedroom apartment in a fifteen-story building the next morning. Since it was furnished, it took but one day to settle down and the third day he was working.

This was his first job in Canada that he had really enjoyed. Working side-by-side with Alex benefited him, as he had explained whatever it was that he wasn't sure of. Entering into a different but challenging world, Andrew absorbed the information with great interest. With complete devotion and bursting ambition, creative rapture overtook him. The inner fire that lurked within him had been rekindled. Being able to work in the career of his dream, he was possessed by the novelty of what he did. It's a rarity, he thought, when a man can work in an occupation he has fun doing and get paid for it. He never had a dull moment. These wonderful days cast an almost unreal glow over his dissolving past.

He was at his mental and physical peak, full of creative energy. Although he realized that while the life he was living was not matched the complete picture in his head, but life was sweet, and his face was glowing with happiness.

Every day brought something new, and his goal was to become as proficient in the trade as he could. His father's advice often rang in his mind to always reach for the top. He diligently studied the trade publications and manuals that came with the products, and as time passed he had a knack for accurately finding the trouble spots, and fixing them with the least amount of waste.

Although Alex was old enough to be Andrew's father, they began to form a close friendship. Watching Andrew's devotion and youthful enthusiasm, Alex quickly realized his potential. He grew to appreciate Andrew's effort and reworded him by raising his salary.

One day, as they were working together, Andrew asked Alex how he started his business.

"I was thirty-five years old when I came to Canada in 1948. I was an electrician at home, but looking around, I realized the potential and I specialized in radio and television. It turned out to be a good investment, as you can see," pointing around.

Then he shared a story with Andrew about how not to do business if one wanted to maintain a good reputation.

"There was a man I was working with, who was very good at smelling people for easy money. In order to create more work, he deliberately did a shabby job, or left some minor faults unfixed. He knew the customer would be back sooner or later for more repairs. He also convinced them that certain repairs had to be done even if there was nothing wrong. He could have sold a refrigerator to an Eskimo. You know, in this business it is very easy to trap innocent people by dishonesty. Needless to say, this kind of 'reputation' we don't need."

* * *

Since Andrew re-established his relationship with his parents, from time-to-time he amazed them with one good piece of news after another. They knew all about his progress in Ottawa, but nothing could have fascinated them more than when he had received his diploma and found his "dream" job in Toronto. They thought that he was a genius. Margie wrote:

"Dear Andrew,

In our amazement, we find it hard to believe your achievement. Your latest letter topped them all! Of course we believe it, but how did you do it? We're hugging each other and crying with happiness, and you cannot imagine how we're wishing to be there to celebrate with you. It is simply incredible. Congratulations! Keep it up, son!"

Andrew trembled with emotion. Their letter sounded as if it were *their dream* that came true, not his. Dear God, how many sleepless nights I prayed for this moment, he thought. He wanted to prove not only to himself, but also to the whole world that he could do it. Although it took him years to climb to the top of the hill, nevertheless he was there, and what an Olympic thrill that was!

Now it was time to phone Cathy to let her know how things were going with him. He could have done it before and felt a pang of guilt. But he was busy, he reasoned. Well, he would be nice and make it up to her.

When Cathy recognized his voice, her own radiated sheer delight. "Andrew! How nice it is to hear from you. I thought you'd never phone. Are you all right?" she bubbled.

"I'm just fine, love. Well, not in every aspect; I miss you so. How is everything with you?"

"Oh, fine, fine, only I miss you too. So, now that I know you are all right, I'll visit you if you don't mind."

Andrew could have been oversensitive, but for some reason that *'if you don't mind'* struck the wrong chord with him.

"Now, Cathy, why would you think that I *would mind*? You don't have to make an appointment to find out if you're welcome."

The moment he said it, the echo of his own voice hit him like icy water. Now why in the hell did I say this?

There was a moment of frozen silence on the other end. "I'm sorry if I offended you, Andrew," she said petulantly. "I didn't mean to. But if this is how you're welcoming me, then it's better if I never come. Bye ... "

"No, wait! Cathy, please!" Andrew pleaded, and he was able to hold her. "Cathy, I'm awfully sorry. Oh God, could you forgive me? I don't know what came over me; I didn't mean it. For heaven's sake, I can hardly wait to see you."

Cathy's voice brightened. "All right, Andrew, it seems like loneliness went to your head, so you're forgiven. Now since I know that you don't mind, give me your address and I'll surprise you."

"That's great, thanks, love," Andrew laughed. "I'm looking forward to it."

He did not have to wait long. The next Friday evening he heard the doorbell ring, and when Andrew opened it, he exclaimed, "Cathy! My, my, what a lovely surprise."

"Hi lover," Cathy said saucily, and she stepped in. They flew into each other's arms, kissing passionately, then Andrew looked her over. "You look great," he said.

"Thanks. Well, the welcome is great. Knowing how difficult it is to get Friday off, you can appreciate the supreme sacrifice I've made," she said mischievously. "But as they say, money isn't everything. Besides, I had to make sure you hadn't forgotten me."

"You mean about loving you," Andrew said with a knowing smile.

"Sure. I don't want you to go around and replace me with a cute Torontonian beauty, if I can help it."

Andrew smiled and kissed her. "That's very reassuring, sweetheart. Though I think you have all the talent to keep me satisfied. But I'm talking too much. Please sit down, you must be tired." Andrew pointed to the sofa.

"Thanks, but I'm not tired."

"That's good. Now let me see," Andrew rubbed his chin, "what would my lovely guest prefer, instant coffee made by yours truly, or perhaps madam would care to go to a romantic restaurant for dinner and a little chit-chat. We have a lot of catching up to do."

Cathy laughed. "We sure do, but not in *that* order. How I adore your innocence. You know me a *little* but not quite enough. Your priorities are way upside down, darling. We can eat later. How about showing me how you've missed me."

She embraced him with all her seductive power, her breasts

rubbing him, and they were swept along by a wave of passion. They fell on to the sofa, kissing and caressing with lusty abandon. Their lips pressed together with burning desire and their shuddering bodies demanded release.

"Oh, woman, you're insatiable!" Andrew moaned with pleasure. He was on top of her, and she was taking him inside hungrily with fire, and surrendered their love with glowing ecstasy, moaning with heightened explosion.

* * *

The next morning Andrew took Cathy to the shop to introduce her to Alex. Usually Saturdays were busy, but he hoped that Alex could give him the day off.

When they entered the shop, Andrew greeted Alex light-heartedly.

"Good morning, Alex. Excuse me for being late, but I have a lovely visitor from Ottawa. Alex, this is Cathy Foldesy, my girlfriend. Cathy, this is Alex Kerekes."

Alex was genuinely surprised. "Pleased to meet you, Cathy."

They shook hands, and Cathy said, "Pleased to meet you too."

Alex glanced at Andrew. "I didn't know you left a beautiful girlfriend in Ottawa. If I were you, I wouldn't take such a risk of losing her. By the way, up until now I thought that all the beautiful women lived in Toronto."

"Then it's just about time for you to get rid of that misconception, because Ottawa is famous for its beauties," Andrew said, winking at Cathy. She smiled shyly. This was typical men-talk and she didn't know what to say.

"Well, you certainly proved your point."

"This is a nice shop, Mr. Kerekes. No wonder that Andrew is so enthusiastic about working here," Cathy said, just to change the subject.

"Thanks, Cathy. We like it too."

Seeing that Alex was in a good frame of mind, Andrew took the chance and asked if he could take the day off.

"Sure Andrew, no problem. Have a pleasant day," he poked his arm. "I'll hold the fort here."

Andrew thanked him and a few minutes later, they were on the street in a pleasant mood. Cathy took Andrew's arm and they walked to the car.

"Your boss is a nice man, what is his name?"

"Alex Kerekes. Yes, we get along fine. Mind you it goes without saying that we have our off days, too. Each of us can get into bad mood sometimes, even from the weather. The main thing is, we know how to compromise. I think sometimes he is more than just a nice man. He has a heart of gold. I know he'd give me the shirt off his back should I need it."

"Yes, he seems like a special man, you lucky devil."

"What I meant to say was that I feel he considers me the son he never had. It's a rarity today to find a real friend to whom you can say things without fear that he might misinterpret them. As you know, in life we don't always say things the right way..."

"Oh I know," Cathy said with a wry smile. "It only means that we're human."

"That's right!" Andrew said, feeling the need to explain himself, but let it go..

They spent some time wandering around Queen's Park, then walked down to University Avenue. Later they stopped by the famous City Hall, which was a unique piece of architecture. After seeing that, they still had plenty of time and Andrew suggested they visit Niagara Falls.

"It's only a two-hour drive."

When they arrived, a warm feeling of recognition flashed through Andrew. Cathy knew that he had lived here, so she was not surprised when he said, "I feel as if I'm coming home."

Cathy looked at the mass of swarming tourists with childlike amazement. "I've never been in Niagara Falls. Isn't that strange?" she said. At the sight of the cataract, she breathed a sigh of delight. "Oh look at that mass of water!" She gasped.

They stopped and admired the perpetually roaring torrent of water plunging down with tremendous force, which produced a huge swirling mist, about which they saw the most spectacular rainbow. The colorful arch spanned over the Niagara River gracefully, like a giant ribbon.

Business was booming and companies were always coming up with something new that would attract the tourists. Recently they had built the famous Skylon Tower close to the Horseshoe Falls. Andrew took Cathy up and they admired the magnificent view. It was a clear day with a pleasant breeze, and from such a height the panorama was spellbinding. Looking down, the cars appeared to be little windup toys, and the people like tiny moving figures.

Coming down in that funny turtle shaped elevator, the hot and sticky humidity hanging in the air, hit them. Joining the strolling crowd, with Andrew's cheerful guidance Cathy enjoyed the colorful scenery tremendously.

Later they went to see the electrically powered floral clock, which was yet another popular tourist attraction. The numbers on the huge round face were made of freshly planted flowers. Then it was getting late and they decided to drive back to Toronto.

On the Queen Elizabeth Way the traffic was normal, the driving pleasant. As Cathy was sitting beside Andrew contentedly, joking and laughing, suddenly Andrew imagined that it was Katie sitting beside him. By now—to his surprise—days and weeks would pass without Katie occupying his mind. But now suddenly he was wondering about her. The love for her was still in his heart, yet he was curious whether it was possible to actually love them both. What would he do should he have to choose? Then he became angry with himself. What the hell is wrong with me for even bothering with such a foolish, impossible question?

That night Cathy slept with him, and the following morning she drove back to Ottawa.

* * *

Monday morning Alex was already in the shop and greeted him with a friendly smile.

"Good morning, Alex."

"Good morning, Andrew. Congratulations on your good taste," he said. "Cathy is quite a pretty girl."

"Thanks, Alex, I'm glad you like her."

"Yes, I like her, and what is more, I think you'd make a nice couple. It's just about time for you to settle down and start a family."

"Wow, wow, Alex, please slow down. You're going too fast. Thanks for your suggestion but I have no intention of getting married—just yet. And as far as I know, Cathy doesn't share your idea either. We're happy the way things are, and as they say, time will tell."

Alex looked genuinely surprised. "Oh, well, you new generation..." he said, making a resigned gesture. "Of course, it is none of my business, but I must say you're strange. From what I've seen, you love each other..."

"That, my friend, you've seen right." Andrew said with a mysterious smile. Then he scurried to the workshop, leaving Alex, shaking his head.

* * *

Andrew and Alex had been working together for almost two years now. On this beautiful autumn day, Alex was in good mood. It was early in the afternoon, not too busy, and he was dusting the shelves. He was joking and laughing with Andrew, when suddenly he felt faint. He swayed for a moment and turned to grab the arm of a chair with one hand, while pressing his chest with the other to ease the pain. He sat down shaking, and muttered, *"Oh, God, please no! Andrew!"* he gasped.

Andrew ran to him. "Alex! What happened?" But looking at him as he was trembling and sweating, his face pale—that said it all. It was fortunate that it happened in the store, and Andrew was able to rush him to the hospital. He watched as the attendants put him on a stretcher and quickly wheeled him through the emergency door. They put an oxygen mask over his face to relieve the immediate pain.

Andrew waited for the report, and when the doctor appeared, he told him that Alex has had a mild coronary attack. "But he is strong, and he'll pull through."

After this crushing news, Andrew left him in the intensive care unit and went back to the shop. He put all his energy and time into his work to make up for Alex's absence. He felt lost for a while and had to think fast. He reorganized his work method, using up every minute in the most economical way. He knew that Alex trusted him, remembering the day when he had told a customer, "Don't worry about it, Ma'am, if it is possible, Andrew will fix it. He is a wizard with these things."

Well, this was the time to prove him right. He loved Alex like a father, and in a healthy way, Andrew had fallen under his influence. So it was only natural that he felt a solid sense of loyalty. In order to get the job done, he stayed in the workshop until ten or eleven o'clock every night.

After a week Alex came home, but it took several more days before he felt strong enough to be back in the store. Even then, he was under Andrew's watchful eyes. He made sure that Alex did not lift anything or rush himself. Inwardly Alex appreciated it, but sometimes it was almost comical the way he complained that he was not a baby.

Then one afternoon Alex asked Andrew to stay after work, as he wanted to talk with him. From the unusually solemn tone Andrew sensed that the subject must be serious.

Seemingly nervous, Alex said, "All right, Andrew, what I was about to discuss with you is simple. During my stay in the hospital I had plenty of time on my hands to think things over, concerning our business relationship. As you know, my wife died five years ago, and I have no children or relatives in Canada. I consider you as part of our success, so should something happen to me (as it just did), it is only natural that I was thinking of you. I want to make sure you'll be in charge. That means I'd like you to become my full partner and own the store jointly. While all the responsibility and profit would be split equally, you'd have the benefit of learning how to manage the store." He paused for a second. "I'm sure this arrangement would contribute to enrich the quality of our business."

Seeing Andrew's startled face, Alex added, "I can understand if you're surprised, but remember this, there is no one else I'd rather have for a business partner. I trust you and consider you like my own son."

"Thank you, Alex. I appreciate it."

Alex nodded. "However, you might find that the responsibility is too much, and you don't want it. I would understand. But take your time and think about it. All I ask is, whatever you decide, please tell me without reservation.

Andrew let out a big sigh. One of the traits that were going for him was his trustworthiness. And Alex's decision had been based on that. However, Alex's magnanimity, his demonstration of pure faith moved Andrew beyond words. This much trust made him a new man. Finally he was able to speak.

"Alex, I don't know what to say other than thank you for thinking of me. I appreciate your generosity; it's a great honor. But you're right, I'm shocked. Do you really think that after one bout of illness you should be making such a hasty decision?"

"Definitely! And I assure you it wasn't a hasty decision. Naturally we don't like to think about dying, but it's better to be prepared before it is too late. And to ease your conscience, you shouldn't worry about my financial position. Hell, I could retire tomorrow if I wanted to."

"I must admit the temptation is overwhelming, but right now, all I can promise you is that I'll think about it before I give you my answer. At the same time, I wish you'd do the same thing. You may change your mind."

"Fair enough."

At first, it made Andrew dizzy just to considering all the pros and cons. It was hard to imagine that all of a sudden he'd be part owner of the business. But no matter how he looked at it, accepting the offer would be a ready-made future, his for the taking. In fact it would be an inheritance, as simple as that. Something like this is once-in-a-lifetime opportunity, and he would be a fool to let it slip through his fingers.

He knew that it meant he'd have to work even harder to make sure Alex would not be disappointed.

Two days later he told Alex that if the offer was still open, he would be honored to become his partner.

Alex seemed to be relieved. "I'm very pleased, Andrew. Thank you. I always knew that I could count on you. It will mean a new lease on life for me, and I'll breathe a little easier."

For the time being, some strange feeling occupied Andrew's mind. The newness of the idea took time to wear off. Two weeks later they went to Alex's lawyer and finalized the partnership. After signing all the documents, they sealed it with a handshake and a warm embrace.

24

MIRACLES STILL HAPPEN

ERDELYI'S HEAD REELED WHEN he learned that he had won a thousand dollars in the Opera House Lottery. (Yes, in the meantime, Australia too had converted her currency to the dollar.) He could hardly wait to get home and celebrate the good news with his family.

When he opened the door, he shouted, "Hey, ladies! Look, I won a thousand dollars on the lottery! Can you believe it? *One thousand,* no less!"

Katie and Annie looked at him in disbelief. "You won what...?"

Only when he produced the winning ticket were they convinced. The joy brought tears to Annie's eyes.

"That's great, Dad!" Katie exclaimed. "At last, you have the chance to trade in your old Holden."

"Oh, no, no, my little girl. We're going to think carefully about what we should do with it. After all, we're not *millionaires* yet. Actually, it was a two thousand dollar winning ticket but of course, I shared it with John. By the way, that reminds me. I might as well give John a call. Let's see if he can come up with some smart suggestion about how to celebrate this marvelous windfall."

On the phone, the two men joked and laughed happily for a few minutes, then Joe said solemnly, "Okay, John, we'll be there. Yes, I know where it is."

After hanging up the receiver, he clapped his hands and said, "All right ladies, let's get ready. John knows an excellent Hungarian restaurant where there is a gypsy orchestra. He is reserving a table for us. We will meet him there."

When they arrived, it was only natural that Frank was there with his family. After greeting each other, Frank congratulated the winners, jokingly calling them the "future millionaires". At the table the parents immersed in their subjects, while Katie and Frank entertained each other.

In the eyes of people they appeared as a happy couple, and their marriage was a foregone conclusion. Since Katie's confession, Frank kept their private agreement a secret, but now it was Frank who hated their false pretense. Since they had known each other for so long, it took some maneuvering for Katie to play her part in a reasonable manner, allowing some intimacy. After all, she was only human, and in her better moods she went into a little heavy petting, exploring her feelings, wanting to know what would it like to be Frank's wife... Morally she was not comfortable with it, but with the safety valve of the confession, she justified it.

At such times, Frank had the impression that Katie was coming around. Of course, Katie knew better. But no matter how she put it, she felt uneasy, for it was just not possible to get away with misleading him.

* * *

When the excitement over the winning had died down, Frank invited Katie for a ride around the city. With his grinning happy mood, he created an exciting atmosphere, at the same time having a hard time to conceal the reason for his happiness. It was as if he were planning some kind of a mischief, forcing Katie to wonder. She could not imagine what the "earthshaking" event could be, but he went as far as hinting at some *big surprise!* Whatever it was, she was glad to see him in a cheerful mood because at times like this, Frank was pleasant to be with.

Driving leisurely across the Harbour Bridge toward North Sydney, he passed through the exclusive Chatswood district, admiring some beautiful parks and manicured golf courses. The luxurious bungalows and villas with their rolling lawns fascinated them. The soft, tranquil green landscape gave the impression they were in the countryside. This was undoubtedly an upper-class neighborhood, which was, in Katie's eyes, to be envied and admired.

She was so impressed with some of the architectural beauty that she instinctively exclaimed, "Ooooh! Isn't that absolutely breathtaking? It would be pure heaven to live in a house like that!"

"That's for sure. Isn't it something?" Frank said, as if he were boasting of his own. He wasn't sure which he enjoyed more, the landscape or Katie's enchantment. "What do you think of this neighborhood, Katie?"

"It's exquisite!"

Getting closer to his destination, Frank's nerves were on edge and fighting for inner calmness. No matter how much he had rehearsed what he will say, Katie was still able to make him feel insecure when he needed to confess something. Unnoticing Frank's problem, Katie went on admiring the houses. Then abruptly Frank slowed down and pulled off to the roadside and turned off the ignition. Katie watched with curiosity as Frank fumbled with the car key, then with a nervous smile he looked into Katie's eyes, gently reaching for her hand.

"Katie, my love, I can't hold my secret any longer. The reason I have brought you here is because I wanted to show you the house that can be yours... I mean ours. In other words, I'm asking you, darling, will you marry me?"

Katie's shoulders sagged, as if an unexpected weight had been crushed on her. Pale faced, for a second she glanced out the window, as if someone had asked her to commit a crime. It flashed through her mind that she should have seen this day coming. After a moment of silence she tossed her head up in a purely feminine manner and looked straight into Frank's eyes.

"Frank, I'm honored that you're asking me to marry you. I know that the outside pressure is upon us but, regretful as it is, I have to remind you of our agreement. As you have seen, I was happy the way things were going between us. I kept my side of the promise—just as you did—that is why I'm surprised. I wish I could make it a happier occasion, but I just can't give you a definite answer yet."

Frank blushed and his lips tightened into two white lines. He made a deep sigh to restrain his anger because he actually expected this. Still, the mystery kept nagging at him: what is it she really wants? She is not getting any younger, yet she is acting as though she is still waiting for some prince to come for her on a white horse to take her to some wonderland. Oh, he knew her reasons, but how long does she want to play this silly game? Swallowing his hurt, he said, "Somehow, I was afraid of this. But I really would like to know, what is there to think about? It just doesn't make any sense to wait for Andrew forever. It's been almost ten years..."

"I'm sorry."

"Yeah...Anyway, I thought you have had enough time, but I was wrong. Of course, I don't want you to jump into something you might regret later," he said, his voice full of sarcasm.

"Thank you Frank, I appreciate your understanding."

Frank made a grumbling sound. "Yeah, God knows, I've enough practice by now. Well, never mind. Since we're here, I might as well show you the house. As fool as I am, I'm still hoping for some miracles, I guess."

Frank stepped on the gas pedal so hard that the tires screeched and the car jerked out, leaving heavy dust behind them. Then he stopped at a handsome cream brick house. The same matching brick fence surrounded the yard. In the back yard, the scent of roses wafted from the well-kept flowerbeds.

Frank had a key to the house and they stepped inside. Katie was impressed. There was a huge living room, a modern kitchen, three bedrooms with beautiful built-in wardrobes with large mirrored doors and windows everywhere. The property was as remarkable inside as it was outside. The backyard had some resemblance to their Matyasfold home, which brought some tears into her eyes.

Frank noticed and looked at her, surprised. "What's wrong, Katie, don't you like it?"

"Oh, it's not that. This house is beautiful. Just that something reminded me of our home in Hungary."

Frank hugged her and wiped the tears, tenderly stroking her hair. "Tears of homesickness, I can understand. You see, this is a perfect proof that everything is replaceable. This home is yours if you want it."

Katie's gaze lingered out the window. She could have made an argument about his statement, but she clung to silence like a shield—it has its own eloquence.

* * *

On the way home they sat in the car in deep silence that created an air of unpleasantness, an invisible curtain between them. They sat beside each other, but actually they were alone with their disturbing, stormy thoughts. Katie was trying to assess the emotional malaise that was their past. What squandered years they had been, she thought. How in the world had she arrived at such a dreadful impasse? What a God-awful muddle they had both got into. Painful as it was, actually it was Frank she felt sorry for. She admitted to herself a million times that she did not dislike him. For someone else, he could and would be a wonderful husband, and it was not his fault that he had fallen in love with her.

She went through it many times that she ought to love him if only for his good qualities. After all, *what was it* that she was waiting for? She hated to admit it but it was time to forget about Andrew. Lying in bed on many a sleepless night, the cold hand of common sense pushed her to grab Frank. What was wrong with her? He was a good man and life was too short...Perhaps she was the biggest fool for throwing away the only future she could ever have.

At the same time Frank came to the conclusion that he must be strong and give Katie an ultimatum. So, when they arrived at Katie's home, he took a deep breath. "Well, Katie, I won't ask what you have been thinking, but this is what I thought. I'm tired of playing games. Both of us are old enough to take the future seriously. Yes, I've accepted your terms of being friends only in the hope that I'll be able to change your mind. I can see now what a fool I was! If you wish to throw away your future, that's your decision. Nonetheless, I can't go along with it anymore. So, to be fair, although I still love you, I'm giving you two weeks to decide. Either we get married or we call it quits."

Katie was moved by Frank's sudden courage. Her face reflected surprise as she looked into his eyes. "Frank, you couldn't be any clearer. Thank you for the last chance. I'm truly sorry for causing you all this trouble, but please don't blame yourself. You haven't failed me; it's just something that I can't explain. Perhaps at another time, it would have been a different story. Thanks again and good night."

* * *

Katie stepped into the house in an upset mood, relieved that her parents were engrossed in watching a movie. She said a forced "Hi!" from the hallway and rushed to her bedroom. In her present state of mind, she did not want to face them. She knew that her mother adored Frank, and did not keep it a secret how much she hoped that they would get married. She felt that their stagnating relationship was a waste of time. The lack of enthusiasm in Katie's attitude concerned her and she looked upon the passing years with apprehension. But out of respect, Annie was reluctant to discuss the matter with her.

Once Katie overheard her mother discussing their affair: "Even if she doesn't love him, she could learn to love him while they're married," she said.

Katie did not believe in that. What kind of freakish marriage would come out of such a union? The only blessed moments would be the time they weren't in each other's way. She did not put much value into the *position* of being a banker's wife. If a marriage was without real love, it would be worthless and empty.

She sat forlornly on the edge of the bed with clasped hands, and her breathing became more constricted and irregular. Her lips quivering, she took a shuddering breath and buried her head into the pillow. In complete frustration, violent sobs shook her body, while with wild, unbearable longing Andrew's image was floating in front of her eyes.. "Oh, Andrew, if only you knew how much I miss you," she moaned. Then she realized that in the end it would make no difference what her answer to Frank would be. Either way her world would collapse within her heart.

Later her mother called her for supper. She did not feel like eating but as upset as she was, she realized she must show up. Choking back her sobs, she took a deep breath and reluctantly came into the dining room. Her parents immediately spotted her red eyes. Realizing she had no choice, Katie explained that she was crying because Frank had proposed.

That's great! Her mother meant to say, but Joe beat her to it. "Gee, honey, I don't remember you crying," he said to his wife. "I suppose we were too happy for tears. And what did you tell him?"

"I asked him for time to think about it."

"Hmm, you didn't ask me that either. We sure were more eager."

"That's not funny!" Annie snapped. Turning to Katie, a shadow of disapproval has flashed through her face. "Obviously that means you don't love him. Then I can't help wondering, what was the sense in giving him hope for so long? You should have been more honest with him. Well, it's too bad but you ought to know better," she said, shaking her head.

"Oh, Mom, you're right, I know. Frank is a decent man and he'd make an excellent husband." And a miserable wave of helplessness gushed over her. "But I'm sorry...I don't...love him." Katie said, and heartrending sobs shook her body.

Joe gathered her into his arms. He did not take their affair too seriously, maybe because he saw into it clearly from the beginning.

"Now, now, my little girl, that's all right," he said with consoling warmness. "It's not the end of the world. Dear God! If you don't love him, you don't love him. So what? This is a free country. No one can force you to love someone, for heaven's sake!"

It is interesting how decisions are made sometimes. Life is like that. A sudden idea ignited a glow in his mind and he hit his forehead. "That's it! Hey, I have a splendid idea. Since you need time to make up your mind, you could have a good time doing it. Why not mix business with pleasure, as the saying goes."

Annie looked at him curiously. "Okay, okay, what is it, get to the point."

"What I have in mind is this: Go and visit Hungary for a few weeks and enjoy yourself while you make up your mind. Many Hungarians are doing this lately, so it's just about time one of us went to see what's going on at home. I was waiting for the right occasion and what better way to spend the money than on my daughter's happiness? What do you say?"

Katie's answer surprised him. "No, no, Dad, first of all, it's your money. I can't take it."

Erdelyi frowned. "Katie, don't talk foolishness. Where did you get that crazy idea? If you didn't know, it is *our money* and I don't know why I haven't suggested it before."

But Katie was stubborn. "Thank you, Daddy. I know you'd give it gladly so I might take it as a loan. Please give me time to think about it."

Erdelyi laughed. "Katie, you're talking to your father, not Frank."

Listening to them quietly, Annie now intervened.

"I don't know why you two make such a big deal out of this. Katie, I happen to know that you have some money in the bank. So, if you want to be fair, all you have to do is split the expenses. The idea makes sense to me. You need a change to sort things out with a clear mind. And what better way to do than this."

Katie looked at her mother with surprise, her jaw dropped.

"Well said, Annie, congratulations! Now, why didn't I think of that? You see, my little girl, your mother is right. As a matter of fact, you could start preparing for your trip as soon as Monday morning, and good luck!" Erdelyi said, leaning over and kissing her forehead.

Suddenly, Katie began to see the light. Yes, she will go to Hungary. She must find out the truth, once and for all! If Andrew was not available, she would feel free to say yes to Frank. She felt strong enough to survive whatever fate awaited her.

That feeling washed over her face like a wind rippling a pond. She must have faith in finding her beloved Andrew! The prospect of going to Budapest began to tantalize her, and she felt a frenzy of excitement. She imagined seeing Andrew's smiling face as they found each other. If that happens, it would change her dull life! Oh, God...She began to hear voices in the back of her mind whispering: '*Here is your chance, Katie*! *This could be the answer to your dreams.*' And like the spring's invigorating sun brings new life into the dormant earth, the hope began to blossom in her heart. She felt reborn, like a prisoner at the opening of the gate.

In this spell of ecstasy, her eyes sparkling, she stood up and with a mysterious smile, she kissed both of her parents.

"I think it's a lovely idea, thank you."

25

SHOCKING NEWS

CATHY VISITED ANDREW almost every weekend. She had her little Toyota car, but most of the time she preferred to come by bus. Together they would explore interesting places within a few hours of driving. They even went over to the American Niagara Falls, but they soon discovered that the Canadian side was more beautiful and more fun.

Once Andrew tried to visit Mr. Balogh to see how he was doing, but a new owner greeted him. He told Andrew that he had sold the motel and moved away from the hustle-and-bustle of the business.

"Just as he said he was going to do," Andrew said.

Next time, Andrew took out a more expensive motel room with a terrific view to the Horseshoe Falls. As usually, he registered themselves as *"married couple."* He smiled about it in their room, dropping himself to the king-sized bed. That is none of their business," he said. "Although I admit that using the word often may lead to real marriage." Then he started to tease Cathy for her belief that marriage—or rather that little piece of paper stifles love.

"Yes, in many cases, I believe it's a psychological trap," she said, dropping herself beside him. "However, until we reach that stage, I certainly intend to enjoy the preliminaries."

"I'm with you there," Andrew said, pulling her into his arms.

"On the other hand, don't be surprised if one day I change my mind," Cathy said, snuggling closer to him. "Let's be honest, it's a matter of attitude. If two people really love each other, a smart wife can prevent a marriage from going stale." She paused, as if surprised. "Hey! Is this me talking? I must be falling in love or old age is catching up with me."

"It could be the '*or*' that you should be worried about," Andrew teased. "So, where do you stand; are you still undecided whether you love me or not?"

"Oh you!...What do you think? Why else would I stick around, huh?"

"Well, one can never know. You might have a hidden surprise," Andrew said, pointing to her stomach.

"Andrew! Why would you even suggest a thing like that! You know I wouldn't trap you if my life has depended on it."

"I'm sorry, sweetheart, of course I know," Andrew kissed her. "You are definitely not a hoodwinker. I think we're getting along just fine. What do you think?"

Now, it was Cathy's turn to tease. "Hmm, it could be worse. But seriously, I don't call you my lover for nothing; I'm happy with you."

Andrew chuckled. "I know, you told me I've earned it."

"That's right, for which I'm taking some credit. The icing on the cake is that you're not only good in bed, but fun to be with. How am I measuring up: are you happy with me?"

"Well, I can put up with you," Andrew said with an impish smile. "But just as you said, if you haven't figured it out by now, you're in trouble. I can't put my finger on it but it seems like we have something in common. I can assure you that I'm not chasing other women."

"I'm flattered. By the way, I'm the same type: I'm a one-man woman."

"That's it! That is what we have in common. But getting back to the subject of marriage, I think that even if it's a lifelong commitment, if a couple grew apart, they should examine their feelings honestly. If they still love each other, then they should extend their marriage license for another five years. If they don't love each other any longer, they should terminate it. It would be better than to drag on a dead marriage."

Cathy frowned. "That's an interesting idea. It certainly would prevent putting up a front in a lot of miserable relationships." Then, with a mischievous smile, she added, "but we don't have to worry about that, and right now I'm in a charitable mood." She nuzzled closer to him, moving her hand down to his thigh.

"Ah, Cathy, how sweet you are!" Andrew groaned, responding to her touches with shuddering as her warm fingers slipped inside his shorts. He started kissing her while he grasped her firm buttocks.

"Ahhh, Andrew," she whispered, as desire flooded her. "As far as I'm concerned, we're still honeymooners."

* * *

The weeks and months slipped by swiftly. To spare Cathy from the hardship of traveling, occasionally Andrew split the visiting routine, and now he was on his way to Ottawa. Although he loved driving, he did not relish spending five hours alone behind the wheel. Therefore, like Cathy, he too, took the bus.

He sat at the window, looking at the scattered snow patches on the roadside. It was a grim reminder of how harsh the winter was in this region. Then, his mind was occupied by the idea of marriage. He was in a taking-stock mood and felt that at the age of thirty, he had passed the playing stage. He felt also that fooling around was no longer satisfying; that settling down and having a family of his own was in order.

Beneath the facade of the "liberated" woman, Cathy was a decent girl. She had qualities that added zest to his life. Her cheerful nature was an asset; it made being with her worthwhile. Although they did not agree on everything—who does?—so far their disagreements had not caused any serious problem. He loved her for her interesting personality, her honesty and he knew that Cathy loved him too.

In those soul-searching moments it surprised him that even after the pleasant years with Cathy, his heart still ached for Katie. At the beginning of their affair he struggled with his conscience, but the reality of life dimmed the memory.

* * *

As far as Cathy was concerned, she had no intention of forcing marriage on Andrew. They trusted each other, so she thought that when the time was right, he would propose. She knew only too well that nothing irritates a man more than a nagging woman. She made sure to satisfy him the best way she knew how, and the rest was up to him. It was true that she was earning good money and enjoying her freedom. But she would give it up gladly, should he propose. She knew well, that aside from not getting any younger, she loved him very much. Why, he was not only good looking and an excellent lover but also a good man and a hard worker.

But marriage or not, it did not really matter. She would not rock the boat, for after all, she had him in every other way.

* * *

With new inventions by the manufacturers flooded the market, the business was growing steadily, bringing with it an increasing workload. It reached the point where one day Andrew suggested to Alex to hire a deliveryman, someone who could be a storekeeper too in his spare time. That would give them more time to work in the shop.

Alex considered it briefly and agreed. "I think it's a good idea, Andrew. The workload warrants an extra man. It'd definitely take some burden off of your shoulders. I know you've been working like a slave lately, so we could even consider an extra technician, too."

Mulling it over, the next day they drew up an ad for the Globe and Mail.

LOOKING FOR EXPERIENCED DRIVER FOR DELIVERY WORK APPLY IN PERSON.

Concerning Alex's health condition, it became a routine that Andrew opened the shop and Alex came in later. The day after the ad, four men were waiting at the shop early in the morning, inquiring about the job. When Andrew let them in, there was a familiar face among them that he would have recognized anywhere. As soon as their eyes met, both made a quick step, embracing each other like lost brothers.

"**Stan Mackay**! My good old buddy, how are you?"

"**Andrew!** Oh, my God, is that you?"

"Sure it is, and still kicking, as you can see. What are you doing here?" But as soon as he uttered it, he added: "Ask a stupid question and you get a stupid answer."

Stan kept turning his head. "Is this **your** shop?"

"Partly. I mean I'm part owner," he said. Then he turned to the other men, watching with an amused puzzlement on their faces. "Gentlemen, I'm sorry but as you can see, the job is taken. Thanks for your interest." Turning back to Stan, he said, "What a nice surprise! It's great to see you. But you haven't changed a bit."

"It's good to see you too," Stan said, still shaking his head in disbelief. "But you sure changed, you son of a gun. What a contrast between the lost man of nine years. How time flies! Are you sure you're the same man? I can't believe this. You really fooled me at the car wash garage. You never told me that you were an electrician."

"Well, one must take some risks in this grinding life to make some progress, my friend. But no, I didn't fool you. At that time I was what you saw and certainly not a tradesman. Although God knows I'd dreamed about it. After we parted, I went through a lot of schooling and I received my diploma in Ottawa. Anyway, it's a long story and that will have to wait for some other time. Let's just say that this is the land of opportunity, wouldn't you agree?"

"Indeed it is. Well, accept my sincere congratulations! I can see the results of your studying: your English has improved a lot. Not that I should be surprised. I told you, you were a good student, didn't I?"

"How could I forget? So, what have you been doing all these years? Obviously you too left the car washing business."

"Hah, years and quite a few jobs ago. After you left, it wasn't fun anymore. I thought a lot about you."

"I did, too. And here we are! It's a small world, isn't it? By the way, I still think you should have opened your own driving school."

"Well, if I had your money I would burn mine. I couldn't afford it. Besides, you have never bought me that new car to begin with," Stan grinned.

Andrew chuckled. "That's true. Well, at least partly I can make it up to you; as a consolation, you can drive the company car. That is, if you want the job."

"Of course I want the job. Why else would I be here?"

"Great, great, just checking. You know something, Stan? There is nobody in this world I'd rather give this job to. In His mysterious ways, God is giving me the chance to show you my appreciation."

"Gee, that's awful nice of you, **boss**, thanks. Now, you can tell me when I should start?" Stan asked with a wry smile.

Andrew let out an embarrassed laugh. "Oh, come on, Stan, that's not fair. We're friends, remember? I know that a lot of water has gone under the bridge since we last saw each other but I hope it won't change anything. So, no more of this 'Boss' stuff, huh?"

Stan smiled and apologized. "I'm sorry, Andrew, I was a jerk,

I shouldn't have said that. I'm awful glad to see you."

One customer came in, so the two friends shook hands.

"You can start as soon as tomorrow, if you like."

* * *

It is the law of life that things do not always go as we wish they would. In late June, 1966, Andrew received a registered letter from his mother. That aspect alone was a bad omen. She wrote:

Dear Son,

It saddens me so much that I have to write this bad news but your father suffered a heart attack, yesterday. He is in the hospital. The doctor hasn't been able to say just how serious it is but I dare not wait any longer to let you know. I just came home and he entrusted me with the difficult task of asking you to come and visit us. It is his fondest wish to see you once more before he dies. So, if it's possible, please try and come home. I realize that it might not be possible for you to come for political reasons, therefore I want to reassure you that should it be the case, we will understand. But please let us know as soon as you can.

Your loving mother.

Andrew stared at the letter in disbelief, his hands shaking. His first reaction was that he would go no matter how dangerous it might be. He must see his father! But what if the communists wouldn't let him in? When he showed the letter to Alex, he mentioned his concern.

Alex expressed his condolences then offered the solution. "Look, Andrew, the situation is simple. Call Cathy up and ask her to go to the Hungarian Embassy and obtain the application form. If they don't object, then you can go home, no questions asked. I know a guy, John Szegedy, who also took part in the revolution and he visited his parents last year. The government is in deep financial trouble, so they want your money desperately. Believe me, they'll overlook your 'crime' for the color of your dollar."

"Our only crime was that we wanted to be free. However, your advice is a good one, so I'll give it a try. But what about you, Alex? Have you got any idea how I hate to leave you like this? I feel like I'm letting you down or something."

"Don't be ridiculous, Andrew. I know you belong here but you also have a duty to see your parents. You can't let *them* down."

"You're right, we both are. My fear is that the burden could be too much for you..."

Alex was touched. He swallowed deeply, then took a deep breath. "You just make sure you come back safely, you big worry-wary. I'll be all right." Then they put every feeling into their embrace that a real father and son would not surpass.

With Cathy's help Andrew's visa was approved and within a week, and he was ready to fly home.

The day he was scheduled to leave, Cathy accompanied him to the Toronto airport. Andrew made a feeble protest, saying that it was too much trouble for her. Nevertheless, she was there. As they stood at the gate, Cathy told him how she would miss him.

Andrew put his arm over her shoulder. "Well, sweetheart, I wasn't joking when I suggested that you come with me. I know my parents would have loved to see you. Actually, I think I should have packed you in my suitcase and smuggled you through customs."

Cathy laughed. "Oh, I don't know. I might be making a mistake by not taking you up on it, but I promise I'll accompany you on your next trip."

"That's a deal then."

"Good. Time is on our side. Besides, just think how sweet your return will be."

"When you say things like that, you make me want to stay. By the way, thanks for the wonderful farewell treatment I received last night, I'll dream about it."

"The pleasure was all mine," Cathy said with an impish smile.

"You know, Cathy, it seems crazy to say this at the most inappropriate time, but I think we should get married when I come back."

Cathy's face lit up for a moment, then she looked at him with piercing eyes. "Oh, my God! Now is this supposed to be a proposal or what?"

"To be honest, I've been considering it for some time. Are you surprised?"

"Yes; but it is a lovely surprise, considering the timing."

"I agree, sometimes I say things left-handedly. But it will give us some time to get used to the idea of being a married couple."

"I sure won't try to change your mind, lover. With this lovely thought in mind the waiting will be much sweeter... I'll have some wonderful dreams. Just make sure you return safely. Oh, Andrew, I love you very much. So take care and *bon voyage*, sweetheart."

They kissed each other, then Andrew moved with the crowd. As he glanced back, he saw Cathy waving. He threw a kiss toward her with his hand, and he was gone.

* * *

This was the first time Andrew had flown in an airplane. As the plane skimmed over the clouds, Andrew sank into the cozy chair, taking the opportunity to untangle the thread of his thoughts. He did not really know what he had expected from the visit, other than hoping that his father would be out of danger by the time he got home.

He was sure that over the past ten years many things had changed. Looking back, those were the stormiest years for him. Not all bad, but he was happy that the lonely years of struggle were behind him. Luck and God were on his side, but he recognized that Canada was good to him. By now he was a Canadian citizen and proud of it.

Winding down these thoughts, it did not take long to arrive at the painful subject of Katie. Meeting Cathy was created by circumstances, and provided some sense of belonging. Katie's memory had been pushed to the back of his mind, but as far as the two women were concerned, in different ways he loved them both. Nonetheless, as the yearning for Katie surfaced, he realized that in the last few years he was leading a double life. In his confusion hope and fear exchanged each other. He hoped that if nothing else, he would at least be able to find out what had happened to her. The painful possibility that he might never see her ever again, always lingered in his mind. Also the fear of their love they once shared might be lost and buried under the ruins of the revolution, was heartbreaking. Well, ten years is a long time. It made him to view their love as an illusion, a beautiful dream. But what if....? So, love affair or not, there was still a faint hope because there never was a crack in his love for Katie.

* * *

Finally, the plane was flying over Budapest and an exciting feeling ran through his body. The outline of the city was in a haze; then suddenly, he was there in his homeland.

After going through customs at Ferihegy airport, Andrew was swept along with the crowd. He found it strange, even amazing to hear *only Hungarian* language around him, as though *he was in a strange country*. While he was absorbing the sights and sounds of the people, his mother spotted him. He did not expect her to wait here, but here she was, letting out a sudden cry, almost a scream, as she ran toward him with open arms.

"*Andrew! Andrew, my dear son!* Oh God," she cried, trembling as happy tears rolling down her face.

"Mom! You're here? Dear God, what a lovely surprise!"

Then the hugging and kissing, the deep emotions choked back the words. All the wasted love, the trials and tribulations, the worries and desperate yearnings of ten years, and the sudden happiness—it was all there and more in that embrace.

Margie looked up into his eyes with such joy, it melted Andrew's heart. "I cannot describe how happy I am that you were able to make it. I was so afraid, but here you are! I was also afraid that I might not recognize you. Now, can you believe that?" Margie asked sheepishly.

"Well, Mom, I'm here, and you are beautiful. Thank God, we lived to see this day!" Then he held his mother at arm's length. "Mom, you aren't a day older than the day I left," Andrew said with a little exaggeration. For ten years of anguish had left their marks on her kind face.

"Oh, come on, Andrew! You don't have to say that. The most important thing is that I still have my health. One cannot hide the years."

"But we are talking too much, how is Dad doing?"

"Good news, Andrew. With the Good Lord's help, he is out of the hospital and convalescing at home. He is weak, of course, but otherwise, fine. Yesterday, he went for a walk with me. He has to walk, you know."

A weight lifted off from Andrew's shoulders. "Great news, indeed. And you weren't afraid to leave him all by himself?"

"I did not want to, Andrew, but you have no idea how much he insisted that I must go to the airport. 'Margie' he said, 'you have to go there to give him a warm greeting, and make sure he doesn't get lost in that crowd.'"

Andrew laughed. "Yes, that's Dad, all right."

Margie kept looking at him. In her eyes Andrew's youthful health and dressing reflected an air of wealth and elegance.

"But you have changed a great deal and to your advantage, I might say. You look so strong and healthy."

"Thanks, Mom. Canada has plenty of fresh air."

Margie chuckled. "The way I see it, there must be more than fresh air. It makes me so happy to see that the good life is showing on you."

As they slowly approached the exit, Margie glanced at Andrew's two heavy suitcases and she became conscious. "You're coming home with a lot more than what you left with. Can I help you carry one?"

Andrew laughed. "Mom, are you trying to spoil me already?"

Looking around searchingly, Andrew caught a taxi and they were on their way home. Sitting beside Andrew, a peaceful contentment settled on Margie's beaming face. She just could not get over it that finally she was seeing her son. While they exchanged some pleasantries, Andrew scanned the street curiously, taking in all the changes and listening to the never-ceasing din of the big city. As he looked at the swirling, constantly rushing people, he remembered that it was always like that.

When the taxi turned into Baross Street, Andrew felt a strange, jerking excitement. It was hard to believe that he was in Budapest. The taxi stopped in front of the apartment and Andrew let out a sigh. He glanced up at the window of their apartment just in time to see the curtain moved slightly, as if soft breeze had fluttered it. Then, he caught a glimpse of his father, watching his son's arrival from behind the lace curtains.

The driver helped to carry the suitcases up to the first floor, for which Andrew tipped him generously. Then, following his mother into the room, there stood his father. Andrew threw himself into his outstretched arms, tears glistening in both their eyes. With constricted throats, they were able to utter one word only:

"Dad!"

"Son!"

They embraced each other tightly with choking, outburst of happiness. In the years of accumulated grief the emotion overtook them, and the joy erupted like a hurtling tornado, twisting and smashing the ocean shore with a wild force, shaking them with a tidal wave of emotion. They clung to each other with all the human love there is, like two lost souls.

When the storm subsided, they slowly let go and greeted each other in a calmer manner.

"Welcome home, son," Mike said, a feeble smile on his tired face. "Come and sit down and let me look at you. Oh, God, how I waited for this moment! Thank God, you made it! Now, I believe in miracles."

"It's great to be home, Dad. It is even greater to see you at home instead of in the hospital. I assume it was not too serious. How are you feeling?"

"I feel fine, especially now that you're here. That is the best medicine there ever could be."

"I'm happy for you. Mom's letter scared the daylights out of me."

"I can imagine," Margie said. "Well, I'll go and get supper ready while you are talking. You sure have plenty of catching up to do. But I'm going to listen, so don't whisper."

"All right, Mom, in that case, we'll skip the dirty jokes."

"Oh, you naughty boy! Is too much freedom corrupting you or what?" Margie laughed.

Happiness radiated on Mike's face. As he kept looking at his son, it seemed as if he were seeing a new person. He saw that his son had turned into a mature handsome man. His thick, black hair was neatly combed backwards, carefully parted on the left.

"This embrace was much happier than the last one," he said. "You have changed from the boy I knew into a man. You look great."

"Well, ten years is a long time, Dad. It doesn't pass by without leaving its mark on us."

Mike chuckled. "You can say that again."

"All right, boys, here I come!" Margie announced happily, returning with the food. She could hardly contain her happiness.

Sitting around the table, Andrew across from his father, he was shocked by his change. Aside from the signs of natural aging, there were scars of pain on his sad face that despair and worry had engraved. Those deeply etched lines, the dark hollows of his eyes, the gray hair and sagging skin were all results of the past ten years.

While he lived at home, he remembered how pleased he was that his parents looked younger than their years. But now, as Andrew towered over them, they seemed to have shrunk; the hard times had caught up with them and the iron teeth of life had mercilessly chewed itself into their bones.

"Yes," Mike said, "I remember the day you said good-bye as if it were yesterday. I'll never forget your frightened face as you looked back at us from the street. It broke our hearts. You have no idea how much we worried whether you'd make it or not."

"Then, when your first letter came," Margie said, "a ton of stone was lifted from our hearts."

Andrew nodded. "Yes, I remember it well."

Then he told them about the episode with the Russian army truck on Rakoczi Street, how he was able to hide from them behind a pillar and escaped.

"I never told you these things because I didn't want you to worry unnecessarily. At the same time one of my worries was that you might go through some harassment by the AVO for my participation in the fighting."

"Thank God, we were saved from that," Mike said. "They came looking for you once but I told them you had left the country with some friends. They did not say what they wanted, but they never bothered us again."

Now, curiosity got the better of Margie and she wanted to know why had he chosen to leave Winnipeg? "You'll never know how upset we were about your mysterious wandering. It just did not seem right."

Andrew told them as much as he remembered, referring to the climate but carefully omitting his fights in the work places. "Anyway, those years are behind me, thank God, and now I have nothing to complain about."

Mike's eyes gleamed and he shook his head with proud amazement.

"Well, son, you sure made us not only happy but very proud of you. No matter how I look at it, what you have achieved is simply a miracle."

"And a lot of hard work," Andrew added. "Naturally, it is double happiness for me to know that I haven't disappointed you. It's the greatest compliment you could have given me."

"I remember you promised us before you left that you'd try and make it up to us. And you did. But you shouldn't have to send us money. We can manage, you know."

"Oh, I know you wouldn't have starved, Mom, but I could afford it and you have deserved it. Besides, it is my payback time for bringing me up."

Margie let out a happy sigh. "Oh, Andrew! Thanks, anyway. So, tell me, now you can understand *English?*"

"Maybe not English, but I understand Canadian pretty well," Andrew said, causing them a few seconds of puzzlement. "One thing I don't always understand is their politics."

Mike chuckled and said quickly, "Just as well. It didn't do you much good understanding it at home."

In his answer all bitterness and hatred of the past seemed purged from him as he said, "Apparently you're right, Dad. But on the other hand, maybe you're wrong. After all, it is Communism that forced me to leave and have a better life."

"Good heavens!" Margie clapped her hands. "What a way to put it!" Then she switched to a more sensitive subject: marriage. "Now, Andrew, I'm wondering, what is your plan? Are you planning to get married or what? You're not getting any younger, you know."

Andrew looked at his father. "Well, it was easy for Dad; he married my mother. Seriously though, there is a woman I'm going with and we might get married. But so far, I have preferred to take the honeymoon and skip the marriage."

Mike laughed. "I can see you have grew up."

"Yes, I remember her because of her similar name. She was also Katie, or Cathy" Margie said. "She lives in Ottawa. But I wanted to talk about Katie. Her disappearance really puzzled us, knowing how much you cared for her."

Andrew's face darkened. "Yes, it puzzled me too. She meant a great deal to me. Probably she is the main reason for my holding back to marriage. But while I'm home, I'll get to the bottom of what happened. God only knows, she could be a mother with three children by now. All I know is I still love her. My guess is that the Erdelyis too, left the country and who knows where they live now?"

"Yes, this is what the revolution brought," Margie said. "Families have been torn apart, and thousands of people lost all contact with their loved ones. It is a tragedy that will take generations to heal. So, what is your plan now that your visit has turned out to be a happy one?"

"Well, other than finding out what had happened to Katie, I don't have any special plans. I'll visit some friends and relatives. But my main concern is to see Dad getting well."

"Your homecoming has put the magic touch on me, son, so I'm on my way."

Andrew smiled and squeezed his father's hand lovingly. "You are a fighter, Dad." Then he said, "I might go down to Lake Balaton for a day or two. Since I'm home, the Hungarian 'sea' must be included in my program. Funny how pleasant memories pull a man to places."

* * *

The following day Andrew have rented a car to "rediscover" Budapest. As he drove around, the changes made him feel almost a stranger. Here I am in a city where I lived for twenty years, he thought. The streets he used to stroll with Katie teasing and laughing, were familiar, but there was something *different* that he could not put his finger on. Then, it suddenly hit him. In his memories everything seemed to loom over him, but in the past ten years he had seen another world. In Canada he was surrounded by high-rise towers and large open spaces, and in ten years he had unaccustomed to the narrow streets and old buildings with peeling paints, which seemed to make this city shrink.

Suddenly a peculiar thought hit Andrew's mind. Reading James A. Mitchener's great book, *"The Bridge At Andau,"* he remembered him saying: *It is tragic how quickly an exile loses touch with the vital currents of homeland...* How right he was!

He parked his car in Pal Street and went for a walk. Passing by the Corvin-Block and Kilian barracks, he felt his heart skip a beat. Vestiges of the revolution were evident still: the old walls were filled with holes from the bullets that hit them. The past came back in waves. As his feet spontaneously followed the accustomed trails, he soon found himself in Prater Street. He swallowed hard; remembering those thousands of fallen heroes, amongst them where George Pusztai had died. He felt a strange closeness to George, and an urge to communicate with him. *I am still here, George, but we had lost our dreams...You know I truly miss your friendship....*

As he continued, one of the most significant changes he noticed was the presence of thousands of tourists that created havoc in traffic on some narrow streets. Police cars drove up and down on the main boulevards; fire engines and ambulances sped by, with sirens blaring. This was new in Budapest.

It appeared that the current political and economical trend was making great strides, and the Hungarian lifestyle began to progress towards capitalism. That seemed a pleasant change. The improved conditions obviously brought about a certain degree of complacency. He attributed this silent victory over Communism as an indirect result of the revolution. Thank God, it seemed that our struggle was not in vain after all, for it paved the road to a slowly seeping freedom into my unfortunate country, he thought.

Although this was still Communism, the most conspicuous change was the lack of heated political debates, the rebellious mood against the system, which had characterized the fifties. The soul of that enthusiastic spirit was missing from this seemingly indifferent atmosphere. On the other hand, further signs had indicated that the communists finally realized that without free enterprise, there is no progress. Permitting private enterprises was significant for Andrew.

He passed by a man on a narrow sidewalk who was mixing cement in his wheelbarrow manually. He heard him talking with a man: "Well, you have received your permit finally, so now you can be a private businessman...."

"I sure did!"

But what really amazed him was the abundance of food. When he went home, he talked about his impressions with some amazement.

After listening curiously, Mike smiled. "The best way to explain the current situation is that since the present time Hungary enjoys the highest standard of living behind the Iron Curtain, Kadar succeeded to sugarcoating Communism. The Soviets simply could not ignore the revolution. But even if the intimidation by the secret police is no longer a part of our lives, we cannot forget that we're still living under Soviet oppression just the same. Many attribute the credit to Kadar for the changes, but this is still Soviet dictatorship, so I am skeptical. Anyway, life has to go on, and true enough, things are going better than under Rakosi's reign of terror."

"No question, I could see that myself."

"The way I see it, it was necessary for Moscow to destroy Budapest as a warning to the neighboring countries. And for consolation they are *allowing* us to live better. Also, what you're seeing out there is mainly a clever political window-dressing for the benefit of the western world. I think history will mark 1956, as a dark chapter of our time, in which the Soviet's purpose was to maintain a firm hold on the territory. But let's put the politics aside," Mike said. "The important thing is that your life has turned out to be all right. A great burden fell off my chest knowing that after all it was the right choice we have made on that dreadful night."

"That is true! God and luck was on my side," Andrew said. "But I wanted to talk about these awful traffic conditions. What is going on out there is sheer insanity. People are parking on both sides of those narrow streets, blocking the sidewalks completely! Can you believe that? No wonder there are so many accidents."

"Hah, you're telling me!" Mike exclaimed. "I've had my share of driving in those streets for a long time, remember? Although Budapest is a charming city, don't forget it was designed for the horse and buggy."

26

GUIDING STARS

THE NEXT DAY ANDREW decided to leave for Lake Balaton. As he dressed, he said to his parents, "I'm sorry you can't come with me, for Dad is not up to such trip. Therefore, as soon as I satisfy my curiosity, I'll make an account on the changes I find."

"Oh don't worry about us, Andrew," Margie said. "Knowing that you're around is enough. You just go and have some fun, but make sure you come back safely."

"I will." Andrew kissed them and ran down to his car.

It was one of those lazy Friday mornings, the kind when one feels he is on top of the world. Turned on the ignition, Andrew headed for Matyasfold to find out what happened to Katie, before taking the road to Lake Balaton. He did not believe she would be there, but he could not give up hoping. Everything is possible....

In his optimistic mood he started to whistling, then his mind began to play the guessing game. He knew how much *he had changed* over the years, but in his mind Katie was still the same little girl he had left behind. He was sure that she has changed, so he tried to imagine how she might look today. He even played with the crazy idea of seeing a fat girl. But he discarded that. Then he tried to conjure up some romantic episode in which they would recognize each other, and in a Hollywood-style scenario, he was kissing her passionately, whispering feverish words of love in her ear. He knew that finding her defied all logic, yet he felt her presence like a hovering ghost.

Ah, the magic of having a car! He recalled using the local transportation system and it took him more than an hour to get there. By car it took him fifteen minutes! When he arrived, the area cast a magic spell. The place had hardly changed, and the Agoston Street was as quiet as always. He felt as if time stood still and he had been here only yesterday.

As he rang the bell, the first thing he missed was the sound of a barking dog. The garden was well kept, so someone must be living here, but they were probably working, he thought. Hesitantly, he looked around, but since he did not see a soul, he dejectedly returned to his car. Sitting there, looking at the gate, he remembered the times they were kissing good-bye. Disappointment swept through him, and suddenly he felt angry, telling himself what a screw-missing fool he was, a hopelessly crazy dreamer who believes in childish delusion.

"Damn! So much for a nice surprise," he mumbled. Then he put the engine into gear and stepped on the gas pedal with a sudden jerk.

The highway to Lake Balaton was a modern one, in fact one of the best in the country. As always, driving cooled him off somewhat, and gradually he began to enjoy the landscape, flickered by in the hiss of speed. Gradually gaining back his good mood, he played with the thought of why was he making this trip? Then the memories, like a magnetic pull, flooded him. There are moments in our lives, he thought, when an inner force, a cosmic power guiding us to our destination. Every move we make from day one, is written in the **BOOK OF FATE**, and altering it is not possible. So, if fate brought him back to Hungary, he *must* go to Lake Balaton to satisfy his urge in seeing their love seat. The mere thought of going there sent a childish delight through him. At this moment he did not care if it would be a painful experience, as long as his heart became lighter by it.

When he reached Balatonfoldvar, he drove through the town with mixed emotion. He remembered the place where he stayed with his parents, so he went there and introduced himself, but of course, the old lady did not recognize him. She apologized for having no vacant rooms, but directed him to another lodge.

After finding it, Andrew made sure he would get a room by mentioning that the price did not matter. And he would pay with dollars. She showed him a room immediately. After settling down, he went for a walk.

It was a beautiful July day, and the beach was as crowded as ever. Strolling around in a bit of a daze, re-acquainting himself with the surroundings, the bittersweet memories came back. No matter how many times he had daydreamed about the place in Canada, it was not the same as actually being there. It seemed that everything remained the same. He even recognized the bench where Katie's parents had been sitting, the children's screaming, the colorful sailboats floating by—it was all there.

As he slowly walked through the sunbathers, instinctively retracing his steps, he could swear he recognized the very spot where Katie had been sunbathing and he "accidentally" bumped into her foot. Reliving the scene, the experience moved him. Then he turned and headed for the bench. It was overwhelming to be back in this little corner of the world, seeing the peaceful, nostalgic setting, remembering how they held each other around the waist.

The familiar rolling hills of Badacsony region made the picture complete. Yes, the bench was still there, empty as if waiting for him. A peculiar thought crossed his mind that if it has been occupied, he probably would feel hurt.

He sat down, put his right arm on the back of the seat, imagining that Katie was sitting beside him. Then closed his eyes, letting his soul to wander into the past, dreaming how beautiful it would be if some magical power would bring Katie here. The memory of their first night floated through the fog with increasing clarity. The image of a lovely girl's face and spirit lingered on the surface of his mind. He could almost hear her voice saying, *"Look at the sun! How red and large it is as it descending behind the hills…"*

Actually it was their hearts that had burst into flame on that glorious night. Mild breezes filtered through the air that relieved the scorching heat, ruffling the surface of the calm water.

He sat there for a long time, staring at the water and remembering the past. He thought of their childish pleasure in playing the heart game. He realized, of course, that with those words they were merely experimenting with their true feelings. *We were both naïve and silly dreamers*, he thought. But how innocent and beautiful it had been! That's right, it was the age of innocence. Glancing into the distance, he whispered, "Oh Katie, what I would give if only you could be here with me!"

When he finally stood up, he felt tired, as though the journey to the past had exhausted him. He turned reluctantly and decided to go back to the snack bar for a drink. He did not relish the thought of going there, for it was always crowded, and he hated standing in line.

His reason for coming here has been accomplished, yet, instead of being satisfied, the difference between his dreams and reality grew wider still. Paradoxically the memories that brought him here, were now driving him back. He felt empty and restless. He felt also as if he had hoodwinked himself believing in something that was not possible. He looked up at the sky, frustration wrenching his heart. He no longer wanted to stay, so tomorrow he would return to Budapest.

He was standing in line indifferently, oblivious to his surroundings. When he received his drink, he instinctively blurted out the question in English, *"How much?"*

"Not much!" came the answer from the crowd, and in *English!* Startled by the voice, because it was from a woman, and uncannily familiar. Turning his head in the direction of the voice, Andrew's face turned white. A beautiful woman with dark hair was smiling at him, but he refused to believe that she was who he thought she was. Even though he couldn't possibly have mistaken her, the chilling disappointment of another optical illusion flashed through his mind. This time he wanted to make sure that fate was not playing a spooky trick with him. But in the next second he gasped, *"My God in heaven! It is Katie!"*

The blood rushed to his head and with a nervous jerk, he rubbed his temple to get rid of the slight dizziness. Then, they were running to each other.

"Katie!"

"Andrew! Ohhh Andrew!" she cried with glowing joy. Oblivious to people around them, they clung together passionately as if happiness melted them. Neither of them could have imagined that such happiness was possible. *Oh, life, life, you cruel and foolish life, how sweet and beautiful you can be!* That was what their hearts were beating, threatening to burst with inexpressible happiness. Whatever happened during the last ten years did not cast the faintest shadow over their love for each other, for it was engraved into their hearts. All that mattered was that they were holding each other. It did not matter either what tomorrow brings, because from now on they would face it together, and this time only God would separate

them. Their capacity of love had been proven —it stood the test of time.

When the emotional storm subsided that was when they really looked at each other. Then, seeing people watching them with amazement, Andrew hastily gave a two-dollar bill to the surprised girl for the drink he never drank, and moved out of the way. Stroking Katie's silky hair, Andrew repeated over and over: "Oh Katie, my sweet love, is it really you, or am I dreaming?"

"Yes, Andrew, it's me. My dear love, my only sweetheart," she said softly. "I...can't...I just can't...believe this is...true," she said, tears rolling down her cheeks.

When out of the crowd, Andrew flooded her with million questions. "Katie, please tell me, what happened to you? What on earth are you doing here? Where do you live? Please tell me before you disappear again..."

Katie looked at him with dazed happiness. "Oh Andrew, I don't know where to start. You'll not believe this, but I've come here after thirty hours of flying. I live in Australia, in Sydney, to be exact."

Andrew's jaw dropped, and looked at her in disbelief. *"In Australia? My good God!* I thought that nothing on earth could surprise me anymore, but this would take the cake. What are you doing in Australia, of all places, for heaven's sake?"

"It's a long story, Andrew..." Then she told him about their escape and how her parents decided to register for Australia.

"Well, that explains a lot of things. But couldn't you at least write me and let me know? I still can read, you know."

Katie smiled, "sweetheart, it's not possible to tell you everything within five minutes. Andrew, you have no idea how desperately I wanted to write, but I couldn't. Please don't laugh because I'm so embarrassed just to think about it. Believe it or not, I couldn't write because I didn't know your address. You know, I always went there with you, so I never really needed to write it down. Our decision to leave the country was so sudden, and there was no way for me to get in touch with you. Ah, you will never know how many tears I shed over my mistake. We make blunders every day in our lives, but I have carried this heavy burden in all these years."

"Now I understand," Andrew said. "But according to your date, it would have been too late to get in contact with me. I was already in Austria. As you know, my escape was much hastier, for my life was in danger. However, I wrote you before I left Budapest, but the letter was returned to my parents with the note of '*occupant moved*'. God, it turned my life topsy-turvy. I almost died worrying about what had happened to you."

Katie looked at him astonished. "Now wait a minute! You say you wrote to me and it was *returned*? My Uncle Bela returned it instead of keeping it and forwarded it to me later? Ah, the misery he could have been prevented! Actually it was me he punished, not you. How could he? Now I remember. He hated you for calling him 'Stalin worshiper'. If he did this, he is an evil man, and I hope God will punish him."

"Well, we were only children then. Raging about it now won't help, so you might as well forget it."

"Oh no! Not before I give him a piece of my mind!"

They kept walking, cherishing every step, wondering whether it was really true that they were together.

"Look around us," Andrew pointed his finger at the crowd. "It seems as if nothing has changed in ten years."

Reaching a restaurant, Andrew invited Katie to eat something while they talked. After ordering, it was Katie's turn to find out more about Andrew's life.

"Well, you know a little about me, now I want to know where you live and what you have been doing in the past ten years."

"Ah, yes! I guess we both have some surprises for each other." Then he told her that he immigrated to Canada; about his lonely years the way he fought his way up to his present position. As soon as he mentioned Canada, Katie could not help laughing.

"Oh, dear, what a world we're living in! Isn't it amazing? Fate couldn't have thrown us farther apart, yet here we are! There is an old saying which couldn't be more appropriate: '*Man proposes but God disposes*'. We will never know why things happen the way they do, but we know that God has guided our steps to meet again. I truly believe this is nothing less than a miracle."

"Yes, but God could have saved us ten years of misery," Andrew said with a great deal of cynicism.

"True, but having you back, I can live with that. The way I look at it is that we should consider those years as forced experience, a bad dream from which we have been awakened."

Andrew chuckled. "I can see I got back my wise philosopher. Yes, I agree."

While they ate, their eyes drank each other's features thirstily, like sponge absorbing water. Observing the changes in Andrew, Katie was struck anew by his masculine appeal. His features had shed their boyish characteristics, replacing them with a new maturity. But other than the fine contour lines the ten years had etched into his handsome face, his coal-black hair and the gentle smile were the same. At thirty, Andrew was a man in his prime.

As for Andrew, Katie had gained some weight, which was making her an even more desirable woman. Watching her innocent face, he thought again that those enchanting black starry eyes were the window of her soul. And he could not help imagining the wild passion in those eyes as they are making love.

With a happy smile, he said, "You know, Katie, ten years hasn't affected your beauty at all."

"Thank you. Although a mere thanks is not quite adequate for such a generous compliment—you deserve a kiss. By the same token, time has worn well on you too. The results are most appealing. Suddenly an involuntary thought crossed Katie's mind. Contrary to Frank, she was amazed how *easy* it was to express her feelings to Andrew. The ten years of Australian reticence had already been stripped off, and she was transformed back into the sparkling, glowing woman she once used to be. She felt—with a sense of delight—that her old inner self had been set free. She looked deeply into Andrew's eyes and let out a deep sigh. "I still can't believe I'm looking at you. How many times have I yearned for this moment, how many sleepless nights have I gazed at the twinkling stars of the Australian sky, dreaming, fantasizing about how sweet it would be to hold each other. In the window of my soul, I could see your image so clearly. I think the bright glowing stars were holding our hands and guiding our steps to Lake Balaton to meet again."

"Hmm," Andrew smiled. "The guiding stars...I like that. You know, struggling with loneliness as much as I did, I had my share of dreaming about you. For many years, I used to believe that we will meet one day. But after such a long time, I must confess, the conviction kind of began fading away. But thank God, the day is here!"

With moisture in her eyes, Katie squeezed his hand, "It's only human that we went through periods of doubting. Who wouldn't?

Certainly the prospect of finding each other was not very encouraging, to say the least."

"I agree. But since life has to go on, I wonder why none of those hot-blooded Aussies managed to get you marry them. For I'm sure you didn't live in a convent."

Katie looked down at her hands. "It's interesting you would bring it up. Oddly enough, that is the very reason for my homecoming."

Startled, Andrew frowned, "Oh really?"

Katie saw his confusion and quickly put him at ease. "You don't have to worry, sweetheart." Then she told him about Frank and his proposal. "My mother was all for our getting married. The only trouble was that although I liked him, I didn't love him. Naturally I didn't know whether I would ever find you, yet when he asked for my hand, I just couldn't say "Yes." So my dad came up with this idea to visit Hungary and think things over before I make my decision."

"One couldn't hope for a wiser father," Andrew said. "I'm glad it happened this way, but crazy as it may sounds, you took a bold chance. He sounds like an excellent man for a husband."

"Definitely. And he has everything going for him: good position, security, and he loves me. There were times when I wished I did not know you. It would have prevented a great deal of misery. You have no idea how I struggled in my sleepless nights that I should try to love him, if only for his good qualities. But loving you as I did, I was stubborn, and maybe even stupid for not going for him. Security or not, the way I saw it, money without love doesn't' make a happy marriage. So why jump into misery?"

Andrew turned his head. "I just realized how lucky I am. One would think that time would kill love, but I love you as much as ever. If I can, I'll try to make things up to you."

"I love you, too. We're both lucky.

Then it was time to leave. But before they stood up, there was one more nagging question Andrew wished to know and get over with. Asking her went against everything he felt, yet...He struggled with the words until taking Katie's hand and said, "Katie, my love, I don't mean to be impertinent, and probably I should not ask it at all because it doesn't really matter...what happened during the ten years is irrelevant and wouldn't change anything..."

Katie immediately knew what he wanted to know and interrupted. "Don't ask, darling, I will answer you gladly. Although I know what life is all about, and I was tempted, believe me. But I am glad that there was no one who could take away what I was saving for you."

Surprised, but with a sigh of relief, Andrew kissed her. "You know, sweetheart, there are many qualities that I admire about you, but your tenacity is the one I love the most. What a special privilege it is to have you back. You're like a fairy tale, do you know that? By the way, do you remember our love seat?"

"Do I ever! The memory of that place brought me back here. I just had to see it once more before I went back to Australia."

"Katie, that's incredible! That is exactly the reason I came here. Would you like to go there with me?"

"Oh, yes, Andrew," she said, happy tears glistening in her eyes.

* * *

Bathing in the rays of the afternoon sun, they headed toward the lake. The sweet fragrance of a warm breeze wafted in from the waterfront that lifted their lively spirits. The air vibrated between them as they walked side by side on the garden path of *"Memory Lane"* with youthful, springy steps. Keeping perfect rhythm with the joyful music that was playing in their hearts, they were floating on the highest cloud of happiness. Holding hands, they felt the old magic of their nearness, while communicating through their souls. As the dazzling sun sparkled on them, in the reassuring reality the accumulated feelings, the passionate and pain-infected longings, the years of intimate thoughts, the beauty of their innocent love, the dreams that came true—all this tear-inducing poetry was written on their smiling, happy faces.

Yet all that was happening was **more** than a dream come true. It was as if a supreme power was directing their every move on the golden path to their destiny, at the same time celebrating their new freedom, which had been suspended by time. How quickly things can change! Sorrow and joy replace each other just like the sun follows the rain. While yesterday appeared as a dark and dreary day, today they saw the cloud's silver lining.

When they reached the bench, they regarded it with reverence. They sat down and looked through the faint wisp of mist that floated above the calm surface of the water, cherishing the place as a cradle of their love. The touch of their bodies acted as a healing balm for their wounded souls. Under the spell of this tranquil surrounding, they felt a deep inner peace as their souls were pervaded with total contentment. In this enchanting setting their thoughts transcended time. It seemed as if they were here only yesterday, and planning their future; a plan in which fate had cut a ten-year-wide gap.

But now God had given them a second chance to plan their future again. No matter how hard it might be, they would have to pretend that the past ten years was just a bad dream. However, the menacing possibility of losing Katie came back to haunt Andrew, and made him search for reassurance. With a look of determination on his face he reached for her hands.

"Katie, my love, now that I have found you, I dare not risk losing you again. Therefore I ask you here and now with all the love in my heart, please will you marry me? I want you to be my wife."

Happy tears sprang to her eyes and rolled down her cheeks as she flung her arms around Andrew's neck, and with a deliriously happy cry she exclaimed, *"Oh Andrew! My sweet love, yes, yes, my heart is yours, it always has been.* I'm so happy that I had the faith and strength to wait for you. I thank God for bringing you back to me."

With emotions that were hard to control, Andrew kissed her passionately. Then, with a graceful movement, Katie took his face tenderly in her soft palms and in her sweet voice, whispering over and over again, *"Oh my love, my only love…"*

27

BEAUTIFUL TO BE ALIVE

THE FOLLOWING MORNING ANDREW and Katie were on their way to Budapest. It was a sweet-scented lovely morning. Katie sat cozily beside Andrew, her smiling face radiating a sparkling glow of youth and vitality. It was like the sun shone from her heart. Luxuriating in each other's closeness, she felt light-headed, as though all her worries and uncertainties had drifted away. The certainty of being able to see each other had a soothing effect on their souls, as though they had discovered a wondrous elixir. It was all there within them, the sweeping sensation and the safe, exuberant feeling of contentment. It was like all the layers of pain were rapidly thawing away in the heat of rejuvenation.

At Lake Balaton, they both had their rented cabins where they stayed for the night. Andrew had considered sleeping with Katie, but he decided against it. He felt that he would be rushing her, and he wanted to give her time for a getting-used-to-each-other period.

As the car sped along, the two lovers discussed their fortuitous meeting. In the mirror of yesterday, some of the moments began to take a humorous slant.

"Exactly when did you recognize me?" Andrew asked.

"When I first noticed you in the lineup, I stared at you, startled, I might add, because you looked so familiar. But I was afraid to believe or trust my own eyes. However, as soon as I heard your voice, I was positive. I can't really describe what I felt."

"I know what you mean. Although you have changed too, I think I'd have recognized you." Suddenly Andrew remembered the episode in St. Catharines, and told her how he had mistakenly taken a stranger for her. "I almost threw my arms around her, can you imagine that?"

Katie laughed. "You were lucky, she could have screamed for help."

"The thought had crossed my mind. Anyway, do you know we found each other on the same spot we had our first drink together."

"Oh, yes! What a coincident! Which reminds me that I fell in love with you head-over-heels on that day," Katie confessed.

"Hmm, you sure had a strange way of showing it."

Katie chuckled. "Oh, you know how it was with all those strong moral values about 'be careful with boys' my mother instilled in me."

"Yeah, I know. And probably we'll do the same things for our daughter, should we have one. And that just reminds me of another thing: My dream of becoming an electric technician came true, thank God, but it's a shame that yours to be a teacher has gone with the wind. You could have been a good one."

"Oh I came to accept it as something I didn't have any control over. To be honest, the notion that *I was the one* who deserted you was the hardest part to live with. Because I was convinced that it was me who left *you* behind."

"Whereas it was I who committed that 'crime'."

"Don't you dare blame yourself." Katie said. "We had ten long years to struggle with our conscience. But in the light of facts we know now that it was the harsh circumstances that tore us apart. And we did the best we could to survive."

Andrew glanced at her. "Yes, we did. Now we have to thank God for the second chance," quoting Katie.

"That's the right way to look at it, because the best part of our lives is still ahead of us."

Andrew squeezed her hand. "My everlasting wise and gracious sweetheart. You know, I almost forgot how beautiful it is to be *truly* in love. However, getting back to teaching, even if you won't do it in school, you still can fulfill your ambition by teaching our children."

"It'll be my pleasure," Katie said, kissing him.

Reaching Budapest, Andrew drove through the frenetic and

noisy traffic on Great Boulevard and parked on a side street, close to a jewelry shop. Then, hand-in-hand, they threaded their way through the crowd to buy their engagement rings. After some searching and trying on, they found the right ones. Having no time for formalities, they slipped the rings onto each other's finger. Fortunately there were no other customers in the store to be concerned about, Andrew looked at Katie and announced solemnly:

"My beloved Katie. I hereby bestow upon you this ring as the symbol of my official commitment to become your fiancé. I promise that with God's help, I'll do all I can to make us husband and wife."

"And I accept your commitment with my own pledge to be your faithful fiancée until I become your wife."

With their eyes sparkling, they exchanged a lingering kiss in front of the delighted sales clerk.

"Congratulations," the clerk grinned. "This is the first time I witnessed such a lovely ceremony. I wish you the very best of luck."

"Thank you," Andrew said. "I can assure you, this is the first for us, too," he joked while shaking hands.

They walked proudly out of the shop, glorying in the beauty of their love for each other. They felt as if they were floating through the air in a golden dream, relishing the fact that they were no longer single. Stepping into a brand new world, their faces were lit with solemnity, the atmosphere bursting with life; it was hard to grasp the reality of it.

Once in the car, they embraced and kissed each other. Then in a dizzy state of mind, they headed to Andrew's parents, their hearts fluttering with anticipation. They knew what a tremendous surprise this would be for them.

"Just watch," Andrew said, laughing. "My parents won't believe that this was not all staged. They're going to think we planned this whole episode just to surprise them."

"That's right! Oh, Andrew, are you sure this is not a dream?"

"Yes, I am, but if it is, I don't ever want to wake up."

When they turned into Baross Street, their excitement mounted. Feeling Katie's trembling, Andrew stroked her hand.

"Relax, sweetheart, everything is going to be all right."

Walking up the familiar stairs together was an emotional experience. At the door, holding his breath, Andrew pressed the buzzer.

Opening the door, Margie gasped and her hands flew to her open mouth, as she stared first at Katie and then at Andrew with complete disbelief.

"*Katie! Oh, my God,*" she cried out and they embraced each other, hugging and kissing. "*What on earth is going on here?*" she asked, drying her tear-filled eyes. Then, as she released Katie, the puzzle-faced Mike had just entered the room. "How in the devil have you met?"

After this unorthodox meeting and greeting, they went in, and an avalanche of questioning followed.

"Well, my dear parents," Andrew said, his spirit soaring. "Herewith we promise you the thrill of a lifetime, so I'd advise you to sit down. But most importantly, I suggest that you start believing in miracles, because I sure do now." And now Andrew put one arm around Katie's shoulders. "Would you believe this wonderful girl has been waiting for me faithfully at Lake Balaton for the last ten years, hoping that I would show up? Isn't she incredible?" Andrew said, flashing an impish smile at Katie.

His parents shaking their heads in mock amazement while roaring with laughter. "Now that's what I call a good sense of humor," Mike said. "Naturally I don't believe a word of it, but I swear it seems that way."

"But wait, there is more to come," Andrew said, enjoying the situation tremendously. "However, before I go any further, may I solemnly introduce Katie as my lovely fiancé." He raised both their hands, proudly showing their rings.

"*Oh, Jesus,*" Margie cried out happily. "This is just too much. How many more surprises will you pull from your sleeve?"

Then it was Mike's turn to congratulate them.

"Well, kids, whatever happened in the last two days, it sure produced the most wonderful result. And it calls for a celebration." He filled four glasses with brandy and he raised his glass to make a toast. "To Katie and Andrew on this miraculous reunion. We wish you both a long and happy life."

"Thank you. And in return, we wish you both a very happy and healthy retirement."

When they sat down again, Mike added, "Life is full of mystery. No matter how I look at it, son, your trip certainly proved to be a valuable one in more ways than one. But now, let's talk about the real story; I want to hear it all."

"All right, Dad," Andrew said.

Then the two of them told them everything, including Katie's living in Australia and Frank's proposal that led her to visit Hungary.

"Good Lord, you're living in Australia?" Margie exclaimed, lifting her hands to her heart. "You mean you came home at the same time? Well, this weird coincidence is as close to miracle as it can be! Are you sure you didn't stage all this?"

Andrew glanced at Katie and they burst into laughter. "You see, I told you," Andrew said. "Well, I admit, it definitely seems that way, and I wish we had. But no, we wouldn't pull a cruel trick like that on you."

"Okay, okay, I was only kidding." Then, as if thinking aloud, she said, "Hmm, who would have dreamed that my letter would have resulted in such wonderful happiness? It seems like God programmed it that way. But what will happen to your fiancé in Sydney?"

"Oh, he wasn't my fiancé as yet, Mrs. Dombrady."

"Poor guy, I'm truly sorry for him," Mike said.

But Margie had not run out of questions. "Now another thing just flashed through my mind. Katie, how come you did not visit us before you went to Lake Balaton?"

Eyes downcast, Katie blushed, for the question was so obvious. It also awaked Andrew's curiosity. "That's a good question, sweetheart. Why didn't you?"

"All right, I can explain. Yes, I could have come, but I was not ready to hear bad news about you. I don't know why, but I expected the worst, and I did not want to go to Lake Balaton with a broken heart. Should I be in your shoes, I can understand and would question it myself. But again, I was almost sure you had either died in the fighting, or left the country. However, it was in my intention to visit you when I came back, for I had to know the answer before I returned to Sydney. I don't know if it was a good or bad instinct, but I think I didn't come because I was a…coward."

Andrew's heart went out to her. "My God, sweetheart, how much fear and doubt we had to suffer because we did not know the answer. Please forgive me for doubting you."

"There is nothing to forgive. The most important thing is that we have found each other and have a happy ending."

"Oh my sweet babies!" Margie gushed joyfully. "It is such a joy to see you together again. So, here comes another hard question. What is your plan now, considering the distance and all?"

"Well, we plan to get married in Sydney," Katie said, glancing at Andrew. "Of course we don't plan on a fancy wedding," she added. "And then, because the business binds Andrew to Toronto, we'll live in Canada. It just reminds me that tomorrow I must go and send a telegram to my parents, letting them know that I'm cutting my holidays short and will return home with my fiancé."

"Just imagine their surprise!" Andrew chuckled.

"Well, it is true what they say, 'you can't make an omelet without breaking an egg'," Margie said, feeling sorry for Katie's parents. "Katie had found her husband, but they will lose their daughter."

"That's a fact of life, my dear," Mike said. "Children grow up and fly out of the parental nest just as we did, only in a better atmosphere, thank God. Our only joy will be derived from the knowledge that they're happy and hopefully getting ahead."

"Yes, it would be all fine and dandy if only they weren't living at the end of the world," Margie cried. "If we have grandchildren, we will never be able to enjoy them."

Andrew's heart went out to her and he tried to console her. "Oh, Mom, it's not that bad. It's a small world, you know. Did you know that it took me only eight hours to fly home? So either we will come or you will visit us, and you could stay as long as you wish."

Mike made a nervous gesture. "Well Andrew, with my heart condition, I'm afraid that my flying days are over. So as far as the visiting goes, it must be done by you."

"No problem, Dad, then that's the way it going to be."

After this was settled, Andrew came up with the idea that they should go out for the night and celebrate the occasion of their engagement in the right fashion. He suggested going to a place he knew, where they could listen to some gypsy music, drink good wine and even dance if they wanted to.

"Oh, I would love that," Katie said eagerly. "Actually tonight is our only chance, for tomorrow we'll be busy preparing for the trip to Australia."

"All right, let's go then."

* * *

While driving home from Lake Balaton, Katie explained that she was now staying at the Hotel Astoria. Besides wanting complete privacy, she had chosen the hotel for emotional reasons, although Uncle Bela's wife wanted her to stay there. "But what I know now, I consider him as my worst enemy, and I'm glad that I did not stay there."

So, Andrew drove her to the hotel to make herself ready for the evening. After he escorted her to her room, he looked around and complimented on the place.

"I'm glad you like it," Katie said, standing beside him. Andrew glanced at her, and their closeness ignited a magnetic desire that drew their lips together. He pulled her to him and started kissing her passionately. Answering his kisses with a passion of her own, she pressed her body to his, moaning with pleasure. She felt the tingling warmth of electricity that set her body on fire, wishing that it would go on forever. But when she felt that her legs wanted to turn to jelly, she gently pushed him away.

"Darling, I hate to say this, but at this rate we will never make it, wherever we go. I think it's better if I start to get ready." A n d r e w took a deep breath. "To tell you the truth, I'd rather stay," he said huskily. "But you'd better go if you must, or else I'll beg you to change your mind."

He turned and went to the window to get some fresh air. As he listened to the sound of the city and enjoyed the view, twilight crept into the room.

When Katie was ready, Andrew looked at her admiringly, feasting his eyes on her beauty from top to bottom.

"You look marvelous, sweetheart."

"Thank you. You're not so bad yourself."

They went swiftly to the car. When they got in, suddenly Andrew's eyes caught on something she wore, and he wondered why he didn't see it before. It was the necklace he had given her on that memorable Christmas in 1955. He stared at it, deeply touched. This was the moment when he understood why their love had not died over the years from lack of nourishment. He leaned over and kissed her as a token gesture of thanks.

"You see, my love," Katie said, "this was the only memento of you, and I treasured it dearly."

And now Andrew reached into his breast pocket and took out Katie's picture. "I must have kissed it a million times," he said.

This time it was Katie who stared at him through misty eyes. She felt her heart throbbing as she said with a constricted throat, "It only proves that true love never dies. While our bodies were wandering so far apart, our souls remained steadfastly together."

Andrew nodded and started the car. He drove across the Elizabeth Bridge and turned toward the Royal Castle. The steep, narrow hilly streets were bordered with weather-beaten centuries old buildings that carried the history of this wonderful city. Andrew stopped close to the Fisherman's Bastion and they walked to the lookout to admire the magnificent view.

They leaned on the stonewall and Andrew looked around wonderingly. The illuminated Parliament Buildings was as beautiful as ever. On the Pest side of the Danube, long flickering lights stretched out along the riverbank, the water mirroring them like long fingers. The long strips of lights, which were an eye-pleasing ornament, also lighted up the many bridges that spanned over the peaceful river. Further on, against the black velvet of the night, the city's lights sparkled like tiny jewels. Even though she had been bruised and crushed many times over the years, it was a joy to see that she had been reborn. The human spirit is indestructible. Although the nation was living under Soviet oppression, this extraordinary city was impossible to identify with Communism, Andrew thought with overflowing admiration. But she will survive it, just as she did the 175 years of Turkish rule.

"You know, Katie, I've seen many cities, but Budapest, the city of lovers, is still the closest to my heart."

"It is beautiful, isn't it? But for us it's obvious; we born here."

"I remember as if it were yesterday how we walked here in 1955, dreaming like two naïve youngsters. Could you have believed that we would leave this place and live beyond the ocean, so far away?"

"*Never!*" Katie said. "And coming back only as visitors. The world is a huge stage, and we all play our parts, whatever fate has written for us. The city of Sydney is beautiful too, but I agree, Budapest is more romantic. When we get there, I'll take you across the Harbour Bridge and show you the 'second Buda'. The Hungarians named it for its similarity."

"I'm very curious. Toronto is also nice, a relatively new and big, modern city. I hope you will like it. One thing I'm absolutely sure of, you'll love Canada. I had never seen a more fascinating and more beautiful country. It has almost everything: freedom, space, and friendly people."

"Oh, I know I'll like it because you'll be there," she said.

With sudden disbelief, Andrew shook his head and kissed her. "You know, I still have the urge to pinch myself to make sure I'm not dreaming all this; that you are here with me!"

"Well, you sure have company on that."

Then they turned and went back to the car.

In a charming row of buildings, the nightclub was elegantly decorated outside and inside. Tantalizing gypsy music and carefree laughter filtered through the window. The moment they stepped into the room, the fragrance of sweet-sour wine tickled their nostrils. A gypsy band played a sentimental Hungarian song, and a group of people were singing near the band.

Soon the waiter came and escorted them to a table near the window. The place was not too crowded, and they found the atmosphere pleasant. Young and middle-aged people sat around them, talking and laughing. When the waiter came back, they ordered a bottle of Tokay wine.

"I drink this to the health and everlasting happiness of my beloved fiancée," Andrew announced solemnly.

Katie's eyes glowed as she lifted her glass. "To the health and happiness to Andrew, my dear fiancé."

After tasting it, she warned herself, "Hmm, this wine is good, but I must be careful or I might get drunk."

"Don't worry about it, sweetheart, I'm the one who is driving."

There was a dance floor in the middle of the club and they watched as some couples began to dance. As Andrew glanced at Katie, an idea hit him. He excused himself and to Katie's surprise, he went to the band. He whispered something to the violinist, slipping a generous tip into his hand. He nodded, and when the next number came, the band struck up the song:

"Should auld acquaintance be forgot..."

Startled, Katie's face lit up and a thrill of delight ran through her. She stared at Andrew with misty eyes.

"My serenade to the most beautiful woman in the world," Andrew said, offering his arm gallantly for a dance. With gleaming eyes, she went into Andrew's arms gracefully, and they danced to the beautiful music. Their glances, the tender touch of hands was ways of paying homage to their profound love. Katie closed her eyes and enjoyed the sensation of their closeness. In their complete happiness they felt as if the moment were an extension of the New Year's Eve party that lived in their memories forever. When it ended, Katie sighed, "Thank you, my love."

"It was my pleasure. I thought this would fit for the occasion," Andrew said, then nodded his thanks to the band.

A few minutes later, the band began to play the beautiful *Blue Danube*, and they were on the floor again, swaying dreamily to the rhythm of the undulating music. In her apricot satin gown with belted skirt, which accentuated her tiny waist, in Andrew's eyes, Katie was the most adorable woman in the world.

After the waltz they sat at the table, their faces flushed, and sipped more wine. Sometimes, just for the sake of privacy, they would switch to English. Andrew enjoyed Katie's lilting Australian accent, which together with her Hungarian one was very amusing. When she said *payday*, it sounded like **pie die**.

Katie chuckled at his imitating her. It brought to mind a joke she had heard on the radio. "When a doctor in a Sydney hospital visited his patients, he saw a little girl in terrible condition. His heart went out to her, and said: 'Oh my poor little darling, did you come here *to die?*' 'No,' she said, '*I came here yesterdie*.'"

Andrew laughed heartily, "That was really cute."

The following number was a passionate Latin tango, one of their favorites, and they really enjoyed dancing to that one. As they danced, they whispered their love for each other, for which the music provided the appropriate accompaniment. Although they were far from drunk, the wine began to work its magic. Andrew's intimate words of love became more and more suggestive, and he told her how he would love to kiss her naked body all over. It took a powerful effect on Katie, as she felt a tingling sensation running up and down her spine. She was glad that Andrew was holding her, for she could hardly control her trembling.

"Oh Andrew," she signed with sheer delight.

When the music ended, they turned to go to their table, but after a few steps, Katie suddenly stopped him and whispered something in his ear. Andrew frowned. "Oh my God," he said, and looked deeply into her earnest eyes, making sure he had heard her correctly.

"Sweetheart, are you sure that is what you want?"

"Yes, I'm sure."

Andrew quickly gave a twenty-dollar bill to the waiter, and then he gently led Katie out of the room, the words ringing in his ear. "*I want you to make love to me...*" The music filtered out into the quiet night. In that sweet moment, Katie looked up at Andrew with radiant eyes, her lips parted as they locked in a passionate embrace. The moon smiled at them as if with blessing, molding their shadows together.

"Oh Katie, I adore you," Andrew moaned. His desire was so strong that it seemed he could not contain himself within the physical bonds of his body. Feeling his hardness of sexual arousal, Katie pressed herself against him with a yearning cry, "Andrew... Andrew..."

"Ah, my Australian angel, I knew all along that you needed to be kissed badly. But my sweetheart, you're starved for love in the worst way. So let's get out of here."

Driving along the abandoned streets, Katie's whisper was still ringing in his ear. Glancing at her, desire filled his stomach with millions of swirling, fluttering butterflies.

The beauty of life transformed their spirit, excited and teased them into happy laughter, as clowns do to children. They felt an overpowering joy that was threatening to burst their hearts. Isn't it sad how those lost ten years of struggle for survival pushed the youthful zest for life to the background? We should never forget that laughter is the music of the soul.

As they got closer to the hotel, excitement and curiosity vibrated between them. With silent appreciation, Andrew smiled at Katie and squeezed her hand for encouragement.

28

ULTIMATE PLEASURE

DURING THE DANCE, a dream had been born in Katie's mind that if she were to give herself to Andrew, it should happen in Budapest. The fact that this was their birthplace, the miraculous reunion, and their engagement was a significant milestone. In her eyes, all that justified her decision and she never had any feelings of remorse. Oh, she knew that she could have waited for a few more weeks, and Andrew would have been patient. But as an adult, she took responsibility for her actions.

She always knew that Andrew was the only man she could be happy with. And now, she was convinced that Andrew was worth waiting for. As they helped stripping off each other's dresses, she was shy, at the same time wanting him fiercely. They stared each other's beauty with the hunger of youth. The happy laughter, the longing was no longer just a dream but reality. In bed in Andrew's arms, his skillful caressing and demanding kisses drove her to unbearable desire. She was afraid at first, but Andrew's hands opened her body up to pleasure. She gasped and moaned with delight, as Andrew buried his face into her soft flesh, kissing her nipples that felt as if an earthquake was rippling through her body. By the sensation tremor she was floating on a buoyant cloud of burning desire, wishing to be lifted higher and higher to the sweetness of heaven.

Her body on fire, Andrew entered her slowly. It felt as if a hot pit of wet fire, a delicious pleasure that gave him the shivers, had engulfed his body. Feeling Andrew's hunger, Katie felt a piercing sensation and bit her lip but her throbbing body could not stop following the rhythm of his movement. They were swept along on a tidal wave high above the silvery clouds into an undreamed world. Rising higher and higher into the wondrous magic of each other, she passionately answered his thrusts with her own. Then Andrew's movements quickened and his body shook with tremor after tremor, bringing her to a glorious ecstasy. Deep inside her a chasm opened and with prolonged shuddering, a wild explosion shook her. Clutching him tighter, she cried out his name, not believing that such pleasure was possible.

Lying satisfied in each other's arm, they felt as though they were really alive for the first time. For Katie, everything coalesced into one moment of perfect unity. She felt that her body was enriched with the new experience and was proud that now she was a complete and happy woman. How could something this beautiful be called wicked, and justified only by a piece of paper? she wondered. Oh, she understood the moral aspect of it but in her case, what difference did it make to have the marriage certificate later? Surely God wouldn't judge them by such an arbitrary standard.

"Before God now we're husband and wife," Andrew whispered after, stroking her hair. He said more sweet and loving words and she felt that his words echoed exactly her own feelings.

Later still, lying beside Andrew, who had already fallen asleep, a silent prayer formed in Katie's mind, thanking God for bringing Andrew back into her life. She felt great gratitude for having the fortitude to wait. She glanced at him and the image of a boy flashed through her mind, the young man she had fallen in love with at Lake Balaton so many years ago. And now she had discovered that she was falling in love all over again but in a completely different way. She was almost afraid to go to sleep for fear of waking up alone; finding that this was only a dream, a figment of her imagination.

The bright summer sun shining through the curtains woke Andrew first. He rose to his elbow and admired Katie's sleeping face. She lay there in a curled-up position, the blanket half way off her bare breasts, her black wavy hair falling around her lovely face like an ornament. Her lips parted slightly, forming a faint smile, as if she were having a pleasant dream. Then, she let out a soft moan. When she opened her eyes, she saw Andrew's smiling face.

"Good morning, Sleeping Beauty," Andrew greeted her, planting a gentle kiss on her lips. "I think that last night of loving brought out some hidden improvement, if that is possible," he said, reaching for her. A tremor went through her body, rekindling the fire between them.

She felt the magnetic power and moaned with shuddering delight. "Oh, Andrew, *You are delicious.*"

Hungry for sex, Katie's mouth opened and their flickering tongues heightened their agonizing pleasure like a flood bursting the shore. Trembling, she pulled Andrew between her spread legs. Their caressing built their passion to a sparkling desire.

When their burning flesh joined, it was like a touch of liquid fire. They made love again and again, as if making up for lost time, savoring every moment for the ultimate pleasure.

*

They arrived at Andrew's parents at about eleven in the morning. For the Dombradys, there was no need for explanation. They had that special glow lovers get, that passionate look only lovers had; Katie's unmistakably radiant face with sparkling, laughing eyes and Andrew's teasing gaze that reflected a special kind of happiness. All the telltale signs were written on their smiling faces. Life seemed a big, wonderful joke that made them laugh; their happiness was whole and complete.

After they greeted their parents and exchanged a few words, they went into Andrew's room for some papers. As soon as Mike had the chance, he whispered to his wife, "Did you see them? They're so happy, they act like they could catch a flying bird with one hand."

Margie was radiated with joy at seeing them so happy. "Sure, I noticed them. I wasn't born yesterday. And I'm happy for them."

"Me, too. They deserve it. They're reminding me of the time when we were at their age. God, how carefree and silly-happy we were!"

"How could we forget? Just like them, we felt the glory of youth, believing it would last forever."

At the dinner table, Mike asked if they had a good time.

Andrew glanced at Katie, and his smile was full of suggestive intimacy.

"Did we ever!" he said. "We went to the Royal Castle where we found the Castle Club. We can still find our way around, you know."

"I've never doubted it," Mike said.

As Margie listened, another question popped into her head.

She wanted to know why Katie had not stayed with her relatives?

"Oh, that's easy to explain," Katie said. And she repeated what she had told Andrew. "The place holds too many memories and I didn't want to spend too much time crying. Besides, I never liked Uncle Bela that much."

"I can understand," Mike said, as if approved.

"Well, now, let's see what has to be done in the next few days," Andrew said. "First of all, I have to go to the post office and send a telegram to Alex. I must let him know that I'm extending my holidays," he said, rubbing his chin. "I must also let him know that I'm flying to Australia with my fiancée and I'll return to Toronto with my wife."

"Well," Katie said, "if that won't drive him crazy, nothing will."

"Poor Alex. Even I get goose-bumps imagining him reading it", Mike commented. " He'll think a tram ran over you."

Katie stood up, ready to go. "I know what I want to do, and if you are ready sir, let's go."

After having done all their business at the post office, Andrew took Katie back to the hotel. She, too, sent a telegram to her parents, but she also wanted to write two letters. The second one was for her Uncle Bela.

"After I'm finished, I'll take the streetcar," Katie said. "So, you don't have to pick me up."

"All right. Take your time, sweetheart."

In her room Katie sat down at the table and started to write. Gradually, she poured out in her letter the whole sordid story to Bela, by which she became aware of his dirty revenge that made two lives ten years of misery. "By destroying Andrew's letter, *you have punished me,* and put *my life* in ten years of hell....

When she finished, she read it again and put it in the envelope. "So there!" she said to herself: "When he reads it, I guarantee, he won't put it in frame."

*

Driving home, Andrew too, had realized that he had some important business to take care of: writing a letter to Cathy. He had not forgotten about her, but fought with his conscience over the misery that he'll cause her... But he had to follow his heart.

When he had arrived to Budapest, he sent her a card, telling her how much he missed her. Then he finished it by saying: *I can hardly wait to see you.* At the time he meant it. He did not really believed that he would find Katie. He was glad he did, but now he must tell her that the affair is over. She was good to him and he came to love her. She waited and wasted seven-eight years of hope... Damn it, she did not deserve this.

Sitting at the table, painstakingly rolling the pen between his fingers, Andrew realized that there was simply no way to tell her without hurting her and himself. So, he wrote:

"Dear Cathy..." Then, he filled up the lines with agonizing apologies and pleads for forgiveness. It was a letter with full of regrets and heartrending hurting, and more apologies....

He was just inserting the letter into the envelope when Katie stepped into the room. Glancing at the envelope, she curled close to Andrew with a wicked smile lurking in the corner of her lips.

"Sweetheart," she said, "there is no need to write me love letters. I'd much prefer it if you proclaimed your undying love in person. It is much more fun that way." She leaned closer and whispered, "I would even enjoy the naughty part if it is good."

Andrew smiled, but he wasn't good at hiding things. With an awkward move, he put the pen down. He had never intended to keep his affair a secret, but since she never asked, it was simply more convenient not to bring it up until he had to. But now, he felt as if Katie had caught him red-handed.

"All right, Katie," he said. "There is s something I have to tell you."

Katie looked at him, surprised. Andrew's strange tone of voice alarmed her..

"What I'm about to say is that I never intended to keep it a secret, but I didn't tell you this because somehow the time wasn't right. But now I feel it is best if I get it over with."

Katie's face turned pale. "Good God, Andrew, you are not already married, are you?"

Andrew laughed. "Of course not! But I came close. I mean, all kidding aside, my story is similar to yours. Just like you, I also had someone back in Canada. Since I didn't know if I'd ever see you again, and being lonely...So, after many years, I met this girl who made me feel wanted. Well, you know..."

"Do I ever! So what? You had a girlfriend. That's no big deal. You really had me scared for a second."

"Well, yes, but she was more than just a girlfriend. You see, we had an affair. She had a special gift of kindness and it happened. I intended to marry her if I went back without finding you. Well, that's over now. That is what I am telling her in this letter."

Katie understood. She had read somewhere that by their biological nature; men are not as strong in resisting sexual temptation as women are. Although she was not convinced of that, nevertheless, she took a deep breath before she spoke.

"You see, sweetheart, this is the difference between me and other women. You had asked me before whether I had slept with a man. Someone in my shoes could have chosen the role of being hurt, hysterical and working herself up into a rage, saying, 'Well, how dare you question my virginity while you were playing the field, I was eating myself worrying whether you were dead or alive?' You had the nerve to sleep around, celebrating your freedom. My God how stupid I have been living like a saint, worshiping you and saving myself while you were fooling around? Now, you can have her! Good luck and good-bye...'

"Oh no, my love, that's not my style," Katie said tenderly. "First of all, I certainly don't intend to run a contest on morality because I'm no saint either. All it proves is that we're not perfect. Sure we loved each other, but we were not married, for heaven's sake! So, I can't even call it infidelity. If I had been in love with Frank, I might have done the same thing. That is how I look at it."

With stunned amazement, Andrew exclaimed, "My God, Katie, what a great relief it is that you did not mean what you just said. You sure know how to put a guy at ease. I don't know if I deserve it but thanks."

Katie smiled. "Keep in mind that I happen to love you," she said. "So, you still have good credit with me." Then, curiosity took over. "Did you love her?"

"Yes, but not as deeply as I love you. I don't know if it makes any sense, but there is a difference between the two of you. In her own way, she was very loveable and very good to me. I hope you won't get me wrong but I feel sorry for her. It bothers me that she will be very hurt, and that she will think I used her until I found you."

"It's incredible! That is exactly how Frank will see it. Anyway, what is so *different* between us? Is she beautiful?"

Andrew feigned some indignation. "Sweetheart, you should

know by now that I'm susceptible only to beautiful women. As for the difference, well, it is mainly in the personality. Nothing to take away from her but you're more my type. Your sweet innocence projects a fresh flower bud, blossoming before my very eyes into a very desirable woman."

"Oh, my, thank you. You couldn't have paid me a nicer compliment. Just imagine, we have been wandering around the world, thinking we had lost each other forever. We can't stop the flow of life, so we sought consolation. It's all fate, destiny."

"I can't argue with that. But you know, I must say that the basic difference between our relationship was that I needed her. We needed each other in a very important way: we had a lifeline between us that you did not need."

Katie nodded. "You might be right, which means that your letter to her could cause more serious consequences than my answer to Frank."

"That's right. But it has to be done. Interestingly, I had invited her to come with me. Can you imagine the shocking situation we could run into?"

"Oh, my God! It just proves that many little things played their parts in helping us to meet."

* * *

Their love had blossomed on a new and a more mature ground. Their closeness enabled them to gradually squeeze out the ten years of misery from their hearts. Katie was reborn, vibrant, glowing with sensuality.

In the afternoon, they planned to go downtown to shop for some souvenirs for Katie's parents and for Alex. But before they went out, Katie always kissed Andrew's parents, then with a touch of elegance, she would reach for Andrew's arm.

Mike looked at them longingly. *"Youth, how I envy them.*

"They're beautiful together, aren't they?" Margie said proudly. "But don't you envy them. Just remember, you had your share of skylarking at their age."

"I'm glad you remember, that speaks for something."

Katie and Andrew walked lazily in the elegant Vaci Street, laughing and talking just like in the good old days, wrapped in a delightful sense of well-being. Stopping at some of the windows to admire the fancy displays, by impulse they turned into one of the shops. Katie saw a beautiful picture album with the Fishermen's Bastion on the cover and bought three of them, one for each set of parents and for themselves.

And when the opportunity presented itself, an intimate glance at each other would be enough for them to run up to Katie's place which Andrew called *our Secret Sanctuary.*

Lying in each other's arms in the afterglow of lovemaking, these delightful days were a dreamlike halts in their lives. In his blissful mood Andrew said, "Sweetheart, you must have had ESP when you picked this place. It's just perfect for us."

"Perhaps. Or, maybe it was my woman's intuition."

"Whatever it was, it gave us a chance to learn first hand that love isn't love until it is shared."

"Ah, and what a sweet lesson it is!" Katie said.

"You know, Katie, I must admit, that even if the feast we're enjoying is coming from stolen fruit, so to speak, I think these are the happiest days in my life. I'm as close to heaven as I ever could be."

"Oh, Andrew, I couldn't have said it more beautifully," Katie said with misty eyes. "And this is only the beginning."

"Amen!" Andrew said, kissing her.

At home, Katie gave the album to Margie with the remark, "Mrs. Dombrady, this will come very handy when we send you all those pictures from Canada."

"Oh, God bless you. What a beautiful gift! I love it, thank you."

"You are welcome."

The following day they went to the Australian Embassy to apply for Andrew's visa. It was all a matter of formality, as Andrew was a Canadian citizen, therefore a British Subject.

* * *

These few weeks of unbelievable happiness engrossed them all. But happy as they were, time ran swiftly and the day came to part. By this time Mike felt strong enough to go with them, so they all sat in the taxi, heading for the Ferihegy airport. It was a quiet, subdued trip with brief exchanges. An occasional muffled moan, sighing and suppressed sobbing—this was the Dombrady's good-bye.

How Andrew hated these heart-wrenching moments.

At the airport, emotionally exhausted, Margie and Katie cried openly. Then with a final painful embrace, Mike and Margie repeated again and again, "Be happy...take care..."

"Take it easy, Dad, Mom, you're the greatest, God bless you."

Then, after more waving, they disappeared behind the door. Soon, they boarded and the airplane sped along the runway, taking them away once again. Sadness and happiness intermingled in their hearts. They felt that as much as they loved their homeland, this time they would not miss Budapest so much because they took the sweetest memories with them. These wonderful days had helped to obliterate the ten years of misery. Finally they have found and come away with the most unexpected treasure—each other. It was much more than a dream come true.

In Zurich, after a long hour of waiting, they were transferred to a huge TAA airplane, which took them to Australia.

29

IT'S A SMALL WORLD

KATIE AND ANDREW ENJOYED the trip immensely. They had window seats just behind the wing, which swayed in a slow, dignified accuracy over the milky clouds. Soon, they were flying above what appeared to be soft and delicate but undisturbed snowy mountains. In its crystal clear and utterly peaceful, mystical quietness, the landscape took on the appearance of a fantasy-world. But this deceptive sight was in fact nothing more than cumulus clouds, floating like a unique wonderland.

"Katie, look at that!" Andrew exclaimed. "That vast rolling whiteness looks like a dream world."

"It's beautiful."

As Katie warned him, it was indeed a long and exhausting trip, but an excellent opportunity to talk over the past ten years. Most of their memories were painful memories but like dying roses, they were able to savor their fragrance.

Andrew told her about his premonition when he last kissed her, promising to see her soon. "I should have known that it was too beautiful to last," he said.

"Yes, I remember. Oh, how shattered we were listening to Imre Nagy's SOS messages on the radio. We all cried," Katie said.

"Yeah, it's funny how things look in retrospect. I thought it was the end of the world."

"I felt the same. For many thousands it was, of course, but for us it was a miserable beginning."

"I think my most miserable time was in Winnipeg," Andrew said. Then he described the vicissitudes of his life in Ontario. One of the bright spots of this part of the story was Stan Mackay. Talking about those days felt like he was telling someone else's story.

"My turning point was Niagara Falls when they sent me to school." Then, he talked about being in Ottawa where he learned his trade, and where their affair started. Alex was another of his warm subject. "I came to love him like he was my father. The way I see it—now I am talking about *us*—our own ways we both possessed the iron will, the mysterious blind faith to carry on. And along the way, fury and stubbornness were an important support for reaching our goals."

Katie mused. "I think you are right." In turn she summarized her four-week ocean voyage, then jumped to the housewarming party in Sydney, which led her to meeting Frank. "Even his getting me a job had not eased my torment of loneliness. Losing you was the hardest part for me; nothing could console me."

"My poor baby," Andrew stroked her hand. "Yet, as hard as it must have been for you, I think I missed you just as much , for at least you had your parents. I was all alone."

"That's true, but you must remember how I resented them for forcing me to desert you. Then, when my dad won the lottery, Frank proposed. The rest is history."

"Yes," Andrew said. "Another miracle: his winning was my winning as well. This just reminds me, Katie, did I tell you today how much I love you?"

"No, but I have a good idea."

"Well, just imagine, *if* you hadn't had that conflict with Frank, *if* your dad hadn't won the lottery, *if* my father hadn't had a heart attack, we wouldn't be here today. Life is full of **ifs.**"

"That makes life interesting. It further enforces my belief that those *ifs* are our destiny. Everyone's fate is written in the Book of Life," Katie said.

Later they turned to lighter subjects and laughed at some of the episodes the language barrier caused.

"I remember Stan asking me once, 'What's your *weight?*' and I said, 'I *wait* for nobody.'"

Then, Katie told him about an embarrassing story that had happened in the office.

"There was a man at the bank who demanded absolutely perfect work. We called him '*Mr. Perfect.*' One day, he came to my desk and made a correction on some of my work. When he left, one of my colleagues waved her hand as if to dismiss his eccentricity. 'Oh, don't worry about him' she said, *'he is nothing but a big...fuss.'* Just imagine my reaction! (*"Fuss"* means penis in Hungarian.) It made me blush but of course, they didn't know why."

Andrew chuckled. "Well, isn't it true what they say? We have to learn so much to know so little. I still can't believe this. Here I am a visitor from Canada, flying a few thousand feet up in the air with my old flame and laughing my head off."

Katie looked out the window to the descending night and the lulling stars made her to fall into a discomfort slumber.

*

Finally the plane landed in Sydney. Andrew and Katie stepped out with relief, stretching their numb limbs and yawning from lack of sleep. After they went through customs, they began debating whether they should call a taxi or phone Katie's parents to let them know they had arrived. But to their pleasant surprise, the Erdelyis were there, waiting for them.

Joe noticed Katie immediately, recognizing Andrew behind her. Then Mrs. Erdelyi shouted Katie's name and they ran into each other's arms.

"Mom, Dad, how good to see you," Katie cried out.

Andrew stayed behind, waiting till Katie reached for his arm and introduced him with a touch of humor.

"Mom and Dad, I'd like you to meet my fiancée. If I'm not mistaken, you've already met Andrew."

Joe held out his hand. "Hello Andrew. It's a pleasure to see you. Welcome to Australia."

"Thank you. I'm happy to see you."

Now, Mrs. Erdelyi stepped forward and gave him a warm hug. "My, my," she said, "I'm glad our lost hero finally found us. It's hard to believe but thank God, you're alive. Who would have thought ten years ago that our next meeting would be here in Australia?"

"We couldn't by any stretch of the imagination have foreseen this happy occasion would happen here. But it had to happen this way, I'm grateful."

"So are we. As you can see, we had made a few jumps from Matyasfold, didn't we?" Joe said.

"Yes, we all had our share of moving around," Andrew said. "But that's the price we had to pay for being free. However, despite the ten years, you both look great." Andrew said, exaggerating a little, for they both had grown a little heavier, and Joe was balding.

"Thank you, Andrew. Although we're not complaining, I think you put it a little too generously," Joe laughed. "I'd rather have the change you have gone through."

"Well, ten years cannot go by without leaving their traces."

"You can say that again. All right then, if we have all your luggage, I say let's get going," Joe said. "I'm sure you have a lot to tell us about your trip. What was Budapest like? Also, I can hardly wait to hear your story."

They reached the car and piled in. Joe pulled the station wagon out of the airport and drove through the illuminated city at a comfortable speed. Long stripes of lights flickered on both sides of the road, and thousands of lights filtered from the high-rises.

"Dad, I don't remember writing when we'd be coming. How did you guess we would be arriving today?"

"We didn't know, my little girl. But we were able to guess it from your letter, so we took a bit of risk; we came out yesterday also. Well, two nights weren't so bad. But what the heck, that's what parents are for," Joe joked, winking at his wife.

"As parents, you're the greatest," Katie beamed happily.

"Thanks, sweetie, we needed that. Well, let's talk seriously. As I can see, the thinking time is over," Joe chuckled. "It didn't take long to make up your mind, did it? Are you glad that I insisted on your visiting Hungary?"

"Oh, yes sir! And you made me the happiest daughter alive."

"In that case, I'm the happiest father alive."

"When we received your telegram," Annie said, "You could have knocked us over with a feather. Such a surprise doesn't hit you very often."

"Well, talking about surprises, nothing in the world could illustrate *fate* more shockingly than our miraculous reunion," Katie said. "I could never ever imagine that this kind of coincidence was really possible. But you haven't heard anything yet. Do you know where we met? At Balatonfoldvar, no less! Where we first met, remember?"

"How could we forget? Especially the night when you stayed out so late, you two rascals," Joe said in a tone, which indicated that times had changed his once harsh view into a sympathetic one.

Andrew smiled. "I hope you'll accept my belated apology, Mr. Erdelyi. But considering that without that night we wouldn't be here today, it was worth it."

"Right on, Andrew! My sentiment exactly," Katie giggled, her face glowing. "So, you see, in the long run it paid off being a little naughty girl."

"Well, if you're happy, so are we," Annie said agreeably. "But what are you going to tell Frank?"

Katie sighed. "I'll tell him the truth, of course."

"That's right, sweetheart. Honesty is the best medicine."

"Poor Frank. He phoned a few times, always asking when you were coming home! You have no idea how eager he is to see you again. We did not dare tell him the news, of course. This is something only you can do."

"And she will," Erdelyi said. What a contrast it was seeing her happy, smiling face again! To him, it was a celebration of a personal victory. The memory of her formerly sad face flashed through his mind. But finding Andrew had finally won back the love of his darling little girl. "But talking about pain, do you remember Mr. Beresh who came with us on the ship?"

"I sure do. He was the one who chose Australia because he said men here treat girls like princesses. And they had that little girl, Marika."

"Yes, that's him. While you were away, I ran into him in Canberra. Poor man, he looked heartbroken. I could hardly recognize him. Then, he told me that his daughter had been killed. She was holidaying with her fiancé at a seaside resort and on the way home, they had a terrible head-on collision. Both died instantly."

"*Marika Beresh? How terrible*! She was so full of life and dreams."

"It's very sad, indeed," Erdelyi sighed, turning onto a side street. He drove by rows of private bungalows then he stopped at a pretty white-stuccoed house, an attached garage beside it, which Erdelyi had built not too long ago.

"Here we are! This is our home, sweet home," Katie said proudly.

Erdelyi looked at her gratefully. She had always been proud of their home.

Andrew looked through the evening dimness, which the

streetlights improved. "It's very nice," he said.

Inside the house, Andrew noticed that the living room was heated. It was August; still winter here and quite cool. After putting the suitcases away, Katie took Andrew's arm to show him around, pointing out the work they had done before moving in. Meanwhile Annie busied herself preparing supper.

During supper, Katie carried most of the conversation, chatting happily about her visit. After supper, they sat at the table, drinking wine, while they discussed Andrew's life in Canada. He told them modestly about his success in the trade, his pride ringing through his voice. Joe was impressed.

"That's wonderful, Andrew. Accept my honest congratulations! Now then, let's talk about the most important question: What are your plans for the future? Because I'm sure you didn't escort Katie all the way from Budapest just to keep her company."

Andrew laughed. "You're right about that, Mr. Erdelyi. First of all, we have decided to get married in Sydney. So I would like to take this opportunity and ask your permission to marry your daughter."

Joe glanced at his wife, then looked at both Katie and Andrew. He cleared his throat and said, "Well, obviously this is what we have expected. We can see that your love for each other is sincere. Yet, I hope you'll appreciate our concern for Katie's future and happiness."

Annie nodded in agreement.

Andrew glanced at Katie who was listening with rapt anticipation.

"I understand your concern and it's only natural. I promise you that I'll do everything possible to make your daughter happy."

Joe nodded. "I believe you will. Well, as far as we can tell, Katie had never been happier, which tells us her choice has been made. So, if this is what she wants, then we give our blessing, and wish you both luck and happiness."

"*Oh, yes, yes, that's what I want,*" Katie jumped up and kissed both her parents. "You know how much I have dreamed of this, and now it came true."

Andrew smiled at her proudly and thanked Joe for his blessing.

After this, they discussed the wedding and their plan to move to Canada.

"I'm sorry that I have to rush things," Andrew said, "but I'm worried about Alex. I know he gets all the help he needs, still with his heart condition, the workload might be too heavy for him."

Joe agreed. They were pleased to see how happy Katie was, and it became a forgone conclusion that she had to live her own life. Yet, it was hard to hide the sadness they felt over her moving away. But that's life, Joe thought, and they would have to adjust to living without Katie.

The discussion stretched well into the middle of the night.

* * *

The following day, Katie went to the office to face Frank with the news. She felt that this was the most embarrassing and unpleasant predicament she had ever faced with. She was absolutely terrified at the prospect of standing before him, for she knew she would have to hurt him deeply. How would she break the news mercifully? If only there was some easy way out. But there simply was not. Every step of the way, her panic grew almost into physical pain.

As she entered the building, she kept sighing to relieve the tension she felt in her chest. When she stepped into his office, to her relief Frank was alone.

"Hello Frank."

Frank's face lit up with delight and he jumped up to greet her.

"Oh, Katie! What a lovely surprise," he said and kissed her. "Finally, you're back where you belong. You look great, sweetheart, I'm so happy to see you, When have you arrived?"

"Last night."

"I hope you had a nice holiday."

"Oh, yes, I had a lovely time," she said, a faint smile on her face, as she disengaged herself.

"Please sit down and tell me all about it. By the way, thanks for the post card. It was nice of you to think of me. I wish I could have been there with you; you would have been a great tour guide, I'm sure. That Fishermen's Bastion is really beautiful."

"Yes, it is," she said, trembling so badly, she could hardly control it. It was like a fever, which Frank's happy babbling just made it worse. Meanwhile, her mind was searching for the right words that seemed to be eluding her. But no matter how, she must tell him. Finally she just blurted it out. "Frank, I came to tell you something. I wish I could say it in a more painless manner, but I've returned to Sydney with my fiancé."

Frank's face turned pale with a twist as if a bucket of icy water had been dashed on him. Stunned, he stood like a frozen statue. When he finally spoke, his tremulous voice reflected sheer disbelief. "Oh, no! Katie, please, tell me you're kidding. It's a joke, isn't it?'

"I'm sorry, Frank, but this is no joke. Forgive me."

Only those who have been hit by an unexpected bullet can understand the torment that rent his very soul. He bowed his head trying to control his emotions while Katie hesitantly told him that she had not planned this; it was rather a weird coincidence. "He is living in Canada and came home to see his ailing father, just at the same time! Frank, you must realize, just as I have, that Fate intervened because our relationship did not really have a chance."

Spiritually bereft and emotionally frozen, Frank listened, but his feeling of emotional reservoir had run dry. Since Andrew's disappearance seemed so final, he had never really believed that this could happen. However, as the reality hit him, he began to feel angry, and the pain exploded in his chest.

"I see," he said, clenching his teeth. "Well, now you just put the cap on my stupidity. I can't say it is okay because it hurts just as much as hearing my death sentence. But what do you care how much I hurt! Finally your dream has come true; your prince has arrived. Congratulations! Good God, was I ever a fool!...."

Tears ran down Katie's cheeks; she was suffering with him. "Oh, Frank, I do care, and I wish I could have prevented this from happening. I'm so sorry for the pain I've caused." Then, she burst into more uncontrollable sobbing.

When Frank's anger subsided, finally he realized that Fate had him meet the wrong girl at the wrong time, which enabled him to turn his response around. "I think you are right. It was one of those situations where things just weren't meant to be. Don't worry about me, Katie, the pain will heal. There is a song that says it all: *You can't lose what you never had*...I did not really lose you because I never had you." He paused to take a deep breath. "I realize that knowing how you felt, even if you had married me, it would have been a waste of time. So, in the long run, this crazy twist of fate actually did us both a favor. After all, you had told me clearly enough that you loved Andrew but I took my chances." With a feather touch, he lifted her chin, "I'm sorry, too, please forgive me. I shouldn't have been so harsh with you. The most important thing is that you're happy. There is nothing left for me to say but to wish you luck and happiness in your new life."

"Thank you, Frank, for making this easier on me. I'll always admire you for being a true gentleman. I too wish you luck. Good-bye, Frank."

She kissed him and left.

As the door closed behind her, she heaved a sigh of relief. Frank looked at the door and felt as if he were at a funeral, all alone. "Good-bye, my love," he whispered with a constricted throat. A man is not supposed to cry but it was hard to control his emotions. The realization that now he no longer had any hope of winning her, struck him. The wasted years, the unrequited love, the disappointment at seeing all his plans turn to ashes, angered him beyond words. Over the years he had played with the idea of what love meant for him. Love, as he defined it, is the ultimate human emotion , a foolish, crazy happiness, a pinnacle of delight that a human being can attain. Love is a tear-bursting passion, the most profound adoration, living in heaven... Love means life itself!

Feeling destroyed, suddenly brought out a powerful desire to destroy the world. For one weak moment it crossed his mind that if he had a gun, he would kill both of them. This is the fictive justification in people's mind; a sweet revenge to commit murder for betrayal...But when he came to his senses, he admonished himself for even being capable of such horrifying thoughts. He was angry, but mainly at himself, realizing that he was the only one to blame. It infuriated him that despite all he knew, the power of her beauty had blinded him. For now, he was able to see clearly that her putting up with him was only a charity. It hurt that both of them were hoping for a miracle, and *she won*. His mind had always told him to wake up, but his crazy heart would not let him.

* * *

After Frank told his father the news, John Nagy had every reason to vent his anger. Guilty, as he felt, Frank had never told his father (partly from embarrassment) about Katie's early confession. Not knowing this, John continued to fume. "Jesus, what did she mean by coming back with her fiancé? What about Frank and the years he had invested in her? Doesn't that girl have any morals? Joe will have to answer me some hard questions, that's for sure! Who in the hell does she think she is? This is sheer betrayal in the truest sense, and she should pay for this!"

His opportunity to confront Joe came soon. Not guessing what was awaiting him, Joe committed the innocent blunder of asking him if he would care to come for supper.

John was surprised.

"Come on, Joe, are you kidding? Don't rub salt into the wound. Did you ever consider that your precious daughter made a fool of my son?"

Joe's face turned red. "John, you have every right to feel that way. But how can you blame me? You must know that parents have no control over their children's feelings. We were just as surprised as you are about what happened, and I'm sincerely sorry. But we had nothing to do with it."

"That may be so, but my beef is that Katie was leading Frank on for all these years under false pretense. Don't tell me you didn't know that! We resent that she was hiding the fact of having a secret lover on the side. She should have told Frank the truth that he was barking up the wrong tree! That would have been the decent thing to do. But no! Instead, she took advantage of his trust. What kind of a...a monster is she?"

Joe's fist clenched and made a step to hit him, but was able to control himself. "Now, just a minute, John," he said with ashen face. "I'm not sure that Frank has told you everything. I think he is just protecting himself. She may have gone the wrong way about it, but I tell you this: as far as I know Katie never told Frank that she loved him. It could very well be that she did not want to hurt Frank's feelings. I suggest you ask him about it."

"Oh, sure, she did not want to hurt him, only break his heart, that bitch..."

Joe flinched, the rage rushed the blood into his head. It took some effort to keep his temper. "John, I don't want to fight with you, but you're going too far. Are you provoking a fight? I am willing to attribute your outburst to your bitterness. I agree, she should have told him about Andrew, if in fact she did not. But she did not go to Hungary to bring Andrew back with her. I assure you that for the last ten years she had no idea whether he was dead or alive. What happened was just a freak accident."

"Well, I don't know," John said, calming down.. "I could be wrong, but Frank is heartbroken. It sure doesn't seem right."

Going home, Erdelyi was bitter about the turn of events because their friendship was a good one. But now, all he could hope for was that time would heal the wounds.

* * *

Meanwhile Katie and Andrew went sightseeing. Erdelyi gave Andrew the car so that they could see as much as possible. While driving, Andrew made a few remarks about the strange traffic rules—in Australia, they drove on the left-hand side. But he got away with only some minor mistakes. They went to see the Sydney Opera House (still under construction), and strolled through the beautiful Botanical Gardens. It was there that Andrew looked up into the blinding blueness of the sky and said, "It's incredible! I've never seen such a deep blue sky."

Katie giggled and cast him a delightful lopsided smile. "So, you've noticed it too? Well, you see, it is because we're still in heaven. Do you remember way back when you said: *'When I'm with you, I feel like I'm floating above the clouds where the sky is always blue.'*"

"You have good memory. Yes, I remember. So, that's what it is?"

"That's right. Do you feel you're still over the clouds? Because right now, I feel I'm in heaven."

Andrew kissed her. "Yes, I feel it in every bone in my body. Can you imagine how hard it is to resist touching you? I'm with the world's most desirable woman and I cannot touch her. This is worse than giving a torte to a starving man and telling him not to touch it."

Katie chuckled. "Relax, sweetheart. When the opportunity presents itself, we'll pounce on it until we get sick."

Andrew laughed. "You're beautiful."

Walking back from Bondi Beach, which was now deserted, on the King's Cross, suddenly Katie's heart stopped. Frank was coming toward them, looking forlorn, even strange.

"Oh, my dear," she moaned, squeezing Andrew's arm, "here comes Frank."

"Hi Frank," Katie greeted him. "What a surprise!"

"Oh, hi Katie," Frank said, just as surprised.

"Frank, this is Andrew Dombrady."

The two men shook hands, saying a polite "Pleased to meet

you," then Frank offered his congratulations.

"I hope you enjoy your stay in Sydney."

"Yes, I do, thank you."

Frank looked at his wristwatch, pretending he was in a hurry. "Oh, my! Excuse me, Katie, I have to run. You know, how busy I am. Bye-bye, now, and good luck."

As they looked after him, Katie shook her head. This was the first time she was really glad that the awkwardness between them finally had been dissolved.

But Andrew was surprised, almost speechless. In the car, turning his head, he remarked, "I didn't expect him to be so handsome. Now I'm more amazed that he could not sweep you off your feet."

Katie sighed. *"Poor Frank, he tried. He really tried."*

* * *

Meanwhile, with the Erdelyi's help, the church wedding was organized. Though Katie did not have many friends in Sydney, she had a few close ones from the office whom she had invited.

When the day came, Katie was so excited she could hardly talk. Andrew too felt some strange excitement but he forced himself to be calm. This is the kind of experience they don't teach in school, he thought, so you have to learn to swim with the tide. To ease Katie's nervousness, he tried to make her laugh by telling some jokes.

During the wedding ceremony, the handsome couple stood solemnly before the priest. At the end of his sermon, he raised his hand in a kind of benediction:

"And finally, always make sure that the sun does not set on your anger for each other. Love is a wonderful and powerful feeling but it has to be cherished and nourished every day of your life."

Deeply moved, the young couple glanced at each other with a faint smile on their happy faces. They were convinced that what was happening today was possible only because of the grace of God. After ten years of loneliness, this celebration was as much of a thanksgiving as it was a marriage.

At the end of the ceremony, Katie and Andrew kissed each other as husband and wife. Then, Katie's friends came to hug and congratulate them, while a photographer appeared and took some pictures.

It was indeed a simple wedding celebration. They sat around

the table: the Mezei couple, another of Erdelyi's friends with his wife, and Katie's two girlfriends from the office. Before supper, Mezei had offered a toast to the newlyweds, which followed a cheerful applause with *"Long live the new couple!"*

After that Andrew stood and thanked the Erdelyis for all their help and for giving him their beautiful daughter. Katie beamed as he continued, "And now, I solemnly promise once more that I'll do my very best to make her as happy as I already am. Furthermore, I wish Mr. and Mrs. Erdelyi a happy and healthy retirement."

*

The following day, Katie decided to go and say good-bye to her co-workers. Not only because it was the right thing to do, but also because they had shared a deep friendship over the years. She knew Frank had taken a week's holiday to restore his "emotional balance," as one of her girlfriends put it. She was grateful for that. They liked her and she was greeted cheerfully. But she had not expected what followed. She didn't know but during her absence, her co-workers had taken up a collection to surprise her. When they excitedly gathered around her, Katie's supervisor presented her a sliver platter with the Sydney Harbour Bridge engraved on it and $450.00.

Katie gasped with complete surprise and was deeply moved. In her farewell speech, the supervisor said, "Dear Katie, with this modest present we wanted to show you our love and appreciation. Although we will miss you very much, we wish you lots of happiness in your new life in Canada with your dashing husband. Congratulations!"

With tears in her eyes, she thanked them for their kindness and expressed her gratitude for their help over the years. "I want you to know how happy I am for having had the chance to work with you. This place will hold the fondest memories for me, as I felt that you were my second family. I'll miss you all." She stopped, for her throat was choking with emotion. "Thank you."

Then they all embraced her with a genuine affection that only years of togetherness can build.

*

Katie and Andrew honeymooned in Melbourne. It was a four-days wedding gift from her parents. When they arrived at the Melbourne airport, the happy couple grabbed a taxi and gave the driver the address of the Hotel Royal where their room had been booked. As they drove down the dazzling Burke Street, once again Andrew was amazed at another beautiful Australian city. On the way, Katie recognized the railway station from the early days when she and her family had passed through as refugees.

Watching the lively city, Katie excitedly pointed out such landmarks as Flinders Street, her enthusiasm as bubbly as a child's. "What a marvelous city," she sighed. "We're going to have a great time here."

"We sure will."

Being accustomed to simple things, they were impressed by the opulence of their room. After a cursory check, they took a shower then went out for dinner. When they ate, there was a new and strange excitement between them, as if they had won a million dollars. Feeling the powerful naked desire that sparkled in their eyes, there was no need for words. The hungry glance, the tingling sensation that sent the blood to their faces, made them hurry to finish eating and rushed back to their room. Like two conspirators, they locked the door and began to undress each other. Teasing and saying sweet, passionate words of love increased the pleasure. "Finally, we have the right to enjoy the fruits of Garden of Eden," Andrew said huskily. "So, I'll give the world's most beautiful wife the love she much deserves."

Katie clung to him, her eyes sparkling from sheer bliss. "Ah, my love, I hope you will."

Then, as they stood naked, trembling with desire, they fell onto the king-size bed, kissing and caressing passionately. "Ah, Katie, what a sweet thing you're; so beautiful, there are no words to express how much I love you. So I'm going to show you." Andrew whispered.

"Oh...Andrew, I'm all yours. I love you, I love you... I..."

Andrew silenced her by pressing his lips onto hers. Then the words were replaced by the fiery caresses, proving that action speaks louder than words. Their touches sent millions of tiny electric shocks through their quivering bodies and they gave and received the greatest pleasure lovers can. Andrew moaned as he guided her, heightening their inflamed desire. Then when finally their burning flesh joined, a shuddering sigh escaped from Katie's lips as they became one. Moaning with delight, Katie took him with all her womanhood, her arms and legs encircling him, like wanting to eat him alive. They moved in exotic rhythm, giving themselves fully to the ultimate pleasure—it was a journey on a magic carpet over the rainbow. Their breathing increased with the speed of their rhythm, until the mounting tension brought forth the shuddering release, as the force of life took them into a contented, timeless world.

Katie's eyes closed, and she let out a quivering, happy sigh. "Ahh, it was pure heaven," she whispered. "Thank you for making me so happy. Such happiness existed only in my dream."

"And I thank you," Andrew said, stroking her silky body. "Now you know. And this is how it is going to be."

Katie snuggled to him, her arms locked around his neck. "My dear husband, this time, it is I who can't get enough of you."

"I'm pleased to hear that, Mrs. Dombrady. Just keep your lips sweet, and I promise you there is plenty more. By the way, I think some celebration is in order. So, let's drink to our happiness."

For the next two days they spent their times between bed and restaurant, and went a little sightseeing and shopping. Ah, it was beautiful to be pretending of living the affluent lifestyle of the rich and famous in a sophisticated wonderland. Too bad it could not last forever. Even if time was pressing, they decided that on their way home they were going to stop at Canberra. It would be a shame to leave the country without having a quick look at one of the world's youngest capitals. But to be able to do that, they had to cut short the Melbourne stay by one day..

Before they left Melbourne, Katie phoned her parents to let them know about the change. Talking to her father, Katie was happy but emotional. With tears of happiness in her eyes, she told him how she was enjoying her honeymoon, sending them all her love.

* * *

The modern city of Canberra nestled within the foothills of the surrounding mountains. As the taxi pulled into the small Civic Center, unfolded before them were the Black Mountains on the left side and the Ainslie on the right. Taking a short tour, they learned about the unique feature in Canberra, the man-made *Lake Burley Griffin*, over which arched the modern Commonwealth Bridge. It was indeed the focal point of the city, for which its citizens were very proud of.

Interesting city," Andrew commented. "Ottawa too is a beautiful capital but because of its unique location, one day Canberra might beat it."

"I heard that it is one of the fastest growing cities," Katie said. "What impresses me the most is the relaxed atmosphere. It seems an ideal place to bring up a family."

When they arrived home, the young couple barely had time to obtain the necessary papers for Katie's entry into Canada. The last day was a hectic one that needed careful planning. Then Erdelyi drove them to the airport.

It was a bittersweet journey, reminiscing what a wonderful time they had together. It was like the good old days, Erdelyi said. What can be more painful than having to part from our loved ones, he thought. Annie cried herself sick and even Erdelyi's lips were quivering. Inevitably, the time came to part.

"Good-bye, Mom, Dad, I love you," Katie sobbed. "God, how I'll miss you!" She clung to them, as if unable to let go.

When the two men shook hands, Erdelyi entreated Andrew to take good care of Katie.

"I will do my best. Thanks for all your help. I hope one day I can return your generosity."

Looking back, it seemed like it was only yesterday the plane landed in Budapest. It seemed incredible how many things had happened in that short two weeks! And so fast, that it appeared as if he were seeing movie actions in high speed. During those beautiful days they had gone through the most significant changes in their lives—they called it *"our turning point."*

Finally they were on the way *home* to Canada to start their new lives. A new life with Andrew, Katie thought, dreaming about it for so long. As the plane began to climb, they looked out the window and admired the magnificently illuminated city. Twilight had already spread its violet veil, and the flickering lights of Sydney waved goodbye to them. Then darkness swallowed the plane and it disappeared into the starlit sky.

THE CONCLUSION

FROM HEAVEN TO HELL
1967 — 1986

30

IT'S INCREDIBLE!

WHEN ALEX KEREKES RECEIVED Andrew's telegram, he was stunned. He frowned and looked at it again, not really believing what he was reading. He went into rage. It can not be real! he thought.

"*That kid is crazy!*" he mumbled to himself. "What the hell does he mean coming back with his wife? From Sydney yet! It's too much even for a joke." Yet he knew Andrew well enough to know that he would not joke about something as serious as marriage.

As soon as he went to the shop, he showed the telegram to Stan, still indignant. "I hope this crazy kid knows what he's doing," he said, pacing up and down. "What a merry-go-round! First Budapest, where he finds himself a fiancé, then he goes to Australia and gets himself a wife. Just unbelievable!" He threw his arms into the air, shaking his head. "I wouldn't be surprised if they brought a baby along with them."

Stan laughed, although he was just as surprised. "They might," he said. "But I agree, it seems weird, not like Andrew at all. Well, we don't know what happened, so we have to wait and see. You know how it is with youth and love. It's a dangerous combination, like a volcano: you can never predict an explosion."

Alex gave him a scornful glance. "Ah, bull-feathers! He is thirty years old, for heaven's sake. It is a wonder that he mentioned his father at all. As if it wasn't him he went home for."

However, when he calmed down, astonishment turned into curiosity. He began looking forward to meeting Andrew's wife. As much as the situation puzzled him, deep down Alex trusted his judgment. So his thinking changed. One sleepless night it crossed his mind that if Andrew was coming back with a wife, he must buy them some wedding present. But what?

The next day, as he was driving home from work, a **FOR SALE** sign hit his eyes in front of a bungalow. From that moment on the problem was solved. The following day was a Sunday, and he went to the Islington area, a nice suburb that he knew Andrew liked. As he slowly drove up and down, the thought of his own home-buying excursion with his wife brought back some bittersweet memories. When they found their home, they called it *Our Private World*. During the waiting period, before they could move in, they often went to look at the house just to be sure it was still there.

Too bad she had not lived long enough to enjoy the fruits of their success. She had died at the age of 44 in stomach cancer.

There were several houses for sale, and about half an hour later one sign caught his eye. He passed by it a few times, and the more he saw the house, the more he liked it. Not only was the house lovely, but it was also close to his own place.

Finally, he stopped, rolled down the window and studied the house for a while. It was a red brick house, facing westward, and it seemed to be in spick-and-span order, with a good-sized backyard. Since it was a private sale, he got out of the car and rang the bell. An elderly woman answered, and Alex asked if he could see the house.

"Sure, come in," she said kindly. Her husband appeared, and together they escorted him around, eagerly pointing out some of the merits of the property. The house was just as neat and inviting inside. The layout seemed practical and cozy. It had two bedrooms, a modern kitchen, a separate dining room, large living room, and an oil heating system. Taking all things into consideration, Alex decided this was the house he was going to buy. He started to bargain, and they came to an agreement.

The next day, he put down a deposit of thirty percent of the price with the condition that the house be vacated within one month.

As he drove home, he murmured to himself with satisfaction, "well, for fifteen thousand dollars, it is not such a bad bargain." He figured that the monthly payment on the remaining amount with the interest rate of six percent would not be that hard to pay. It might be even less than what Andrew was paying for rent for his one bedroom apartment. He knew that Andrew lived comfortably there, but it was going to be too small for a couple, especially if children came along. At the end, he was quite pleased with his brainchild.

Eventually he thought about Cathy. They seemed to care for each other, and for the life of him, he could not understand what could have gone wrong between them. He had to admit he was very fond of her. He always assumed that one day they would get married. That obviously was not going to happen, and for that he felt a pang of regret. Well, that's life, he thought. Let's hope Andrew knows what he is doing. He could not help but wondering whether this woman, Andrew's wife, was as pretty as Cathy.

* * *

It was early evening when Andrew and Katie had arrived in Toronto. They were just as tired as when arrived in Sydney. After going through the Customs, they took a taxi to Andrew's apartment. The strange feeling of being back in Toronto again, overwhelmed Andrew. In the taxi the recent incredible events occupied him. He could not have imagined of going through with such terrific changes during this trip. It was like being transported to another world in centuries ago, then dropped back to Toronto, transcending the mundane world he had inhibited before—but now with his wife on his side.

Katie was happy to be with Andrew, but she felt strange. After all, she was in a foreign country and needed a transitional period to adjust to another uprooting. But sharing Andrew's excitement, she could show her appreciation.

Finally they reached the apartment. While Andrew searched for the key, Katie clung to him like a lost child in the wilderness. Andrew looked at her with admiring smile, and to Katie's surprise, he lift her in his arms and carried her in.

"Sweetheart, this is your home now, welcome to Toronto."

Katie kissed him with overwhelming love. "Thank you, my dear husband."

"*Husband*," "*Wife*" The words were still new and they played with them like children do with a wonderful toy.

After showing her the place, he said, "All right, sweetheart, you just sit down and make yourself comfortable. I'll put the coffee on, then I'll phone Alex to let him know we're here."

"Hello, Alex."

"**Andrew!**" Alex exclaimed with joy. "Thank God, I can hear your voice again. I can't believe it. Are you in Toronto?"

"Yes, we've just arrived. It's nice to hear you, too."

"I'm glad. But listen, what the hell is going on with you? Well, never mind. You will explain it later. How are you? And how is your.. wife?"

"Everything is fine, except that we're a little tired. How are you? I hope all is well with you."

"Fine, fine, other than we have missed you."

"That's good. To be honest, I felt very guilty and worried about being away longer than I planned."

A wave of annoyance and joy changed place in Alex's reaction.

"*You worried?*... Listen young man, I could say a few well chosen words...But anyway, congratulations are in order here. You rascal, if you pull a stunt like this again, I'll twist your nose. I can hardly wait to meet your wife."

"Alex, I'm sorry if I've caused you any trouble. But you know, there is a Chinese proverb: *'There are only two perfect men—one is dead, the other is unborn.'* However, my dear friend, as I said, we're tired, so please excuse me for cutting it short. We will visit you first thing in the morning."

Alex chuckled. "Sure, sure, Andrew. Have a good rest and see you tomorrow. Give my best regards to your wife. And thanks for calling."

Andrew hung up the phone with a sigh of relief and turned to Katie. "It could have been worse, but everything seems to be all right. He is such a loveable guy. I know you're going to like him."

* * *

The next day they woke up to a bright, lovely morning. The rays of the Canadian sun radiated through the colorful horizon. Having some rest gave them a fresh, renewed feeling physically and mentally. Andrew was in the kitchen stretching when Katie joined him.

"Good morning, beautiful," Andrew kissed her. I hope you feel better."

"Good morning. Seeing you in a happy mood, I could not feel any better. Only you'll have to show me where the things are, because I'm lost," she smiled.

"Yes, of course."

When they arrived at the shop, Andrew opened the door for Katie. Seeing Andrew, Alex's face lit up and greeted him with open arms. "Andrew! Welcome back. How good it is to see you!" he said, hugging him.

"I'm happy to be back. But let's not neglect my lovely lady. Alex, this is my wife, Katie," he said, with pride in his voice.

The woman's beauty did not escape Alex's attention, but he was taken aback by hearing her name. Not only was she beautiful, but it seemed as if Andrew had changed one woman for another, but kept the name. He stepped forward with a welcoming smile.

"Alex Kerekes. I'm delighted to meet you. Welcome to Canada."

"Thank you. I'm pleased to meet you too."

Alex cast a puzzled glance at Andrew. "*Katie, you said?* Well, kids, my heartiest congratulations. I must say I've never heard of a more romantic storybook marriage in my life."

"We have enjoyed every minute of it," Andrew said. At the same time he sensed the confusion in Alex's voice about the name, so he wanted to put him at ease. So he turned to Katie and began to explain. "You know, sweetheart, there is one more thing that I forgot to mention. You see, Alex is confused by the fact that... I mean, he doesn't know that you know... oh hell! Let me rephrase it. I forgot to tell you that the name of the girl I was going with was also Katie. Except she changed it to Cathy in Canada." Turning to Alex, he said, "I hope that will clear up the confusion."

Alex nodded, but this time it was Katie who was surprised, and she started to laugh. "Cathy?" she asked, "My goodness, does that mean I have a twin sister out there, Mr. Kerekes?"

"Well, I wouldn't go that far," Alex said. "She was pretty, too, but you're definitely more beautiful."

"Oh, thank you."

At this moment, Stan came in from the backroom and as soon as Andrew saw him, he greeted him effusively.

"Hi, Stan, my good buddy. It's awful nice to see you."

"*Andrew!* Nice to see you, too," he said, and they shook hands.

"Stan, this is my wife. Katie, this gentleman is Stan Mackay."

Katie extended her hand. "Pleased to meet you, Stan."

Surprised, Stan took her hand with a bow. "Pleased to meet you, Mrs. Dombrady. Welcome to Canada."

"It's Katie, please. My husband told me some very nice stories about you. He said if it were not for you, he probably still would not be able to drive."

"Oh, Andrew has a way of exaggerating," he said. "But yes, we have some nice memories. It is very easy to get along with him."

"I'm pleased to hear that."

Stan glanced at Andrew, puzzled. This guy is something else, he thought. How in the world did he manage to find a beauty like this in such a short time? "My sincere congratulations!" he said, then turned to Andrew. "I'm glad your trip had a happy ending in more ways than one."

"It sure had, but I could not have anticipated it in my wildest dreams."

Several customers entered the shop and Stan excused himself. "We will talk later, Andrew. I have to go."

"Sure Stan, duty first, see you later."

Alex was busy, too, which gave Andrew the opportunity to show Katie around. There were neat rows of television sets and radios, parts and fixtures hung or stacked neatly on the shelves.

"It's a nice shop," Katie complimented. "I'm impressed. I guess you have to know all these little gadgets by name."

"Yes, if you want to stay in this business," Andrew said with pride. Katie looked at him with new respect, while they walked into the workshop where they greeted Charlie, the new man. After exchanging a few friendly words, they moved on. The back door was open and Andrew noticed that Stan was about to leave for a delivery. With a quick excuse to Katie, Andrew went to the truck and stopped him.

"Stan, I want to thank you for the extra work you took on for me while I was away. I appreciate it."

"Sure, any time, buddy, although I'm glad you are back." Then he glanced at Katie and smiled. "Congratulations on your taste in women. You bloody Hungarians; you know beauty when you see it. She is a knockout, you dirty dog."

Andrew chuckled. "Thanks Stan. It just proves that we both have the same good taste in women."

"Right! Well, I must go. See you later." He turned the ignition and waved.

When Alex was free again, they talked about Andrew's father and how quickly he had recovered. Then Andrew said, "Alex, I feel guilty for never telling you anything about Katie. I should have. So it is understandable that you think we got married on the spur of the moment. When you come over for dinner, I'll explain it all."

"Oh, come on, Andrew, you don't have to explain anything. Your private life is none of my business."

"I know, I know. But ours is not an ordinary story. The reason I have never talked about it is because I never dared hope that this could happen."

"All right then, if Katie doesn't object."

"Not at all. In fact, I'd like to hear it myself."

At this moment Stan returned, so Andrew thought it was time to distribute the gifts they brought: a typical Hungarian china set, and a very special Hungarian wine, Tokay Aszu. Then Andrew started to excuse himself to move on, but to his surprise, Alex stopped him.

"Wait a minute, Andrew. This time it is my turn to show you something. So allow me to tell Charlie to take care of the store, and we will be on our way..."

"Hmmm," Andrew said, "I wonder what Alex is up to this time."

When Alex returned, he said in a peremptory manner. "I want you to follow me with your car, no questions asked. All right?"

Stan, who was included the invitation, was just as surprised as the Dombradys were. He knew nothing about the surprise.

They drove for about fifteen minutes, then Alex turned into a gently curving street and stopped in front of a bungalow. When Katie and Andrew joined him, Alex pointed to the house. *"Well, kids, this is your home, my wedding present."*

Katie gasped, and both looked at Alex then the house with stunned expression. Finally Andrew broke the silence.

"Come on, Alex, you must be kidding. We certainly cannot accept such an extravagant gift."

Alex frowned. "*Why not?* Anyway, it is too late for that. Heck, if you don't like it, you can always sell it."

They were deeply touched. Turning his head, Andrew said, "Alex, what can I say? I always knew that you were generous to a fault, but this is too much. All I can say is thank you very much." He stretched out his arms and embraced him.

Katie, who had already looked upon him like a father, flung her arms around his neck and kissed him. "Mr. Kerekes, it is a beautiful house. Your generosity is beyond my wildest dreams. Thank you from the bottom of my heart."

"You are welcome, Katie. And there is nothing more to say, except one thing: No more of this 'Mr. Kerekes' stuff, huh. Just call me Alex, please. It makes me feel younger. So let's go inside and see if you like it."

Inspecting every room inside, Katie was delighted. "Oh, Alex, it is as beautiful inside as it is outside. How did you pick such a perfect place?"

"Let's not forget, Katie, I was married once, too. I'm happy that you like it."

Meanwhile it bothered Stan that he forgot about buying a gift. Not wanting to be left out, he said, "My contribution to the wedding is that when the time comes, I'll take care of the moving."

"Stan, that's a wonderful idea, thank you!" Katie said. "We'll appreciate it very much."

Looking at his best friends, Andrew proclaimed: "Gentlemen, I feel I'm the luckiest man in the world. I could have not imagined a more wonderful reception from my two wonderful friends. You are just incredible! So the least we can do is to invite you both for a Sunday dinner to celebrate."

* * *

After his lengthy absence, Andrew made an effort to make up for the lost time. So, if the workload required, he was willing to work ten or twelve hours a day. Now that he was married, he had the profound satisfaction of working for Katie, too. His soul was in peace. As he promised, it was a matter of supreme importance that he did everything to make her happy in Canada. Gradually things fell into proper order, which provided him with a new source of energy.

As for Katie, she had to learn in a hurry how to be a wife, and to create a home in a new environment. At the beginning there was always missing something from the household. She called it "discovery time." Silly little things could annoy her, which was a sure indication of uncertainty. It was difficult to come to grips with the reality of being married, and being on her own. Not having anybody, like her mother, to give her advice, she often tried too hard.

It took her several weeks before she found her surroundings congenial, and could actually feel at home. But she never complained because Andrew was very considerate and helpful. He insisted on her phoning him whenever she had any problems.

Then, she was concerned about the neighbors, for they were reserved at first. But as they got to know her, they could not help but to fall in love with her. She was candid, friendly, and charming when given the chance. She made all the effort to say the right things at the right times.

It was fortunate that the Dombradys had not met those 'poison ivies', as Andrew used to call prejudiced people. These were friendly people, sensitive to the little world in which they were living.

When the neighbors found out that Katie had escaped from Hungary, but lived in Australia, she became a local celebrity. They felt flattered that the Dombradys had chosen to live in their corner of the world. The young couple's unassuming ways won the neighbors' respect, and when they talked to each other, they referred to the Dombradys as "*that nice couple*".

31

HAPPY YEARS IN CANADA

FIVE MONTHS LATER KATIE suspected that she was pregnant. All the signs were there, not only her missing periods, but also several bouts of morning sickness. Her first reaction was surprise, followed by elation. But she decided not to tell Andrew the big news until she was sure. So she went to the doctor, who confirmed it.

"Mrs. Dombrady, you're as pregnant as any woman can be."

Back on the street, she felt a feverish color on her cheeks. Knowing she was going to be a mother, a new wave of excitement came over her. Walking home, she started thinking of how to break the news to Andrew. She could not just say, "Hi Andrew! Guess what? I'm pregnant!" That would be too...ordinary. Then she began to wonder how Andrew would react. She pictured the look of surprise, then joy on his face when he will hear the good news.

Lately Andrew wondered why wasn't she pregnant, and he teased her about it. What's wrong *with you,* sweetheart? As if something could not be wrong *with him*!

Then her thoughts flew across the ocean, imagining the parents' happiness over being grandparents. A shadow of sadness passed over her face, for she knew how much her parents would like to be with her and share her happiness.

Andrew is going to be a father, she thought. Such a unique occasion calls for celebration. After all, being pregnant with our first child is one of the highlights of a lifetime. She would go and buy a bottle of Hungarian wine to go with Andrew's favorite meal of roast chicken. She was glad she bought a Hungarian cookbook some months ago, and her painstaking efforts had paid off. To her delight, she was now able to prepare what he liked.

The minute Andrew walked into the house and greeted her, he knew that something special was going on. Not only because he caught the wonderful smells wafting in from the kitchen. Because living with Katie was an everyday feast, but he felt that he was in for a special treat. Katie's face was radiant that reminded him how beautiful she was. The special atmosphere she had created perplexed him. He quickly tried to remember a special occasion he might have forgotten, but he could not come up with anything. Watching her for a few seconds, he went along with the guessing game. But his patience reached the limit when she took out the best tableware.

"All right, sweetheart, I give up. Would you like to tell me what this is all about? Either you have won a jackpot, or spent too much money and want to be forgiven."

Katie smiled then reached for his hand.

"Come on daring, sit down. I have some fantastic news to tell you, and it is bigger than any jackpot." Then, despite all the fancy words she had come up with on the way home, she blurted out, "Imagine, sweetheart, I'm pregnant!"

Andrew's jaw dropped. He stared at her as if he had never heard the word before. It took him a few seconds to come to grips with the implications of what she had said. Then his face beamed with glorious happiness. He pulled her onto his lap. "My love, are you sure?"

Katie nodded. "As sure as I'm sitting here," she said happily. "I saw Dr. Smith this afternoon and he confirmed it."

"Oh man, this is wonderful. Congratulations!" he said, kissing her deliriously. "Now I can see that we really do have something to celebrate."

* * *

Andrew went overboard trying to protect Katie from just about everything: from tiredness, from too much heat or cold. He got into the habit of calling her a few times a day to check if she was all right. Sometimes Katie laughed.

"Oh come on, Andrew, give me some credit. I'm not made of porcelain."

Alex and Stan were just as happy. Now the three of them collectively worried about her well being. As the baby grew, one day Katie said, "When I go out, I feel as if I'm walking the baby."

Andrew laughed. "You sure do. Only you can't hold his hand yet."

Then the day came when she excitedly told Andrew that she could feel the baby moving. "*Imagine, Andrew, I just felt the baby kicking. Here, can you feel it?*"

Andrew placed his hand on her swollen belly. "*Well, I'll be darned! Isn't that something?*" he said, amazed. They were both overwhelmed by the fascinating experience, the mystery of creating another human being. Sharing it was like taking a daily joyride to "Mystery World".

It did not take long to learn that there was another surprise in store for them. At the next visit, Dr. Smith said, "Mrs. Dombrady, I have one more piece of news for you. You are pregnant with twins."

"Oh, really?" she exclaimed. "I think that is wonderful."

She went home elated. She thought having twins was an added bonus. When Andrew came home, she told him, "Just imagine, sweetheart, we hit two birds with one stone, figuratively speaking. I'm having twins," she said, stroking her swollen tummy.

"Oh?..." Andrew said, confused. He did not share her enthusiasm, for he thought she was too fragile. "Yeah, it seems that way. Only it scares the daylights out of me. I'd hate to see you hurt in the process of...."

"Oh come on, darling, don't worry about me. I'm strong, nothing is going to go wrong."

Katie was 28, a late bloomer, but to his amazement, she was the embodiment of courage. He began to call her "my heroine."

"I hope so," he said and kissed her.

* * *

At the end of October Katie's water broke, it was time to go to the hospital. Katie was ready and prepared.

"So, this is it, little mother," Andrew said. It was a hesitant statement. Before they got in the car, Katie remarked, "When we return, we'll be a *foursome*. Won't that be something?"

Andrew nodded but said nothing. It was a beautiful autumn day. Toronto's morning peak was over, but due to Katie's condition, Andrew drove carefully. When they arrived, a nurse provided a wheelchair and helped Katie get in. She looked at Andrew's gloomy face.

"Cheer up, sweetheart, and don't worry so much. Remember,

I'm strong and healthy. Everything is going to be just fine."

Andrew made a forced smile and kissed her. "Good luck, sweetheart." And then she disappeared.

Sitting and looking around in the waiting room, he saw people—presumably expecting fathers—reading magazines. Some were even sleeping! How can they be so calm, he wondered? It did not help his nerves seeing doctors dashing down the hallway. He was convinced that all their rushing was related to Katie's delivery. He was so consumed by fear, he forgot that he was in a hospital with full of sick people.

During the first six hours, nothing happened. Then the hours stretched into the night and still nothing changed. A nagging suspicion crawled into his brain that something must be wrong. His eyes darted back and forth nervously from his wristwatch to the clock on the wall. To control his nerves, he left the room and paced the corridor. Once he saw Katie's doctor and stopped him.

"Dr. Smith, what's going on?" he asked anxiously.

"Well, we're dealing with some unexpected complications," he explained. "Because Katie is so narrow, it means we have to be more patient. But relax. She is all right, there's nothing to worry about."

"I hope so," Andrew said, not too convinced.

Then the doctor suggested Andrew to go to the cafeteria and have some coffee. It would make the time pass more quickly. But Andrew did not want to drink coffee; it would make him more nervous. The doctor's explanation did not satisfy him either, for he saw some concern on his face.

The hours dragged on, drilling the worry deeper into his heart. When the doctor approached him again, he looked more tired. Nothing had changed, he said, and this time he suggested Andrew to go home.

"You must get some sleep, Mr. Dombrady. As it is, you'll exhaust yourself, and you won't be any good to anybody. If it is necessary, we will consider a caesarean operation. I can promise you that I'll call you as soon as I need you, or if there are any changes."

Seeing Andrew's hesitation, he quickly added, "Of course, we're doing our best for the safety of your wife and the babies."

Yes, Andrew was tired, so he agreed. "All right, Dr. Smith, I will go. It's just that I'm so scared."

"I understand."

"But before I go, I'd like to say that if there are any complications, it is my wife's safety that you must consider first and foremost."

"That's only natural, Mr. Dombrady."

Reluctantly, he left the hospital. In contrast with his dejected mood, it was a beautiful morning. From East the sun was slowly rising brightly to the sky in pinkish color, and its brilliant rays flooded the sleeping city, which was just beginning to awake. Its glitter reflected from the windows of the spires of Toronto's high-rises. The dampness of the fleecy grayish mist of clouds that settled on the ground, began to rise by the heat of the sun.

Walking slowly with a heavy heart and burning, blood-shot eyes, he examined the sky. Life is amazing, he thought. The law of eternal nature provides us the days and nights, while countless new lives born into this mysterious world. Any other day he would be greeting this life-giving day like a wondering child. Today, however, fighting with his desperate fear of losing Katie, he looked at it with a dull indifference.

In the car he was thinking of her. In their short lives together, the beauty of their marriage and the heavy weight of the events created a storm in his heart. Only God knows the ten years of anguish she went through till she fond her happiness. After all, she had sacrificed her youth for it. But now they could lose it again. What they felt for each other was more than love. Katie was his wife, but she was his friend, a mate who stood by him no matter what. He could not bear to see his love story ending in their happiest of time. Without her, he would not want to live. No one knew better than he that she deserved the happiness she was finally enjoying.

Although the traffic was light, in this emotional state he decided to stop at the side of a wooded park. He was tired, but his mind was clear. Sitting there quietly, he couldn't get rid of his tormenting thoughts of how fragile human life was. Watching people drove by, rushing to their destinations as though their lives had depended on getting there. In the meantime, they don't even notice the beauty of the wonderful morning. The most precious things in life are free, yet we're ignoring them as unimportant. While everything is fine with us, we live the life of a blind man, not even noticing the dazzling colors of the leaves and the flowers in the park. Then—when it is usually too late—we would willing to give anything to bring back the lost time and enjoy the hues of the rainbow...

Perhaps ten minutes later the storm subsided within him and he slowly drove home. The moment he opened the door, the eerie silence struck him. Without Katie, the place felt cold, almost as if he had walked into a crypt. He stood in the middle of the kitchen, feeling the urge to call out to her. He looked around as if expecting her to greet him. A staggering loneliness gripped his heart; the notion of living without her horrified him.

He went to the refrigerator and, again by force of habit, he opened it. A warm feeling pervaded his heart, and he squeezed his lips together to suppress his emotion. Katie had prepared food to last him a week. "Who knows how long I'll have to stay?" she had said. "And I don't want my darling husband to be hungry."

Though Andrew had not eaten much in the hospital, he could not touch the food. He drank a glass of milk and went to bed. In the bedroom he looked at the empty king-sized bed, above which hung their beautiful wedding picture. Slowly he stroked the pillow where Katie used to sleep, curling up to him. Then fully dressed, he fell into a fitful sleep.

It was three o'clock in the afternoon when the phone awakened him.

"Hello."

"Mr. Dombrady?"

"Yes."

"This is Dr. Smith calling. Please come to the hospital immediately. We don't want to wait any longer for a natural delivery, so we decided to go through with the operation. In order to do that, we have to have your signature of consent."

"Of course. How is my wife?"

"Considering the circumstances, she is fine."

"I'm on my way."

Andrew hung up the receiver, quickly threw on his coat and ran to his car. He drove recklessly, passing cars as if they were parked on the road. He did not care about being stopped by a policeman for speeding. He was convinced that it was written on his face that he was on an emergency call; that his wife's life depended on him. Surely anybody would understand that.

Arriving at the hospital, he bolted out of the car, ran up the stairs two steps at a time and darted through the corridor into the doctor's office. The form was on the table ready, waiting for him to sign. When done, the doctor thanked him and Andrew turned to leave. But half way he stopped and turned back.

"Dr. Smith, before the operation, I would like to see my wife if that is possible."

Rubbing his forehead tiredly, the doctor said, "All right, Mr. Dombrady, but only for a few minutes."

Andrew thanked him and he walked swiftly to her room. He stepped in gently, holding his breath for fear of startling her. She lay under the white blanket, her pale face grimacing with pain. She was hooked up to a respirator. Looking at the ceiling, she attempted to stifle a moan.

Oh, my love, Andrew wondered, is it worth suffering so much for someone we don't even know yet? At that moment he realized why there is such a special bond between mother and child.

Recognizing Andrew, Katie's eyes fluttered with joy.

"Hi, my love," Andrew greeted her. "How do you feel?'

"They will have to do an operation," she whispered. "But they say not to worry, I will be all right. So that is what I'm telling you."

"I know," Andrew said, swallowing deeply, his eyes hot from mist. "You are brave and beautiful, I'm proud of you. I came to wish you good luck. My heart will be with you."

He kissed her and left.

He went back to the waiting room again and sat down, feeling as if the room was a freezer. The anguish he went through before was nothing compared to what he was going through now. Every moment seemed a lifetime until the doctor joined him. He was exhausted but smiling.

"Well, Mr. Dombrady, accept my sincere congratulations. *You have a beautiful son and daughter.*"

"Oh my God!" The words involuntarily burst out of him with a mixture of disbelief and joy. "Thank you, Dr. Smith. And how is?..."

"She's fine. The babies are fine too. They are in an incubator, and You may peak at them if you wish. But I suggest you let your wife have her rest for obvious reasons. However, let me say this:

you're a very fortunate man. She is one hell of a fighter, the most courageous lady I have ever met. Once again, my heartiest congratulations!"

Andrew's heart was bursting with pride. "Thank you, Dr. Smith. Thanks a million. You have just made me the happiest man alive. I truly appreciate all you have done."

After a warm handshake, Andrew went to the nursery. Among the long line of tiny babies, there was a double incubator. Andrew stood there in awe, staring at the two tiny babies. He was deeply touched and amazed by the power they held over him. Shaken, he felt his heart was beating in his throat. They seemed so tiny and fragile, that the nagging doubt struck him: would they survive? It was such a strange feeling knowing they belonged to him and Katie. His mouth twitched as if wanting to call out to them, "*Hi kids! Welcome to this world!*"

So now he was a father to a boy and a girl. Dear God, this is incredible! After he tore himself away from the nursery, he ran to the telephone and dialed with shaking hands. He called Alex to tell him the good news.

* * *

After the difficult birth, Katie and the babies stayed in the hospital for two more weeks. During that period, Katie recovered beautifully, and the twins also became stronger. In Andrew's eyes, the autumn roses could not have been more beautiful than their tiny bundles of energy.

Before Andrew took them home, he put a bouquet of roses on the table, and a **WELCOME HOME** sign hung from the ceiling.

When Katie looked around she was moved by Andrew's thoughtfulness.

From that day on their lives had a new focus: raising a family. It was a new and exciting adventure that brought them a different kind of pleasure: caring and protecting two innocent human beings. When Andrew held the babies in his arms, he said to Katie with pride, "they're the fruits of our deep love."

"They are, indeed," Katie beamed.

When they asked Alex to be the babies' godfather, he took it as a great honor. He was so happy that he responded with misty eyes. In edition, it was a unique situation as he was also considered to be their substitute grandfather.

As for the babies' names, Andrew entrusted Katie to make the final decision. So she decided that the boy would be named after his father. But because they wanted to give Alex some consideration, his name became Andy A. Dombrady. The girl's name was Aniko M. Dombrady, after Annie and Margie, to please both grandmothers.

.As time went by, naturally there were difficulties, like getting the babies to adjust to bottle-feeding, since Katie could not provide enough milk.

One day, while changing a diaper, Andrew joked about how his life had been turned upside down. "Ten years ago I was cleaning motel rooms, and now I'm cleaning after two babies."

Katie laughed. "So which one would you rather do?"

"It cannot even be a question, my beautiful sweetheart," Andrew said.

Every day brought some changes; things they had to deal with on a day-to-day basis. It was the school of life; teaching them how to become parents. From time-to-time they stole into the babies' room when they were sleeping. They stood over their cribs marveling at their peach-pink faces and damp silky hair, their tiny fingers curled as they breathed peacefully like two little angels.

"Just imagine what we would be missing by not having them," Katie whispered.

One of their favorite pastimes was dressing up the babies and, like a typical middle-class couple, going for a leisurely stroll on Sunday afternoons along the pathway by the Lakeshore Boulevard. In that peaceful setting, pushing the double baby carriage, they would talk about the children's future.

"You know Katie, growing up in a poverty-stricken dictatorship with complete uncertainty, where the future was so bleak, we really can appreciate how fortunate these kids are living in a prosperous country like Canada. Here, if you have ambition, the choice is yours, and the sky is the limit. While it all seems perfectly natural here, should we heard them in Hungary where the choice was dictated to you, our jaws would have dropped in disbelief. So I'm willing to work my fingers to the bone to provide them with the education they need."

Katie smiled at him proudly, "They are lucky to have you for a father."

"And even luckier to have you for a mother."

Other times Alex would accompany them and they would be sauntering in the park, rustling gold and scarlet leaves crunching under their feet, like a colorful carpet on the ground. They called it the Festival of Fall. Along the way, people often stopped to admire the bubbling twins, with remarks like: "Oh, look at those cute, happy-faced babies." "Hello, beautiful, how are you?" "Are they twins?"

Katie would smile and answer, both bursting with pride.

Then came the days when the babies uttered their first words: mama and papa; and took their first steps. Katie and Andrew couldn't help but laugh at their struggle as they fell down on their soft fannies. But Katie would encourage them, standing two steps in front of them, cajoling them "come on, sweetie, come to mama..."

Although twins, they were special in their individualities. Aniko's charm lay in her cute dimples, which made her mouth curve into a smile, as if nothing but happy thoughts were in her mind. She inherited it from Katie. Andy had an impish, devil-may-care expression on his face, ready for mischief the minute you turned your head. Each had a zest for life, and a healthy curiosity.

Naturally, Katie was terrified at the thought of childhood diseases, and for prevention, she made sure they received every available immunization to protect them.

Over the years they sent many of snapshots of the babies to both sets of grandparents. They captured them in every possible position: smiling, laughing, crying, and playing with their toys or with Andrew.

They were a happy couple in most ways, with one disagreement: how to bring up the children. Andrew felt that Katie was too overprotective, and that she was spoiling them. (And seeing a spoiled-rotten child disgusted him.) On the other hand, Katie felt that Andrew was too strict, and that he sometimes acted like a military sergeant. Fortunately they were able to compromise by using common sense.

Until their second birthday, the children didn't speak English. It was a topic on which their neighbors were consulted, and they agreed, "English will come naturally." They were right. As soon as they started to play with other children, it was amazing how quickly they picked up English.

That is when they reached the glorious stage of experimenting with the magic power of words. They learned to skillfully imitate their neighbors in a cute teasing manner. They were rambunctious and mischievous, but without malice; not angels but endearing little devils. Watching them grow produced a treasure house of countless heartwarming memories.

How could they forget the burbling, impish laughs that went with their games? Or the passion with which the children tore open their presents under the Christmas tree; their glee over making a snowman, tobogganing down the slopes, reveling in the icy flow of air across their faces.

The children loved Alex and Stan, for different reasons. They adored Alex for spoiling them, and Stan for being their 'playmate', running and clowning with them.

The twins' minds were as vigorous as their bodies. For them everything was new and amusing, the simplest thing was delightful and funny. Friendly squirrels amazed them, and they watched in rapt attention as they ran on the lawn, or up in trees. Mounties parading on horseback, or pigeons in the park were endless sources of fascination.

One winter day, little Andy held a snowball in his hand, shouting, "Daddy, be careful! I'm aiming at your head, so you better duck or I might hurt you."

The snowball landed ten feet short of its mark.

"Oh well," he said, "maybe next time."

"Next time you better not aim at my daddy or I'll aim at you," Aniko told him, wagging her finger at Andy.

"Oh yeah, you little teeny-weeny ninny," Andy said, and they started pelting snowballs at each other vigorously.

Andy was born first, so he was considered Aniko's older brother. In many subtle ways, he was reminded of that, so protecting her was something he took seriously. But that was an unwritten law, rather than a manifestation of brotherly love. For given the chance, they would have some terrific fights.

Although Aniko occasionally still hit Andy, he no longer hit her back. This was because one day they had a fight and Andy hit her on the face. When Aniko began to scream, Andrew put down his book and called him in to another room for "serious talk."

"Look Andy," Andrew said, sitting before him. "You may have had your reasons for getting angry with Aniko, but you have to find some other way to settle your arguments. You must know that a boy should never hit a girl. It is easy to hit a girl because boys are generally stronger. She might have been wrong, but it is cowardly and degrading to hit her."

"But she hit me first, Daddy."

"You could have stopped her. What would you think if I hit Mommy when we are arguing? It wouldn't be nice, would it? Of course, I will talk to Aniko too, but I don't want to see you hitting her again. All right?"

Andy stood there with his head bowed. "Yes, Daddy. Daddy, what is *degrading?*"

Andrew was caught by surprise.

"Degrading means that by hitting her you take advantage of your physical strength. So you make her feel less worthy and ashamed for not being able to protect herself."

* * *

Playing outside with friends, they observed life around them. Naturally it was just a matter of time before they came home with some embarrassing questions.

"Mommy, why does the lady across the street have such a big tummy? She looks so funny," Andy said, making a face.

"What a silly question!" Aniko interrupted pretentiously. "Because she eats too much, stupid."

"That's not possible because last year she was so skinny, silly yourself! And if you are so smart, why just ladies?"

"Not just ladies. Mommy isn't fat. Besides, I have seen lots of men with big bellies, or even bigger. So there!"

Katie turned her head to stifle a laugh. What can be more touching than the sweetness of an innocent child? she thought.

There was nothing wrong with the question, but she was not prepared for an answer. And she did not want to make a foolish remark. To gain time, she dismissed it with a simple reply. "Okay children, it's a long story, and I'll explain it some other time."

The ploy worked, but it would not hold for very long, because a few days later, the kids 'discussed' the matter on the street and Andy's knowledge expanded. So at home they turned the question around.

"My friends say the lady has a baby in her stomach. If that's true, how did it get there?" Andy asked.

"Yeah! And how will it come out? That's what I'd like to know," Aniko added with a puzzled tone.

Katie was speechless. She could not imagine that they would come up with such questions at such an early age. They sure get more education on the streets than from us, she thought. Luckily the phone range and she pretended she was too busy to talk. When she hung up the phone, she diverted their attention with their favorite dessert. But she could hardly wait to discuss the matter with Andrew. At night, after the children were put to bed, Katie brought up the subject, telling him the events of the day.

"Can you imagine?" she asked. "You know, being parents is not as easy as some people would have you believe."

"Why not?" Andrew said flippantly. "Just tell them the truth."

Katie frowned. "You certainly can't mean that. At three they would not understand it even if I did."

"So, that would be the end of it."

"Aha, that's what you think. Why, did you learn the facts of life at that age from your parents? Because I certainly did not."

Andrew chuckled. "I don't remember asking them. Just imagine, bringing up a question like that in the thirties. They would have said the devil possessed our souls. But I think our parents got away with it more easily. Or was our generation more disciplined? The notion of *runaway* kids didn't even exist in our vocabulary."

"It was a different world with different attitudes," Katie said. "Anyway, coming back to the present, you are a big help, I must say."

Andrew kissed her. "Okay, sweetheart, you may be right. So let's talk more seriously. The best way as I see it is to try not to overcomplicate things. You can explain that people fall in love, get married and naturally they want to have children to share their love with. At this age you don't have to bring the sex stuff into it. The important thing is to make them see that the essence of life is based on loving one another. And if they persist, you can say, 'we'll figure that out at another time'. You see what I mean, love?"

"Yes, you have some good points. I think next time I'll send them to you," Katie said.

"That would be fine, sweetheart, except you must be careful with that. Because if they think 'father knows best', it would not help to maintain your respect."

* * *

When the time came to enroll the children in school, Katie prepared them with all kinds of stories about what they could do there. With her encouragement, they were ready to go and meet new friends. The school was within five minutes walking distance, but for the first two weeks, she walked with them every morning, teaching them how to get there safely.

"Now you remember, sweethearts, what mommy always says 'use your eyes and use your ears before you use your feet'."

"Yes, Mommy, we know," Andy said.

Then in the afternoon she waited for them at the school gate, so they could get home safely. When she finally let them go by themselves, secretly she still watched them from a distance to see how they managed. One evening she told Andrew about it.

"You should have seen how they were holding each other's hands as they looked from side to side at the street corner before stepping off the curb—just like I told them. They were so cute."

Andrew listened to her happy account with a smile. "You're doing a splendid job, little mother, just like I always knew you would."

* * *

Most of the letters from Australia was written by Joe. He wrote it in a style as if he were talking to Katie at the table. Katie also was a conscious letter writer, letting them know in a happy tone about her pregnancy, then the birth of the twins. They were ecstatic, wishing to be with her, and wanted to know all that was happening with her. When the pictures had started to arrive, that eased a lot of pain. Through Katie's letters, they came to know Alex, and loved him. They knew also that Katie was not only happily married, but loved Canada and was very happy to live there.

The friendship with the Mezeis and the Nagy family was still strong. (Yes, as soon as Frank told his father *that he had known* about Andrew, John apologized to Joe for his unfair accusations.) Missing Katie as they did, they were glad to have that solved.

Usually Joe was avoided mentioning Frank, but he made two exceptions. Once, when Frank married to an Australian girl, and again when they had a baby girl. But once came a letter that brought a great surprise to Katie. Joe wrote that they had received a letter from Bela's wife, telling them that after receiving Katie's letter, Bela's wife had agreed with Katie. They had a big fight over it, which ended up with divorce. Soon after that, Bela committed suicide. With a big question mark, Erdelyi wanted to know what that letter was all about.

When getting over the shock, she gave this letter to Andrew to read, with the remark: "It is true what they say, *God is not punishing sinners by strap.*"

32

FATE OF THE GRANDPARENTS

IN THE SUMMER OF 1974, Andrew received a letter from his mother, telling him the sad news that his father's health condition was steadily deteriorating. The graveness of the situation was such that his condition took a toll on her as well. By this time, the children were seven years old and, in his answer, Andrew wrote that it was time to pay them a two-week visit.

Soon he took a trip to Ottawa to obtain the necessary visas at the Hungarian Embassy. Naturally he could not visit Ottawa without thinking about Cathy. No, he had not forgotten about her. After he and Katie arrived in Canada, he tried to get in touch with her. His conscience bothered him, so he wanted to talk to her, to explain that he had not planned what had happened. He hated the thought that she might despise him. But when he dialed her number, all he got was a message, telling him the number had been disconnected.

Another time, on a business trip to Ottawa, he went to the restaurant where she used to work. To his enquiry all they could say that she had moved away, vaguely remembering that she had considered going to Calgary.

"We were puzzled by her abrupt move," one girl said, "but she refused to offer any explanation."

Coming home without any answer, Andrew discussed the news with Katie, voicing his concern for her safety.

"What do you think, Katie, why would a woman do a thing like that?"

"I haven't got the faintest idea, sweetheart. But it seems to me that there must be a more serious reason than just feeling hurt.

No matter how betrayed or resentful she might have felt, that is not a good enough reason to uproot her home like that."

Andrew agreed. "Thank you, Katie." Deep worry was written on his face, for after all his relationship with Cathy was a big part of his life. Oh, he guessed the reason, but should that justify a drastic step like that? He remembered her telling the first night they met: "*Nothing can shock me anymore*". And now he had added yet another bitter chapter to her memories.

Later, discussing the matter with Alex, he was shocked too. "Hmmm, what would drive a woman to do something like that?" His fear went as far as connecting Cathy's disappearance with the possibility of suicide.

"God forbid, no!" Andrew exclaimed.

He kept hoping that one day he would solve the mystery, but the years went by and he had to accept the fact that Cathy was only a bittersweet memory.

* * *

Returning to Toronto with visas in hand, he was preoccupied with preparing his family for the adventure they were about to embark on. The children were consumed with excitement. This would be their first flying experience, and Andy's main concern was to figure out how in the world could such a heavy machine get off the ground, and what keeps it up?

Aniko's concern was more practical: she wanted to know which clothes she should take to show to her grandparents.

The last time Andrew had waited at the Toronto airport for the Budapest-bound plane was eight years ago when his father had been ill with a heart attack. He remembered standing with Cathy just about where he stood now, kissing her lovingly, promising to come back to her. He had even proposed marriage. It was embarrassing just thinking about it. He could see her waving to him. Life is a mystery, a blind bargain, he thought, and the results are unpredictable.

Eight years later he was standing there once again, but this time with his wife and two children. He glanced at his family with pride, then had to cast the thoughts aside, for it was time to board the plane. Soon they were airborne, climbing swiftly away from the earth. The children looked out the window with amazement.

"Daddy, aren't you afraid the plane might crash down?"

"Of course not, son. Are you?"

"Well, if you aren't afraid, then neither am I."

"Don't forget, Andy, it has been proven that flying is safer than traveling on the road."

"But why are we going so slowly?" Aniko asked. "It seems as if we aren't moving at all. When we see them from the ground, the airplanes seem to be going like zoom!" indicating with her arm.

"You have a good point, sweetheart," Katie explained. "It is because when you are looking at them from the ground, you are standing still. Now, we're moving with the plane, you see?"

"Oh I can't wait to see Budapest," Andy said. "You and Mom sure talk about it a lot."

"It is a beautiful city, you'll see," Katie said.

Andy frowned. *"Then why did you leave?"*

Well, that's a kind of hard question, Andrew thought. How could he explain to a seven-year-old who never had experienced terror and fear for tomorrow, about the political and economical situation that caused such repercussions? How could he understand when one's homeland is ruled by one of the most evil systems on earth; a system that has no other rule but oppression, where there is no other choice to have a decent life but to leave your country....

"Because Canada is even nicer," Andrew said finally.

"Well, I like Toronto, too," Andy said.

* * *

It was early afternoon when they arrived in Budapest. After going through the Customs, the family got into the taxi and headed for the city. The children were tired, but still the amazed look never left their faces. Getting closer to Baross Street, Andrew told them about the places they were passing by. Soon the taxi stopped and Andrew said excitedly: "Here we are!"

When Andrew pressed the doorbell, Margie opened the door and gasped, shouting: "Mike, it's them! Andrew, Katie...how lovely. Come in."

After some hugging and kissing, Margie looked at the children. "Dear God, look at these two beauties! You look just like your pictures," she said, hugging and kissing them with all the love a grandmother can give.

Then Mike was there to greet them.

"Well, here is my family," Andrew said proudly to his father.

"We have increased in number since last time!"

"In the most pleasing way," Mike said. "They are beautiful. Thank you for giving us the chance to see our grandchildren."

"It is my pleasure. They're a little tired from the long trip," Andrew explained, excusing their quietness.

"Oh, that's all right, they'll get used to us in no time."

Mike was right. Soon the children began to warm to the loving attention of their grandparents, which pleased them immensely.

"What a joy it is to see you again," Margie said, wiping the tears from her eyes. "You have no idea how much we dreamed for this moment."

When they heard the children speaking Hungarian, their tired faces lit up with amazement. Seeing their happiness moved Katie and Andrew. How cruel life can be, Andrew thought. Just being able to see their grandchildren made all the difference in their lives. It transformed them from lonely old people into exuberant grandparents. The happiness made them almost children themselves. Remembering his once active father, trying to imagine his purposeless life of today, what could be more boring than an un-challenging, idle life? He could see that boredom was slowly eating him away. There was vagueness about him as though he was living in a constant twilight, knowing that his days were coming to an end. His tired face revealed that existence was a chore, and the magic of being alive had vanished. Even in his last visit, there had still been some spark of life in his father's eyes. He was eager to take part in political discussions, showing some concern about what was going on. But now he seemed unconcerned about life outside of his own. When Andrew brought up political points, Mike simply waved his hand and dismissed it as unimportant. That is what time does: we are all prisoners of time. "*If there is nothing to get up for, there is nothing to live for,*" he had once said.

Indeed, what was there for him to live for if he could not even enjoy his grandchildren! Human nature demands physical and mental attachment to those we love. There was desperation in their happiness, a longing that underlined how joyless their lives were.

Seeing Andrew's concerned face, Mike smiled and nodded with understanding. "I know what you think, son. But you know, I keep saying to myself, it is one thing to reach seventy or eighty, but why do we have to get *old?*"

* * *

During the days that followed, Andrew scheduled their activities in a way that his parents could be included. The next day, walking on the street, Andrew's father's raspy breathing indicated the toll of his efforts, which said they have to slow down. It was a painful sight for Andrew because in his eyes, his father had always been a tower of strength.

While exploring the city, Andrew derived a great deal of enjoyment from telling the children interesting stories about the places they passed by, especially around the Corvin-Block and Kilian barracks where he had fought in the revolution. He pointed to the spots where they had burned out a number of tanks. Then when they passed by the Hotel Astoria, Andrew smiled at Katie.

"I'm not going to tell them our secret memory of this building," he whispered to Katie.

"You had better not, or else I'll bite your tongue."

During the last eight years the city of Budapest had undergone monumental changes. Now many intersections were connected to an efficient subway, called METRO. It was fast and inexpensive, and they made good use of it.

The next day was a lovely balmy afternoon and they went up to the Royal Castle. While admiring the beautiful panorama, they stopped at the Fisherman's Bastion. The children's curiosity was endless and they asked all kinds of questions about the buildings around them. Naturally, the Parliament Buildings were the big attraction.

"Well, children, how do you like Budapest?" grandpa asked them. "Would you like to live here?"

"It's very nice," Andy answered.

"I wouldn't mind living here with mommy and daddy," Aniko said.

"Of course, dear," Margie said. Turning to Mike, she added, "They're so smart. It's refreshing just to look at them."

"That's right," Mike said, and with a glint of pride he added, "No wonder, Dombrady blood flowing through their veins!"

Andrew overheard them and smiled.

"As far as their living here is concerned, it wouldn't work, Dad, because economically they are hopelessly spoiled."

"I can believe that."

When suppertime came, Andrew embraced his mother, "Mom, you deserve a day off. We're going to a nice restaurant for Hungarian goulash. So relax."

"Oh, no! *That will cost a fortune.* I don't mind cooking, you know that," Margie said, but she was pleased, nevertheless.

The following day, as a special treat for the children, they decided to go to the amusement park. On the tram, Andrew told the children about the many wonders that were in store for them. "When I was a little boy, I went there often and enjoyed many of the rides."

"Oh great!" the children shouted. They could hardly wait to get off the tram.

When they entered the noisy, carnival-like atmosphere with all the rides, the children's faces lit up. Even the grandparents were caught up by their enthusiasm. Andy wanted to try out everything, and now grandpa had his chance of thoroughly spoiling them. He eagerly bought one ticket after another." Thank you, Grandpa, you are wonderful," Andy shouted, accepting yet another ticket. This time it was for the merry-go-round airplanes.

Aniko sat between Katie and Margie.

"I think I'll skip this one and stay with you," she said to grandma.

"Nothing would please me more, sweetheart," she said, stroking her hair.

They stayed there all day, and in the evening they went to the Capital Grand Circus, which was right beside the amusement park. The acrobats put on a magnificent show, and the children laughed at the clown's crazy antics. While enjoying the show, Andrew noticed how fast the children reverted to the Hungarian language even when speaking to each other. They had never done that before. At home, he mentioned it to Katie.

"Yes, I've noticed it, too," she said. "I think that at their age they pick things up very fast, but I'm afraid they forget them just as quickly. Should they live here for a year, returning to Canada, they would need a few weeks to get back to English.

The next day Andrew rented a car because they decided to visit Lake Balaton. It was Katie's idea to finish their holidays that way. The trip was filled with excitement; a very happy family affair.

Andrew drove at a comfortable speed while reminiscing about the day Katie and Andrew had met.

"It's interesting how the human mind works," Andrew said. "I remember as if it were yesterday when I was walking among the sunbathers, suddenly I saw this young girl lying on a blanket. For the life of me, I could not explain why, but I decided to deliberately stumble into her foot."

"**Deliberately**?" Katie stared at him. "You never told me that, you...big cheat. Well, whatever way it happened, it was love at first sight with me."

"Yes, the same with me. And it turned out to be one of the happiest summers of my life," Andrew said. "I even predicted that very night that I would marry her. And I was right."

"You sure were," Mike confirmed.

"Yes, but listen to this," Andrew chuckled. "I remember also how upset Mother was when I told her I was going to take Katie out for the night. She thought that Katie was too young to go out with me."

"*Oh, you rascal! You still remember that?*" Margie blushed. "I hoped you had forgotten about it by now."

"We have come a long way, haven't we?" Katie said.

"Yes, and the world has turned upside down with us, but the happy ending gives us a sweet memory," Andrew said. "Those were *our* good old days."

"Well, that first night when you told us about Katie, we didn't know her, but I liked the romance right away," Mike said. "But who would have believed that we would end up living so far apart."

Andrew heard the pain in his father's voice. "Well, Dad, we have to look at it from the bright side," he consoled him. "It could have been worse. I'll never forget the night you insisted that I must escape. It broke my heart, but you were right. Just bear in mind that if I had stayed, I could be dead somewhere in Siberia, like so many others."

"How true, son. Yeah, I was the one who put the pressure on you to run while you still could. Sometimes we need a harsh reminder to make us realize why things are the way they are."

It was early afternoon when they arrived. Looking for a suitable cabin, again the almighty dollar smoothed the way. After they rested awhile, they were ready to go to the bench. The children ran in front of them while Andrew held Katie's hand, walking between his parents. There was an overwhelming joy on Katie's and Andrew's faces that radiated their fulfilled dreams.

Reaching the bench, they fell under the spell of the past. Memories rushed back from their first meeting, bringing with them the vivid picture of their reunion.

"Well, Mom and Dad, this bench is the landmark of our happy love story. Our love started here, and the fruits of our reunion are here," pointing to Andy and Aniko, throwing pebbles into the water. "They are our hope in the continuation of our family tree."

"And ours," Mike added.

As Katie listened to the conversation between father and son, it was like a log had been thrown on the fire; it warmed her heart. She remembered how she and Andrew sat on that very bench the first time, just children themselves—what a beautiful moment it was! Enjoying the rays of the sun, the memories blended with the sounds of her children's carefree laughter. She had to turn her head to wipe the tears that clouded her eyes.

"What an uplifting moment," Margie said, deeply moved.

Feeling peace and contentment, Mike said, "You know son, your homecoming and sharing these moments means the world to us. I haven't felt this good for a long time."

Yes, it was amazing how the visit revitalized him. He realized that his purpose in life had been fulfilled: he and Margie had not lived in vain. And this new awareness of having done their duty soothed his soul.

A warm feeling ran through Andrew and he looked at his father with misty eyes. "It means a world of happiness that I was able to make you feel that way, Dad," Andrew said. Then they embraced each other for a long time.

* * *

The two week holiday passed much too quickly, and it was time to part.

"We have just lived some of the most beautiful days of our lives," a somber Mike said, at the airport. "It's too bad we can't stop time for our own pleasure. Thank you again for visiting us. You have given us the greatest treasure humanly possible, and we will cherish this for the rest of our lives."

"We are just as happy that we were able to bring a little sunshine into your lives," Katie said, her voice trembling.

Feeling the weight of the occasion, the children behaved solemnly. Margie was too shaken to say much. She kissed and clung to them as if by doing so, she would delay the parting. As always, it was a bewildering moment for Andrew. People who don't have to live through this, have no idea how fortunate they are, he thought. It was excruciating to see the withering, tormented faces of his parents, as the monumental weight of their good-byes crushed them into bottomless grief.

33

HOME, SWEET HOME: CANADA

IT HAS BEEN WONDERFUL to visit his parents and share some happy moments with them. Yet no one can go through life without undergoing some changes, and Andrew certainly had gone through them in a huge way. Painful as the parting was, arriving back in Canada, they felt great relief, and an overwhelming contentment. It was not surprising—but amazing to Andrew—that after almost twenty years, they were able to cut the umbilical cord with Europe. Their roots were firmly entrenched in Toronto —Canada was their home now.

During the first few days they were busy getting things in order. The lawn and garden were in fairly good shape because Stan has been taking care of them.

Yes, Stan was still with them. But during the past two years he had gone through some changes too. He met a divorced woman, Rose, a thirty-five year old redhead, with a similar sense of humor. They were living together and seemed to be getting along fine.

Andrew went back to work with renewed ambition. By now Alex was considered a member of the family, therefore it was a matter of routine that he came to the Dombrady house for Sunday dinner. When he made his visit the following Sunday, Andy jumped up joyfully, leaping high into his arms.

"Oh, Godfather, it's so nice to see you," the children shouted. "We missed you very much."

Their genuine love melted Alex's heart. "I missed you, too, more than you'll ever know," he murmured.

After playing with them for a while, he sat down with Andrew and Katie to discuss their trip and drink some Hungarian wine, *Bull's Blood*. Although he was interested in what was going on in Hungary, Alex had no close relatives there, and had no desire to visit the country.

When they exhausted the subject of the visit, Andrew suggested they play cards. It was one of their favorite pastimes.

"It beats watching some of these TV programs," Andrew smiled, referring to a musical show they had once watched, during which a so-called singer screamed with all the energy he could muster. The concoction was supposed to be a love song, and he repeated the words "*I love you baby*" at least twenty times, followed by a convulsive body language. As the show continued, a boldly composed vulgarity rolled out from the "Rock Star's" mouth with hot, suggestive whispers.

"God in heaven, is this *music?*" Andrew asked, thinking of the soul soothing loveliness of the Big Band era, with Guy Lombardo or Billy Vaughn. "It's unbelievable! This revolting trash makes my skin crawl. And I'm sure he thinks he's a *singer*. A horde of cornered dogs could do a better job by howling for help."

Alex laughed. "I agree. It's a disgrace that a handful of fast-buck-minded individuals find the airways through television to sink the cultural taste to the lowest level of entertaining trash. And by injecting obscene dirt into the lyrics, they trample the beauty, replacing it with spiritual prostitution while forgetting that moral value and good taste are the lubricant of civilization. When they constantly pumping this kind of filth into the next generation's mind, they not only erode beauty, but make them believe that this is the *norm*."

"Amen!" Andrew said. "But let's hope that this is just a passing fad, and they won't be able to poison the minds of the youth permanently."

* * *

Soon autumn was upon them again, and the bright leaves fell from the trees, beaten by the wind and rain. The way they lay on the ground so wet and limp, was a bleak reminder that winter was just around the corner.

Then came the long and bitter cold months of snowy winter. The Dombradys took up hiking and riding around and were in good shape. After surviving the winter, the refreshing beauty of spring was upon them again, and the month of June arrived. Life was good and fulfilling.

One beautiful Saturday, before closing time, Andrew had an idea. "What would you say, Alex, if I invite you to come with us tomorrow? We want to make a little tour with the family to Niagara Falls. I think you would enjoy it. I know my family would."

Alex was pleased. "I'd love it, Andrew, the time is just perfect."

"Great! Then I'll pick you up about ten in the morning."

When Andrew told his plan to his family, the children looked at their father with wide-open eyes. They loved to go to Niagara Falls.

"Oh, splendid!' Andy exclaimed.

So the next day they were driving along on Queen Elizabeth Way. The atmosphere in the car was cheerful. Being his pet subject, Andrew described how mesmerized he had been when he saw the Falls for the first time. "I was so sad," he said, "because I could not share my enjoyment with Katie. I felt as if I were cheating her."

"That is exactly how I felt," Katie said. "You remember when I said 'I wish my parents could be here with me'. There is such a strong desire within us to share things we enjoy." By now Katie was just as proud to live in Canada as Andrew was. "*These are the happiest years of my life,*" she used to say whenever the chance is presented itself.

To which Andrew could not resist putting in his two-cents worth of humor by saying, "Of course, it must be, *I'm her husband!*"

"Oh, you conceited bragger," Katie would say, tousling his hair.

Crossing the bridge at Hamilton, they saw the high chimneys of the steel factories pointing at the sky like giant candles, belching torrents of black smoke and flame into the air.

Driving by the side of Lake Ontario, Alex remarked how rich Canada was in water.

"Oh, yes, water and forestry. They are plentiful here, along with freezing rain, snow and ice," Andrew said. Then he changed the subject and played the role of a tour guide. "Not that I'm telling you anything new," he smiled at Alex, " but now we are passing by the famous orchards of the Niagara Peninsula, where I worked for a few weeks. And we're about to reach St. Catharines, where I attended school to learn English. You know, the language that we used to love to hate."

They all laughed.

"Well, you certainly have been around," Alex said, "probably more so than in your own country."

"Oh, yes, I've seen quite a few places all right. But in retrospect, it was fun and a good experience."

"My dad even lived in Winnipeg and Ottawa, too," Andy bragged proudly.

"Thanks, son. You bet I have."

After driving through the winding bridge at the outskirts of Niagara Falls, they reached the main attraction. It was a beautiful warm day and the heavy traffic indicated they were in the middle of the tourist season. The sidewalks were crowded with leisurely strolling, camera-toting tourists, and along the Clifton Hill cars inched forward bumper-to-bumper, making driving slower than walking.

After parking the car, they stood in awe before the handsome ornamental iron fence, looking at the Seventh Wonder of the world. Like a magnetic pull, they watched the measureless amount of water thundering down into the frothy river in a turbid bluish mass, forming a mist that had accumulated into a huge gray cloud.

"It's fascinating!" Katie said. "You never get tired of watching it."

Then they mingled with the hundreds of strolling pedestrians, heading toward the American falls. It was interesting to see the huge stones that had been pushed down hundreds of years ago by the force of the water. There was that magnificent park on the Canadian side Andrew knew so well and further on the Rainbow Bridge. It was like a dream world.

A minute later, as Andrew looked down at the swirling river, he turned to Alex. "Look at those small boats with tourists on them. They're going right up to the Horseshoe Falls, as close as possible. I've already been there, and I assure you it's quite an experience. If you're not afraid of a little water, we could try it out. What do you think?"

"Oh great! Let's go Daddy," Andy cried, clapping his hands enthusiastically. "You'll come, won't you, Godfather? You'll love it; I know you will."

Smiling, Alex looked at his handsome godson, and put his hands on Andy's head. "I wouldn't let you down, son, not for all the treasure in the world. It's a hot day, so a little water won't hurt us, right?"

"Right on!"

Before buying the tickets, Andrew turned to Katie and Aniko. "What about you, ladies? Will you come along?"

"Oh no. You men just go. We would rather wait it out here, right, Aniko?"

"Yes, I'll stay with Mom," Aniko said, snuggling close to her.

"*Chicken*," Andy said, glancing at his sister. Then he tagged along with Alex. "Can you see the name of the boat, Godfather? It's called '*Maid of the Mist*'. Neat, huh?"

"Very appropriate."

Before boarding the boat, they were each given large black waterproof coats. When they put them on, Andy burst out laughing.

"We must look like teddy bears," Andrew said.

"You sure look funny, Dad. How do I look, Godfather?"

"*Like a cute little bushwhacker.*"

As the boat pulled out, the tour guide started to talk about the history of Niagara Falls. But the noise of the rumbling cataract, blended with the speaker's voice, made it difficult to hear. The excitement grew by the moment as they edged closer and closer to the gushing waterfall. Looking up at the plunging Horseshoe Falls from below, the sight was beyond imagination. It was awesome! They heard the speaker say, "Well, folks, **this is Niagara Falls!**" The rumbling noise intensified, while they received a steady shower of mist, even though the actual falls was still quite a distance away. It felt like a heavy rain had hit them, which brought on some screaming and laughing, as people tried to protect their hair and cameras.

"Oh my hair is getting soaked," screamed a woman.

They had not received rubber boots, so their shoes and socks were completely soaked. When they came up from the tour dripping wet, Katie burst out laughing.

"Well, you guys, if it is water you wanted, now you have got it. Looks like you just came up from a storm."

Andy settled down on the grass between the two men, sighing happily. "Ohhh, that was fun!" he said, squeezing the water out of his socks.

"If you call that fun, you can have it," Aniko chuckled, shaking her head. "I'd rather have a shower in my bathroom."

When they were ready, they continued walking around, passing through Clifton Hill. Then Andrew saw a restaurant and suggested they eat.

"Just in time," Katie said, "I'm starving."

* * *

The next Sunday they went for a boat tour along the Thousand Islands. They drove to *Ganonoque Way Boat Lines*, located near Kingston.

The ship swam gently down the St. Lawrence River, which divided Canada and America, so they enjoyed two of the most beautiful countries in the world.

They all leaned against the handrail, quietly observing the lovely summer cottages nestling peacefully at the sides of the river. They passed by some magnificent castles, like the picturesque *Bolt Castle*. It was an architectural wonder.

"Just look at that fantastic castle," Katie said, marveling at the mass of stone-built beauty.

"My goodness, isn't it something?" said Alex.

Then they passed by the world's shortest international bridge, located in the middle of the river. The tiny structure spanned the Zavikon Islands, flanking the American and Canadian border, national flags fluttering on each end.

Andy and Aniko ran up and down, having their own fun, paying attention only to the major sights, like the long international bridge at Kingston that connected the two countries.

"Children, be careful, don't fall," Katie warned them. "And watch out for people around you."

When the excursion was over, they drove home. Alex was sitting in the back seat, talking and playing with the children. He kept reminding himself how blessed he was for having them, saying that they were his lifesavers.

"It was a lovely trip, wasn't it, Godfather."

"Oh, yes, I enjoyed it very much."

"Too bad Stan couldn't come with us," Andy said.

"Well, he has his own life to live, you know. But I'm sure he would have enjoyed the trip. And there's always a next time."

"Yeah, I guess so."

"Did you see those hundreds of birds on that platform, Godfather?" Aniko asked. "Around that statue?"

"Ah, yes. Seemed like it was their gathering place."

Andrew glanced at Katie, then at Alex with a mischievous smile. "It's always a pleasure to see how well the children are behaving," he said. The remark was aimed to tease Alex.

"You just keep your eyes on the road, for I'm getting hungry and want to get home safely," Alex retorted, winking at Andy.

"But you're having supper with us, aren't you, Godfather?"

"Of course he is," Andrew said, before Alex could speak.

While Alex hesitated, Andy said, "Let's put a seal on it."

The three of them put their hands over to each other's, and as a symbol of agreement they counted: "one-two-three."

"So there! Now that's official," Andy said. "You can't change it."

34

REMINISCING

MANY YEARS HAD ELAPSED since the trip to the Thousand Islands. The wheel of time spun fast as autumn turned into winter, spring into summer, and the seasons rolled into years. When the Erdelyis received Katie's account of the visit to Hungary, with pictures of the Dombrady's enjoying their grandchildren, Joe expressed his sadness at the misfortune of not having the same opportunity.

. Contemplating his promise he had made to Joe at the airport, he was happy at the chance of being able to return their generosity: two years ago Andrew sent them two tickets to visit Canada.

During their one-month stay, enjoying their grandchildren, the Erdelyis were fascinated by Canada. They became best friends with Alex. Using up the time wisely, they were seeing as much about the country as they could. The Erdelyis had a marvelous time, and the visit was a huge success. Seeing Katie's established lifestyle, and her happiness, they returned to Australia with great satisfaction.

* * *

Then in 1983, Andrew fell ill with a stubborn flu and by the doctor's order, he had to stay in bed for a few days. The slanting rays of sun filtered through the window shutters in scanty streaks, making an effort to brighten the room. In the radiant light the dust sparkled in the air, and the peaceful quietness made a holiday-like atmosphere. When he awoke, he looked around at the familiar light green wallpaper, which depicted a snowy landscape with pine trees and a lake with boats, nestled between the mountains. A large wedding picture on the wall was surrounded with pictures of a smiling girl and boy, taken at various ages.

No matter how many times he saw that strikingly handsome couple—Katie and himself—, he looked at it with great nostalgia.. He had, of course, gone through some changes over the years, and he could not hide some wrinkles on his forehead. His hair had begun to turn gray at the temples, but at forty-seven, he was still in excellent shape with a youthful look. When his friends were teasing him, he used to boast that a man's real creative power begins after his forties. But if it came to it, he would be the first to admit that he was not without fault. "You are a tempered, extremely stubborn and sensitive man to the fault," Cathy told him once. And he agreed.

Having nothing else to do, he closed his eyes, allowing his mind to wander deeper into the past. Through the struggled years he was proud of his achievement that he had accomplished by his two hands. He could not imagine life without working. With his ambition he viewed life a challenge, in which the accomplishment was the purpose. A man has to have a goal in life, a challenge in order to be a worthwhile member of this society. It was easy to understand his attitude, for he knew he had inherited this from his father.

His father... Andrew glanced at his picture, almost sensing his presence. He had died three years ago at the age of seventy-two. He felt an inextinguishable love towards him that transcends time and gains immortal stature.

Later his thoughts spread in many directions, as if trying to embrace a lifetime of memories all at once. The mind holds millions of pieces of memories that constantly come in and out of focus like a turning kaleidoscope. And in a quiet moment like this, Andrew wondered about people he had met over the years. During certain periods of time, they were an integral part of his life, filling a void, like Meszaros in Winnipeg, Mr. Balogh in Niagara Falls, Margaret from the school in St. Catharines, his friend, Lovas in Elliot Lake. And Cathy... What had happened to them?

The gentle opening of the door interrupted his thoughts. "I'm sorry if I woke you up, sweetheart," Katie apologized with a smile.

"But you did not. Actually, my wandering thoughts carried me into a never-never land, which means I was lonely. Anyway, you should know by now that I still enjoy your company," he said with a flattering smile.

"Yes, I know, but a woman never gets tired of hearing that," she said. "From your mood, however, I delude myself that you are getting better."

"Yes, Madam. But the trouble is that while I'm shaking off this bug, I'm getting another disease—terminal boredom. And I don't know which is worse: this blasted flu, or people avoiding me like the plague."

Katie smiled, "Oh poor thing! When you get well, I'll overwhelm you with kisses and caresses, so that you'll beg me to stop." Then she reached for a small bottle on the night table and said, "It's about time for your medicine."

Andrew tried to wrap his appreciation into humor. "Ah, I know you love me, beautiful. Your only fault is that one of these days you'll kill me with kindness. Did we get any mail today?"

"Just the telephone bill and some junk mail. It is amazing how much money they waste on those silly advertisements. I, for one, never bother to read them, let alone buy from them. I think most people throw them into the waste paper basket without even looking at them."

"Well, apparently, you're wrong because if there was no money in it, they would stop printing them."

"You could be right," she said, frowning, as if searching for thought. "What else did I want to tell you? Oh yes. Before I came in, I spoke with Alex on the phone. He was very charming and in a good mood. He joked about your getting lazy. He wished you a speedy recovery with the message of don't worry. Although he misses you, things are under control, so you're not to go back until you're all right. He doesn't want to catch the flu and end up changing place with you."

"Ah yes. You know, Katie, sometimes we don't realize how fortunate we are. I love decent, honest people. Life is full of chances, but we could not have been luckier in meeting him."

Katie nodded, "So true. But as far as Alex is concerned, the two of you are very compatible, to say the least."

"I think so. But speaking about luck, are the kids still in school?"

"Of course. This morning I gave Andy five dollars to buy you some fresh fruit and lemon for your tea on his way home. Before they left they said 'hi' to you and wished you well."

A warm feeling pervaded Andrew. "Well, that's nice, thanks." Then he added in a musing tone, "you know, Katie, it's amazing how quickly the children are growing up. Can you believe that in eight months they will be sixteen years old? It seems as if they were born only yesterday. Only the growing numbers of candles on their birthday cake is an incontestable reminder of how old *we are getting*. Boyfriends and girlfriends are coming and going through the house, but thank God, the so-called usual teenage trouble hasn't caught up with them as yet. Their friends seem decent, so their rushing and laughing doesn't bother me. It rather reminds me of my youth."

"That's an interesting way to look at it," Katie said, then suddenly she started to chuckle.

"What is so funny?"

"I just remembered one of our arguments on how many children would make us happy. 'Two boys and one girl' you said, remember?"

"Oh yes. But that was hundred years ago. In any case I can live with what we have," Andrew said. "'*Man proposes but God disposes*', as you used to say. The important thing is that they are good kids. I feel I'm one of the luckiest guys in the whole world."

As if suffered an insult, Katie put her hands on her hips, putting up a fake argument. "Now wait a cotton-picking minute, Mister! In case you haven't noticed, you are speaking in the singular. Perhaps I should remind you that it's not only your luck, I was there when they were born, remember?"

"Excuse me, sunshine. How could I ever forget?"

"Good. As long as you remember it's all right," Katie said, smiling. Changing the subject, she asked him if he remembered their first Christmas present. "Do you remember way back when we exchanged our presents? We used the proverb: '*My heart is given for yours with pleasure*'."

"I sure do, why? Do you think I'm getting senile in my old age?"

"Hmmm," Katie mumbled, swaying her head as if considering it. "Let's see. You're forty-seven. If I wanted to be generous, I'd say you still have one or two good years left in you."

Andrew stared at her in mock shock. "Thanks a lot, lady! You really have the nerve of a double-dealer. Some respect I'm getting here. 'One or two years', my foot! You sound as if you agree with that old saying."

"And what is that?"

"Of all the things I have lost over the years, it is my brain I miss the most."

Katie laughed, then kissed him. "Oh come on, stop being such a crybaby. It is not that bad. You still have me to take care of you," she said, and left the room. When she came back, Andrew asked her to sit on the edge of the bed.

"Sweetheart, I have something important to talk about."

That grabbed Katie's interest and she sat down.

"I was just thinking about the possibility of taking an extended holiday this summer. Actually, I've been dreaming about driving through the Canadian Rockies up to Vancouver. We have already been to Prince Edward Island, now it is time to go west."

Katie loved to travel, so her eyes lit up. "Oh, Andrew, you know how I love the beauty of nature, so I'm thrilled with the idea. The children will be itching to go once they hear about it."

Andrew laughed. "Just hearing your happiness makes me glad I thought it up. As for the children, aside from the pleasure of traveling, there is a saying: the wider a man's horizon of knowledge, the freer he is."

"I couldn't agree with you more," Katie said. "But first, you'll have to get back in shape, my vagabond husband."

"Don't worry about me, sweetheart. The problem is that Vancouver is so far away that we need at least four or five weeks to make it worthwhile. Anyway, I'll discuss it with Alex and see what we can come up with."

* * *

Later that day Andrew got out of bed and went for a walk. The pleasant, healing rays of the bright, caressing sunshine lifted his sprits. Fleecy clouds feathered the blue sky, while the light breeze brought out the scent of the soil that was bursting with new life. Spring is upon us, Andrew thought, sending a contented sigh towards the sun.

Shortly after he got back, the children burst into the house like balls of fire. How much they have grown in just a few short years, Andrew thought.

"Hi, Mom, hi, Dad!" they shouted. "Look at these beautiful lemons I bought you, Dad," Andy announced. "Five for a dollar! Nice, huh! Are you feeling better?"

"As far as I can see, he is just fine," Aniko answered for him, planting a kiss on his cheek. "What's a little flu bug to my strong daddy?"

"That's the spirit, my angel. After that kiss, I feel even better."

"Well, men don't kiss, so I'll have to make you feel better with something else. Ask me a favor, Dad," Andy said.

They laughed. "By making me laugh, son, you have done me a favor already."

"Gee, that was easy. So what are we waiting for? Let's celebrate daddy's health. What should we start with?"

"Not so fast, young man. Whether we celebrate or not, it will have to be after you've done your homework—if you have any that is." Katie said.

"Darn it!" Andy said, gesturing with his arm.

Andrew laughed and invited the children to sit beside him.

"Now tell me, kids, how are things in school."

"So-so," Aniko said.

"What about you, Andy?"

"Hmmm, not so-so, I'm afraid."

"Oh? Do you want to talk about it?"

"Well, Dad, to tell you the truth, I just had to punch a guy on the nose at the schoolyard during the break."

"Go on, I'm listening."

"You see, the way it happened was, he was making fun of my name. He kept calling me *Dumb Dombrady*."

Katie looked at Andrew and burst into laughter. "*Like father, like son.*"

"Come on, Katie," Andrew glanced at her, annoyed. "I think Andy was right." But as soon as he said it he stopped, realizing that it was an instinctive reaction, being conditioned from years of defending himself. He felt that he would have done the same thing. But now, seeing himself in Andy, he thought about his parents. Suddenly his father's' advice flashed through his mind. *"You can't catch a bee with vinegar."* No, he doesn't want to experience what his parents had experienced with him. So he turned to Andy with a changed voice.

"Andy, I'll tell you something that might surprise you. When I was a young man like you, I also was quick to fight because I was as sensitive as you are when someone had hurt my feelings. But thinking back, I realize that some of it could have been avoided by using common sense, instead of my fist. Of course there are *times* when you could get into situations when you must defend yourself.

However, you have to make sure that solving it with your fist is the last resort. In this case we may think that you were right, but you could have told him first that what he had said he would not repeat again, or else... *In another words, I'd have given him a second chance."*

"Gee, Dad, you could be right. Next time, I'll try to remember," Andy said. Then he turned and went to look for Aniko, who had left them in the middle of the discussion.

Sitting at the table chin in hand, quietly listening, Katie echoed, "Gee, Dad, that was nice."

"Thanks, Mommy," he said, and they laughed.

Sometimes Cathy's words crossed Andrew's mind, saying that boredom stifles love in marriage. But over the years they had managed to keep boredom out of their marriage. What he felt instead was that their youthful passion had blossomed into a deeper kind of love and appreciation.

"You know, Katie," Andrew said, putting his hands on hers, "I don't know if we're the exception to the rule, but after sixteen years of marriage, my love for you hasn't changed a bit. You're just as desirable to me as ever. It seems that we're one of those so-called 'perfect couples'."

It was true. Katie was able to retain the texture and resilience of youth, and she knew that Andrew was proud of her, which pleased her.

"You have just made my day, sweetheart. You know, in a good marriage people become bonded like one body and soul, as if they were born twins."

Andrew laughed. "Interesting way to put it."

Also, it may be a trite, but our ten years of separation proves it, love should never be taken for granted. Although there are times when I used to wonder how our lives would have been changed had we already been married when we reunited at Lake Balaton. Would we have considered divorce? Because I'm convinced that I would have never stopped loving you. I know it's crazy even to think about it, yet one can't help reflecting upon how strange life is."

"You can say that again! So you're not sorry about marrying me? You could be -."

"Now that's a silly question, Mr. Dombrady."

"I'm sorry, love. But what I meant to say was that had you married Frank, as a banker's wife, you could be much richer."

"I never cared about that. And if you keep referring to Frank's money, you'll make me angry. Are you sorry for not marrying Cathy?"

"I see...Well, one silly question deserves another. Of course not."

"Besides, with Frank I might have had more money, but who is to say that I'd be blessed with two wonderful children like Andy and Aniko."

"Oh you still could have had children, although maybe not twins."

"Oh, you men! Sure, but they wouldn't be **yours,** you big dummy! That is why it would not be the same."

At this moment Aniko rushed in and interrupted by asking when supper would be ready?

"In half an hour, honey."

* * *

After supper, Andrew announced the big surprise.

"Well children, your mother and I have decided that sometime in July we will embark on our longest journey yet in Canada. If all goes well, we shall be on our way to Vancouver, British Columbia."

The children gasped and looked at each other, shouting in delight, "Oh boy! Hurray!" Then Andy added, "Gee, Dad, how sweet it is! Just like Jackie Gleason would say. This is going to be our best trip ever!"

"We certainly hope so," Katie said.

The next day Andrew went back to work. When he came home, he was a little tired, but the satisfied smile on his face suggested that he had some good news. "I've talked things over with Alex and came up with a brilliant plan, if I may say so myself. We decided that the best solution would be to close up the store for two weeks during the summer holidays. This way they would be working without me for two weeks only."

"Sounds like a good idea," Katie said.

By now Katie got along fine with all her neighbors, but since she loved gardening, it was Mrs. Miller who was most appreciative of Katie's neat gardening efforts. Consequently, it was Dorothy, (as Katie called her,) with whom she had the most in common.

"You know, Dorothy," Katie said over the fence, "we're planning a trip to Vancouver next week."

"Really? Well, I must tell you that when you go through those magnificent Canadian Rockies, you will love every minute of it. You must not miss seeing Lake Louise and Morain Lake, among many other beautiful places. But be prepared that you'll have a sore neck from looking up constantly. We have seen them a few times. Oh, what a marvelous trip that was!"

* * *

Planning a trip of this magnitude was a major source of fun and excitement. Katie solicited the children's help in making up a list of what they would need to take with them. They already knew from previous experience what a nuisance it could be if they forgot to pack something important.

But being teenagers, this time their "help" created a certain amount of bargaining. Because they wanted to take everything, things they just wouldn't be possible to make room for. It came to the point that Katie has regretted asking their help.

"Now wait a minute, children. We cannot take the whole house with us."

Fortunately they had a new Ford station wagon, roomy enough to feel comfortable for the trip. They even had an extra lockable box on top of the car, which came in handy for storing warm clothes and blankets. They had heard how cool the nights could get, no matter how warm the days were. As Katie pointed out, Canada is such a big country, one can never know. After all, they would be driving through the snowy mountains....

35

THE CANADIAN ROCKIES

THEY LEFT ON A SATURDAY. Along with the radio, Andrew had a built-in cassette player, so they could listen to their favorite music. Katie also made sure that Andy and Aniko had plenty of books to read, and games to play. But even with all that, sometimes they would become restless and Andrew had to make frequent stops.

Andrew loved driving, but experience had taught him that no matter how good a driver you are, it is always the other guy you have to watch out for. He had seen so many careless and dangerous drivers on the road. During his wandering years, Andrew had driven through this area, but for Katie and the children, Sudbury, the copper-mine town was the first interesting sight. It was a hot and humid day, yet on the charcoal colored rocky hills, there was no trace of grass or any type of vegetation, other than some isolated stunted trees here and there. Everything looked dull and dirty—even the air smelled like soot and smoke. As Katie put it, it was as if they had landed on the moon. It reminded her of a television documentary on Tasmania's copper mines.

"Look how black and barren those hills are," Andy said. "I sure wouldn't like to live here."

When they entered the city, the first thing they noticed was more stunted trees along the street that was lined with stores and workshops. But despite the stores' pretty facades, the offensive smog hung in the air, which overshadowed everything that might otherwise have been attractive. When they left the city, they breathed a sigh of relief.

The first stop for the night was in Sault Ste. Marie, where they rented a family cabin with a kitchen.

They started early in the morning. Driving along on Highway

17, passing through Wawa, north of Lake Superior, Andrew suddenly saw a car coming toward them on the **wrong side** of the road at ominous speed. It appeared that the driver was trying to pass two cars, presumably miscalculating the distance between his and Andrew's car. Terror hit Andrew with its icy grip, for it was not possible for him to pull over, as the road was cut into the rocky hill. All he could do was to apply the brake. Expecting the oncoming car to ram into them, horror filled Katie's heart. She was clinging to Andrew's arm as if her very life depended on it. This was one of those moments when the end of life flashes through the mind, for the crash seemed inevitable. But her scream froze in her throat and was replaced with a sigh of relief, as the car was able to zoom back into its right lane at the last second, almost hitting the other car. The whole incident lasted but a few seconds, but for Katie and Andrew it was the most dramatic experience they have ever had; one that would be with them for the rest of their lives.

Trembling violently, she slumped in the seat and let out a painful moan. Glancing at each other in astonished silence, both felt that the wind of death had brushed past them.

"Oh, Andrew, I have never been so terrified in my life. I thought it was over for us."

Andrew's heart was beating wildly and a cold shiver ran up his spine. He gripped the steering wheel so hard, his knuckles were white. Realizing that their lives had hung on by a thread, he was terrified over the thought of what *could have* happened... Fortunately, he was able to stop a minute later to calm down. *"God was with us,"* he murmured, bowing his head as if in prayer. "Relax, sweetheart, it's all right now," he said, stroking her hand.

The children were so deeply absorbed in their game that they noticed nothing until Andrew stopped, and they heard Katie's moaning. Andy asked what had happened. Instead of explaining, Andrew dismissed it with a few well-chosen words concerning that idiot driver.

As the hours passed, gradually they were able to relax. To divert their thoughts, they observed the farmhouses in the fields. Occasionally they passed by dilapidated old buildings, flanked by ramshackle wooden barns with sagging roofs and tilted walls. But here and there, they saw new homes, appearing like shiny gold teeth among the rotten ones.

"Look at that beautiful farmhouse!" Katie exclaimed, pointing to a particularly pretty one. "In Toronto, a house like that would be priceless."

"It would be, indeed! It almost seems like a waste to build such a beautiful mansion in a godforsaken place like this."

"I disagree," Katie said. "If they have the money and love the lifestyle, they certainly deserve to live well. Why shouldn't they enjoy the fruits of their hard work?"

"I think you are right; indeed why shouldn't they?"

Reaching the wide-open spaces of the Manitoba prairies, they realized the vastness of this country. It took them three days just to travel out of Ontario. Driving along the long stretch of flat plains, Andrew remarked that he could drive ten miles with closed eyes and fifteen minutes later he would think that he was on the same spot. Passing by huge tracts of lands lying fallow because there were not enough people to cultivate them, Andrew thought.

"In Europe, this land would be an agricultural goldmine!" Andrew said. Noticing the quietness in the back seat, he glanced back. The children were asleep. Taking advantage of it, Andrew changed the subject. "Katie, I can't get over how fast the kids are growing. My goodness, Aniko could come home one day and announce that she wants to get married. Then in no time grandchildren would come along. Can you imagine *us* as *grandparents?* You as *grandma?* For God's sake!" Andrew shuddered at the mere thought, as if it were inconceivable. It was so amusing the way he emphasized those words, Katie laughed.

"In our youth," she said, "old people's lives remain a foreign notion, like death, and it has little relevance to our daily lives. When I was a little girl and saw an old person, I always thought that they were *born old*. At that age, you can't see yourself ever being old. *Me? Oh no! How could that be! I'll never get old.*"

"I think you were right," Andrew said. "You will be *aged* but never old."

"Oh, you wonderful flatterer. Anyway, I hope it won't be that soon, I mean being grandparents. But when it happens, let's hope we will have more luck enjoying them than our parents had."

Andrew nodded. "I hope so too. Can you imagine how much they must have suffered? Well, at least my father doesn't suffer anymore. You know, my father's death tore me to pieces. Perhaps I didn't show it, but I remember feeling a furious knot tide inside me. I said to myself a million times, 'Is that all?' All those fights, the risks, the worries, the everyday struggle, for what?"

"Yes, I've seen your suffering. It is so easy to say *'that's life'*, until tragedy hits you right at your very soul," Katie said. "Your father was a symbol of kindness, a ray of sunshine in your life."

"Yes, he was. But of course those words could be said about your parents as well."

"I agree. But what I meant to say before was that fate robbed them of the pleasure of being with their grandchildren," Katie said. "Another thing: It's a shame that our parents never had the chance to get to know each other. As if we were living in a different country. We could have been such a close-knit family."

"I think so. What I used to be wondering about is that since God blessed us with two beautiful children, wouldn't it be nice to see our descendants for a few generations to come."

Katie laughed. "Your dreams are a little far fetched, my dear. I don't know about you, but I, for one, don't relish the idea of becoming a nonagenarian. But I don't think you should complain. What would you say if we had only daughter, like my parents?"

"You're right, it's not fair. After all, they have just as much to do with our progeny as my parents. Yet in the future, only the Dombrady name will survive, provided a male will be born to carry on the name. The Erdelyi name is doomed and will be forgotten."

"What can you do about it, unless the child gets the mother's name?"

They reflected upon the subject for awhile, then Andrew jerked his head. It was like a light flashed in his head and shone through his face.

"Katie, a marvelous idea struck me. Next year we should visit Australia. What do you say?"

"Oh, Andrew, need you ask? It would be like another dream come true. But as much as I love the idea, the cost for the four of us would be out of the questions."

"I dare say we could manage. The children already have seen Hungary; it's time for them to see Australia."

"Hmmm, just imagine how happy my parents would be," Katie said, a dreamy look lingering on her face that Andrew could not miss.

"Well, that's it then. My decision is final. You have just given me the encouragement I needed." Along this train of thought, his good mood gave way to a streak of teasing humor. "Who knows what fate has in store for us? Your parents said that Frank has a beautiful daughter. Perhaps Andy will fall in love with her and marry her. You could still be related to Frank by marriage, even it is not your own."

Katie's eyebrows arched with amusement. "Your wit is very sharp today," she said. "Nothing is impossible—no one knows it better than we do. However, we don't have to worry about it yet. After all, Andy will be only seventeen next year. So let's set that aside. I'd rather talk about *their dreams* for a change. Could you ever imagine Andy wanting to be an *airplane pilot*, and Aniko a *TV broadcaster*?"

"Well, at first it surprised me, but what I like about it is their early discovery of what they want to do with their lives," Andrew said. "Even if they change their minds later, at least they aren't saying '*I don't know what I want*'. On this note, I agree with my father who once said that it is wrong to accumulate financial wealth for our children, because they can't put much value on something they did not work for. To be able to appreciate it, they *must feel* the triumph, the power of achievement. He strongly believed that the parents' duty is to provide them with the best possible education and all the moral and spiritual tools they need to be strong to stand on their own feet. The rest is up to them what they want to do with it."

Katie smiled. "His philosophy is a sound one, but I think it is easier said than done."

At this moment Andrew hit a bump on the road and he heard the children's blissful yawning; a good indication that they had awakened. Andrew joked with them about whether they had dreamed of some prince or princess, from which they were sorry to wake up.

"No, I'm not wasting such precious dreams in the car," Andy said. "I pass that kind of romantic silliness to Aniko."

"I don't need your charity, thank you."

Andy leaned over the back of his father's seat, watching him drive with envy. The whole operation seemed so simple, and lately he was increasingly interested in driving a car.

"I really would like to learn to a drive a car," he said finally. "I think it's just about time. Many of my friends can drive already."

Although Andrew sympathized with Andy, he smiled at Katie as if saying, *"I'm not going to touch this subject."* When it came to important matters, usually Katie was the diplomatic one to solve it.

"Darling, you'll have to wait at least another year or two. There are just too many teenage accidents on the road as it is."

"That's not fair! Anyway, you know how to drive, how come you don't take over sometimes."

"The truth is, I only drive when I absolutely have to. Besides, highway driving makes me nervous. This madness best suits your father."

"Of course. *It's a man's job, anyway.*" Andy boasted.

Aniko's pretty mouth puckered with disgust. ***It is not!** Perish the thought, you male chauvinist pig!*" she shot back. "Sometimes it's a nice virtue to practice saying nothing," she lectured, shoving him away.

"Oh brother!" Andy said, a hidden amusement on his face.

Andrew laughed then interrupted. "Okay, kids, cut it out. When the time comes, you will both have a chance to prove who is the better driver. Until then, go back to your games or books." Glancing at Katie, he chuckled, "my goodness, wrinkles are hereditary; parents are getting them from their children."

Katie laughed. "There must be some truth in it."

When they arrived in Winnipeg, they planned to spend a little time in the city. Andrew talked about the Patakis many times, so Katie knew whom he meant when he said, "I wonder if the Patakis are still alive. It is only proper to try and visit them."

It felt strange but exciting to be here again. His memory of it had faded somewhat, but it slowly came back as he drove through the city. Hew as surprised to see so many new high-rise buildings. But then he had left Winnipeg twenty-six years ago!

Once he turned into the familiar street, he recognized the house immediately, even though its weather-beaten façade had been painted over and over.

He stepped out of the car with mounting curiosity, and walked up the familiar steps and rang the bell. A middle-aged man opened the door, and after a brief greeting, he politely listened to Andrew's enquiries about the Patakis. "I used to live here with them," he concluded.

"Well, sir, that must have been a long time ago because the Patakis have passed away. We bought this house from them fifteen years ago, and they moved into an old-age home."

A shadow of sadness flashed through Andrew's face. He guessed that might be the case, but he thought that until one knows for sure, it is hard to accept the fact that time is running out on all of us.

"Thank you very much. I'm sorry for bothering you."

When he got back to the car, he said, "Yeah, they're both dead," and turned the key. They toured around for awhile, showing them the hospital where he had his very first job in Canada.

"Nice city," Andy said, "but I like Toronto better."

"Me too!" echoed Aniko.

After a hearty meal in a quiet restaurant, the Dombradys hit the road again. In the peaceful surroundings a train flashed by them, otherwise only a few scattered houses, resting securely in the heart of the countryside, changed the view. So far the whole journey had given them an impression of space and infinity. But between Regina and Calgary the scene began to change. They saw many fenced-in oil wells that operated twenty-four hours a day, perpetually pumping up the black liquid treasure from the bowels of the earth.

*

It took them five days to reach Calgary, Canada's famous rodeo town. Here they also spent a few hours sight-seeing. Roaming around, Andrew thought about Cathy and wondered whether she lived her somewhere. Naturally, he did not believe that there was a ghost of a chance of finding her, yet wouldn't it be something after all these years? I might not even recognize her, he thought.

As soon as they left Calgary, the countryside began to change dramatically. In the dazzling rays of the sun, from the distance a breathtaking landscape loomed out of the mist, and gradually unfolding before them was the immeasurable beauty of the Canadian Rockies. And just as the camera lens brings the picture closer, the mountains began to turn into soaring giants. The solid mass of frozen snow, covering the tops of the mountains, was the winter wonderland, a continuous panoramic delight. It appeared as if the mountains were resting contentedly upon the earth, like sleeping children on their mother's lap. The awesome wilderness made them gasp, and strange excitement came over them. What a delightful contrast it was to the flat landscape they had been traveling through!

In the startling brilliant blue sky the breaking clouds slowly rolled above the undulating peaks. As they progressed, the beauty of the landscape made Andrew muse upon this amazing nature. No poet could fail to be inspired by the changing hues, or the sudden rush of the waterfall cascading down the crags; the sublimity of the towering mountains in their glittering colors; the awesome drama of their silence, and the tangy fragrance of the pine forest. He summed up his thoughts by saying, "No man could ever create perfect beauty as well as nature can."

The immensity of the majestic snow-capped peaks were a natural splendor. The hard-packed crust of ice with its craggy ridges took their breath away. It was fascinating to watch, as the sky appeared to rest upon the giant mountains as if their tops were lost in it. One could not help but feel closed in, as though the world beyond the mountains had disappeared.

"*Canadian Rockies, here we come!*" Andy whooped exuberantly. "What a magnificent sight! Dad, your idea to come here is worth a million bucks."

"Ohhh, look at that!" Aniko exclaimed, pointing her finger at a peak of an especially brilliant whiteness, her eyes wide with fascination. "I'm getting goose-bumps just looking at it."

"What a truly enchanting land," Katie gasped. "The contrast is so great, it's like we're having winter in July."

Lifting his head, Andy said, "This is the first time I am being in two seasons at the same time."

"Right on!" Aniko applauded. "I feel as if I'm in a dream world, floating over an unreal landscape."

The descriptions Katie had heard turned into exact images. "It is hard to describe this exotic place; there is a soul-soothing tranquility in the scenery. One has to see this to believe it," she said.

In Banff, they looked around the beautiful city, then took a chair lift up to the peak where they enjoyed a fascinating view of the city and the mountains.

An hour later they left Banff. As Andrew was driving along, he glanced into the rearview mirror and discovered the glaciers from yet another prospective. No matter which peaks they gazed at, each was reflected differently by the sun. Crystal clear blue lakes nestled peacefully between the cliffs, in which the stately pines and the peaks were gracefully mirrored in the smooth surface of the water.

"This exquisite, unspoiled world is more than just a beautiful picture," Katie said. "Strauss wrote music for the *Vienna Woods*. Someone ought to compose a symphony for the Canadian Rockies."

"Nice thought. And I'd call it the Hymn of the Mountains." Andrew said.

Among the many famous spots they visited were Lake Louise and Moraine Lake. Andy was the photographer, taking pictures of every marvelous sight. Standing at the edge of Moraine Lake, admiring the row of marvelous mountains that radiated tranquility. Andrew surprised them with a bit of trivia.

"Did you know that these magnificent mountains are on our twenty dollar bill?"

"Oh, really?" Andy asked excitedly. "Let's see."

Andrew showed them the bill.

"Yep, that's it all right!" Aniko verified. "How about that! And we're standing right here," putting her finger on it. "But seeing it live is nicer."

But above all, it was Rogers Pass that fascinated them the most. Arriving to this amazing wonderland in the afternoon, they stopped at a small bridge, and got out of the car. Unfolding before them in the horizon were the nature-invented gigantic peaks that glittered in the sunshine like diamonds. In the infinite silent surroundings they felt the vibration of some sense of peace and tranquility.

They stood there and looked up, their faces transfixed and mystified by its grandeur. In the descending rays of the sun, the peaks stood erect, which provided an everlasting beauty that was suspended by time. The shadow of the forest grew slowly, creeping toward the peaks, creating the image of a shaggy foot of a giant. There was magic in its unspoiled intactness.

Mother Earth was settling down to sleep for the night. One could be lulled by the welcoming quietness. A tiny river rushed below, flanked by evergreen pines. The soft emerald velvet moss along the side looked like cool, verdant cushions encasing the crags.

"What a wonderful country!" Katie exclaimed. "It is hard to believe such beauty exists."

Still looking in amazement at the peaks, Andrew said, "Yes, it is a great treasure of British Columbia."

Enjoying the pristine landscape, Andrew observed the silky

rustling of the falling leaves. His nostrils were tickled by the fresh, pungent smell of the wilderness, and the crispy scent of the trickling stream, washing its way through the crags. He felt the uplifting power of nature, which brought out some religious fervor, and found himself philosophizing about the mystery of life.

How sad it is that human life is so short and limited, he thought. These magnificent wonders will be here for time immemorial, but we may never see them again. Everyone should have the opportunity to breathe the fresh air and enjoy the smell of the intoxicating scent of pines. Seeing this awesome, unique world of trouble-free reality, only here, and here alone, can we fully comprehend the true meaning of life. If mankind were ever to attain the innate grace of nature, it would be here that he should find the heights of peace and contentment. We may be able to conquer the moon, and destroy the universe, but this majestic wilderness will be here as a symbol of an everlasting kingdom of victory. We can pretend strength and power, but we are fragile to conquer the power of nature.....

The huge red globe of sun slowly slid behind the hills. As a final thought, Andrew paid homage to the grandeur before him. You everlasting beautiful glaciers, we imperfect human beings bow our heads and salute you.

* * *

The next day they continued their journey and ran into an extreme heat wave. They drove through some steep, sharp winding curves. As they looked down into the bottomless yawning abyss, Andrew had to drive with the brake on.

Passing through Hope, they soon reached the suburbs of Vancouver. As the silhouette of the city took shape, they held their breath again, as an unusually beautiful city began to come into view. It was built around the sides of the mountains, overlooking the Pacific Ocean.

"*Oh, look!* Isn't that something?" Katie exclaimed.

"Yes, it is beautiful," Andrew agreed.

"Looks like it beats even Toronto," Andy said.

They made a short ride into downtown, then settled into a cozy motel on Hastings Street. Studying the map that Andy got from the motel owner, Andrew said, "It seems, the best place to start with would be *Stanley Park*."

Like experienced travelers, they had no problem getting there. Fascinated by the surroundings, they strolled through the charming park, curiously admiring the totem poles, carved by the West Coast Indians. Looking around, the beautiful landscape caught Andy's attention, and he persuaded his parents to pose for a picture in front of a group of totem poles. While he peered through the viewfinder, Aniko jumped between her parents at the last moment, Andy was struck by his mother's youthful shape.

"Gee, Mom, you're as beautiful as a shining star," he complimented. When they burst into laughter, he snapped the picture.

"This will be one of the best picture," he said. "You will probably want to enlarge it, unless Aniko spoils it." He was always eager to tease her in their continual cat-and-mouse routine.

"Oh, yes? If anything, I'll be the icing on the cake."

"Hah! More like sour cream!" he remarked.

"Ah, you conceited meany. I'll get you for this," she said with wounded pride, and quickly tousled his hair. She knew how he hated it. "So there! For poking holes in my charming presentation."

They continued walking down the path, Andy and his father leading the way. He was almost as tall as his father. His strikingly handsome looks would have been the pride of any parent. His dark eyes seemed to dance with laughter, which, in Katie's opinion, were a strong reminder of Andrew in the early days of their courtship. Andrew glanced at his son with pride.

Sensing his father's eyes upon him, Andy glanced up smiling. "You know, Dad, I'm really impressed with Vancouver. Wouldn't it be terrific to live here?"

"It probably would, Andy, but as you know, we have to live where we earn our bread and butter."

* * *

The following day they drove around the downtown area, ending up at a nice beach. Strolling leisurely in Jericho Park, they ran into a pleasant surprise. They saw an elderly couple sitting on a bench, the woman carrying a tourist bag with the word: "AUSTRALIA" on it. Katie approached them and asked if they came from Australia.

"Yes," the woman said, "we're from Sydney."

"Really? How nice," Katie said, telling them that she too had lived in Sydney. Soon she found out that the couple lived in the district of Burwood, not too far from the Erdelyis. Katie gave them the address and asked if they would visit her parents after their return. "I would very much appreciate it. What a lovely surprise they would have," she said.

"Isn't that something?" Katie said later. "It sure proves that it's a small world."

From there they went to see the beautiful Queen Elizabeth Park, where newlywed couples went to pose for wedding pictures. It certainly provided a beautiful setting.

Two hours later, they drove across the *Lions Gate Bridge* and went to see the Capilano Hill's *Suspension Bridge*. Dorothy, Katie's neighbor, had advised them to go and see it. Just getting there was an adventure.

After entering a lovely garden, they spent some time studying the long, narrow bridge above a deep precipice, suspended by thick wire cables. As people walked on it, the bridge swayed, making it difficult to move. The Dombrady family joined the crowd to experience the peculiar sensation. At the other end of the bridge was a forest, where they walked along the cool path. The children made two more trips across the bridge, then Katie suggested they leave.

"Oh, come on, Mom, it's so much fun," Andy protested.

In the souvenir shop they bought some presents for Alex and Stan, and then headed back to the city. Coming down the hill, they turned into the residential area, leisurely circling around. Noticing a great lookout spot, they stopped to admire the breath-taking view of Vancouver. It was indeed an extraordinarily beautiful landscaped city, spreading along the side of the hills.

When they decided to move on, they realized they were lost. Andrew spread out the map on the hood of the car, debating how to get back to the city, when an elderly couple walked by. Noticing that Andrew had a problem, the man asked, "Can we help you by any chance?"

"We seem to be lost," Andrew said and told him where he wanted to go.

"Oh, we can fix that," he said. "Wait here a minute, I'll be back." He left his wife there, and while she chatted with the Dombradys, her husband came back with his car. He instructed

Andrew to follow him and he led them back to the Lions Gate Bridge.

* * *

The next day they wanted to see the famous steam-powered clock in Vancouver's Gastown. As it was still early, they decided to visit Victoria, the capital city of British Columbia.

The two-hour ferry-ride offered plenty of time for the travelers to read the brochures, informing them what a peaceful and beautiful city Victoria was. It boasted about its favorable climate and beauty, which ensured a pleasurable place for retired people to live.

Arriving to a strikingly clean city, they drove to the impressive Parliament Buildings and the famous Empress Hotel, that was flanked the harbor. These attractive landmarks in the heart of the city were a magnetic pull for tourists.

After a long walk around the Parliament Buildings—which Andrew named as *"People's Place"*—they enjoyed the beautifully landscaped *Beacon Hill* Park. In Katie's eyes Victoria's flower culture was one of the most obvious sights. Then, seeing those double-decker buses stationing at the Empress Hotel, they took a tour around the city. Enjoying the ride, they learned from the tour guide that no one should leave Victoria without visiting the marvelous *Butchart Gardens*. So that was their next program.

Entering the gate of the gardens, an almost theatrical setting received them. The fascinating, riotous profusion of colors were an eye-pleasing wonder—a feast for the senses. They marveled at the overwhelming artistically shaped bushes, trees and velvety green lawns. "Oh, look at that beautiful star-shaped pool!" Later, sauntering along a charming winding path in the *Sunken Garden*, a dignified art of spectacular colors rolled before them like magic carpet. Katie gasped in delight. "I wouldn't even try to describe the beauty of this magnificent garden. There was a gently swaying fountain in the middle of the lake that people stopped to watch. Unlike Niagara Falls, with its flamboyant wealth of colors, *Butchart Gardens* was a manmade wonder of the world.

They spent two more days in Victoria, exploring some museums and interesting places, then had a pleasant walk along *Dallas Road*. It seemed to be another *"People's Place,"* where kite enthusiasts had fun showing their skills. The Dombradys strolled leisurely, and enjoyed the view of the Pacific Ocean. They were amazed how on a clear day they could see the American snow-capped mountains on the other side of the ocean.

"Besides the beautiful view, I also enjoy the scent of the ocean," Katie said. "I sure don't blame people for loving to live here."

"I would love it myself," Andrew said. "It was worthwhile coming here, and I'm sure we will come back some day."

."Great!" Andy applauded. "And next time I'll do the driving."

"Or I, if you don't mind," Aniko sniffed.

"The answer is a big question mark, my lady."

36

FROM HEAVEN TO HELL

AFTER ONE MORE WEEK in Vancouver, it was time to return home. When they left the city, they felt a sense of sadness: a part of their hearts stayed behind. At the same time they could hardly wait to see those magnificent mountains again.

On the road Andrew evaluated their vacation. The trip was a marvelous success, in fact the best they had ever enjoyed. Spending weeks on sandy beaches and lazing under the sun held attraction for them, too, but staying in one place was not their style. Thank God, Katie had the same adventurous blood in her, Andrew thought.

Whenever they stopped for the night, they took two rooms for privacy. After six days on the road, they were only one day's drive from Toronto. Although it was only five o'clock in the afternoon when Andrew saw a motel with family cabins on a lakeside, he decided to stop. He was a little tired, and this quiet countryside motel promised a cozy rest. The ominous dark clouds covering the sky, were another reason for the early stop.

"I think we will turn in here for the night," Andrew said. "We still have a few days of vacation left, so why rush it?"

There were good choices of vacant cabins, and after taking one, Andy flopped down on the bed sighing happily. "I feel as though we traveled around the whole world. It was fun!"

"It was wonderful, wasn't it?" Katie said, while preparing something to eat. "This trip surpassed everything we have done before. And thank God, we have made it without a scratch."

"It is because my daddy is an excellent driver," Aniko said, kissing him.

"Thanks for the confidence, sweetie," Andrew said, kissing

her back.

After supper, sitting around the table, Katie said, "So if all goes well, at this time tomorrow we will be at home, safe and sound."

"Without any question," Andrew said.

"It is funny, no matter how wonderful a vacation is, it is always a special feeling to return home."

"In a way, it is," Aniko interrupted, eating an apple. "But I feel kind of sad that the trip has to come to an end. I think I could go on living like this forever."

"I don't think so," Andy said. "I enjoyed it, too, but I think you'd get tired of it after awhile. I, for one, can hardly wait to get home and tell all my friends what fantastic places we've seen."

"Oh sure, I know how good you are at bragging," Aniko teased. Then her saucy smile disappeared. "Oh, I'm sorry, Andy, I shouldn't say that. Will you forgive me?" She stroked his face. "I think you're right, we sure have a lot to tell."

"It's all right, sis, I forgive you. I know that under your naughtiness, deep down you're almost as good as I am," he smiled.

"You're something else," Aniko laughed, poking at him. "But I love you anyway, you big hunk," and kissed his cheek, while their parents watched with a great deal of amusement.

Andy turned to his father. "So, where do we go next year, Dad? Shall we explore Vancouver again, or maybe sunny Florida?"

Andrew smiled mysteriously. He did not want to talk about their plans for the Australia trip just yet. He meant it to be another surprise.

"As we used to say in the old country, '*the truth will come out at the interrogation*', son. In other words, time will tell. One year is a long time, many things can happen. So let's sleep on it for a while."

"Dad is right, of course," Aniko agreed. "Who knows, maybe I'll be on my honeymoon in Hawaii a year from now, for all we know."

Andy could not help but burst into laugh. "Now that will be the day! And who would be the dream bridegroom, may I ask? I want to congratulate him."

"Aside from the fact that it's none of your business, I know you've no imagination, lover boy, because you're blind," she retorted, making her parents laugh.

"Just be sure you don't rush into anything, honey," Katie advised her. "Time is on your side."

In the morning the sky was still cloudy and the blasting wind wailed furiously before the storm, bending trees, ripping off branches and hurtling dead leaves in the air that flew like birds before the wolf of wind. Suddenly, a loud crash of thunder ripped through the valley and the sky blackened as though a magician had snuffed out the flame of the sun. Blue-white lightning flared across the ruffled water and sprang back into the swaying trees. Then after some more claps of thunder, heavy rain began to fall from the dark clouds, pounding the roof with savage vehemence, lashing at everything that stood in its way.

"It's a good thing we're not on the road," Katie said, standing beside Andrew at the window, watching the wind driving the rain hard against the glass.

"Yes. Thank God, we had the good sense to wait. But I think it's a passing storm, and we probably won't have to wait long."

He was right. The heavy wind soon subsided to a hushed whisper and as the gray, tattered clouds floated across the sky; the sun broke through in its glittering, silvery rays. The earth and trees smelled deliciously fresh, and the leaves sparkled in the bright sunshine. The heavy downpour had formed some small puddles on the bumpy ill-paved parking lot, so people jumped over them as they started preparing their cars for the journey.

Andrew also did his routine of checking the car, while Katie and the children did the packing. Soon all the baggage had been set neatly in the trunk and they were ready to move on.

They were on Highway 400. Having plenty of time, Andrew drove within the speed limit. Despite the rain, the road was good and dry already. Occasionally Katie and Andrew smiled at each other as they listened to the children's chatter about how exciting the trip has been.

Then, glancing in the rearview mirror, Andrew noticed with blood-chilling horror as two cars were racing side-by-side at breakneck speed. It seemed that one was trying to pass the other, but he would not let him. Both cars were pushing the speed limit to the point where skill gives way to chance—as if wanting to outstrip the wind. The speed kept escalating, and Andrew witnessed this insane racing with stunned helplessness. His mouth went dry.

"*They are out of their minds,*" he mumbled. "What the hell are they..."

But he did not have the chance to finish the sentence, for in the next moment the passing car finally managed to pull in front of the other. But doing so at more than 100 miles per hour, he had no choice but to smash into Andrew's car. In reaction, Andrew hit the brake, further increasing the impact. After the thunderous explosion of twisted metals, a red glow of lightning sensation flickered through Andrew's eyes. He was faintly aware of being thrown back and forth like a puppet on a string, banging his head onto the door and then onto the steering wheel. Then his grip on the wheel loosened and he sank into darkness. The car swerved off the road and came to a screeching halt, hanging halfway over the ditch. The engine shuddered and died.

The car that ran into his, was demolished beyond recognition, but the third car had managed to avoid the collision and disappeared.

Katie had been hurled towards Andrew by the impact, which momentarily knocked the air out of her. The world was spinning crazily, but miraculously she stayed conscious. Shaking uncontrollably, she noticed that the door on her side swung wide open. Gasping for air, she felt as if all the strength left her. By force of will she looked back, and with horror, she saw a tangled mess that froze her into immobility. The tail of the car has been crushed in, and amid the crushed metal lay the children, crumpled in the wreckage like smashed dolls. On their faces blood streaked down, dribbling from their foreheads. The sight froze in her mind forever.

Drawn by the awful sight, she knew she should act and wanted to move to get her babies out of the wreckage, but she was paralyzed by the horror of it. Then she heard a heart-piercing scream, her own, frantically calling their names.

"Oh, Andrew, please help me!" she begged. But it was useless, for Andrew leaned slump against the door, his face was a mask of blood. Katie looked at him with disbelief, her hand on her mouth, as passing motorists stopped. They pried Andrew out of the wreckage and laid him on the grass, while some women gathered around Katie to calm her, as she was screaming hysterically.

Fortunately a police patrol car passed by and summoned an ambulance on the radio. They soon heard the shrieking ambulance as it arrived reasonably fast, along with reporters.

Katie was aware of things only in an abstract way, as if she were detached from the whole scene. With a sick sensation in her stomach, she watched the swiftly moving attendants, but heard only the urgency in their voices as they put Andrew on the stretcher, then, very gingerly, they freed the children.

A rift in the gray clouds let through a stream of sunlight, illuminating their limp bodies. As Katie stood there staring at them with tear-blinded eyes, the stark reality struck her. She felt a sudden excruciating pain, as though a knife had passed through her heart. Millions of black dots whirled before her eyes, And with a sighing sound, she sank into a blessed blackness, falling into the arms of a man behind her.

On the way to the hospital, Andrew's semiconscious mind barely registered the shrieking wail of the ambulance, which sounded like dying screams from the pit of hell.

* * *

The following day a policeman came to the shop looking for Alex Kerekes.

"That's me," Alex said. From the solemn face of the officer, an instant suspicion flashed through his mind. "What is it, officer?"

"I have some bad news to tell, I'm afraid." A notebook in his hand, he asked his relationship to Andrew Dombrady, then he said, "*There has been a serious accident.*"

"Oh my God!" Alex exclaimed, and the blood rushed out of his head. The strong dizziness he felt was like a silent earthquake and a tremor of fear shook him. Stan quickly gave him a chair to sit down. What the officer said after that was a blur. Wildly shaking, he glanced at Stan with a look of total disbelief.

After the policemen left, they jumped into the car and rushed to the hospital, while Alex's mind echoed the terrified words: "*There has been a serious _accident...*"

In the hospital the nurse on duty permitted them to see Katie only, so they rushed to her room. When they stepped in, they were shocked to see her shaking and crying hysterically, afraid she was going insane with grief. Seeing Alex, all she was able to moan was, "Oh, Alex...my babies...my...poor babies...what am I...going ...to do?"

"It's all right, Katie, it's all right, calm down," Alex hugged her, doing his best to calm her down. Then he told Stan to stay with her, and he went to look for the doctor. When he finally heard the horrible, ugly story, he broke down and wept bitterly.

"We will do everything that humanly possible," the doctor told him, "but their lives ultimately rest in the hands of God."

Because Andy and Aniko had been so close to the impact, both had suffered serious internal injuries. They were put in the Intensive Care Unit, hooked up to the life-support systems, with round-the-clock surveillance.

* * *

Andrew lay one floor lower from the children. In his nightmare he cried out, "No, no, oh God..." his body bathing in sweat. The room began spinning, and the pain made him wince when he tried to move. Then he fell back into darkness.

When he opened his eyes, the memory slowly came into focus from the foggy blanket of confusion. A dark figure loomed over him, checking his pulse. "Good." he said, making a note on Andrew's chart while the nurse straightened out the sheet over him. He touched the bandage on his head.

"Welcome back, Mr. Dombrady," the nurse greeted him cheerfully. "Boy, you have had a rough journey in your dream, but thank God, you will make it."

"What happened to my children? Where is my wife?" Andrew demanded.

"Your wife is fine. Your children are in another ward. They're in bad shape, but they're still alive."

Doubt crept into Andrew's mind, thinking that she was only saying these reassuring words to spare him from the tragic news.

"I want to see them."

"Oh, no, that'll have to wait; you're not in any condition to leave your bed. But I'm telling you the truth."

Only Katie was able to convince him when she came in. They both cried—Andrew in relief that at least Katie had been spared.

When the doctor told them that the children had a fifty-fifty chance of surviving, Andrew interpreted that they had a fifty-fifty chance of dying.

* * *

After a thorough examination, three days later Katie was allowed to go home. Alex came for her but he dared not take her home. Instead, he set up a room in his house and hired a woman to take care of her.

Being alone, and knowing how seriously her children were hurt, Katie's pain was mixed with guilt. Why them? She would have changed places with them any day to ensure they would live. She was on the verge of losing her mind. Her brain was on fire as if millions of burning pins were being driven through it. The hideous, gruesome sight at the back of the car drew her mind into its murky depth. The terrifying thought that the children could die at any moment tore at her heart. I will die with them, she thought, as shuddering sobs shook her body.

When Alex found her crying like that, he tried to subdue her, only to realize that he had no adequate words to console her. Instead, as Katie put her head on his shoulder, both their sobs filled the room.

* * *

Andrew's emotions were at war. The suffering of his family, the feeling of guilt at not being able to help them, tormented him. Looking back, he could visualize the menacing advancement with gut-wrenching clarity. And he had done nothing to prevent it! How could he have been so dumb, he thought, hardly able to control his exploding rage. At times he was seized with uncontrollable shaking, as if he had been electrocuted, other times his brain felt numb.

In his recurring nightmare, Andrew struggled with the steering wheel, trying to keep his car under control. But in spite of his superhuman efforts, the machine was like a huge monster with a mind of its own. And his dreams would always end with the sounds of that horrible thunderous crash, mixed with the screaming of his children. Then he would awake, drenched in sweat. Lying in bed he would see the children's happy, beautiful faces, and whisper their names. In his mind's eye, he could see them bursting with carefree happiness. Their energetic bodies would appear before him, until the shadow of that terrible accident threw a dark blanket over them. Then tears would gather in his eyes and trickle down his cheeks; a sensation that he would be aware of only vaguely.

* * *

Katie visited Andrew every day. Although her own suffering ravaged her like a cancer, when she entered his room, she would always greet him with a smile. She was deeply concerned about Andrew's tormented state of mind. The psychological pain of the accident had left its mark on his face, and there were new wrinkles on his forehead. His obsession with guilt was alarming. So, she took it upon herself to be strong, to keep his hope alive. She could not let him lose the will to live, for she knew if he lost that, all the medicine in the world could not heal him.

"Dear God, please let him get well," she prayed.

* * *

As soon as Andrew was permitted to leave his bed, they went to visit the children. Before they stepped in, Katie gently prepared Andrew for their conditions. But seeing the children, rippling shockwaves ran down his spine. They lay there like crumpled leaves, torn and fragmented, struggling for life—life that only the waving lines on the cardiograph machine indicated that they were still alive. As he watched them, tears rolled down his cheeks that he did not try to stop. It reminded him of another hospital, looking at their tiny bodies in the incubator. He remembered how shaken and deeply touched he had been. But unlike then, this time he wanted to beg for their forgiveness. To control his burning pain, he pressed his quivering lips together, desperately trying to keep from screaming, from breaking down. Silently praying, the thought flashed through his mind that in our young minds everything is so permanent and lasting. But now he realized that in any moment our children could be gone...

From that day on he and Katie sat at their bedsides as if their presence somehow would prolong the children's lives. Generating enough strength to talk to them, they developed a pattern of telling them **anything** that came to mind: their favorite TV programs, about their godfather, Stan, their friends who came to visit them—pretending that they were hearing them.

The most painful moment was when they had to leave. They felt that with every departure they are breaking that imaginary magic power of connection; that there may not be a next time. Indeed, the shadow of that possibility hung over them like the sword of Damocles. Andrew, who never had been afraid of dying, was now afraid of living. It was pure hell waiting to see what tomorrow *might* bring.

Whenever they had a chance, they would ask the doctor for more information, for more encouragement on which they could build some hope. But from their answers Andrew sensed they were bargaining for time. "We're doing our best, but we don't want to give you false hope," they would say.

The insurance man, who was working on the Dombrady's behalf for a large settlement, told Andrew that the nineteen-year-old teenager, who ran into them, had been drunk. It was no consolation at all that he died instantly.

When he heard this, violent rage seized him. But his anger was directed toward the law. Why cannot they see that drunk drivers are a menace on the road, potential murderers?

Then suddenly Andrew remembered the tragic story that Stan had told them some time ago...

* * *

"I grew up in Toronto's poor section," he said, "and in that environment, I had to fight to survive. It did not help the situation that my Irish father was a hopeless drunkard, who had been beating my mother and me mercilessly, abusing us mentally and physically for no reason. Just for being there, I guess. In his drunken state he often accused my mother of bringing a bastard into his life—that I was not his son."

"Oh Stan, what a terrible way to grow up," Katie exclaimed, shocked.

"Well, I didn't think I could ever say this, but it seems one can get used to anything. So, as you can see, I grew up in a hateful environment with no love or affection, only terror and insecurity. My father found fault in everything: in the taste of food, my mother's spending too much on 'junk food', calling her a no good lazy tramp. But these were only made-up reasons to build up his righteous anger, then he would turn over furniture, break anything that got in his way. It came to the point where it became a routine for him.

"Sometimes I used to run from the house screaming because my father would threaten to kill us with the kitchen knife. Then the neighbors would rush over to subdue him.

"My father's cruelty affected me as a child. For a long time I felt guilty, believing that my parents were fighting because of me. When my mother tried to protect me, he always turned his fury against her. Innocent as I was, I often asked my mother, why did daddy beat me last night? I don't remember doing anything wrong.

"He didn't know what he was doing, son,' she would say. 'He is a sick man. You see, he doesn't even remember that he gave me this black eye,' as if it would have justified it.

"If he is sick, why doesn't he go to the doctor?' I asked. But it was hopeless. She thought that I was too young to understand. Oh she knew that it was crazy to put up with him, but—as she told me later—what could she have done? There was no help, and she had nowhere to go.

"Then one day my father disappeared. Just like that: vanished. He went to work one day and simply never came home. I remember we both breathed a sigh of relief. I was about ten years old. After that, we moved into a government housing project, and lived on welfare. Surviving those tormented years, I developed a certain behavior pattern that helped me take things in stride. I guess I was covering my pain with my sense of humor. Actually it was an instinctive search for love and attention that I missed so much as a child.

"I have been working very hard since I was about eight years old. I quit school at grade six to help my mother. She died of tuberculosis at the age of thirty-eight. I was sixteen years old. So you can see why, when I see a drunk on the street, my blood runs to my head, and my fists clench. I hate them with a passion."

A shiver ran through Andrew's spine just remembering his story. Now he felt the same way.

* * *

Katie kept postponing writing to her parents. First, she did not want them to know what had happened, for she was convinced it would kill them. Second, she could not tell them the truth, because by the time the letter reached them, she did not know what the reality would be. In her logic, she thought that by revealing the condition of the children, she would be tempting fate. She believed that the less they knew, the less they would suffer.

She had sent many postcards during the tour, telling them what a marvelous trip they were having, so that should satisfy them for the time being. When Alex suggested that he would do the writing if it would make it easier on her, Katie reacted violently.

"Oh, no!" she protested frantically. "It would make things even worse! They would think the reason you were writing is because we were dead. Thanks, Alex, but please let's wait."

A week later, Katie felt strong enough to move back into her own house. Alex protested at first, but seeing her determination, reluctantly he agreed with the condition that she would let Stan help her with whatever had to be done. After taking her home, Alex and

Stan left her alone.

She walked around slowly. The house that once was filled with laughter and joy was like a silent tomb. Death seemed to vibrate in the air, and the cryptic silence was choking. She felt as if she were in a morgue. She looked around and wanted to scream to break the eerie silence.

Her mind flashed through the inventory of her happy memories. And like a movie camera, it played back some of the children's innocent chatter. With a faint smile in the corner of her mouth, she heard Aniko's voice as she argued with Andy: *"She eats too much..." "Everyday?...Silly yourself..."* They had dreams, but now they might never have a chance to become a TV broadcaster or an airline pilot.

She walked into Andy's room with a constricted throat. The room was exactly the way he had left it—in hasty teenage-style "order." She saw some books on the shelf, a small amount of change beside his radio, and music tapes in a box. Some sports equipment was on the floor at the edge of his bed.

Katie sat on the edge of his bed, moaning softly. She looked at the children's smiling pictures. Then, she succumbed to her pain and began to sob disconsolately.

Alex phoned or visited her whenever she needed something. With Stan they worked out what had to be done around the house. He agreed to cut the grass, rake the fallen leaves, and drive Katie for shopping. As Andrew used to say, one of his "weaknesses" was that he always put other people's needs before his own.

Only long years of friendship can build such genuine love what he felt for the Dombradys. So their tragedy was his tragedy as well.

37

DEEP HIDDEN SECRET

ONE MONTH HAD PASSED since the accident, but the children's condition had remained the same. Andrew was still in the hospital, but not so much for his injuries, rather because of his nervous breakdown. Meanwhile Katie persuaded him to see a psychiatrist twice a week. At first he was vehemently against it, but later Andrew was grateful he had agreed. He learned from Dr. Saunders the importance of accepting reality. Blaming himself was self-destructive, and would not solve anything. The doctor also has been successful in making him realize how unfair he was to put an unnecessary burden on Katie's shoulders by his self-punishing attitude.

Being hospitalized for so long meant having plenty of time to think. In a place like this, time moves sluggishly for a man who never knew idleness. Doing nothing was the hardest thing to endure. It seemed such a useless waste of time. Working in the hospital in Winnipeg, he remembered how seriously ill patients were reduced to total dependency. What an undignified and depressing sight it was to be completely at the mercy of others! That must have been the hardest thing to take, he thought. And here I am. Who could have believed that one day I would be in the same predicament?

Spending many a night alone, searching for strength and consolation, by sheer chance Katie came across a book, called "*The Way of the Bull*", by Leo Buscaglia. From it she learned the horrendous suffering that people in the Third World countries had to endure; tragedies they had to surmount. Somehow it gave her a new perspective, a reason to believe that there is hope even in hopelessness. Then at one of Katie's visits, Andrew discovered for the thousandth time that life is a treasure house of inexhaustible surprises. Even with a broken heart that left her mortally wounded—with her iron strength that lay hidden under the blanket of femininity—she was still able to divert her attention from her tragedy by accepting a greater power, which she took as the grace of God's will.

"We cannot fathom the power of the higher wisdom, but there must be a reason for everything," she said. "Remember how hopeless we felt when we lost each other? Life did not seem worth living. But we survived because we had faith. So, as long as there is life, there is hope. The right attitude is that we take each day with that hope in mind."

Andrew smiled but said nothing. Who could argue with her? Oh, he could have come up with some down to earth argument, a sharp protest against senseless and needless suffering, but he did not have the heart to destroy her belief. He had always considered her a little over credulous, living in some glorified optimism, which creates a false illusion. He hated to admit it to himself, but his faith was wavering.

Before she went, she left the book for Andrew to read. There was a passage in it that she particularly brought to his attention. "Read this, sweetheart. I love the way this psychologist analyzes the waste of living in the past, and the great value of the moment," she said.

Later Andrew started to read:

"Life is now. Yesterday is past and gone, and therefore unreal, only real in its effect on the moment. The future is not real, and possibly it will never be more than simply a dream. This leaves simply the now, the moment, as reality. Yet so many people live only under the shadow of the successes or mistakes of the past or the possibilities and hope of the future. They do not seem to realize that when they deal with these worlds of the unreal, they are missing the 'moments', the accumulation of which makes a life. Life, then, becomes a series of moments, either lived or lost. Since moments pass, as time, there is soon nothing left, and life is over, leaving some poor, unfortunate souls having never lived at all .... "

* * *

The next day, with this book in hand, Andrew stood at the window, looking out at the courtyard, musing. In the relative safety of his lofty perch, he enjoyed the soothing golden rays of the autumn sunshine that broke through the window. Outside russet-yellow leaves floated in the gentle breeze, glittering like goldfish in an aquarium. Observing this colorful, yet fragile world that offered beauty, pleasure and happiness so generously, it was easy to relate human life to those falling leaves. At this moment, their life-span was over, sending him the message that *all that glitters is not gold.*

Life is a tragedy, he read it somewhere, for we all born to eventually die. Even if one is fortunate enough to attain a certain amount of happiness, and has the luck to enjoy the fruits of his hard-earned success, he can lose it all at the most unexpected moment. Thinking of his children, a shudder ran through his body. Why must innocent children suffer for the crimes of irresponsible adults? "Please, God, give them a second chance," he murmured.

When he turned away from the window, he involuntarily glanced at the calendar on the wall and noticed the date with surprise. *October 23rd.* It was the anniversary of one of the most dramatic events of his youth. An almost forgotten image passed in front of his eyes. *He saw himself as a youngster twenty-seven years ago, sneaking up to the Russian tanks with George Pusztai to jam and burn them.* He would have come with him, if he...It is unbelievable how one's memory can fade into oblivion.

As one plunge into the swift current of daily life, wrapped up in the fight for survival, hardly notice the widening gap that time builds. Then, when one looks over his shoulder, he realizes with surprise that *time runs faster as one moves slower.* Andrew used to dwell on the futile subject of what might have happened had the revolution really won? What he just read was right: only the present moment is real. The past is gone and the rest is nothing more than luck, destiny. *Our future is a toy in the hands of Fate.*

Living in the hospital has a certain effect on one's outlook on life. It's a different world. Musing over his life through the wandering years from the revolution, in retrospect, it was easy to realize that time has a way of embellishing the past and smoothes away the rough edges. So even the most troublesome days can be recalled as pleasant, because our youth is in it.

Andrew turned and climbed into bed; he wanted to read more from the book. Meantime, the nurse came in to check if everything was all right. When she had gone, he read for a while, then for some strange reason, suddenly he thought about Cathy. Lately, he had been thinking about her more often. It still bothered him that she had disappeared with such finality. God knows, he had not meant to burn the bridge between them. Then he drifted into a light sleep. He didn't know how much he slept when a soft knock on the slightly open door woke him. He jumped out of bed and reached for his cloak, for he did not like to receive visitors in bed.

A woman walked in hesitantly, and in a heart-stopping moment, grabbing the arm of the chair, Andrew could not believe that the woman standing before him was Cathy. For a moment they stared at each other in mute disbelief, neither of them believing how much the other had changed. She stared at Andrew's lean face, as the skin drawn tightly over the bone, and saw the streaks of grayish hair on his temple. At the same time Andrew saw wrinkles around her sad-looking eyes, that the years had engraved. Gone was the teasing glitter from her smiling eyes. Their hearts were throbbing wildly, as Andrew stepped forward with open arms.

"**Cathy!**," he gasped.

"Hi Andrew," she greeted him timidly, with a constrained smile. "Thank God, you're alive," she said with relief.

Andrew kept looking at her as if he were seeing a ghost.

"Yes, I am, as you can see. But I can't believe I am looking at you. How are you? Please sit down."

"I'm fine, thank you."

Andrew still had a difficult time talking. "I don't know what to say, except how did you know I'm here?"

Cathy took her time sitting down, as if she too were having a hard time collecting her thoughts. "Andrew, I'm sorry about the tragedy that happened to you and your family. I was so terribly shocked. How are the children?"

"They are fighting for their lives. *But how...how do you know all this?*"

"It was quite accidental," she said. "I was in Ottawa, visiting one of my girlfriends who subscribes to the 'Globe and Mail'. By sheer chance I picked up the issue that carried a picture of the car accident with your name under it. You can imagine my shock; I just could not believe it. I kept reading it over and over again. That is when I decided to find out where you are and how you are doing."

"That was very nice of you, thanks," he said with a mild sarcasm in his voice. Slowly Andrew became himself. "It seems this accident should have happened a long, long time ago. It would have saved me a lot of worry about what happened to you."

"Well, I might as well tell you I never ever intended to let you know that I was alive, unless fate brought us together. But your accident brought me to my senses, so to speak. I could not remain silent any longer."

"But why for heaven's sake?" Andrew cried out angrily, shaking his head. "For the life of me, I could not understand why you had disappeared without a trace. Oh, I had some idea but..."

There was a mysterious look on Cathy's face.

"Yes, I believe you had, and I thought about you, too, believe me. But... well, life has to go on."

"Cathy, did you come here to reopen old wounds? I thought I made myself clear in my letter. Do I have to explain it to you all over again? Sure I understand your resentment, and I'm terribly sorry that I hurt you, but I always wanted to tell you..."

Cathy shook her head. "No, no, you are wrong! I understood you perfectly. I knew you could not help it, although it did not help me much. I tried not to judge you too harshly because after all *there was no way that you could have known*...Oh before I forget, I brought you a present. Almond chocolate—it used to be your favorite."

"It still is. Thank you," he said and kissed her cheek. "However, you still did not answer my question, and I won't let you go until I find out. Why did you disappear so mysteriously? It did not make any sense..."

"It's a long story, but I'll burden you only with the important detail."

"Cathy, please..."

"I'm sorry, Andrew," she sighed, then abruptly lifted her head. "Andrew, before I tell you more, could we see the children?"

"We can try." he said, a puzzled look on his face.

They walked to the intensive care ward where they were given permission. As soon as Cathy saw the children, she gasped. She kept staring at Andy, "*What a resemblance!*" she said. "They are twins, aren't they?"

"Yes."

She clasped her hands and whispered, "Dear God, let them get well."

While she prayed, Andrew took the opportunity to observe her more closely. She was still attractive, but her sad face reflected an air of resignation. Her brown eyes, once so bold and teasing, were veiled, and the smile she used to have at the corner of her mouth was gone. Well, sixteen years is a long time, he thought. She must be forty-nine years old.

They returned to Andrew's room and Cathy sat down. When she began to speak, her voice was trembling. "Andrew, I hope you'll appreciate how difficult it is for me to talk about the past. But I want to be fair, for I feel I owe you an explanation. I'll never forget the deep, dark emptiness when I received your letter. For a few seconds, I hoped it was just one of your jokes. But of course, I knew better. The hurt and pain, the abandonment engulfed me. Then the feeling of how powerless we are in the grip of destiny, shocked me. Yet, what hurt me the most was the clear realization that I had lost you. My first reaction was to disappear from your life. I did not want you coming around and looking for me, and having me stand in the way of your happiness. I remembered an old Indian proverb: 'it is useless to wash the coal to change its color—what can't be cured must be endured'. But there was a deeper reason for my disappearance," Cathy said with a sad glance. Then she paused and took a deep breath.

"*Andrew, I will tell you something that I never ever intended you to know. Just a few days after I received your letter, I discovered that I was pregnant with your child. Imagine my state of mind: receiving your letter of rejection and finding out that I was pregnant.*"

As she paused, Andrew's jaw dropped. He looked at her in mute disbelief on his ashen face; the stunning revelation of her hidden secret, the long years of mystery struck him like lightning. He was moved beyond words visualizing the loneliness she must have been suffered. He groped for words to ease her pain but his mind paralyzed, all Andrew could utter was a moan, "*Oh my God!*"

After a moment of heavy silence, Cathy continued. "But instead of bursting with joy, I was in a state of shock for not only had I lost you, but also my baby had lost his father. During my pregnancy I struggled with the thought that by looking for happiness, we find someone and fell in love. Then when we think we have it all, in an unexpected moment, our hearts are wrecked, like a peaceful village after a tornado. The loneliness crushed me hard, and life suddenly became meaningless. I felt as if I was standing at the edge of a cliff, afraid to make a move. I loved you so much that I felt I could not go on without you. I cried for days, knowing I was carrying your baby but you could never be his father."

Cathy paused, but Andrew could not speak. These are the moments in life when happy memories are flashing through our minds; memories that choke our throats, and the pain squeezes the tears out from our eyes. *Nostalgic music makes the same effect when a lonely old man sitting alone on a park bench with gray head, amid the green landscape and sparkling sunshine, feeling the breeze that prickles the skin; and through the golden haze children's laughter fills the air that mixes in with our thoughts, while listening to music like* **"Misty Blue."**

While Cathy shed some light on the mystery, it was like when the sun clears up the fog and brings with it the harsh lesson of the past. Andrew felt Cathy's pain. But there was no sense to search for atonement— it was too late to make up for the misery he had caused her over the years. Instead, he edged his chair closer to hers, and took her hand.

"Cathy, I just don't know what to say. I know that it is not good enough, but all I can say is that I am very sorry. Naturally I had no idea of what had happened with you. When I wrote that letter, I felt guilty for letting you down because I did love you, and knew I was going to hurt you. But I just had to make my choice. Do I make any sense?"

"Yes, you do. I knew you still loved Katie, and although your letter hurt me, in retrospect I have realized that I was dancing on thin ice. But I could not hate you.

"What I meant to tell you was that when we came back to Toronto, I tried to phone you. I don't know what I wanted to say— probably that I was sorry, for you did not deserve it..."

This was when honesty overrode emotion, and Cathy answered candidly.

"Oh Andrew, you should not blame yourself. After all, it took two to tango, you know. This is not a perfect world," she said. "Naturally, I considered abortion, for under the circumstances that seemed to be the best solution. However, I had neither the courage nor the heart to go through with it. But my decision to keep the baby had nothing to do with those 'pro-life' extremist hypocrites. God, I can't stand them, as I'm a 'pro-choice' woman all the way."

Andrew nodded.

"You have no idea how I yearned to share my secret with you. I made up a million plans how I should approach you, but I was in constant struggle with my wounded pride. So I forced myself to remain silent. In my moments of anger I told myself never to let you find out about the baby. That was why I made a resolution to erect a wall around my secret.

"Well, if it was intended to punish me, you sure have succeeded."

"I was too confused. What gave me some solace was that no matter what happened, I would always have your child. Through him, I could still love you."

Cathy's face darkened. She closed her eyes in an attempt to collect her strength, she keep a grip on her emotions.

"First, I went to Banff where I worked as long as my condition permitted me to. Then when little Andrew was born, I waited a year before I moved to Calgary. When people asked about his father, I simply told them that he had died in a car accident. Now you can imagine the remorse I felt when I read about the accident. It was as if I have tempted fate—that what happened to you was some kind of retribution for my lies. It begun to haunt me, so my guilty feelings forced me to come."

"Oh come on, Cathy! Surely you know that it is preposterous. How could anyone but God know that this was going to happen so many years later?"

With her head bowed, Cathy nodded. "I know, yet I felt that it was too much of a coincidence. By the way, how is Katie and Alex doing? We haven't even talked about them."

"They are fine, thanks. Thank God, Katie suffered only minor injuries. The business is doing fine, which keeps Alex alive. He will regret missing the chance to see you."

"Anyway, I didn't finish my story. I got married shortly after I moved to Calgary. My husband adopted Andrew and considers him as his own child. I must say he loved him dearly from the beginning. But it was not hard because Andrew was such a smart, loveable little boy. Well, now you know you have two sons."

"I wish I had known sooner. But thank you for telling me, I appreciate it very much." Then seeing again her resigned face, there was a telltale sign of an unfulfilled life. He felt compelled to ask, "I hope you're happy with your husband."

"I can't really complain. He is a good, hardworking man. He is a cabinetmaker and he owns his own business. Compromise is an art; it takes time to make the best of any situation. Besides, there's a saying, *'if you can't have the man you love, you have to love the man you have'*. The only happy note I have that relieved my misery is that keeping little Andrew turned out to be a blessing, for otherwise we could not have any children. So you see, God works in mysterious ways." Glancing at her wristwatch, she realized how much time had passed. "Oh, my goodness," she said, "it's time to go. And we hardly talked about you."

"That's all right. Now that we've seen each other, I hope there will be other times," Andrew said. "But for now, I must tell you that it is wonderful to know that you're all right. You've cleared away my fear by sharing your secret. Regretfully, we can't change the past, but now I hope the past will no longer hurt us."

"I hope so, too. As far as I'm concerned, I have accepted that what had happened was meant to happen. Please let me know how the children are doing." She reached into her purse and pulled out a piece of paper. She wrote down her name and phone number. "Your call will be welcome any time."

"Thanks, Cathy. Should there be any change, I'll certainly let you know."

While she stood up and smoothed her skirt, Andrew glanced at the paper. Mrs. Cathy Faludy.

In a moment of hesitation, she pressed her trembling lips together. Her pain-stricken face reflected a superhuman emotional restraint that showed that the phantoms of the past still haunted her, as if saying: *"I hate to leave you, Andrew."* She composed herself and extended her hand.

"So long, Andrew. Please give my best regards to Katie and Alex. I wish you all a fast recovery and the best of luck."

Andrew, also fighting with his own emotions, took a deep breath. "Thank you for coming," he said, and kissed her.

Then she turned, but before she reached the door, she

glanced back once more with misty eyes.

"Cathy?"

"Yes?"

"Please, take care of yourself, and... our son."

She nodded with a smile that blended with longing like a pleasant pain, and whispered, *"I will."* Then she was gone, letting the tears roll down her cheek..

Andrew remained rooted to the spot, staring at the door. The sight of Cathy, and the incredible turn of events brought a strange solace to his lacerated heart. Yet her haunting words and accusatory glances penetrated into his conscience like a twisting knife. Memories from the mist of time flooded his mind, like walking along the Ottawa River Parkway. One of her remarks especially stood the test of time: *'Like dream and reality, they tend to proceed in opposite directions.* She had predicted her own fate.

Andrew admitted that Cathy had represented sweetness. She was bright, and added sparkle to his life. Naturally, she had changed, and her philosophy on life had softened with the chemistry of time. The most powerful impact was the shock of her confession. He could never in his wildest dreams have connected her disappearance with pregnancy. Had he known she was pregnant, he might have stood by her. At least he would have made an effort to contribute to her financial welfare.

So I have another son, Andrew thought. *Everything happens for a reason, she said.* This accident was a terrible price to pay to discover this secret.

Life is full of secrets, he thought, some of which may be revealed in time, while others remain buried forever. Yes, there are moments in our lives that we are not proud of. If we are really honest, there are episodes in our lives of an embarrassing nature that lingers in the back of our minds, and flash back at the most unexpected moment. It remains a constant reminder of how imperfect we really are. Someone said once, and he remembered agreeing with him. "We have many small and great sins that we keep hidden which, if it were known, would make the moralists horrified. Otherwise, whatever it is that the world knows nothing about, the truth will be lost forever in an infinite silence, and we remain, on balance, decent people.

It is not a consoling picture, is it? he asked himself.

Now he remembered Cathy's exclamation as she looked at Andy, "*What a resemblance!*" It did not mean much to him then, but now it made sense. She must have seen the resemblance between the two boys. It is too bad that he grew up without knowing his real father. The way Cathy described him, he felt a sense of loss. Some day he definitely wanted to see the young man. The prospect gave him a pleasant feeling—a feeling that Cathy's visit had a therapeutic effect upon him. A dark curtain had been stripped away, letting in the light that revealed the mystery.

Andrew hardly could wait for Katie's arrival, so he could share his surprise with her. He had no intention of keeping Cathy's son a secret, but he would not tell her just yet. It would have to be at a more appropriate time. Katie had enough worry on her mind as it was, and she did not need more upsetting thoughts added to it. The news had shaken even him, and he needed time to let it all sink in.

* * *

When Katie arrived, she was pleasantly surprised to find Andrew in such a good spirit.

"Hi, sweetheart! How is my lovely wife?" he asked, hugging her. "I could hardly wait to see you."

Startled, Katie placed a bouquet of freshly cut flowers on Andrew's bedside table, saying, "Well, well, well. What is happening here? Do you have some good news, or did they give you some miracle cheer-up-pills? Whatever it is that makes you this happy, I would like some myself."

Andrew laughed. "I like that. But no, pills would not do it. Listen, sweetheart, before we go to see the children, I have to tell you I had an unexpected visitor. But I bet you will never guess who it was."

"Oh really? Well, let me see." She paced the floor up and down, clapping her hands, seemingly enjoying the challenge.

"Are you ready to give up? Let me tell you; you'll never guess."

"No, no please give me a chance, will you?" Katie continued mumbling to herself. "No, it couldn't have been him. Only a woman could make such an impression." Suddenly, her face brightened. "*I have got it! It was Cathy, your old love.*"

Andrew looked at her dumbfounded. "That is impossible! How in the devil could you figure that out? Can't I even surprise you?"

"Of course you can, sweetheart," she said, with a twinkle in her eyes. "But you see, that was easy. Your cheerful voice made it too obvious. It had to be someone you were pleased to see. All I had to do was to put two and two together. Now, I'm dying to hear how could she have traced you, and what on earth had happened to her?"

"Yes, my surprise was indescribable as you can imagine." And Andrew told her all he knew, mainly about her marriage, and that she had read about the accident in the papers.

"Hmmm...I can imagine her surprise. It was nice of her to show concern for the children. Now about the big secret. Why did she disappear so mysteriously?"

"She said she was so terribly hurt, that vowed never to see me again, which is what I always thought," Andrew said. At least it was half of the truth, which Katie also found acceptable.

"To be honest, I can relate to how she must have suffered, and my heart goes out to her," Katie said. "She must have loved you very much."

"That is what she told me."

"Well, life can be cruel, we know. At least this mystery has been solved. But she sounds like a good person, and I'd like to meet her one day."

"You will, I'm sure of that."

38

DEAR GOD, LET IT BE TRUE

JUST LIKE EVERY DAY, sitting by the children's bed, Katie and Andrew praying as always. Then they began their small talk about the weather, Alex and Stan, how everybody loved them. Andrew told Andy about Johnny, his friend in the street, who had received a little puppy for his seventeenth birthday. For the very first time they were both noticed the faint sound that was coming from Aniko. It was more like a faint whisper, like a gentle sigh, and with a hardly noticeable movement of her lips, she said: "*Hi... Mom...*" Not even sure that it was real, they looked at each other with tremendous surprise. But the heavenly miracle lit up their very souls.

They quickly bent over her and poured out the sweetest words of love. "Hi, my baby! Yes, yes, we're here, sweetheart, can you hear me?" Katie said, desperately trying to establish some communication. "Please say something…"

Perspiration on their foreheads, now Andrew looked at Andy whose mouth also twitched and whispered some incomprehensible word. They kept talking feverishly to them, hoping they would hear that faint whispers again. It did not happen, but with a flicker of hope they clung to it with all their might. Yes, it *was* true, there was no doubt about it. Life was coming back! Dear God, **they are** alive! After such a long time of frantic waiting, finally they are coming back to life! Oh what a blissful, exciting moment it was! Katie and Andrew clung together, shaking, crying and laughing.

"My God, Katie, I can't believe it!" Andrew whispered, hugging her with joy. "You were right! You never gave up hope."

Katie cut the visit short and rushed home to Alex to report the wonderful news. When Alex let her in, by sheer excitement she fell into his arms. Gasping for breath, with delirious happiness she reported what had taken place in the hospital.

"Alex, you won't believe it, but *it has happened*!" she shouted, and told him everything. Both of them trembling, Alex let out a deep sigh of relief, "*Thank God*!" he said, and they were hugging, jumping, dancing and crying ecstatically, as if they had lost their minds.

* * *

The following day, Katie, Andrew, Alex and Stan stood next to the children's bed. Katie and Andrew bent over and greeted them as they always did. This time, however, Alex and Stan spoke too, to make them feel their presence. It seemed as if the children heard them, for things began to happen. During Katie's talking Aniko's eyelids fluttered feebly and a faint smile appeared on her face. Recognizing her mother, she repeat the whisper in a barely audible voice, "*Mom...my...*"

A cry of joy escaped from Katie's throat, and the fountain of emotion filled her eyes with happy tears. "Oh my sweet baby," yes, mommy and daddy are here," she said, as both of them bent over and whispering the most profound words of love.

At the same time it appeared as if the twins' souls were communicating, for now Alex noticed that Andy's eyelids were fluttering. He touched Andrew's arm to get his attention, just in time to hear Andy's feeble whisper, "*Hi...Dad...*"

"Hi, champion," Andrew said in a trembling voice. He kept talking, but Andy's eyes stayed open for seconds only, then it seemed as if tiredness pulled his eyelids down to return into his mysterious world. Nevertheless, those amazing moments conveyed not only life, but also thousands of words, that evoked the greatest relief and happiness to all of them.

The next second Katie rushed out to report the miracle. While they witnessed the most moving experience, Alex struggled with his emotions. He nervously placed his head in his hands and silently said a prayer: '*Dear God, let it be true*'!

One of the nurses called the doctor and he arrived within minutes. He had listened to Katie's rambling account, nodding occasionally with satisfaction. He made some notes, then he said, "Well, that's great! The healing process had been pleasing us for some time, and gave us hope to be optimistic. However, it must be said that this positive result was a combination of our, and your effort, and of course with God on our side. Also, their strong bodies fought off the adverse effects their systems were subjected to. So, as the progress indicating, if all goes well, there is a possibility that you might spend Christmas together. Now wouldn't that be great?"

"Oh, God!" Katie cried, embracing the doctor gratefully, with happy tears in her eyes. "Thank you."

A sudden wave of hope, a new faith and inspiration swelled in them. After they thanked the doctor, he left, then Alex and Stan started to hug Katie and Andrew, congratulating them.

"Well, now," Katie said, her eyes sparkling in happiness. "God has chosen this blessed day to give our children back to us. *Did you know that this is their birthday?*"

"That's right!" Alex said. They all bent over the children's beds and whispered, in unison: *"Happy birthday, kids."*

Well, this miracle calls for a celebration," Andrew announced solemnly. "It means that tomorrow morning we are going to church to thank God."

"Count us in, my friends," Alex said.

Andrew stood between the two friends, his heart swelling with joy. He looked at Alex with relief, for he had been concerned about how the worry would affect his health. He put his arms over their shoulders. "I must say that I'm more than lucky to be blessed with not only two wonderful children, but also with the greatest friends in the world. Thanks my friends, thanks a million for standing by us."

"Well, sure. What are friends for?" Alex smiled. Then he added, "There is one more thing I have to say: I have never been much of a believer, but what I have witnessed today, it has changed all that. I feel as light as a feather. Finally I can go home as a relaxed and contented man."

"I am happy to hear that, Alex," Katie said. "We appreciate your being with us. We love you both very much."

Before they wanted to go, Alex sensed that Katie wanted to stay a little more. So he extended his hand to Andrew.

"Well, it is time to go, kids. Katie, we will wait for you in the car. *So long, Andrew.*"

As soon as they left, Katie and Andrew looked at each other with such a tremendous sigh of relief that only the most loving embrace could express. It felt good to cry, to let the tears wash away the weeks of long, heart-wrenching anguish.

"Oh, Andrew, at last it has happened!" she whispered, her eyes sparkling. "After the rain, the sun is shining again! Our prayers have been answered, as I always believed they would be. We are the happiest parents in the world."

"Yes, it is incredible, isn't it? I feel the urge to cry and laugh with joy at the same time. God has given us another chance. But I must admit, your faith was stronger than mine. Only people like us can imagine how wonderful it is to see the ominous clouds finally disappearing. I've never ceased to wonder how mysterious life is. We cannot comprehend why things happen the way they do; we simply have to accept the wisdom of a higher power."

"That is how I always felt." Katie said.

"There were times," Andrew continued," when I felt the world was falling apart, and I would never be able to cope again. But, just like Alex, today I have been cured too. Tragedies are great teachers. When the gate of life narrows, it knocks a lot of unimportant things out of our heads. It helps us to recognize and reject the non-essentials from our lives, so that we can pay more attention to each other's needs and love. It helps us to search for the true meaning of our purpose in life. You know, sweetheart, as we stumble down the long road of our short lives, collecting the crumbs of our failures and successes, one thing stands out in my mind: that you have always stood by me no matter what. For that I wish to express how much I cherish…"

"I know, sweetheart. But I stood by you because you have earned my love and respect with your devotion to me and the children."

"You were just as devoted. This tragedy has fortified our love and brought out the best in us. The most important thing is that God gave us the chance to accomplish our mission in life. There is a lot more to be done, and we will resume our duties as soon as the children come home."

"Oh, Andrew, your words are the most heartwarming melody to my ears. Just imagine, with God's help we will all be together again!"

"I can hardly wait to return to the real world. I will let you go now, my love, and start to write those belated letters to our parents. Tell them that if all goes well, we will visit them in the near future.

That will be the culmination of our fondest dreams."

"Oh, yes, yes, definitely. But before I go, I must tell you once again that I love you more than life itself."

"I love you too. Without you, my life would not have any meaning." Then Andrew glanced at the children's beds with adoration on his face. "Andy and Aniko," he said with pride that only a father can have. "It was a tough and long fight, but they triumphed over the menacing giant of death. They are winners. Thank God for the chance, the future is still ahead of them. Katie, do you remember what Andy said on that beautiful day at the Rockies."

"Yes, I do. *'This is the first time I'm in two seasons at the same time'.*"

"When they come home, it will be the second time: *We will have spring in the winter.*"

EPILOGUE

SINCE ANDREW'S CAR was declared a total wreck, the insurance company took care of the towing, while Alex and Stan salvaged all of their belongings.

Andrew was released from the hospital in the middle of November. But the children's homecoming had to be delayed longer than the doctor had predicted. He wanted to eliminate all possibilities of complications that might occur. So instead of Christmas, they were released from the hospital at the end of January.

When the two fragile, bundled-up teenagers walked out of the hospital, it was a day of victory; one of the happiest occasions in all their lives. Reaching their new car, they stopped for a moment.

Andy gasped. "**A new car!**" he exclaimed, a flicker of longing in his voice. "It's beautiful."

Andrew embraced them with radiating love. "Yes, Andy, a new beginning."

"I love it!" Aniko said.

As Katie hugged them, the sudden emotion, like a boiling lava, forced the hot, happy tears into her eyes.

"Don't cry, Mom," Aniko said, but her voice trembled too.

"Oh, I'm crying because I'm so happy. Daddy is so right," she said. "This is a new beginning."

"But I feel so...funny." Aniko said in a musing tone. Being outside again gave her an awkward feeling, as if being resurrected.

"I think you will have to get used to the real world all over again," Alex said. "For a while you might find the change overwhelming, but happiness will compensate for it, I guarantee. How you feel, Andy?

"I feel fine. Ah, what a great feeling is to be free again."

Moving along, the teenagers scanned the streets with interest, a wondering look on their faces.

The accident had not caused any "driving-fright" in Andrew, but he wondered whether the children felt any "car-fear." They seemed all right, but he was afraid to ask.

Seeing their home again brought up more emotions. With their parents' help they stepped out of the car. "Here we are!" *Andrew said solemnly.*

The children stopped for a moment and slowly looked around. Inside the house, the Christmas tree was still in the living room, decorated and surrounded with presents.

"Oh it is beautiful!" *Aniko said.*

Alex was a silent observer. The occasion has touched him so deeply, that he considered this celebration as a miracle of life, and he did not trust his emotions enough to talk.

"Welcome home, kids," *Andrew and Katie said.* "This is your home again. Your rooms are waiting for you just as you left them."

"Thank you, Dad, thank you, Mom. My God, what a feeling it is to be home again! We dreamed about this a lot."

"Just as we did, sweethearts," *Katie said.* "Having you back is the most precious gift we could have ever received."

The circumstances definitely presented a new and different world. It was as if the youngsters had been reborn; they had to learn how to get back to live again.

* * *

Naturally, the children were still weak and needed plenty of rest. Katie made sure they took their medication, and that their lives were as comfortable as possible. "Tender loving care is the best medicine," *was Dr. Smith's advice.*

As the children's strength gradually returned, their attitude and mood changed along with it. To Katie's delight, one of the best signs of improvement was their increasing appetite. They were always hungry. (Dr. Smith warned them about that too.)

However, being together again as a family was the most effective medicine. Alex's and Stan's frequent visiting was also a great therapeutic help in their healing process. The twins enjoyed their company, especially Stan's clowning humor. Sometimes Andrew joined in, and together they were able to make them laugh.

Then when the harsh winter months were behind them, and they were strong enough, they went for a walk, as almost like a family tradition. It was a great pleasure to see that their family was whole again, strolling leisurely in the park and enjoying the wonderful power of the sun, which they had been deprived of for so long. They appreciated simple things, like listening to the singing birds, flying from one branch to the other... However, watching the children, Katie noticed something that was new, a maturing sign perhaps: they no longer bickered. Instead, they displayed a deeper love and appreciation for each other.

The tragedy has changed them. The wounds may heal but the scar will stay in their souls indelibly forever.

Another day, after a long walk in the park, they sat down for a rest. After a few minutes of cheerful chit-chat, Katie glanced at Aniko and out of the blue an emotion had swept over her, and tears dropped out of her eyes. Having no idea what had happened, Andrew and the children looked at her with concern.

"What's wrong, sweetheart?" Andrew asked.

With an embarrassed smile, Katie dried her eyes and said, "Oh, nothing really, just a little sentimental silliness crossed my mind. I was exactly in the same age as Aniko when I fell in love with you at Lake Balaton."

With relief, Andrew burst into laughter. "My love, that is the fondest memory that you could have ever shared with us. Thanks for the memory," Andrew said, and kissed her.

"Oh, Mom, that is beautiful! One day I want to learn a lot more about it," Aniko said, and they both kissed her.

"Same with me," Andy confirmed. "It should be interesting. Too bad that we could not have been there."

Andrew and Katie looked at each other, laughing their heart's content, which prompted Andrew to say happily: "You know, Sweetheart, I have learned it a long time ago, that as long as one can laugh things off— even if tears shining in the eyes, life and hope is still exist."

"How true, Darling! I'll try to remember this. But you know," Katie glanced at him, "when it comes to think of it, our first happy ending had occurred with our reunion at Lake Balaton. But I think **this miracle** is far surpasses **that one**."

"Yes, this is indeed the sweetest, although one could not have happened without the other. And we will do our best to make it last for a long, long time...."

By the time they were ready to return home, the bright red sun was sinking ever so slowly, spreading the horizon with its beautiful scarlet veil.

* * *

Message from Budapest:

Dear Mr. Ling;

I am happy to inform you that the flame of *Guiding Stars* had not died out from the sky of the Hungarian literature. By a professional jury in Budapest, your book has been rewarded with the honorary title of the *Second Best Novel in the last Decade of the 20th Century!* Both fellow compatriots are living abroad. The first title went to T. K. *"Trilogy of the Danube,"* which itself indicates the high level of evaluation in which your work has been recognized, and the success will remain engraved forever. Accept my sincere congratulations!

Gyula Nyitrai, chief editor of Nation's Guard.

****

GUIDING STARS
WOULD MAKE A PERFECT BIRTHDAY OR CHRISTMAS PRESENT!

It is offering you beautiful literature, much excitement and dramatic, real-life events. But above all, it is informative, tasteful, and provides a rare, clean entertainment. What more would one want from a fascinating book?

==================================

ABOUT THE AUTHOR

There is a resemblance between Julius Ling and Andrew Dombrady, the central character in GUIDING STARS. In 1956, Mr. Ling and his wife were Hungarian refugees, landing in Australia, knowing no more than "yes" and "no" in English.

After starting at the bottom, Mr. Ling worked as a machine operator at the Commonwealth Bureau of Statistics in Canberra, where he learned some English. In 1966, he and his wife emigrated to Canada, and worked at Statistics Canada, in Ottawa.

Mr. Ling is now retired and living in Victoria, British Columbia.

This is his first novel in English.